Death in Focus

SR GARRAE

This is a work of fiction. All the characters and events described in this book are fictional, and any resemblance to real events or persons living or dead is entirely coincidental.

DEDICATION

Thanks are due to my family, who didn't laugh at me, and to all the people who encouraged me, criticised me, and helped me to write, but in particular Daniela, who never let me give up.

CONTENTS

Chapter 1   1

Chapter 2   3

Chapter 3   12

Chapter 4   22

Chapter 5   30

Chapter 6   41

Chapter 7   50

Chapter 8   52

Chapter 9   62

Chapter 10   70

Chapter 11   79

Chapter 12   87

Chapter 13   89

Chapter 14   98

Chapter 15   106

Chapter 16   113

Chapter 17   122

Chapter 18   131

Chapter 19   141

Chapter 20   151

Chapter 21   159

Chapter 22   161

Chapter 23   170

Chapter 24   180

Chapter 25   188

Chapter 26   197

Chapter 27   206

Chapter 28   208

Chapter 29   216

Chapter 30   224

Chapter 31   233

Chapter 32   235

Chapter 33   244

Chapter 34   253

Chapter 35   262

CHAPTER 1

Belvez swore viciously in Spanish at his equipment. He didn't get it. He was absolutely sure he had followed every single step exactly, and it still wasn't working. The others could make the compound freaking *dance*, and he couldn't even get it to limp.

He'd got to have screwed up somewhere. He just couldn't see how that compound was so much better than his, but there were millions of dollars riding on the pair of them so he'd better work it out or he wouldn't be seeing many of those dollars for long. Telagon only funded the guys who got results.

He ran chemical-stained fingers through his shaggy black hair, loosening it from its ponytail. With an angry noise, he re-tied it, and scowled at the optical instruments and their unhelpful readings. He'd tried to replicate the synthesis five times so far, all on his own time – he didn't need the rest of the research group knowing he wasn't good enough: he was brought in because he was *supposed* to be the best in optical compounds and Telagon funded them another five million on that alone – because he would have sworn to the Virgin, Father, Son and the freaking Holy Ghost that his should outperform this one by miles.

But it didn't.

Well, it did. But only when he made the other compound. Then, his own one performed hugely better. When the others made that compound, it was reversed. He was missing something. He'd got to be missing something. He was part of the best research group at Columbia, one of the best in the country, he was one of the best in the country – and he couldn't replicate the results.

It had got to be something he was doing wrong.

Somewhere in the back of his head, though, a nagging niggle said *what if it's not you, it's him?* But that couldn't be. No-one in John Terrison's group

1

would fake results. Terrison was a straight up guy, and the group was a good group. He'd been in other groups where a new boy coming in to take the top spot – ha! He couldn't even replicate results here, so that wasn't going to be true – would be ostracised, but it wasn't like that here. Just the kind of place he wanted. Terrison didn't care about anything but getting the science right, and he was pretty liberal with the credit.

Plenty of credit to share around, too, to go with the plenty of dollars sloshing in. Not that he would be getting much of either if he didn't work this out. His compound *should* be better. He just couldn't see how it wasn't.

"Hey, Ricky."

"Hi."

"Still working? It's after nine. Put it down, and take a break."

Belvez straightened up, the light catching the silver ring in his ear and illuminating the turquoise set into it: his reminder of his home in New Mexico.

"Guess so," he said. "You know, I just can't see how you work your magic on that compound. It's outperforming by a mile. How'd you do it?"

"It's the placement of the di-imide group," It was said easily.

"Yeah, but I ran your synthesis and I *still* can't get your results."

Belvez didn't notice the other man's eyes widening: he was still lost in chemical confusion. He tapped his pass, and they left the lab, lights going out behind them, into the dark spaces of the campus.

"I don't know," still coolly confident and easy. "Tell you what, we can both go through it tomorrow" –

"I'm teaching tomorrow afternoon. Won't be time before that – how about the next day?"

"Sure."

He started to wander off, but only got a step before Belvez carried on.

"I might talk to John about it. If yours is that much better, we shouldn't be wasting time on mine. Gotta keep Telagon happy, no?"

"Dammit," his colleague said, distracted as he tripped. "Give me a sec, my lace is undone. Don't want to be mistaken for those boozed up undergrads." He sank down to the pebbled path, fussing with his sneakers.

"No way."

His companion straightened up again, hands and face all in shadow.

"I think we should go with both. Yours'll come through."

CHAPTER 2

Her cell phone rang loudly.

"Clement?"

She knew what it was, took the details, cut the call, and groaned, flopping back on the pillow and grumbling. Death should not have disturbed her. Death didn't disturb her, only her nightmares did that.

NYPD Detective Katrina Clement, otherwise known as Casey, hated mornings with a passion, and hated even more being dragged out of bed by Dispatch calling. Murders at six a.m. on a Wednesday were simply unkind, she decided for the hundredth, or maybe ten thousandth, time. Long habit forced her through the shower and into clothes, adding a swift slick of make-up, swallowing scalding coffee as she went, pulling back wet dark hair into a clip rather than wasting time on drying it. Her practised routine had her out of the door in less than thirty minutes, though it didn't cure the yawning. If she slept better, or earlier, she might have liked mornings more, but she didn't.

The body was up near to Columbia, round the back of West 111th. She got there first, which was extremely satisfying and which she had every intention of marking up on the team score sheet. O'Leary, her partner, normally won that race, and he wasn't shy about pointing it out. She tugged down her dark blazer over her plain blue t-shirt, shivering a little in the September morning chill, wishing she'd put on jeans rather than navy pants. At least it had stopped raining, though she could have lived without the murky puddles in the alley. She avoided them. Who knew what nastiness might lurk in them? After all, there was already a dead body.

She inspected the corpse carefully. It was almost tidy, stuffed behind a Dumpster, fully clothed. The clothes weren't disarranged, which argued against a simple mugging, and there were no obvious bloodstains, brains or other bodily emissions on the body. On the other hand, there were no

3

obvious wallet sized bulges in his pockets. A light-fingered mugging would be surprising: if the criminal were that good at pickpocketing, why kill the mark?

She looked at the man again. Hispanic, mid-height, not overweight, and dead. No noticeable tattoos, no clear clues to his occupation. Her conclusion that it wasn't a mugging was enhanced by the presence of an earring: a silver ring with a turquoise set into it. It wasn't from Tiffany's, but it would have been good for a few dollars so a druggie could get another hit.

His clothes were equally ambiguous: stained jeans and a sloganed t-shirt, a beat-up denim jacket thrown over them. Sneakers, and eye-wateringly jazzy socks. The sneakers had bleached patches: the socks' luminosity made up for the lack of colour on the shoes, and indeed for the lack of full light in the early morning dimness and the shadows of the surrounding buildings.

"What happened?" she asked, steeling herself to deal with Medical Examiner Dale McDonald, who disliked her, her team, and indeed the whole wide world. M.E. McDonald would only be happy, Casey often thought, when the Earth was denuded of humanity, with only himself remaining. However, McDonald had one redeeming feature – he was stunningly good at his job. So she put up with his many and varied foibles, and daydreamed about shooting his angular form so that she was never tempted actually to do so.

"Ah, Detective Clement," he sighed. "I should have known it would be you and your eccentric little band."

"Leave the complaining for where I can't hear you. What happened?"

"He appears to have suffocated."

"That's weird," rumbled up behind Casey in a sidewalk vibrating sub-bass. O'Leary had arrived, trembling small items of street furniture with his sizeable tread.

"Indeed it is, Detective O'Leary. A tad more interesting than my normal fare. However, if you wish me to be able to comment further, please remove yourself from there. You are, as ever, blocking the light."

The sun had barely risen, so calling it light was somewhat hopeful. McDonald was already in full pomposity, however, which didn't bode well. O'Leary rearranged his immense self so as not to cast a shadow, and received no thanks.

McDonald prodded the body, oblivious to Casey and O'Leary. On another look, it was revoltingly suffused, scarlet-tinged about the lips, the reason for which was not obvious. Not to the cops, anyway: that was what they had MEs for.

"Why's it that shade, McDonald?"

"It looks like carbon monoxide poisoning." He poked a little more. "I shall have to run toxicology, because that is deeply unusual." He sniffed. "I am not fond of the unusual." No doubt, Casey thought sardonically, that was why he wasn't fond of cops. They specialised in the unusual. If murder were usual, the global population would have been a great deal lower, which wouldn't have bothered McDonald in the slightest.

Casey leaned over his shoulder, at which he tutted fussily. "Space, please." He delicately pried open the battered jacket. "There are no obvious gunshot wounds, and it does not look as if he was assaulted, other than this" – he indicated – "damage to the head. I shall check the exact injury, and for stab wounds and other matters, in the morgue."

His thin fingers in their blue gloves explored further, examining the hands. "Stains."

"Nicotine?"

"Potentially. I shall test. It is far too early to assume." His mouth pinched. McDonald never allowed an assumption to pass unpunctured.

McDonald's assistant sidled up, regarding the ME with justifiable caution. McDonald's irascibility was legendary.

"Don't touch," he snapped. "I'm not done yet." The assistant scuttled away.

"Are CSU on the way?"

"I expect so. They were summoned."

At that point the rest of Casey's team rolled up.

"Hey."

"Andy. Tyler. What kept you?"

"My calligraphy practice," Andy grinned wryly. "I do an hour each morning, after my tai-chi class."

Casey snorted. "Calligraphy? You? I've *seen* your handwriting. Chickens write better than you."

"That's why I'm practicing," he flipped back, amused. "Can't be outdone by a bird, 'specially one that can't even fly."

"What've we got?" Tyler asked. He was a man of few words, most of which he seemed to have learned in the Army. Five years in Casey's team hadn't made him any more loquacious.

"Corpse."

"I got that much."

"McDonald said he'd been suffocated. Could be carbon monoxide."

"Huh," was all Tyler emitted.

They grouped themselves around the dead man. Another bright Manhattan morning had begun for the Thirty-Sixth Precinct's crack homicide team.

"Have we got any ID?"

"No."

"Wallet?"

Andy's gloved, delicate fingers delved into the pockets of their victim's denim jacket.

"Not here."

"Weird. Phone?"

"No."

"Definitely weird. Who goes out without a wallet and phone?"

Tyler pulled on gloves and patted the pants' pockets. "Cash," he pointed out laconically. "Store thataway. Keys." He extracted the keys. They didn't help. It would have been a lot more useful if they'd had an address tag on them.

"I guess," O'Leary drawled, "that he ran outta milk for his coffee, an' ran out on to Amsterdam to get some."

"He has been dead for several hours," McDonald corrected prissily. "And there is no milk carton in evidence."

"Bedtime cocoa, then." O'Leary grinned. He was permanently amiable. It was one of his most useful qualities, though Casey knew it was simply because at six-ten tall and wide in proportion, he never needed to get mad. He was quite scary enough if he only forgot to smile.

"Muggers don't usually go for milk," Andy grinned back. "Maybe we got a crazy version of the Milky Bar Kid?"

Tyler groaned at his partner. "Too early."

"I would not assume that it was any form of drink as yet."

"We know." Casey managed not to snap. McDonald was a complete pain: the stick up his ass surgically implanted, probably at birth – but he was the best ME available, so they all put up with his prissy, pompous formality for the sake of the results. He turned away to instruct his assistant, which let the team inspect their corpse more closely.

Around them, the city was beginning to bustle: a little after seven, the light clearer even in the dingy alley: in fact, surprisingly bright, as if something were reflecting….

Casey's head snapped up. That had been a flash, and she didn't like flashes. She didn't like any press around her corpses. She hated photographs and photographers at any time, in any circumstances. She took a few strides away from the body, leaving her team to continue, and glared at the prying photographer.

His height and good looks didn't endear him to her. She had the odd feeling that she ought to have recognised him, but she had no idea why: her life didn't encompass photography except by the CSU techs. She supposed she might have seen him making his grubby stringer living around other scenes, but she couldn't place him and had no reason to try. Anyway, he shouldn't have been invading her crime scene.

"Back off, you. This is a crime scene. Put that camera away."

The photographer didn't. Instead, and infuriatingly, he took another swathe of photos, and only stopped on her second instruction. On closer acquaintance, he didn't improve. Too tall, too broad, too pretty. Well, handsome. Definitely handsome. She ignored that, and the little curl of appreciation in her stomach. Too used to checking women out, and regarding her with an assessing blue gaze which she didn't like at all. Nor did she like his curiosity, or more likely voyeurism. There were always ghouls crowding round the corpses. If Casey had had her way, she would have had her team issued with some tech that would block phones and cameras, to stop the constant prurient watchers and their social media accounts. Deaths were not a suitable subject for increasing one's followers on Twitter or Instagram.

The ghoul took another set of shots. The disrespect did nothing for her temper. "Stop that. Respect for the dead." And he could stop taking shots anywhere near her too.

"He's dead," the man pointed out. "He won't know." He smiled smugly, which only annoyed her more.

"Not the point. This is a crime scene. You're in the way. Scram." She turned away, back to her work. Too-handsome men with charmingly smug smiles did not help her in her job.

"What happened to him?"

Would this pretty boy ever just take the hint and be gone already? She flipped back, eyes blazing. "That's what we're here to find out."

"Hey, Casey," O'Leary called. "We got something. Come see."

"'Kay." She wanted to get back to the important matters, such as the corpse and the nature of the death, not to deal with lookers-on.

"Casey?" he asked.

Say what? Not just a ghoul, but an idiot as well? Crime scenes were not the place for social interactions with strangers, no matter how tall and broad.

"My name. Excuse me," she said with chilling formality: barely civil, leaving him unwanted and ignored behind her.

She dismissed him from her mind as soon as O'Leary summoned her back. He didn't require any of her attention.

Unfortunately, whoever that had been didn't dismiss himself from the scene. She tapped O'Leary, whose height and width made him a good man for suggesting that rubberneckers should move along at speed. For some reason, once they'd managed to focus on the top of his head, they complied. Speedily.

"Go move that jackass with the camera along, will you? He's getting in our way."

O'Leary shrugged, and obeyed. A moment later, he returned.

"Casey, he's a professional, not a rubbernecker."

"So? We got our own professionals."

So what if the guy was a professional? She didn't need photographers: they had CSU for that, who were already contentedly sweeping the scene. At least, she supposed, if he were a professional he wouldn't take photos of her.

"Name's Jamie Carval," the man called.

The name meant less than nothing, right up until Andy reminded her why he was faintly familiar.

"Carval?" he blurted. "Casey, he's the one who had the exhibition about city lowlife. Remember? The one you went to. You told me so much about it I went myself. You gotta remember."

"I don't," she said flatly. "Can we get on with the case? You know, this dead guy?" She flicked a contemptuous glance across Carval and raised her voice to make sure he heard. "The dead don't care much about culture." She paused, to point her moral. "Or photography." She didn't show her recognition, either. She had a job to do, and that was what mattered, not some misery tourist.

The next time she looked around, he was gone. CSU were all over the scene in their usual efficient fashion, McDonald's stork-like form was fussing around the body and preparing it for transport, and the team could pack themselves up to get back to the bullpen and start the real work. She was keen to get going.

Casey loved her job. Always had, and she was pretty sure she always would, despite loathing the early morning calls. She wasn't bothered by the late night working. She'd entered liberal arts at Stanford, aiming for future admission to the (or any) law school, thinking she'd be a lawyer and aiming for the top, but pretty soon she'd discovered, talking to graduates in the law school, that the case analysis involved in law, while interesting enough, didn't really pique her passion. Even working part time in an advice centre somehow wasn't enough, even though she was dealing with real people with real problems: making a difference – it just didn't do it for her.

She found that she didn't want to read about crimes or cases, or prosecute them – she certainly didn't want to go into commercial law, which simply bored her. All that boredom and sense that law was going to be the wrong direction didn't coalesce into a different view, however, until she went to listen in on a criminal justice module, discovered more about policing, and re-targeted her life with the same ambition she'd applied to entering Stanford.

Her parents had been – well, likely they had been a little disappointed, but they hid it pretty well. They wanted her to be happy, and she was. They were as proud of her at her Police Academy graduation as they had been when she graduated from Stanford, and took the obligatory million parental photos of her on her first day in uniform. She had kept one on display, showing her with both of them, in her neat apartment on the East

Side: proudly framed on her little side table, together with the small stone bird that they'd bought her in Quito, years before. It was a good memory. She needed some good memories, to balance out the bad. It was a good photo, too. She needed one of those. She'd never told them how much she hated photos.

Back in the bullpen, the motley gang congregated around Casey's pristine desk. She didn't like clutter or mess, and her desk reflected that. No-one commented on its emptiness more than once, except her team, who joshed her about it every other minute. Most of her co-workers had tried it once, received a chilly reply, and rapidly decided that it wasn't worth it. She wasn't bothered by that at all. She was quite happy with her team: she didn't need to be popular as long as she was respected.

"Have we got anything?" she asked rhetorically.

"A corpse," O'Leary flicked back at her.

"I think I got that. Anything useful?"

"Less than two hours later? C'mon, Casey. You do this every time. You know it takes CSU more than ten minutes."

Casey favoured Andy with a mild glare, to which his only response was an inscrutable, irritating grin. He was good at inscrutable grins. He had fit right into their team when the Captain had brought him in, swiftly paired up with Tyler, though two cops less alike than Andy and Tyler could hardly have been imagined: Tyler burly, black and terse; ex-Army and proud of it; Andy flippant and quick. Still, it worked. One of Captain Kent's better decisions. And they'd needed someone. Three was unbalanced, and Casey and O'Leary had worked together for years, which had left Tyler a little lonely.

"Okay. So what're we going to do for the gap while the techs do magic and read chicken entrails in the background – and *don't* say harass McDonald. The first one suggesting that gets to do it."

There was a certain amount of shuffling as everyone closed their mouths again. No-one wanted to be sent to beard the McDonald bear in its den. He had all sorts of ways of making them miserable if he felt harassed, and not one of them would have dared to accept so much as a glass of water for fear of the potential outcome.

"Waalll," drawled O'Leary, "we c'n chaw the fat 'bout carbon monoxide poisoning."

"If we're gonna do that," Andy said, "can you lose the cornfield? You don't need to pull that on us. We know you've never been out of New York City in your life."

"That ain't true," O'Leary contradicted comfortably. "I went to Albany, once."

"That for the Bigfoot ball?" O'Leary bared his teeth at Tyler's comment. Tyler wasn't noticeably scared, and fist bumped Andy.

"Wait till I get you sparrin', little man."

"You kids finished?" Casey enquired in a bored tone that stopped the fun cold. "We all know they issued you a brain along with the shield, O'Leary. So how about putting it into gear? Let's talk about carbon monoxide, even if McDonald hasn't confirmed it yet."

Some discussion later, the team had come up with a list of ways in which carbon monoxide poisoning might have occurred. Top of the list was the victim having been bashed on the head, stuffed in a closed car with a blocked exhaust, and then being dumped in the alley where he'd been found.

"Who found him?"

"Some dedicated student" – Andy's face indicated what he thought of supposedly dedicated students – "who was coming off an all-night study session."

"Bender, more like," Tyler noted cynically.

"Most likely."

"Is someone interviewing them?"

"Uniform, for now. They were pretty shook up."

"So we'll get that in a bit."

Casey tapped her pen restlessly on the desk. She wanted *something* to get going on. Even something to give her an ID would have helped. She didn't much like the idea of working on cold cases when she could play with a nice new murder which she would have a much better chance of solving. Cold cases were cold for a reason, and while each unsolved case was an irritation which she'd have liked to remove, the faster she could get going on the new one the more likely it was that they'd clear it.

Before Casey had a chance to take out her frustration on the desk or her co-workers, her e-mail pinged up. "We got an ID," she exclaimed. "Finally."

"Yeah?"

"Ricardo Belvez," she read off. "Hm. He came up – hey, that's unusual. He came up because he's got clearances."

"Clearances? Like government?"

"Ain't that the same as criminal? Lowlifes, politicians, politicians, lowlifes" –

"Tomayto, tomato" –

"Let's call the whole thing off," Casey said briskly, "and do some work, hmm? Clearances."

"So, is it government clearances?"

"No, not exactly. Security, though. Says he's a researcher. Chemist. Let's find out about his life."

Over the rest of the morning, Casey dug into the ID and from there found and ran a social security number and then the driver's licence.

Belvez had been a man who scoffed at speed limits, from the citations, though they were all back in New Mexico. Some further digging proved that he wasn't married. The state of his clothes and the tastelessness of his socks had clued them into that. Not much mileage in a slob. Her mind wandered for a moment or two, clearly without her conscious permission, because it was thinking that the pestilent photographer was very easy on the eye, even in jeans and a soft leather jacket. She firmly pulled her mind back to business. Easy-on-the-eye didn't make up for pestilent.

Andy, claiming a background that included high school chemistry, also claimed that that gave him the best chance of investigating Belvez's clearances, and thereby the possibility of a work history. Tyler would have to take point on anything arising which wasn't clear from the ME's report: not because he had any specialist expertise in medical terminology beyond what was expected of any experienced detective, but because his laconic speech and lack of social chatter (except where sport was concerned) made him least likely to irritate McDonald. Up until the ME could tell him it was autopsy time, however, he would marshal the canvass and seek out street camera footage.

Casey looked around, surveying her team, and, content that everything was progressing on the normal, well-oiled path which they had evolved in their four years together, turned back to the necessary, but tedious, business of analysing the evidence they needed and starting the process to acquire it. That would take the whole afternoon. She wished that she could have the same magically instant information that cops got on cop shows. It would have made her life so much easier. Still, it gave her plenty to be going on with.

CHAPTER 3

It had been the perfect shot. The cop's head had been up, and he had had a clear view, perfectly centred. He had pressed down, and it was done.

In the preview of the shot that Carval had taken, the cop's head was indeed centred, framed by the grimy walls and service doors of the alley, drying puddles on the sidewalk; contrasted with the sharp blue sky above. The other heads were, deliberately, a fraction unfocused, leaving hers pinpoint clear among them. Her expression was fierce, intent; focused on the scene.

It had been so fortunate that he always carried a camera, even for a brief trip to the store early in the morning. He kept on taking shots: gradually moving closer and closer to the group. He ended up almost on top of the yellow tape blocking off the area, and it was only then that anyone noticed him, or, perhaps, paid any attention.

"Back off, you. This is a crime scene. Put that camera away."

Her voice was clear, educated and cool: each word carrying command. Close up, Jamie Carval, celebrated photographer of the underbelly of New York, could see the dark, cold eyes focusing on him. When the cop straightened up, he couldn't help taking another set of shots, hoping that the speed of snapping wouldn't leave them all uselessly unfocused or misaligned.

"Stop that," the cop ordered. "Respect for the dead."

Carval stopped taking shots, mostly because he was looking at the cop instead. She was... interesting: only moderately tall, most of her height coming from legs; dark brown, almost black hair pulled smoothly back in a neat, controlled clip, but curling where the ends spilled out; tailored, formal pants and jacket – and a face which he thought could have been photographed for cover shots. She didn't acknowledge his look in any way: making it obvious that she was thoroughly bored. The dark brown eyes should have been warm and friendly, but they were disconcertingly unemotional. Carval wasn't used to such extreme disinterest, and it didn't sit too well with him. He was almost relieved when this Casey-cop was called away.

The rest of the group had stayed with the corpse, as uninterested in his presence as Casey-the-cop, who had first tried to drive him off, and then, when he tried to establish a connection – and indeed a way of finding her again if he needed more photos – brushed him off as if he was something nasty that she had found on her shoe. Smart, mid-heeled shoes, not too high. Very practical, and surprisingly elegant.

Carval scanned the scene again, refusing to be dismissed so easily, and took a few more shots. With Allan nagging him and insisting that a new exhibition would need to be scheduled for six months' time, he desperately needed to discover a new angle. His last show, studies of the panhandlers and street life of New York, had been acclaimed, but he needed to find something different – and preferably less odorous. The cop noticed him still photographing, and nudged the man who'd called out. He stood up...and up...and up. It wasn't a man, it was a giant. Hagrid, perhaps. The mountain moved towards him, at which point Carval, not himself a small man, reckoned that the titan stood at least six-ten. He would barely fit in shot.

"Thought Casey told you to stop?" he drawled. He sounded as if he'd just come off a cornfield, but the sharp gleam in his light eyes put paid to any thought of flannelling him.

"No law against it," Carval pointed out. "What happened to him?"

"Got dead. Why'd you care?"

Carval smiled. Normally, people responded quite well to his smile. The cop didn't. "I'm a photographer. The scene caught my eye."

The mobile mountain, still nameless, softened a little. "Photographer?" he said with some interest. "Professional, not some tourist?"

"Professional," Carval confirmed.

The huge cop gazed down at him. "Wait there a second." He crossed the gap to the scene in two immense strides. Carval couldn't hear the exchanges, but they didn't look encouraging, which already didn't surprise him.

"Name's Jamie Carval," Carval called. Casey didn't react. The giant turned back towards him. Strangely, it was a slightly built, Asian-American cop who reacted, clearly recognising it, and exchanging a series of still-inaudible words to Casey-the-cop. She appeared even more unimpressed, if that were possible.

"The dead don't care much about culture." She flicked a contemptuous glance across Carval. "Or photography."

Ow! Just out of sheer spite, Carval took another round of shots, and then swiftly departed. As far as he could tell, not one of the cops noticed, and certainly they didn't care if they did.

He returned to his studio more than mildly irritated. He was, after all, *famous*. Known, lauded, awarded and applauded. He'd even made money from his talent, which wasn't common, or indeed expected. Then again, it wasn't why he did it, either. He simply had to take photographs. Okay, he wasn't entirely public spirited about it – he had to eat, and pay the rent, and while a starving artist in a garret might have been a staple of fiction, the reality was likely very unpleasant. Carval liked the transitory pleasures in life: good food, good wine; good company. He wasn't short of that last, either.

Still, what had he expected from a bunch of cops? They couldn't move in his milieu. He didn't move in theirs. They were only interesting because, for the first time in a few months, he'd found a scene he wanted to shoot. That he *had* to shoot. He could feel the bones of the next exhibition aligning. There, in the grimy back alley off West 111th, not far from Columbia, he'd finally found some inspiration. He'd known something would turn up, and now it had.

But he was still rather irritated. His shots were *memorable*. And they were definitely part of the cultural scene.

His irritation lasted until he got a good look at the shots he'd taken. He whistled to himself, and ran fingers through already-tousled hair. Unposed and fast they might have been, but he'd caught the mood, caught the scene. The slightly unfinished, rough quality added to the atmosphere, rather than diminished it; gave the scene a certain sense of urgency, contrasted with the finality and stillness of the corpse. The focal point, though, was that female cop. Casey. Seen through a lens, she was – he couldn't resist the pun – *arresting*. She was going to be the show-stopper moment: the centre of the exhibition.

He began to plan: seeing the exhibition in his mind's eye, sketching out a rough plan. All he needed now were some more – a lot more – shots. The theme, he decided, would be *Murder on Manhattan*. Yes. That would be it. Short and to the point. He began to work up the shots he'd got already.

As ever, a third of the shots were discarded immediately: out of focus, or not properly aligned, or just plain wrong, in a way that defied description but that Carval instantly identified. Now that he'd got a theme in mind, he could pick and choose: instantly able to remove those shots that wouldn't fit his concept.

When he'd finished his first cut, he was left with more pictures than usual. But the first shot he'd taken: the fierce, intelligent gaze in sharp focus; the blurred forms around her – *that* was going to be his centrepiece. It was perfect. He'd caught a gleam of light on the shield; there was just a hint of the shape of her gun in the gap between the other forms; and then the suggestion of the corpse below. Utterly perfect, taken in one of those moments of sheer instinct.

He stared at it for a while, committing it to memory, and then began to arrange some of the other prints around it. He liked to work with physical prints at that stage: shifting and rearranging: he'd pin them to a large expanse of corkboard covering fully half of one wall so that he could absorb how they would come across in an exhibition: how they would strike an onlooker. Later, he would play with filters and colours and washes, cropping and angles: a little artistic manipulation in the digitisation – but never *retouching*, never any digital manipulation to make the humans more perfect. These shots would stand or fall on the reality of the cops on which they were centred: their humanity needed to shine through, imperfections and all.

He continued to play with his prints. More were discarded. The composition of the cop team was, to say the very least, intriguing: as if it had been specifically picked to be diverse. Casey: female; the big man a mountain in human form. He would add scale, a sense of massive presence, to the scene, set against the fragility of the dead. A small, slight Asian-American, almost delicate. Carval was quite certain that he wasn't delicate at all: there was a certain tinge to some of the shots where his eyes were as hard and cold as Casey's were. Finally a tough, fit African-American; close-cropped hair: even through the covering of his jacket he provided a burly sense of muscle and physicality: a fine contrast to Casey. In fact, they were all a fine contrast to Casey. It wasn't that she hadn't looked in good shape – she surely, surely had – but even bored, cold and irritated she'd exuded a certain sense of curves beneath the blazer, where the men around her were all straight lines.

Finally satisfied, he regarded his corkboard delightedly, and picked up his phone.

"Allan, I got it."

"Got what?"

"Got my next theme. I went out to the store and there was a bunch of cops with a corpse. You gotta come to the studio and look. We're gonna be busy. C'mon."

"I guess it stops me fielding calls about how you're going to fill the walls," Allan said dryly. Carval snickered.

"C'mon. When have I ever let us down?"

"Well…"

"Stop. I haven't. Not since I made it. You gotta come see. This is going to be as good as the panhandlers. Just get here, okay?"

Some few seconds later, since Allan normally resided only one floor down in the office, he arrived. Carval regarded him fondly: a small, dapper man who dressed sharply but absolutely refused to allow Carval to shoot him. Allan claimed it would ruin their working relationship. Carval thought that he was simply scared of being famous. Still, Allan kept him in some sort of order and didn't annoy him by doing so, which was a major improvement on the disorder in which Carval had previously survived. Electricity, Carval had found, was a necessity, but it did have to be paid for. Allan, among many other good qualities, kept the lights on.

"So what is it this – oh. Wow. Okay." He stared at the corkboard.

"Isn't it great?" Carval enthused. "It was just right there in front of me. I told you something would turn up."

"Yeah, yeah. I should have more faith in you, yada yada yada. That doesn't cut it when the gallery's calling up wanting a strapline."

"I got that too." Allan raised a cynical eyebrow. "Don't look like that. I can do straplines. We're going to call it *Murder on Manhattan*."

"Mm." Allan turned back to the display. "It's not enough."

"I know that. I'll get more. Now I know what I'm looking for, I'll find it," he said with simple arrogance.

"How?"

A fair question. Carval hadn't really thought about that. It needed to be *this* group. This team. Actually, it needed to be *her*. Casey the cop. With her team.

"And what are you going to do, anyway? Are you following the dead or the living?"

Ah. He hadn't got that far, either.

"Stop spoiling it by wanting me to *plan*," he complained. "I got my inspiration and you already want me to do everything. Genius can't be *planned*."

"Which would be fine if you were a genius. Since you're a photographer, not Einstein, maybe we could think about how you're going to turn this into a full show? Your bills don't pay themselves."

"No, you do that for me. C'mon. Stop fussing."

"You pay me to fuss. Though I prefer it to be called *organising*."

"I've got plenty of money. Just the royalty stream" –

"Won't last if you don't keep doing exhibitions."

"Will so," Carval grumped. "You told me I was made for life."

"You're being childish."

"So?"

"So when you're thirty-three, it's not attractive."

"It works on everyone but you." Carval's eyes twinkled mischievously. "'Specially on women."

Allan cast up his eyes to the ceiling. "God knows why," he sighed. "I mean, what about a tall, fit millionaire would attract any woman? It's a mystery."

"It made me a success. That first exhibition…"

"Yeah, yeah, yeah." Allan had heard it all before. Often. "You'd still be doing hack 'glamour' shots if you hadn't done that series of snaps down in Palo Alto, and you got most of those by looking pathetically cute at every pretty woman you could find."

"I still did hack glamour shots, after. Paid the bills."

"And then you got lucky. I *know*. You tell me every week."

"I get lucky every week," Carval smirked sleazily.

"Oh, for God's sake. Keep your catting around for somewhere else. Can we just concentrate on how you're going to flesh out this show?"

"Lemme think."

Carval stared at the board, thinking. Should he follow the life, or the corpse? Death had its own attraction: people were reluctantly drawn to the morbid, but… he didn't want to be Gunther von Hagens. Apart from anything else, such as trying to *avoid* horrible smelly scenes, it wouldn't be original.

"The cops." He turned back to Allan. "It's gotta be the cops. Look at them. Look at the contrast, the details, the *life*. It's not the corpse. It's them."

"Ri-ight."

"Don't be like that. It's all of them together. It's not just the woman."

"Hmmm. Really?"

"It is. Look at the contrasts. Use your eyes. They're all so perfectly different. The visuals are astonishing. Even you stopped cold when you came in. If you will, everyone will. I gotta shoot them. It's going to be mega."

"Mm," Allan hummed again. "How're you going to find them? You don't even know their names, or their precinct, and they're cops, not models. You can't just call them up and hire them."

"Will you *stop* introducing logic? It's depressing. Anyway, I bet I can find them. One's called Casey. The woman. And look at him – the giant. Surely it's easy enough to find someone that big? They'll be part of the Thirty-Sixth precinct, most likely. It'll be easy."

"Jamie, it might be easy to *find* them, but who says they'll want you hanging around?"

"They can't stop me. No law against photography in public. Anyway, like Warhol said, everyone wants their fifteen minutes of fame. I'll make them all famous. Who'll object to that?"

"I did."

"You're an exception. Course they won't object. Everyone else wants to be famous."

Allan wandered away, muttering. Carval dismissed the mutterings as Allan's normal dyspepsia, and carried right on arranging and considering his shots and pondering how best to get to the cop team again. There had to be a way.

Unfortunately, he knew no cops. Nor did he have political connections – in fact, he avoided those like the plague – a plague on all their houses. He paid as little attention to politics as he could possibly manage, and he had flatly refused to allow his panhandler shots to be used by any party. Consequently, he had no idea how to negotiate the access he would need. Cop shops and precincts were most unlikely to allow random blow-bys in to take photos, even ones as famous as he. He could, he supposed, try to bluff it, but being thrown out wouldn't be a good look, and then he would be ten steps back from his present position of unhelpful neutrality.

He stared hard at his board, hoping it would give him an idea for access. It didn't, unsurprisingly, but gradually another thought began to nibble at the edges of his mind. His central shot was entirely unposed and original, but something about it seemed very familiar. He hoped he hadn't seen it in some other exhibition. He didn't want to be accused of copying. Whatever it was that was nagging at his mind, though, wasn't making itself clear. How irritating.

A lot later, he left the studio, Allan long gone from the office, for the upstairs apartment rooms: open plan main room and kitchenette, separate bedroom. Small, but perfectly adequate for his needs, and those of any company he chose to bring back. He'd got lucky with timing: bought straight after the crash on a wing, a prayer and most of the proceeds of his first exhibition and his parents' life insurance. He still missed them, seven years on: still kept the photo he'd taken of them – an early shot, before he acquired skill, but not, even then, without talent – on a wall.

Just as he was about to drop into sleep, the elusive familiarity of his shot sneaked into his mind and woke him up with a jolt. It wasn't the pose or the looks. It was the expression in the eyes. He'd seen it – he'd photographed it – before. He had – somewhere, somehow – photographed Casey the cop before. All he had to do was find it, which wasn't going to be easy, since he had kept copies of every photo he had ever taken – and he'd taken lots.

Carval decided that he couldn't wait to think about that tomorrow: now that he had remembered, he needed to find it. He bounced out of bed in his boxers, realised it wasn't that warm and grabbed a robe, enthusiasm sparking around him, eager to get on with it. He was going to chase down that elusive familiarity. Allan would no doubt chide him for it, and complain that Carval wasn't paying attention to the real world, but then Allan was there to recall him to reality and to make sure that the mundane details of his life were attended to without Carval having to waste energy on it. Allan made his life much easier, and Carval paid him well for it, but he was distressingly focused on reality. Carval liked photographing reality, but he didn't want to live there. He liked his comfortable bubble of creativity much better.

He pulled up his extensive files of photos, thanked heaven that photography was digital and all the shots were in the high spec computer system for which he'd paid a fortune, and started searching. It was easy enough to discard everything that didn't include humans.

His real joy was photographing people. He'd tried a bit of architectural photography, and swiftly been bored. He liked expression and movement and life, not the stillness and chill of stone or brick. He'd tried some wildlife photography too, back in the day, but that hadn't suited him either: the animals wouldn't do what he wanted – mostly, they hadn't even been visible - and he'd had no patience to wait for them. He wasn't good at patience or waiting, generally. His best shots had always been instant, taken on the fly by instinct and (he could admit it to himself) luck. Still, he'd had a good time down in the Don Edwards reserve, though he'd had a much better one on the Stanford campus a month or so later, twenty-three and confident that the world was his playground. He'd taken a lot of informal campus shots, and then he'd talked quite a few girls into some more carefully posed shots. When they'd been up for it, those meetings had founded the glamour photos that originally thrust him on to the stage. Good times. He'd had a lot of good times.

He sank into a reverie as he looked through the early files of shots, remembering the days when he'd been footloose and fancy-free; when there was no pressure to meet exhibition deadlines or to come up with the next plan – truthfully, his only plan had been to come up with the next meal, beer and pretty girl; and that was exactly what he'd done for four months, from early April through to the end of the summer. Definitely good times. He should do it again, he thought, just take a time out – but not yet. Maybe after he'd caught his cops on camera.

He didn't even realise that he was already thinking of them as *his* cops: in his head and on his corkboard.

A time out might be good. He could travel, mess around, simply enjoy life. It wasn't as if he couldn't afford to, and Allan would keep everything ticking over here till he came back –

Oh. Oh, oh, *oh*. No wonder the look was familiar. He stopped hard on a shot from the Stanford campus. It was Casey-the-cop. It was almost exactly the same shot: the face in sharp focus, her gaze fierce, concentrating on something that was out of shot. He looked down at the date. June, 2007. End of semester, more or less. She'd been in the centre of a group, but he couldn't remember what they were doing. It wasn't relevant: only the shot had mattered.

He stared at it. It was so similar... And then he grinned, smugly. Good to be reminded that even then his instincts for the snapped shot were right on track. He flicked through the rest of the shots of the group, but there was nothing else there. Since he was two-thirds down memory lane, he kept going, lost in that period nine years earlier.

And there she was again.

He didn't remember a great deal about that evening. He'd bluffed his way into a club, still near enough to looking like a college student that everyone had thought he'd come with someone else, claimed to be doing a photography elective and taken as many shots as he could manage while enthusiastically socialising (that was, drinking. Some of the party might even have legally been allowed to drink, though he doubted whether it was all of them) with everyone in sight. All he remembered about her was dancing with her, too briefly, snatching a kiss as she revolved away, and then losing her in the crowd as he'd stopped to take more photos. No more impression than that. He'd never thought about it, or her, again. She'd not been interested in more photos of any sort, or he'd have had more of a memory.

He clicked the files closed, and the smug grin expanded. Now he'd got a reason to contact Casey-the-cop. Renew old acquaintance, or something like that. He reopened the file, and looked at the photo: a fresh-faced young woman in a dress the size of a handkerchief and sky high stilettos: hotter than hell and the poster girl for the sort of trouble that ended up in a ruined bed. He'd used it as part of a much bigger collage: an advertisement for the – er – social side of college life. Glam shots paid. In those days, reality series didn't. They did now, but he wasn't ashamed of the shots he'd taken then. In fact, he was pretty proud of some of them.

He slipped back into bed, stretched out into space, and remembered that he'd ditched his most recent companion for sharing good times a couple of weeks ago... no, longer than that. Maybe a month. He hadn't really noticed or been counting, too worried about finding a new theme to care. She'd wanted to be part of it, but... well. He didn't need to do glamour shots any more, and he certainly wasn't going to use them for an exhibition, however pleasant it was to do the easy, lucrative sessions. Too easy, too slick, and in the end, too boring. His latest idea wasn't going to be boring at all.

He idly wondered what Casey-the-cop would look like dolled up for a glamour shot.

That had been a very bad idea, he realised an instant later. His ability to visualise was emphatically not an asset here and now. Because now he had a whole series of visuals, absolutely none of which would assist in achieving his *Murder on Manhattan* theme.

It was ridiculous, he told himself: it was only because he didn't currently have a girlfriend. Besides which, she had been pretty unwelcoming, and he didn't – didn't need to – go where he wasn't welcome. In intimate terms, that was. He went a lot of places where he wasn't welcome for the photos, starting with yesterday morning's crime scene, where he *definitely* hadn't been welcome.

A naughty little thought wormed its way into his devious mind. It squirmed around for a few seconds, and then curled itself into clarity. It said: *if you were friends with Casey-the-cop then you'd get all the photos you needed.* Yeah. Well. That was about as likely as snow in the Manhattan summer. Sadly, common sense chipping in also seemed to be as likely as snow in the Manhattan summer, because he just couldn't get the idea to leave his head. If only his head had had some idea about how to make friends, it would have been more use.

He plunged into sleep, dreaming only of the next exhibition – and its centrepiece.

CHAPTER 4

By shift end, and somewhat beyond, every form of investigative line to tug upon had begun. Annoyingly, not one of them had yielded any interesting results as yet – though that was normal, it didn't amuse Casey any better five years after she became a detective than it had on her very first case.

"C'mon," O'Leary said, watching her restless fingers tapping Chinese tortures into her desk. "Beer time."

"I wanna toss his apartment," Casey complained.

"Bit hard, without an address yet."

"Stop spoiling my life with reality. Why don't we have an address?"

"Because he didn't have a wallet. An' he paid attention to all those warnin's about not puttin' your address on your keys, so's you don't get your home invaded. Musta been security conscious."

"It's not helpful," Casey growled.

"Beer," O'Leary said firmly. "You need a break. You guys wanna beer?"

"Nah," said Andy. "Not tonight."

Casey raised an eyebrow at him. "Back on the dating trail?" He simply smiled. He never rose to that bait. He was never very forthcoming on the subject, either. "Tyler?"

"Not me. Gym."

Tyler worked out. It was the closest he came to religion: in fact, sometimes it sounded as if it *was* his religion. He sparred with O'Leary, who despite his size was the best around, and Tyler sometimes won, which considering the nine inch height difference was pretty good going. Casey didn't even try to spar with those two. She was good, but there was searching for improvement and then there was absolute insanity. She worked out with Andy, or a couple of the other guys in the bullpen who would stretch her but where she didn't run the risk of being inadvertently badly hurt. On the other hand, she could outrun all of them, whether it was a sprint or a longer chase.

"C'mon," O'Leary rumbled. "Iffen you don't pack up, I'll need to do it for you. An' you hate it if I muss up your desk."

"Touch my desk and you die," she threatened, and grinned at him. "*Okay*. Stop hassling me. I'm coming."

There was no point in resisting the O'Leary juggernaut. There never had been. He was unstoppable when he had an aim in mind, and he generally did have an aim in mind. She thought back to their first meeting, only a few months after she'd graduated from the Academy.

Not long into the NYPD, Casey had been tapped up to go on a Vice operation. It had been a bit more interesting than the usual Dumpster diving and canvassing which had been her lot till then, because it had been part of a much bigger sting, involving a couple of other precincts. She had been moving precinct soon, so it was by way of a last hurrah.

She certainly hadn't been sorry to move on from the Vice operation, though realism had told her she would be going to be doing a lot of them, especially… well, especially after the Academy. She might not have been tall, but she was pretty, so it would probably have been inevitable no matter what. Anyway, as a rookie she had to do as she was ordered. (She had been desperate for Homicide, but she would need to serve her time before she had been in any way fit to apply for that.) The op was down in the Meatpacking District, and it would have been a little uncomfortable even if she had been wearing more than two oversized belts and six inch dominatrix heels. The caked on make-up had protected her face from showing her blushes, though. She'd been staking out the patch for two or three days, passing on everything she had noticed. *Eyes on the ground*, her boss had called it, so she'd guessed she could stand the embarrassment, and the commentary. She'd got used to dealing with the commentary in the Academy. It hadn't been any different.

When it all got loud and busy with red-and-blues and sirens and cops of all sizes and shapes flooding the area, Casey, leaning on her lamppost, had watched with interest, right up till two of the cops had tried to arrest her. She hadn't liked that, and had been about to protest and show her badge, when she had remembered that she'd been ordered to stay undercover – and then one of them had copped a feel, and she'd lost her temper big time. He'd ended up on the floor in a hurry, his likewise-wanderingly handed pal had followed, but then suddenly a giant uniformed officer had appeared right next to her. Casey, thoroughly displeased with the whole situation and unable to treat the unprofessional cops as they had definitely deserved, hadn't hesitated before she'd taken a kick which only just missed his testicles and then followed up with a textbook haymaker to the solar plexus.

It had seriously hurt. Her, not him. He hadn't so much as flinched. She'd tried for another punch, which Bigfoot had caught, and then he'd dumped her head down over his shoulder without even a deep breath, while she'd tried and failed to hit him hard enough for him to notice and sworn at him up hill and down dale in two languages. She'd wanted to shoot him when he swatted her ass, though she'd managed to resist and landed some scratches and at least one hit that made him huff, but eventually she'd stopped. The Bigfoot had cuffed her, and stuffed her into his cruiser in regulation fashion. It hadn't been the plan.

"Er... hey?" she'd said, when the cruiser doors had shut. "Um, I'm Officer Katrina Clement, badge number 56364. I was undercover for Vice, but I'm at the Eleventh Precinct."

"You're a cop? Little bitty thin' like you?"

"I'm not little!" she'd whipped back indignantly. "You're a monster."

"Nah," the mountain had rumbled. "Now then, I'm Officer O'Leary, an' I think I'd better find out if you're tellin' me the truth." He'd made a call, listening for a moment or two. "Yessir," he'd said. "Yeah. Dark hair, dress matches. Badge 56364. She ran it right off, like we do. Yeah, that's the name she gave. Yessir. I got her here. She's okay."

He'd cut the call and turned around. "Guess you're who you say you are. Let's go around a bit an' when we're clear of the funfair I'll take the cuffs off an' you can come up front. We oughta get acquainted a bit, seein' as you been tryin' to beat me up an' I swatted your ass for it."

"Doesn't that make us practically siblings?" Casey had asked him pertly.

"Prob'ly," Officer O'Leary had grinned.

He'd made a few quick turns and pulled up to uncuff her and let her slip into the passenger seat.

"Um... sorry about that," she'd said. "I didn't know what to do, and I was told to stay undercover till it was all over."

"'S okay. Ain't no way a teeny little thin' like you was gonna hurt me."

"Hurt my knuckles trying," she'd groused.

He hadn't been sympathetic. "Ain't my fault. Anyways, pleased t' meet you, Officer Clement. How long you been on the job?"

"Ten weeks since my Training Officer signed me off. First Vice operation. Nice to meet you too. Most people call me Casey."

"Clement?" he'd rumbled. "Have I met you before?" A faint bell had obviously been ringing in his head. Casey knew what that was. She was notorious.

"No." She'd shivered. "Could you turn the heating up a bit? It's cold in here."

"Not surprised you're cold. You ain't wearing more'n two handkerchiefs." He'd obligingly turned the heat up. "So, Casey. I'm O'Leary. I'm with the Third. Bin there a year."

"Third? That's where I'm moving to next." She'd smiled at him, which, oddly, hadn't had the usual effect. She wasn't now and hadn't been then a model-type, but her smile turned heads. Also oddly, unlike the two meatheads, he'd been strangely calm. "Do they know you're gay?" she'd blurted out, and the atmosphere had splintered in an instant.

Officer O'Leary had choked. "Say what?"

"You're gay. Aren't you?"

Enormous Officer O'Leary had not been at all impressed. "How'd you know that?" he'd growled. "No-one knows that."

"Um…" she'd stammered, a little scared in a way that she hadn't been when he'd arrested her earlier, reminded herself that she probably couldn't be shot by Officer Bigfoot O'Leary, and decided on truth. "You didn't cop a feel. All the others did. Um…. I won't tell anyone. Um… we didn't meet, but…er… I'm the one that those photos were about?" Might as well get it out there. He would have worked it out pretty soon, since he'd already half-recognised the name.

He'd stood down, somewhat. "Okay," he'd said, slowly, and extended a massive hand to her. She'd put her own in his, contemplating its likely crushing. In fact, O'Leary had enfolded it with considerable delicacy, and shaken very gently. "Heard about the photos. Don't make no never mind to me, 'cause I don't judge on rumours." Casey guessed that his particular secret made him a little less biased than the rest. Plenty of them judged on rumours. "You say you're comin' to the Third?"

"Yeah. Wanna tell me a bit about it?"

"Okay…"

The rest had, as they said, been history. She'd made it to the Third, and they'd been paired up quite a lot. She'd covered for him – the NYPD not, even those few years ago, having been as tolerant as it might have been – and if she'd needed a plus one, he'd obliged. They'd quickly become friends, as well as partners. She'd needed a friend, a little later.

She turned her mind away from that thought. It still bit, agonisingly. She still needed a friend, some days. God knew, she didn't have much of a family.

Suddenly, a beer or two seemed like a really good plan. She already knew where they would go – the Abbey Pub, on 105th. O'Leary claimed Irish roots, and wore green every St Patrick's Day to show it. If it was true, the roots were long buried. Still, it made him happy. Guinness, on the other hand, did not make Casey happy. It was disgusting stuff, though O'Leary knocked it back like soda, and with about as much effect. Ugh. She stuck to bottled beer.

"We can start again in the morning, y'know."

"Yeah. I just want something to work with."

"Yeah. Anyways, you made a new pal," O'Leary said mischievously, and acquired an evil smile.

"Uh?"

"Waalll, that photographer was certainly checkin' you out. He was quite pretty, though he ain't a patch on Pete."

"I'll tell Pete your eyes are wandering," she threatened.

"Nothin' to tell. Anyways, it's my duty as your pal to let you know. Since he ain't a suspect, you're allowed to check him out right back again."

"Not interested." She wasn't, she told herself. She had enough on her plate, right now. She didn't need complications, and the too-pretty photographer would have been a complication sufficient to fuddle Einstein. Besides which, photographers took photographs, and she hated being photographed.

"Shame. I always wanted to do cover shots."

Casey's mouthful of beer hit the table as she choked and spluttered. "You? Cover shots? What for?"

"I dunno," he grinned. "How 'bout Mr Universe?"

She couldn't answer for coughing. "No way," eventually emerged.

"Waallll," extended over her red-faced wheezes, "he was sure takin' a lotta shots. An' if you're not interested, mebbe you should stop blushin'. Might give me the wrong impression." She growled with indeterminate fury, which had no effect whatsoever on O'Leary's rhino-hide imperturbability. "Gotcha."

"I hate you," she sulked.

"Naw, you love me. Always have."

Casey gave up and laughed. O'Leary was unbreakably amiable. She saluted him with her beer bottle.

"Now," he said, abruptly serious, "how you doin'?"

"Okay." O'Leary simply regarded her piercingly. "I'm okay."

"An' your pa?"

She shrugged. "Same as always."

"'Kay." He didn't say anything more. He didn't need to.

"D'you think we'll get the address first thing?"

"How would I know? I ain't the database whizz. Hope so," he said, and followed her lead to talk shop till all the beer was gone.

***

"I got where he works," Andy said, the next day. "Clearances are for working at Columbia. Looks like he was a chemist there. Part of a research group run by a Professor Terrison. *Doctor* Belvez."

Casey wrinkled her nose as she contemplated the information. "Okay. You keep on with that. Let's see if we can find anything on next of kin, or cameras. I don't want to talk to his workplace till we've got a little bit more – and it's a bit mean to tell co-workers before we tell the family. Wish he'd had his phone on him," she said gloomily. "Now we have to do it the hard way." Andy made a sympathetic grimace, and set to.

Before she could begin, Casey's phone rang. "Clement."

"Detective Clement. Do you wish to attend the autopsy and receive the results first hand, or would you prefer to receive my report?"

It was pretty clear what McDonald would have preferred, but the team had set everything going, and waiting was not something at which Casey was good. In fact, she hated waiting.

"I'll come to the morgue." She flicked a glance around, considering her options in less than a millisecond. "Tyler'll come with me."

If McDonald had ever had enough emotion to express, he would surely have given a sigh of relief.

"I shall expect you shortly."

"Tyler, McDonald's invited us to the autopsy."

O'Leary's deep snickers filled the bullpen. "Goin' to the dance with him too? Iffen he's invited you over, he must be keen."

"You know he only likes Tyler 'cause he doesn't talk."

"It's good to talk," O'Leary grinned. "Stops a lot of problems. If more people talked, we wouldn't have so many murders."

"And we'd all be out of a job," Casey said cynically, turning to Tyler. "Let's go."

Casey and Tyler departed post haste for the morgue, where McDonald, gowned and gloved, was waiting for them.

Belvez looked no better laid out on the slab than he had in the alleyway.

"As you can see, there are no tattoos or distinguishing marks."

"Likely not military," Tyler noted briefly. Tyler had a small tattoo high on his bicep. They'd never have known about it, if O'Leary hadn't seen it when he was changing for sparring. Just another thing they didn't need to discuss, most times.

"I'll get O'Leary to check. I don't think so either, but let's knock it off the list. He doesn't look old enough, or fit enough."

"No."

"If you are finished chattering?"

Casey simply looked at McDonald.

"There are also no stab wounds, gunshot wounds, or significant defence marks."

"What is there?" Tyler asked.

"There is some slight bruising to the wrists and torso, consistent with ante-mortem transport while unconscious."

"Unconscious?"

"Observe this contusion and depression of the left parietal, approximately one inch above the occipital bone, which is likely to have rendered the victim unconscious ante-mortem."

"Can you tell what caused it?"

"Not yet. I shall take measurements and swab for particulates. Results will not be instant." Casey frowned. "I can tell you that it was a rounded object. There are no indications of a sharp point having been used."

"So he got whacked on the head?"

"That is what I said, yes."

Yeah, if she spoke fluent medical. She was sure McDonald did it to annoy her.

"But that didn't kill him."

"No. As I surmised at the scene, Mr Belvez was suffocated. I am still of the opinion that carbon monoxide was used, from the coloration of various areas. Note, in particular, the bright red lips and pink skin. Toxicology will confirm. Again" – he cut across Casey's question – "that will take a little time."

"Can't you speed it up?"

"Detective Clement," McDonald snipped irritably, "you ask that every time. Surely by now you have learned that it is not possible. Repeated questioning will not change the answer. No, I cannot speed it up. You will have to wait."

"I don't like waiting," Casey huffed under her breath, and said more loudly, "Thank you, ME McDonald. Is there anything else?"

"I estimate that he was killed around ten p.m., with a margin for error" – McDonald abhorred the precision of certain TV shows, which he frequently stated to be invariably ridiculous – "of approximately two hours either way. His last meal appears to have been a hamburger with fries. No vegetables. He drank soda. I estimate that it was consumed some three to four hours before death."

Casey opened her mouth, and was forestalled.

"There will be no further information until I receive toxicology results. Do not waste my time by asking."

She suppressed a growl. Sure, she'd rather have accuracy than speed, but why couldn't she have both? "Thank you, Dr McDonald," she emitted, and stalked out, followed by Tyler.

"Not much new," Tyler said laconically.

"No. Maybe Andy or O'Leary will have found next of kin."

"Yeah."

Back in the bullpen, Andy had indeed discovered next of kin.

"He's got a brother. Leon Belvez, back in New Mexico. He's a teacher – high school Spanish."

"I guess I'd better call him, then."

She picked up her phone.

"Leon Belvez?"

"Yeah? Who is this?"

"Mr Belvez, this is Detective Clement from the New York Police

Department."

"Police? Have you got Ricky? He's not picking up his cell phone."

"Mr Belvez, I'm sorry to tell you that we found a body" – she got no further.

"No! He can't be dead. He just started his new job a few months ago."

"I'm so sorry."

"I was gonna come up for the weekend in a couple of weeks to see New York. I've never been there before, but with Ricky" –

Realisation suddenly hit Leon. "Oh God. Ricky…" There was a shattered, ghastly silence, and the phone went dead.

"Poor guy," O'Leary said.

"Yeah," Casey said flatly. "But now I'll need to call him again when he's calmed down a little and ask the questions I need to ask."

"You think he's involved?"

"Not yet. But if he's next of kin, and Belvez had assets…"

"Not too likely, if he's a researcher."

"You never know." Which was so self-evidently true that Andy was silenced.

"Seein' as you told next of kin, we c'n go see his workplace now," O'Leary pointed out.

"Yeah, okay. You just want a trip out. You're as antsy as a first-grader."

"He's the biggest first-grader I ever did see," Andy singsonged. "Hey, do Bigfoots go to school?"

"'Course they do," O'Leary grinned in his usual amiable style. "How d'you think we learn to leave confusin' footprints an' suspicious tufts of fur without gettin' caught an' put in the Zoo?"

"Are you telling us you depilate, then?"

"Sure. Otherwise I'd be all furry. Can't be Mr Universe if I'm all furry. You lose points that way, an' besides, the oil don't do my fur no good at all."

Tyler snickered. Casey outright laughed.

"Come on then, Bigfoot. Let's go terrorise the university. Terrison, you said, Andy?" Andy nodded.

"I always like some good terrorisin'," O'Leary rumbled happily, and they started off for Columbia in the thin September sunshine.

After some threatening, O'Leary moderated his pace and they walked companionably down Broadway to Columbia's Havemeyer Hall. Even at a moderated pace, it was still a brisk walk for Casey. It was a relaxed ambulation for O'Leary.

CHAPTER 5

A passing student in a dirty lab coat directed them to Terrison's office, through the open door of which Casey could spot a small, neat man bent over a desk.

"Professor Terrison?"

"Yes?" he said distractedly, not really looking up. On shelves around him were brightly coloured stick-and ball models; a Periodic Table decorated the wall with a framed certificate next to it which she couldn't read.

"Detective Clement, NYPD."

"What?" He jerked up to meet her gaze, shocked. "Police? Why? What?"

"I'm sorry to tell you that Ricardo Belvez has been found dead."

Terrison's face paled. "Dead? They said he called in sick, so I asked Mike to take his class this afternoon. Dead? Ricky? *Ricky's* dead?" His face collapsed, suddenly old and sad. "He only joined our group a few months ago. He really knew his stuff." He looked grieved. "Now he's dead? What a waste. He was shaping up to be brilliant. His papers were getting cited a bit more than a post-grad might. He's dead? What happened?"

"He was found on West 111th. He'd been hit on the head." Casey was certainly not going to give any unusual details. She also didn't mention the timing. Called in sick? When, she wondered.

"He was mugged? That's dreadful. What a *waste*."

"Okay," Casey said sympathetically. "I'm afraid we'll have to ask you a few questions now, and then talk to all of your group. Can you give us their details so we can do that without needing to disrupt anything?"

Terrison produced all the details without a fuss. Casey didn't point out that this was unusually co-operative and that normally the university

30

bureaucracy would have forbidden it. She never looked a gift horse in the mouth.

She began with the easy matters.

"How and when did he start here?"

Terrison acquired a slightly smug smile, despite his upset. "I recruited him from New Mexico State. I read the papers he'd co-authored, and it was clear he was doing some really brilliant thinking in the opto-electronic compounds field."

"Huh?" grunted O'Leary.

"New substances to make lenses, or fibre-optics. All sorts of ways of improving vision or transmission – it's all about how the light behaves as it travels through the compounds."

It didn't look as if that explanation had really improved O'Leary's understanding.

"So he came in as the new boy?"

"I guess so, but he was five years post-doctorate, so he wasn't a *junior* hire."

"How did the rest of the group take it? Was there anyone he didn't get on with, or who felt put out?"

Terrison thought about it. "Not really. We're a pretty friendly bunch, and new blood that can bring in new grants benefits us all."

"Grants?"

"You get a grant from someone – for us, we get a lot of funding from Telagon, you know, the telecoms company, because we do optoelectronics and they're obviously keen on that – for a period of time or a specific project, and when that's finished so is the money, so you need to apply for a new one." He sighed. "We have to spend a lot of time on grant applications."

"But why's that important?" O'Leary rumbled.

"If you find an important result, you'll get more money, more often," Terrison simplified. "So even if you're a split-new post-doc, you'll be contributing to the income of the whole group. The more papers you publish and contribute to, and the more your work is cited, the better your reputation and the chances of getting bigger and better grant funding."

Casey considered that. She thought that Terrison was being astonishingly naïve about the effects of a new, brilliant, incomer. She wasn't an academic, and she wasn't tapped into the academic world, but she surely did understand the corrosive effect of professional jealousy. She shivered. Terrison noticed.

"Would you like coffee? Tea? Some people find it cold in here, but I can't say I notice."

"Coffee, please. Black."

"An' me, please."

Terrison's small, neat, efficient hands made swift, efficient coffee from a pot by his desk.

"You said your work was funded by Telagon?"

"Yes. They're huge. They're very generous, too. They spread it around, and, well, I won't say I wouldn't like more of their dollars, but... we do a lot better than okay. They fund us in the millions, if they think there are practical applications, and they always have. We've got a really good relationship with them. Mike runs it, though. He knows what they like to see and" – he looked a little embarrassed – "well, if I'm head down in work I'm not always as organised as I need to be and Mike saves my ass by keeping Telagon happy – and he does great work, too. Nearly as good as Ricky."

"Mike?" O'Leary asked.

"Mike Merowin. My senior post-doc."

They would follow up that name.

"Dr Belvez had clearances. Is that normal?"

"Oh, sure. We all do, because Telagon work with the Department of Defense, so we get them as standard. Do you need to see them?"

"Not at the minute, thanks."

Well, that explained that. Casey was already pushing Terrison lower down her suspects list – he was totally unguarded and open and he had been genuinely shocked at the news of Belvez's death – but a little more pushing wasn't going to hurt. Better to be safe.

"Who's your main competition?"

"It's not really competition," Terrison said, which Casey, and from his cynical expression, O'Leary too, thought was remarkably naïve. "Research gets published, so we all get to know about it and test it in the end. Research has to be replicable by someone else before you can say it's a breakthrough. I suppose when you come up with something patentable, that's a bit different, but that's uncommon. A big breakthrough in this field, though, would definitely be patentable, and that would really be worth a lot of money. If we manage that Telagon will fund us even more."

"I see."

So there was a lot of money sloshing around this group. Mm. As motives for murder went, money was right up there with sex. Pretty much always – barring psychopaths – it was one or the other, and sex often went with psychopaths too. This murder, however, was beginning to sound like a money crime already. Belvez's general appearance hadn't left her thinking he had been a sex god.

A little flicker of memory of the photographer tried to dawdle through her mind, and was kicked out before she could think that he'd been pretty sexy. He'd been a pain.

"Was there anyone you knew about that knew him well?" O'Leary asked. "Girlfriend, family, anything? Anyone outside the group that'd got a beef with him?"

"Not that I knew. He was head down in his work, and I'm afraid I usually am too. I don't really know much about them. Can I help some other way?" he added, pathetically keen to assist.

"If we find out anything that involves his work, would you be able to help us with it?"

"Surely. Anything. What a *waste*," he mourned. "He had all his future ahead of him. Poor guy." His sincerity was patent.

"Thank you. I'll contact you if there is anything you can do." She handed over a card. "If there's anything else you can think of, call me. Anything could be important." She paused. "One more thing."

"Yes?"

"Don't tell anyone else that Dr Belvez is dead. We'll do that. Let them all think he's still sick."

"If it's going to help. Poor Ricky."

Casey already knew that there would be matters he could help with, but Terrison needed a little time to get over the shock, and *she* needed time to interview the members of his group to ensure that he really was the naïve scientist which he appeared to be, rather than a Machiavellian mastermind with several Oscars under his belt.

"Anything," he said again.

The cops rose. Terrison did too, consulting his battered, old watch. "I'll come out with you," he added. "I think…. I want to clear my head. Poor Ricky."

"What did you think?" Casey asked, after they'd left Terrison contemplating the fragility of life from a bench on campus.

"He seemed pretty cut up."

"Mm. That's what I thought. I can't discount him – will you *slow down*? I don't want to jog back – but he's not top of my list. I'm thinking there's money in the mix."

O'Leary dropped his pace to allow for Casey's shorter legs. "Slowpoke," he grumbled. "Yeah. I'm thinkin' that too. Sounded like there's more cash about than we knew. Money don't buy happiness, but it sure do buy murder more often than we like."

"Yeah. I think I'd like a look at this Mike guy. If he's got the lock on the money source, that's interesting."

"Sounds like that's one for the list."

"Yeah."

"Iffen you needed another chemist," O'Leary drawled, "I been thinkin' that photographers do a bit of chemistry?" He said it very innocently. "You could call him. I'm sure he'd be keen on helpin' you."

"You," Casey bit out, "are the biggest damn Cupid in creation. Just 'cause you're all loved up, you think everyone else should be. Well, just leave it. I don't have his number and photographers don't do serious chemistry. I don't even think they do darkroom developing much anymore. That's what computers are for."

O'Leary regarded the back of her head and her stiff spine with amusement, but dropped his ragging. "Okay," he said equably. "Just sayin'."

After that *helpful* little suggestion of O'Leary's, Casey didn't quite stomp back the last few yards to the precinct, but there was certainly no chit-chat. She growled to herself, and turned to the haven of her case.

So. Belvez was Terrison's new boy, or bright shining star, more like. She looked down the list of names that Terrison had provided (so *useful* when people didn't stand on ceremony, or indeed the letter of the law).

"Andy, Tyler?"

"Yeah?"

"Huh?"

"I've got the list of names of Terrison's research group. He thinks that everyone would be peachy keen to have a new boy come in – one who's already aiming for the top."

The three of them exchanged cynically disbelieving glances.

"Yeah, right," Tyler commented.

"Have his chemicals fried his brain?" Andy asked rhetorically.

"Yep, I thought all that too. Terrison's dropping off the top of the list pretty fast, but could you two split the list and just run them quickly: see if anything pops up that we should know about?"

"Hoping one of 'em's an axe murderer?"

"I'd prefer a list of suspicious suffocations, but axe murderer will do too," she laughed.

They set searches in train on the research group, and a further search to eliminate Belvez from a military connection, in the hope that by running them overnight the databases would have spat out something useful by the morning, and decamped.

"Y'know, it's late. Nothin' more's gonna happen tonight, so it's me for home."

O'Leary's suggestion found substantial support, and the team dispersed.

***

Early the next morning, Casey applied her brain to the case.

She sat down and pulled a piece of blank paper towards her, on which she started to sketch out a plan of campaign. She ticked off what she had, then she ticked off *who* she had: naïve professor, brother back in Albuquerque – and a senior post-doc. Plus the rest of the research group, of course. Once she had done that, she started to plan the next steps. Not long later, with the application of some logical thought, she had an extensive — and rational — to do list. Things had been a little scattergun so far, and now it was time to impose order — now that they had some, still sadly few, matters upon which to impose it. She grinned nastily at her basic list, and began to expand each section, flicking her attention back and forth from her murder board.

Casey looked at her expanded list with considerable satisfaction. It was neatly laid out, though the less said about her handwriting the better, and covered everything she could think of in perfectly logical and detailed sections. She stretched widely, and swung briskly off to get a coffee from the break room, mulling over her lovely logical list as she did. She downed a large slug of coffee, hummed happily, and grinned, all untoward feelings caused by O'Leary's matchmaking and the annoyingly persistent memory of the photographer dissipated in the contented knowledge that she had a trail to follow.

When the team arrived, she grinned fiercely at them. "I made a list. Let's all get some coffee and work out what happens next."

Casey with a list was a sight to be feared. On the other hand, coffee was a good plan. The four detectives whisked into the break room, and shortly whisked back out, taking possession of a handy conference room and spreading themselves about.

"So what've we got now?" Casey opened, two sips into her coffee. "This Merowin guy seems to figure a lot, so O'Leary and I will go and have a little chat with him. Anyone else pop in the research group?"

"No," Andy said disappointedly. "Nothing. None of the others had so much as a speeding ticket. No prints in any systems for them."

"None of 'em popped for anything else yet either," Tyler said, equally disappointedly. "No reason to haul anyone in and frighten them."

"Shame," Casey agreed. Tyler could get a little edgy if he didn't get to do a bit of intimidation every now and then. On the other hand, he could intimidate that photographer any time he liked. Win-win. Happy Tyler, happy Casey, unhappy photographer. Perfect. "Still, we can get uniforms to do the first canvass, and ask them about Belvez. Cover it off."

Tyler liked that idea. "Sure I can. I'll set them up after this. I think we should do that while you're seeing Merowin. Don't want them tipping him off, huh?"

"No," Casey agreed. Tyler could always be counted on to make sure that the right timing went in. He was good at tactics: probably because of his military background. "Guess that means we're back down to Columbia, O'Leary. You'll be bored of it."

She received a very innocent look in return. "Yep. You thinkin' we should soften this Merowin up?"

"Can't hurt."

"So we're going to have a chat with him?"

"Yep. I was just about to get his schedule."

She went to find the number, returned, picked up the phone and had a brief conversation with Columbia's chemistry department. "Okay, he's teaching the rest of today. That gives us Saturday morning. Tyler, you take the uniforms, and O'Leary and I will take Merowin."

"Unfair," Andy said. "You get to go out again. We never get to go out."

"I get to speak chemistry, too," Casey said dryly, "which is worse than high-school German. Give me Spanish any day."

"I can speak Cantonese," Andy said happily. Everyone glared at him. Bilingual didn't count.

"If we find any international transfer students who need to be spoken to in Cantonese, you'll be going right down there. You can bond over calligraphy and tai-chi classes at six a.m."

"Yep," Andy said equably. "That's my style right there. You should try it, Casey. Tai-chi is very soothing. Good for the soul."

"Nothing is good for the soul that starts at six a.m."

"You're only saying that because you haven't tried it. You should."

Casey grumbled wordlessly. Andy knew perfectly well that she only did mornings because she had to. She hated mornings. Sleep was much nicer, when she could find it. He smiled sweetly at her. She growled. Everyone returned to the plan and the work.

***

Carval woke with a plan in mind. He'd got all those crime scene photos. If he printed them off and took them up to the Thirty-Sixth precinct, then he could say he'd thought they might be helpful. He didn't know what cops needed, after all. He wouldn't be lying. And then he could simply ask the team if he could tag along. He might as well be up front about what he wanted, and he was pretty sure that he would get a positive response. He didn't want to hang around the precinct for hours and hours at all: that would be no fun and not consistent with his theme; though a few shots inside wouldn't hurt, for contrast. He just wanted to tag around behind their investigations so he could track their movements and expressions. He was sure it wouldn't be a problem. Everyone wanted to be famous, after all.

He meandered through shower, coffee, breakfast and printing copies of all yesterday's shots except his centrepiece; thought for a moment and then printed, unsure why, copies of the shots from Stanford. Preparations made, he ambled off to the gym, spent an easy hour with the rowing machine and the weights, and came out feeling good.

Not far into the morning, he'd spruced himself up a little – he told himself that it was respect for the majesty of the law in the form of the NYPD, and certainly didn't allow himself to consider that it was because

Casey-the-cop hadn't regarded him with any approval at all, where most women showed at least a flicker of appreciation – and was on his way to the Thirty-Sixth. Naturally, his camera was in his pocket.

Despite his dislike of architectural shots, and the fact that the sand coloured, blocky building had no redeeming features whatsoever – it certainly hadn't been designed by anyone with taste, and those shields on the glass doors looked like carnival masks from a distance – he snapped off a few shots of the building and the bustle around it, catching the light on the marked cruisers, the mixture of uniformed officers and plain-clothes cops identifiable only by their shields, cuffs and guns on hips, and the stressed civilians pushing in and out on waves of emotion.

Possibly fortunately, no-one noticed him taking surreptitious shots. He slipped inside, and approached the desk.

"Hey," he said mildly. "My name's Carval. Um, yesterday I was taking photos and some of your detectives were dealing with a corpse, and I thought afterwards that maybe there might be something useful in the shots?" He was deliberately uncertain, all good-concerned-citizen who wanted to help but wasn't sure it was worth disturbing the cops for something that would likely be nothing.

The rangy desk cop gave him a smile which contained no recognition at all. "Thanks for coming by. Do you know who any of the detectives were? We got a lot of teams here."

Carval made a pretence of thinking. "Didn't catch the names, but a woman, and a guy the size of a house."

"O'Leary," the cop said immediately. It seemed that there was only one skyscraper masquerading as a cop in the Thirty-Sixth, which was faintly reassuring. "That'll be Detectives Clement and O'Leary. I'll give one of them a call and get someone to escort you up."

"Thanks." He hesitated, and decided to go for it. "Er, could I take a few shots in here? I wouldn't show anyone's face."

The cop blinked, surprised. Carval looked innocently hopeful.

"Naw," the cop drawled. "Wouldn't be appropriate."

"'Kay." He hadn't really expected to be allowed, which was why he'd been taking surreptitious further shots ever since he came through the door. He had no idea at all whether any of them would be in focus, useful, or anything other than a waste of memory. He'd worry about that later. For now, he'd got what he wanted. He leant casually on a wall and whistled tunelessly to himself, watching the world go by in all its infinite variety, his fingers pressing on the camera and hoping: hoping that he caught the old, bitter pain in the face of the hunched, wrinkled woman; the military gait and posture of a white-haired man; the mischief of the small toddler wobbling on a rein but determined to escape and explore this whole new world. He waggled fingers at the toddler and received a wobbly wave back again, with a brilliant smile.

"Mr Carval!"

Ah. Oh. The uniformed officer had clearly tried to attract his attention several times already, from the note in his voice.

"Sorry."

He followed the officer to an institutionally whitewashed stairwell, from which a slight whiff of unpleasant bodily odours oozed, and then along endless corridors. Finally he was deposited in a small interview room with uncomfortable plastic chairs and a Formica-topped table. It had no windows, just a one-way glass wall. It occurred to Carval that it was an interrogation room, not a conference room. He was not encouraged by the realisation.

Still, no time like the present... and he took proper shots, which involved him actually having a chance to raise the camera so that he could see the shot and ensure it was, at a minimum, in focus. There might have been some interesting reflective effects from the one-way glass, too: he tried a few with flash, then without, then at some other angles. He heard a hard clack of brisk, authoritative steps and quickly stowed the camera away.

"Mr Carval," Casey-the-cop pinched out. She didn't look at all pleased to see him. "Sergeant Marnock called me. You said you had useful photos?"

"I said I had photos and I didn't know if they might be useful." He tried a warm smile on her chilly gaze. "Better that I asked you." She huffed, disbelievingly. "That's a little unkind. I just wanted to help." Her face was stonily blank. "Look, I brought the shots I took." He laid them out on the table. She didn't react at all. She shuffled through them and put them down.

"Nothing there," she noted. "Thank you for trying." It was as sincere as a shell game hustler. Carval realised that his tactic wasn't working, and went for the last resort. Truth.

"I wanna shoot you."

"So do lots of people, but I guess you mean with a camera. No. I'm no model."

"No, you're at least six inches too short and you've got a figure," he tossed out casually. "But you take good shots. I want to follow you – all of you – around."

She spluttered. "Get lost. You're interfering with my work. If you show up anywhere near me again I'll arrest you."

"For what? I'm not in the way and photography in public isn't illegal. First Amendment, or don't they teach that in the police academy?"

"It's not a First Amendment right," she snapped. "That's free speech. Photos don't count."

"You still can't arrest me for it," Carval pointed out. He was surprised.

Normally cops weren't that hot on the finer points of constitutional law.

"I can if you obstruct me," she growled, dark eyes sparking angrily. Behind the anger, there was just a hint that there might be a different spark.

Now that was even more surprising. She hadn't even tried to argue that she could arrest him for photography. He'd had a few run-ins on that subject before. She'd gone straight to the one that worked. Obstructing a police investigation. Who *was* this woman? She was smart. He liked smart. He liked sparky, too, and she was certainly that. Not to say feisty. If only she weren't so *angry* with him. It just wasn't fair. He tried a repentant smile. It received a chilly stare. Okay, cute wasn't going to work today.

"What's your beef with me?" he asked, with an edge of irritation.

"You're wasting my time. Your photos don't give me squat to work with – I don't need so-called art, I need evidence. This isn't evidence, and in the half hour you've been messing me around I could have been doing something useful to find the perpetrator." Passion rang through her tones.

Carval looked blankly at her. He hadn't expected that. Truthfully, he hadn't even thought of it like that. More accurately, he hadn't thought. He certainly hadn't thought that her need to find the killer might be as strong in her as his need to take the photographs to fill the gaps in his theme: the shots that he could see in his head.

"Thank you for your" – he heard *wasted* – "time." She opened the interview room door, and spun back round. "What the *hell* are you doing?"

He was photographing, of course. What did it look like he was doing? He smiled sweetly. "Nothing." They both knew it was a lie. He watched furious frustration bleed into her face as she realised that she had no legal grounds to confiscate his camera.

"Delete them. You've no reason to take photos here."

"I've got a plan for my next show. Cops in Manhattan. Specifically, you and your team. So nope, I've plenty of reason to shoot here and I won't delete them," he said brightly, and made sure his camera was firmly in his hand. She sized up her options, very obviously – and most unfortunately worked out that he was enough taller than her that trying to take it from him wouldn't work. Shame. He really wouldn't have minded her trying. Without a blazer on, she was definitely curved in all the right directions. In fact, as he passed her on the way to the door, he idly noticed that even in her moderate heels she was neatly about his shoulder height. Very tuckable – *what?* He was going crazy.

He was definitely crazy. Because he had just said, "You know we've met before?"

"Yeah. Yesterday. So?"

"No. Years ago. When you were at Stanford."

She stared at him, frozen. "I *met* you?"

"Yep."

"I've never seen you in my life," she said in disbelieving cynicism. "You're just spinning a line to get into the crime scenes for your photos."

"You did." He pulled the prints from his jacket pocket, and put them on the table. "See?"

She looked down and the colour drained from her face. "What the actual *fuck*? You?" she breathed. As quickly, she recovered. "Doesn't change a thing. Leave, and stop disrupting my investigations."

"You remember me," he said. "You didn't before but now you do."

"Not relevant. Go."

"You danced with me," he provoked, and then, "What's wrong?" he diverted, noticing the lack of blood in her cheeks.

"Nothing. Leave. We're done here."

She walked out without a backwards glance. Since Carval was dead in the water anyway, for a reason he didn't understand, he took a whole series of shots of the drab corridors and grimy stairwell. He left the prints – all of them – on the table before he departed. She could collect them, or not, as she pleased. He'd struck out. There wasn't a hope that she would talk to him sensibly today.

But his undisciplined mind suggested that he could hang around for a little bit, just in case she came outside. It was ridiculous, and she surely wouldn't, but he'd got nothing to do and nowhere to be and he had to take some chances to get and keep his show firmly on the road. He was not giving up on doing this theme. He didn't get to where he was by caving in at the first hint of resistance.

And besides, now he was really intrigued.

CHAPTER 6

Casey preserved her composure until she was out of earshot and then shut herself in an empty conference room. The day had just gone to hell and it wasn't even eleven in the morning. She should have known as soon as the desk sergeant called up, telling her that there was a Mr Carval here who thought he had some evidence for her. She'd instantly disbelieved it, but she couldn't afford not to investigate. Being suckered into his game hadn't done anything to sweeten her temper. The little voice in her head that had said *mmm* hadn't helped, either.

And now she'd been thrown right back into the memory of a stage she'd long ago left behind, just from one photo.

So that had been where that picture came from. She'd never understood that. She thought back to two months or so into the Academy, about the point that friendly competition had stopped being friendly.

Mark Marcol. Came from a family of cops. Good cops. Commendations and awards all over the shop. He'd come into the Academy already expecting to succeed: be the best, graduate top. And for the first three weeks, that's exactly what had happened. He had been popular, sociable, and just where he expected to be.

Right up till he hadn't been.

Casey knew that she was possibly a tad competitive. Okay. Insanely competitive, but she hid it quite well. She had been used to doing well. She had been used to coming top. Succeeding. And three weeks in, she had already been so totally over the casual sexism; the mostly-joking commentary about how she'd be fine because if she wore a short skirt the criminals would chase her; a few snide comments about uptown girls slumming it. So she had decided to prove she was as good as any of them.

On balance, that might just have been a mistake. Because once she had really put her mind to it, she had started doing well. Really well. And then she had started to come top. She had been a competent shot – her mom and dad had taught her – but she'd practised hard, and got better. She'd started to exercise more, and become much fitter. Still curvy – she was never going to be catwalk model slim – but tauter, more honed. Her times, reps, scores: they had all improved, and kept improving. Her classroom work had already been top notch: the one area in which she'd excelled from the beginning.

She'd driven herself hard, and then harder; competition had become its own reward and excelling its tangible proof. Her class had begun to notice, and comment. She'd ignored them, and kept on pushing herself.

When she'd come top of the rankings for the first time, she'd found that Marcol hadn't liked coming second. The next time, he had been top, and he hadn't won gracefully, same as he hadn't lost gracefully. Casey, also not a good loser at the best of times, had fought back by coming top the next time, and compounded that mortal sin by totally failing to notice that he had also been trying to cosy up to her. She hadn't had time for a boyfriend: she had been wholly focused on the Academy and pushing herself on. Besides which, sleeping with her co-recruits would have been a very short way to mess up any hopes she might have had.

Three months in, when she and Marcol had been fighting it out for top spot every time, she'd begun to notice whispering among Marcol's cronies. Soon it had spread. It had been pretty clear it was about her. Nasty stuff, but she'd shrugged it off. *Sticks and stones may break my bones, but names will never hurt me.* She'd had her supportive, loving family; so she'd simply worked another level harder, pretended she hadn't heard any of it, and resolved to beat the pants off Marcol and his pals. If they had thought that silly name calling would faze her, they had been totally wrong.

And then they'd upped the ante. That photo. Somehow someone – she still suspected Birkett, who'd been a dyed-in-the-wool technogeek and a total weasel – had found it. Copies had been everywhere. Recruit-officer Clement wearing a dress the size of a dishtowel and looking like a centrefold: smudged eyes, lush lips, and legs a mile long.

She turned her mind forcibly away from the memories of brutal commentary and the occasional attempt at going further. Marcol had obviously thought that she'd quit or back off in the face of an orchestrated campaign to denigrate her: rumours designed to reduce her to a slut who had been doing it on her back not by the book. Well, she hadn't had any of it. She'd retreated completely into herself: developed a hard, cold shell in short order, and decided that the best defence was to watch him eat her dust.

Before, she'd been driven. Then, she'd become obsessed.

She had graduated top by a margin that caused the instructors to blink, but along the way she'd lost any ability she might have had to make friends whom she could trust. The key lesson she'd learnt was that everyone was out to bring you down, and the best way to avoid it was not to get involved with them.

That didn't change till she met O'Leary, and even now she knew that if she hadn't guessed he was gay straight off the bat, it wouldn't have changed then either. He'd had a far bigger secret than she. By that time, though, it was too late. She was known, sometimes in consecutive breaths, as Centrefold Clement, and as Ice-Cold Casey. Or alternatively, That-Cold-Bitch-Clement. So she buried herself in being the best cop she could be, worked her ass off, did everything asked of her and then more – and enjoyed every last minute that she learned and worked and helped *solve* cases, in whatever capacity. And later, it gave her respite.

But still. Even now, years on, she was respected by everyone in the bullpen, but she hadn't got many real friends. Everyone exchanged a smile and casual conversation, but they didn't draw her into conversation. She and her team were an airtight unit. They each had their own secrets, or demons, and they didn't let them out to play where others might have seen. Tyler had left friends out on the sand, and sometimes he startled when a truck backfired, though he was always at the top of the range master's score sheet, and when he was bored, he gave tuition. Andy: well, he didn't always sleep so soundly. He was slim, and delicate enough to be pretty, and his teen years had been – they would say *difficult*, and let that single word cover a lot of ground. He was the first to call out abuse, the one who worked hardest to solve any case where that was in the mix.

And Marcol? She never thought of him. For all she knew or cared, he was in Podunk, Ohio.

She sat, slumped, in the small conference room, shocked cold by the resurrection of a long-buried skeleton. Now she knew where the photo had come from. She'd almost forgotten that evening after graduation. Now she knew why Carval had carried a vanishingly faint hint of familiarity. It hadn't been the exhibition at all. It had been the long-ago dance, and the kiss. She'd remembered the kiss, for months. She remembered the kiss *now*.

Oh, *hell*.

She dragged herself out of the conference room, returned to collect the shots just in case there proved to be something useful, and pocketed the two prints from Stanford. Better not let those get mixed in. She didn't need to make any slip ups like that. The past was a foreign country, from which she'd emigrated long ago.

She didn't want to be part of any photographic show. Not now, not then, not ever.

O'Leary looked up as she slid back into the bullpen.

"Where you been?"

"Wasting time," she bit.

"Mm?" She wished O'Leary wouldn't hum. Apart from the fact that he sounded like a giant bumblebee, it hurt the bones of her ears.

"That photographer turned up with his shots from Wednesday pretending they might be useful. That's an hour of my life I won't get back." Bitterness spilled over.

"Mm," her mountainous partner hummed again. "You look like he hit you."

"Want me to *talk* to him?" Tyler grated. Menace pervaded his posture. Tyler was occasionally a little over-protective.

"It's fine," she said wearily. "I'm just pissed that he wasted my time. All he wants is to take pictures of us working. Wants us to be his next show."

O'Leary had extreme disbelief written all over his face, which, fortunately, Tyler (and Andy, coming up on track one to see what was going on) couldn't see.

"I'm going out to get a decent cup of coffee."

Nobody asked her to bring them one back. O'Leary made a slight move as if to join her, and then thought better of it on comprehending her expression.

***

Watching from a conveniently sunny point with a clear view of the front entrance of the precinct, Carval was rapidly coming to the conclusion that waiting to see if anything interesting – for which read one of his targets exiting – would happen had been a bad plan. Worse, it was boring, and he hated being bored. There was nothing more interesting here for him. He put the camera away, and took a step –

She came out of the door, and he whipped his camera out of his pocket. He was snapping off shots before his brain had caught up with his instincts. Through the lens, she was pallid: the dark eyes dull. All the fire and spirit which had informed the first photo, the centrepiece – all that was gone: drained. The contrast was astonishing, and it would be brilliant. She turned to her left, oblivious to the hurrying bustle which concealed both his camera and that he was following her. She wasn't brisk: head down, steps heavy.

She ghosted through Old Broadway, made two turns, arrived on Broadway and kept walking south, turned again and disappeared into a black-fronted espresso bar. Carval waited a beat, mentally girded his loins and reminded himself that he wouldn't get shot in a public place, and followed her in.

It was tiny. Fortunately, it was also quiet. Casey-the-cop ordered a double espresso, added a mini pain-au-chocolat, and stowed herself in a corner. Carval quietly ordered an Americano, didn't take a pastry, and in an astonishing display of courage also known as suicidal stupidity, sat down opposite her, not entirely accidentally blocking her from general view.

He was dumbfounded to see the print which had so upset her on the table. She was staring at it, and since she hadn't so much as twitched an eyelash at him sitting down, he guessed she wasn't in the same universe as he was, right now. He stayed very, very quiet, and didn't give in to his unexpected impulse to cover her slim, long-fingered hands with his. He'd have *liked* to shoot those hands: still, cold and pale.

He did: a stolen shot which she didn't notice: just like she hadn't noticed anything outside her head since she sat down.

Before she lifted her cup – that was, before she absolutely would notice him, drop the cup and both lose her coffee and destroy the print – he spoke.

"Hey," he said softly.

Her head flicked up, almost panicked, he thought; and then her eyes dropped again. "Stalking is a crime," she said dully.

"The photo upset you."

And he wanted more photos, but saying that was possibly not conducive to his continued existence.

"And this is your issue how?" There was barely a spark of fight, or even irritation.

"It's my photo. When I took it you were sky-high – legally," he added quickly, just in case she thought he meant something else. "You were all celebrating graduating. You were really happy. I wanna know why it's so upsetting now."

"Do you?" she said flatly: heavier than concrete. "Well, you'll just have to want." She stared into her coffee.

"Casey" –

"*Detective* Clement, please." The bite on that should have cut oxen in half.

"If you're Detective Clement, why did everyone call you Casey?"

"My *friends* call me that. Not strangers."

Ah. An opening.

"But we're not strangers. I danced with you." Irritation rose in her face, which was marginally better than the defeated misery of a moment earlier. He decided to push his luck, in the interests of cheering her up. "And I kissed you."

"I don't remember." But a tiny hint of colour limned her cheeks. Carval raised his eyebrows, indicating that he'd clocked her lie. "It was a long time ago. It's not relevant now."

She drained her espresso, disposed of her pastry in two fast bites, and stood.

"Leave me alone," she said. "You did enough damage with the first photo."

It was the break he needed. He caught her hand, and stopped her motion towards the door.

"Damage? What damage?"

She tried to free her hand, and failed. "Let go of me," she hissed.

"Sit down and talk to me, then. I wanna know what happened, 'cause I never did anything to damage you. I didn't even know your name."

"I have to get back to work." She tugged.

"So talk to me after."

"I don't want to talk to you at all."

"I noticed. I'm really quite nice. I promise not to kiss you again, if that's what's worrying you?"

"If you try to kiss me I will shoot you. Now let go."

"I'll let go if you come back to talk to me later."

"I won't arrest you if you let go."

"Arrest me for what? If I'm in the cop shop, someone'll tell me about the photo. And I'll get more photos."

She hissed furiously. "No talking to my precinct. No photos."

"Deal. So I'll see you at six, here."

"Seven. At Starbucks on Broadway and Tiemann." He wasn't even sure she'd realised she'd agreed.

"Later." He let go. She left with an irritated clack of heels and an angry swish. Carval gave her a second to clear the doorway, left the coffee bar himself, and then started to count. He reached twelve before she stormed back to find him gone. He reckoned she had just worked out that she had no way to contact him to cancel. Now he was simply relying on her not standing him up. It was as tenuous as spider silk, but… it was worth a go.

He wandered off, whistling.

***

Casey stomped back into the bullpen infuriated by her own stupidity and not in the least calmed by her coffee, the soothing effect of which had effectively been cancelled out by that damn photographer. Her pitch-black mood was not improved when she found Captain Kent flicking through the photos on her desk.

"Where have you been, Clement?" He never referred to her as Casey.

"Following up a lead, sir." Kent's interested gaze tempted her to further words. "The guy who took these thought he might have information."

"Did he?"

"I don't think so," she said bleakly. "He didn't have anything useful."

"Mm." Kent examined the photos again. "Carval's work. I'd recognise it anywhere."

"Sir?" No harm in letting Kent pontificate, even if she knew it already.

"Photographer. Lowlifes and panhandlers. Quite well known, if you like that sort of thing." His tone implied that he could take or leave it. "My wife likes it. We've been to all the exhibitions and lectures." Ah. Much was explained. Rumour had it that Kent's wife imposed culture upon him. It hadn't taken as yet. Kent was pretty keen on football. Art, not so much.

"So he took these at the scene?"

"Yes. They don't show anything we don't know already."

"Colour of the face?"

"Dr McDonald postulates carbon monoxide poisoning, sir. He was hit on the head ante-mortem."

Kent picked through the other photos. "Stained fingers?"

"His work history said he's a chemist. Tox will show if he was a smoker, too. Either could cause the stains. We should have results soon."

"Hm," Kent said. "Okay." His slightly stern demeanour softened. "Carry on, Detectives. Seems like you've got everything on track for now."

The four detectives looked at each other. "He's happy?"

"If he said so, he is."

Andy found a different scent to follow. "Took you a while to find your coffee." His nose twitched in the manner of a curious hamster. "What kept you?"

"I… that damn photographer was there and hassling me."

O'Leary cast her a querying glance. "No, I didn't shoot him." She faked a grin. "Too many people about."

"He's pretty desperate to get these photos, ain't he?"

"I can have a word," Tyler added. Clearly there had been a discussion. Her team all knew why she didn't like photos.

"It's okay. I can handle it."

"Mm," Tyler hummed, very dubiously. "If you say so." He thought for a moment. Tyler didn't generally say a lot, and though he was as tough as they came he also generally didn't push points; but when he put his two cents in it was worth listening carefully. "You don't think it'd be easier just to let him take 'em?"

"Say *what?*"

"Let him show up at the scenes. Tag along. Take his pictures. Give him what he wants an' he'll get bored or finished an' go. All done. No drama."

"Never thought you wanted to model," Andy grinned. Tyler flexed a bicep, and looked admiringly at it, until O'Leary flexed a bicep, which almost tore his shirt. Tyler scowled at him, and then grinned.

"No drama, Casey. Isn't that worth a moment or two's annoyance? I know you hate photos" – his tone came as close to sympathetic as Tyler ever could – "but if you fight about it you'll have no control. This way, maybe you can keep it manageable." He grinned nastily. "And I hear you need a new picture for your targets at the range."

"Captain wouldn't like it," she said laconically.

"What wouldn't I like, Detective Clement?" came from over her shoulder. Oh, shit. She looked frantically at the rest of the team. Kent was not precisely keen on surprises, important information being withheld from him, or assumptions. This was going to cover all three. Three strikes and she would metaphorically be out. Or carpeted, which would be no fun *at all*.

"Um..." she mumbled inarticulately.

"This guy Carval," Tyler started. Kent blinked. Tyler voluntarily explaining – indeed, talking – was so unusual that Kent was blindsided. "He was takin' pictures. Wouldn't leave."

"Those shots," O'Leary took up the tale, Tyler having exhausted his limited supply of words, "Waallll, he wants to base an exhibition on them. Us. Sir."

"He *what?*" Kent expostulated. "That's ridiculous!" There was an interesting undercurrent of red below his summer tan. Kent was not happy with the idea. Good.

"That's what we thought, sir."

"So what wouldn't I like, Detectives?"

Dammit.

"I thought we'd get rid of him faster if we let him take his shots." At least Tyler was prepared to stand up for his opinions.

"And why did you think that?" Kent inquired, delicately cutting.

"Because we can't arrest him for photographing in public, as long as he's not obstructing us," Casey pointed out bitterly. "He knows the law." She sounded as if she wished he didn't. "All that'll get us is bad publicity."

"Hm," Kent didn't sound impressed by that.

"But I don't want him around," she added. "He'll just get in the way."

Very loudly, everyone around her heard *I don't want to be photographed*. Everyone knew why, but no-one was unkind, or stupid, enough to say it.

"I don't approve," Kent said, and Casey's spirits rose. "But" – and they crashed – "we can't stop it. I am not going to court bad PR. We get enough of that when we're in the right." He frowned, thinking. "He can't come in here, so he can't interfere with your work; he has no right to follow you around and obstruct your witness interviews, and if he tries that we can close him down. But we can't stop him photographing you all in public." He harrumphed. "This is a fine mess. Detective Tyler has a point about getting rid of him faster, but civilians have no place around crime scenes and detection." He made a very dissatisfied noise under his breath. "I'll think about it. Don't do anything for now."

Oh, *hell*.

"Um, sir?"

"Yes?" It was entirely discouraging.

"Um..." Oh God. This was *not* something she had wanted to disclose, but if she didn't 'fess up she would be up the creek without a paddle. "Er…. I've met him before. Years ago. And, er, he wants to meet tonight."

"Why?" Kent rapped out. The three other men looked dumbfounded, and O'Leary then acquired a smirk. Fortunately, he didn't say anything. Even O'Leary wouldn't be immune to *enough* bullets.

"He *said*," Casey bit out, "he wants to talk about old times."

Kent's expression was sternly disapproving. "And?"

"And as it was a choice between him disrupting us here and meeting him elsewhere I chose elsewhere. But I think he just wants access for his photos." There was a slight softening.

"I see. Lesser of two evils."

Quite. Casey definitely agreed that Carval was an evil.

"Okay, Clement. Carval has no place in my precinct or my Detectives' investigations. *But* I can't prevent him appearing at crime scenes or indeed anywhere in public. *So*" – Casey's guts clenched – "I agree with Detective Tyler's sensible suggestion. We will allow him to appear in public places and nowhere else, unless I approve it. You will allow him to take any shots he wishes. We can't stop this, but we can control it, and we will." He frowned impartially at all four flabbergasted detectives. "You will so advise him this evening, Clement."

Hell. Now she couldn't even stand Carval up, which had been her best plan. Dammit, dammit, *dammit.* Why her? Why now?

Kent strode off, exuding Captainly decisiveness. Casey slumped at her desk. At least he'd missed the reference to *old times.*

"I got an idea," Andy chirped. Casey did not appreciate the chirpiness. She was utterly morose. "This Carval is expecting you, yeah?"

"Yeah," she growled. "And now I have to go."

"Well, he's not expecting the rest of us," Andy finished evilly.

Casey developed a feral grimace as the full beauty of Andy's suggestion became apparent. "I *like* it," she gritted out. "Oh, I like that idea."

Everyone smiled, very nastily. Casey was their own, and this Carval guy was going to discover what that meant.

CHAPTER 7

"Terence, it's me."

"What d'you want?"

"There's a cop sniffing around the lab. Two of them. In seeing Terrison."

"So?"

"What if they find something?"

"We can't have that. Hang on a moment. Let me patch in Carl."

"What's going on?"

"Cops around the lab. What if they've found out?"

"Found what? You covered up all the deviations from the norm. You said no-one else in the group knew. What's a bunch of meatheads going to find?"

"But..."

"No. We're all in this together. We've funded you millions and on the back of your results our stock price – and our bonuses – went through the roof. You benefited plenty too. Don't bring it down now."

"I guess they're only cops. If they had brains, they'd be doing something else."

"Exactly. Don't lose your nerve now." There was a menacing pause. "And make sure you don't draw attention to yourself. Don't go snooping, don't ask too many questions. You're the one who'll hang for faking it. You're the intellectual superstar who fooled us. Just keep your mouth shut and your head down. Got it?"

"Got it. But..."

"Yeah?"

"What if he took stuff home to work on? He was trying to replicate my results. What if it's there?"

"Did he ever take papers out the lab?"

"Never saw it." He sounded happier.

"Where'd he live?"

"Brooklyn. 3323 Nostrand Avenue."

"Okay. We'll go take a look. Who's the landlord?"

"Guy called Ahlbrechtssen. Karlen's ex. 135 Clarkson, Brooklyn."

"He know anything?"

"No. Karlen knows what side her bread's buttered on. Wouldn't say a thing."

"That better be true. We'll make like there's an infestation, and go in." There was a slow, thoughtful pause. "I got a better idea. Let's make it look as if he was taking secrets home. Get hold of some papers from the lab, get his laptop. By the time we're finished he'll be the fall guy."

"I've got something to make that look even more likely."

"Bring it along. No-one'll be looking at us if Belvez looks like he was on the take."

CHAPTER 8

Buoyed on considerable satisfaction, Casey turned to her searches, in tandem with the rest of her team. Much hard work was undertaken, to depressingly little effect. Everything was out there, but there was nothing coming back. Specifically, Dr McDonald's lab had not provided tox, confirmation of the carbon monoxide theory, or indeed any results at all. She could have screamed.

Shortly before she exploded with frustration, Belvez's residential address arrived, just in time for Casey not to call the searcher and threaten them with murder of their own. Belvez had lived in Brooklyn, until he got dead.

"Okay," she said to her screen and the team, "I'll call the landlord."

The landlord, one Mikael Ahlbrechtssen, was relatively forthcoming, once Casey told him that if he didn't spill his guts (actually, she'd said *talk to me* in tones that implied that not talking would be a really big mistake) she would have him hauled in by the two biggest uniformed officers she could find.

"So he moved here from New Mexico? Did he say why?" She knew exactly why. This was just a cross-check.

"Dunno. Expect he needed a job," the landlord grumped. "Paid me on time, though. Deposit, too."

Casey made a note. *Check bank.*

"Any visitors? Girlfriend? Boyfriend?"

"I don't have none of that shit," the landlord said angrily. "Ain't having no boyfriends round here."

Casey's eyes widened. Pretty unusual to have hit that attitude in NYC in 2016. She had no reason to suspect the landlord - yet, but if he was going to make that sort of comment she'd have loved to haul him in on general principles, so he could have a friendly discussion about the unacceptability of homophobia with O'Leary. O'Leary had strong views in that regard, and he was not at all shy about sharing them.

"Okay. We'll need in. I'll need the spare key. We'll pick it up from you" – she checked her watch: it was too late to get to Brooklyn and back before the unwanted discussion with Carval – "tomorrow, first thing." She would need to defer Merowin. Searching the apartment had to come first.

"Okay." The landlord sounded unhappy, but too bad. She had an investigation to run.

She called CSU, but they hadn't got back to her at ten to seven, and, extremely reluctantly, she had to leave to meet Carval.

On the other hand, her team would be there too.

"Guys, time to go," she announced. It wasn't the most popular invitation she'd ever issued.

"Where?"

"Starbucks." There was a collection of groans and grumbles, not all of which were related to the quality and strength of the coffee. "C'mon. We can go to a bar after."

She was pretty sure she heard *too damn right we will*. Strangely, nobody's lips had moved. None of them hurried their packing up, either.

The four of them ambled out. Well, that was the plan. O'Leary ambled. Tyler walked at a moderate pace. Casey and Andy trotted to keep up, until Casey poked O'Leary in the ribs and told him to slow down.

"We don't all wear seven-league boots."

"Not my fault you're all tiny," he muttered plaintively. "I can't tiptoe through those teeny little dance steps that you all do. My boots are too big."

Casey snickered loudly at the thought of O'Leary trying to do ballet. He drooped at her, trying to look pathetic and failing miserably. "I can't see you doing ballet, Bigfoot."

"I can't either. Now, Andy there" –

"Nope."

"I don't dance, 'cept in the ring," Tyler said quickly, in case anyone should think he might.

No-one mentioned Casey dancing. Just the same as no-one would ever have mentioned PTSD, or child abuse, in the team.

Far too soon, in Casey's view, they reached Starbucks. It wasn't even as if they all liked coffee. Casey might mainline espresso, but Andy drank tea (usually green tea), Tyler eschewed anything that wasn't energy drinks with exaggerated health benefits, with occasional forays into beer, and O'Leary drank anything that came his way, especially if he could plead, beg or con one of the others into providing it. Mostly, they didn't.

Casey entered first. Carval was already there. He acquired a look of utter delight that she had arrived, which began to slide off his face like paint from wet canvas as the three men followed her in. She smiled very nastily, and ignored the effect of his smile on her nerves.

"I'm here," she said bluntly. Carval gazed round the group, preserving strict calm. She might have shown up, but she'd played her hand and called his bluff and now he couldn't do anything except talk about photography. He might have been impervious to hints when trying to take his photographs, but he certainly knew how to read body language. The three men in front of him might not have been actively hostile but they were certainly not friendly, and they were clustered around Casey very protectively, not that she seemed to need protection. Unlike earlier, she was wholly enclosed in her professional persona. Her eyes were cool, her stance relaxed. The men were behind her.

It was just too damn perfect. He whipped out his camera and flicked off half-a-dozen shots before she'd blinked.

"What d'you think you're doin'?" the mountain growled.

"*My* job. Taking photos."

Carval's statement was deliberately provocative, but he was also intending to set a boundary. Hostile mountains growling at him or not, these cops weren't going to stop him taking photos in public places. He smiled sweetly, with a hard underlying edge. For a moment, nobody said anything.

Abruptly, on some signal that Carval couldn't detect, the men stood down their hostility, although Casey's cool professionalism remained unaltered. She sat down, and they followed: still surrounding her: the giant on one side, the burly black cop on the other. Their last member took the final seat: up close he was almost fragile looking, but his eyes were a thousand years old.

"We have a deal for you," Casey stated flatly. "This is the best you'll get. Captain said you can tag along in public, as long as you don't obstruct us. Nothing more. No coming into the precinct, no butting into our interviews. You can take your snaps" – it was obvious she'd chosen the word to insult him – "when we're in public. That's it. Take it or leave it."

It was equally obvious that she'd like him to leave it. The burly cop clearly agreed. The slight Asian didn't seem to care. (He needed to learn their names.) The Titan, however, was exuding an aura of smirking, though his enormous face was bland. Suspiciously so.

"Done," he said briskly. "So you'll tell me when you're leaving the precinct, and I'll tag along."

Casey smiled nastily. "No."

"But" –

"We don't have to tell you anything. If you find us, then you can work. But we don't have to help you." She stood in one lithe movement. "Good night." She was gone upon the word and an angry clatter of heels on lino. He watched her go, and admired the sway of her walk.

Carval gazed at the remaining cops. They gazed back, neutrally. Hostilities appeared to have been suspended for a few moments: though the likelihood of that continuing was finely balanced.

"Don't think she likes you," O'Leary rumbled.

"I'd guessed that," he said dryly. "Wanna introduce yourselves properly?"

There were a selection of shrugs and exchanged looks. Finally a collective decision appeared to have been made, and despite the hayseed drawl and shambling demeanour, it was the titanic O'Leary who gave the decisive nod. Clearly there was more to him than the immense bulk which met the eye.

"I'm O'Leary."

"Tyler."

"Actually, he's Jayvon," O'Leary said mischievously. "But iffen you call him that, he don't answer, so I wouldn't. He might shoot you. He don't miss, either."

Tyler growled ominously. Carval filed the snippet of background away.

"Andy."

"An' he's An-Cheng Chee," the largest imp in creation added even more mischievously. O'Leary was clearly a man of some considerable gentle humour. "Casey wouldn't let me call him Annie," he added dolefully. "She was real mean about it."

"And I told you that if you tried it I'd poison your lunch," Andy pointed out. "I'll get something untraceable in Chinatown."

O'Leary faked terror. With Casey's departure, the atmosphere had lightened a fraction. Very cautiously, the men were sizing each other up.

"Why're we here?" O'Leary asked almost rhetorically. "Three of us don't got a drink, an' you" – he gestured, and a small tornado passed through – "got some teeny little wussy thin' that don't count." He grinned broadly. "We should go find a proper drink."

From the astounded expressions on their faces, this came as just as much of a surprise to Tyler and Andy as it did to Carval himself.

"O'Leary" – Andy started. Tyler merely scowled.

"Iffen he's gonna tag along, might as well be civil. I don' like it when there's bitchin' an' unhappiness."

Who was this hayseed? Carval had never heard anything like it. He sounded like an ambulant cornfield – and was nearly as wide – with about as much brain as the corn would have had; but for entirely unclear reasons he *also* seemed to be treating Carval as if he was a normal human being rather than Satan incarnate. Carval was immediately suspicious. In his extensive experience, cops were not instant best buddies with anyone, still less with photographers who wanted to use them for an exhibition.

"Abbey Pub," O'Leary continued, and stood up. "C'mon."

"But" – Andy was still trying to work out what was going on.

"Naw. C'mon. If he knows what we're like he won't make dumb suggestions an' dumber comments. He won't ask us to do dumb thin's like we wouldn't ever do." He grinned again. "'Sides which, he needs to work out what my good side is. Wouldn't like it if he got that wrong."

O'Leary heaved his bulk into motion. Perforce, the other cops did too, probably on pain of being conveyed, one under each arm. Carval, completely confused by the whole situation, but well aware of his own best interests, did as he was told. He thought that he would take better pictures if he knew a bit about his subjects. It had always worked well in the glamour shots: a bit of story, a bit of chat, a bit of flirting. He wouldn't try that last on Casey-the-cop, though. It was likely to be an epic failure.

On reflection, Carval thought as he was blocked into a too-small table by the three cops, he should have been much more suspicious of Hayseed-O'Leary. *Much* more suspicious. That damn persona had had him totally fooled. Because there might have been a drink in front of him – and in front of each of the others – but O'Leary was now giving him the hard stare and wasn't down-home friendly at all.

"What'd you do to Casey?" he rapped.

"Uh?"

"You barged in, claimin' to have info 'bout our dead chemist, 'cept you didn't, she spoke to you, she came back upset. What'd you do?"

"Nothing. I showed her the shots, she got angry there wasn't anything useful, and stomped off."

"Really?" O'Leary said: suddenly, shockingly different from his earlier slow drawl. "I don't believe that's it. Not one tiny little bit. Spill."

"No. I haven't done anything to her. She's upset, you ask her why. I got no idea so I can't tell you."

"Don't believe that neither. There's something you're not tellin' us." O'Leary sat back, picking up his Guinness and throwing it back like soda, fixing Carval with a deadly stare.

"Gotta be about photos," Tyler said sharply. "Nothing else you do that connects."

Oh fuck, someone whispered. It might have been Carval. It might have been any of the cops. Maybe it had been all of them together.

"When'd you meet Casey *first?*" Tyler, now taking aggressive point, demanded. "When'd you *first* take photos of her?" He was scary enough when he was calm. Now, when he was riled up and on a trail, he was much more so: leaning forward, fists clenched, glowering. He might have been a couple of inches shorter than Carval, but he was a lot fitter. Leaving didn't seem to be an option.

"Nine years ago. So?"

"So it was him." Andy's light tenor scalded Carval. "We found the asshole."

"Ain't that a shame?" Tyler agreed, very sarcastically.

"What the hell are you talking about?"

"Don't give us that crap."

"It's not crap. I don't have a clue."

"You know more than you're sayin' though. So you're the bastard took the photo of her all dolled up."

"What's that got to do with anything? It was part of a college recruitment poster."

The three cops looked at each other. Carval was simply confused, and very, very worried. If these men took against him, no-one would ever find the body. Metaphorically. Maybe. The glint of their guns was not reassuring.

"You ever sell the negative? Or the rights?"

"No." A horrible suspicion began to dawn on him. "I never sell the copyright in any of my works."

"Hope you can prove it."

"What?"

"You better be able to prove it. 'Cause someone – an' we ain't convinced it wasn't you – spread that photo around the Academy, tryin' to bring her down. If you sold it, we need to know about it. Who an' when an' where."

"I can't prove a negative. But I can prove I licensed it for the poster, 'cause it wasn't the only photo there. I can show you the whole poster."

Now Carval understood the whole fiasco earlier. Some thieving bastard had stolen his photo and used it with ill intent. No wonder she'd reacted as she had. He'd been an unwitting pawn – must be eight or nine years ago – to screw with her, and how would she have known he had had nothing to do with it?

"Someone used *my* photo to mess her around?"

"That's right."

Carval downed half his beer in one go, took a breath and downed the rest. He then began to swear softly and sulphurously for some time, during which interval the cops didn't say a single word and didn't drop the intimidation level by a fraction.

"What happened?" he eventually asked.

"Photo got spread around. People took it as proof she was easy. Gossip spreads fast, 'specially if not everyone's keen on bein' beat to the top."

Carval indulged in considerably more swearing. Andy quietly put another beer in front of everybody.

"So I wouldn't reckon on her bein' too friendly for a good long while," O'Leary rumbled.

Carval regarded the cops as balefully as they were regarding him. "And you?"

"We haven't decided yet."

"And none of you are going to tell me anything about where or when you'll be outside the precinct?"

The cops shuffled in their seats.

"We haven't decided yet."

"Fine," Carval said exasperatedly, and dropped ten dollars and three business cards on the table. "When you do decide, let me know. Till then, I got better things to do than listen to you guys threatening me." He stood up, and squeezed out from the corner they'd blocked him into. "Nice to meet you," he said sarcastically, and left.

There was a meditative pause behind him.

"Waallll, *that* was interestin'," O'Leary hummed.

"Sure was."

"D'you believe him?"

Tyler shrugged. "Swore a lot."

"So do you."

"He looked pretty shocked," Andy said thoughtfully. He was usually the voice of reason. "Pretty pissed, too."

"Didn't crumble." O'Leary smirked happily. "Tough guy." He sounded very approving. Everyone else went on alert.

"What're you playing at, Bigfoot?"

"Nuthin' much." The smirk widened.

"Oh, fuckit. You're playing Cupid. Not again. Just 'cause you're married you think all the rest of us should be."

"This is not going to go well," Andy added dolefully. Past history did not incline Andy to think that this was a good idea, and somehow he always ended up in the firing line.

"You saw he looked pretty pleased to see her."

"Till he saw us," Andy said gloomily. "Anyways, you've scared him off."

"Naw. He wasn't scared. Pissed, sure. Not scared. Don't look like he scares easy."

"That'll change," Tyler muttered blackly.

"She didn't shoot him."

"She'll shoot *you*. And you'll deserve it, too. This is a really bad idea. Like, *really* bad."

"Casey won't shoot me," O'Leary said happily. "I'm her oldest pal."

"You reckon?" someone muttered.

"Anyways, she was blushin'. Proof."

"You're crazy."

"Naw," he chuckled. "I'm just gonna put them in, um, *proximity*. That's the word. Proximity. Ain't no matter to me what happens next."

Another round of beers appeared. Tyler and Andy clung to theirs like lifebelts.

"Why are you doing this?"

"Casey needs some fun. Somethin' that ain't the job or worryin' 'bout her pa. So this guy showed up an', well, it's Providence. Even if she just yells at him it's somethin' to liven her up." He grinned. "An' those photos he took are pretty good, too. You seen 'em? Worth lookin' at. I always wanted to be a star."

"Not me," Tyler muttered bleakly.

"Even your ugly mug looked good in them." Tyler growled. "So think how good I'll look."

"What about me?"

"You?" O'Leary tapped his chin. "Um… can't rightly remember. You there at all? Mebbe it was before you showed up. You were last."

It was Andy's turn to growl. "Dispatch never calls me first."

Tyler emitted a cynical grunt. "Beer," he said laconically, and got the next round in. He thought that O'Leary was batshit crazy, but it would be O'Leary's head that would have ventilation holes when – not *if*, definitely *when* – Casey found out. He was going to leave well alone. Much safer that way.

***

Carval marched out with a cadence only one beat short of a stomp. He admired Casey's tactics – there could never have been a conversation with the rest of her team around – but he was certainly not impressed by being grilled, intimidated, threatened (even by implication) or by the creative use of imprecision in her interpretation of what must surely have been an order to allow him to shoot them.

She was really far too clever for his good.

Still irritated, he downloaded the day's efforts from camera to computer, and took a look. He must have been lucky. Lucky at shots, unlucky in improving his acquaintance with Casey. These would be a great addition. All life, from the toddler's mischief through the bitter old woman to the elderly military man, reflected in the passing trade of the precinct's doorway. Perfect. He printed them off, and arranged them around his board.

The shots in the interrogation room weren't quite as effective. There were a couple of interesting ones: those where he'd used flash and achieved some clever reflection effects from the one-way glass, but mostly they weren't interesting or useful. He dragged them to a folder out of the way of the ones with which he could work.

Now, those were better. His camera simply *loved* Casey-the-cop. Photogenic was not the word. He'd caught her framed in the doorway: the mundane municipal whitewashed walls and grim corridor behind her emphasising and focusing on the emotion and life in her face – albeit it had largely been anger. Oh, yes. Casey-the-cop was his centrepiece. (He had to try really hard not to revise that last word to *centrefold*, but she wasn't exactly exuding availability or indeed liking.)

And those – oh, *those* photos were better still. He printed and pinned them. The contrast between the fierce focus of his first shot and the weary, burdened feeling from these was, as he had hoped, shockingly brilliant: the still pale hands on a cheap café table, with the small espresso cup giving scale to the long, slim fingers and neat unpolished nails, the edge of the print just in shot, but unfocused. He wasn't sure yet whether that one would fit with the main theme, but he might use it as a single print. He left it pinned up anyway, in case inspiration struck later.

Finally, he dealt with the second set of group shots, taken as the four came into the bar. Perfect. Team cohesion and dynamic was bursting from every pixel, every line. Casey up front, a sardonic, knowing smile on her face that lacked any genuine humour; the massive height and bulk of O'Leary almost surrounding her, guarding her, displaying a mildly rueful look, as if he wasn't entirely in agreement but would support her in public; Tyler's sharp, honed size and fitness with his cold eyes boring into the lens; and finally smaller, delicate Andy, barely taller than Casey, but with that odd, faraway stare, as if he was far older than his apparent years.

The real strength of the images, though, was their solidarity. This was a group – everyone looking, even for a brief glance, would see it – that stood and fell together; that existed as a single unit. This team was an island, entire of itself.

He wondered what bound them together; these four very different seeming people. And yet… and yet. He looked to the original shot, and had his answer: that same fierce focus written on each face; applied to the death below them. Dedication. He recalled the NYPD's motto: *Fidelis ad mortem*, and saw in the four detectives a different kind of faith: the faith that they would find this killer and so find justice for the victim. He would show that faith and focus to the world.

He carried on arranging and thinking and selecting and re-arranging until he was finally satisfied for the time being. Done, he located his phone to call Allan to come and admire, and was only prevented when the phone told him, unbelievably, that it was nigh on one a.m., and Allan would object forcibly to being disturbed. That wouldn't have stopped Carval, but the three weeks' constant reminders and complaints if he did disturb Allan would. Not even Carval's need for validation of his artistic genius could defeat Allan's well-thought-out methods of training him to control his impulsivity. He regarded his board with utmost approval, and betook himself upstairs and to bed, perfectly content with his shots.

He was not perfectly content with Casey's behaviour, but that was a problem for the next day. Allan would know how to track the cops. And if he didn't, he knew how to use Google to find a gadget that would. Carval fell asleep on the right side of satisfied.

CHAPTER 9

Casey, having made an unmatchable exit, didn't wait for the rest of the team. She had the distinct impression that the hard word was going on Carval, and she didn't mind that one tiny little bit. She could always count on her team. They'd always been there for her, since the day she met O'Leary, then went to the Third and teamed up with him; since Tyler joined them at the Thirty-Sixth and two became three; since Andy arrived and three became four. And four became solid, gradually, over four years of tricky cases and mundane murders; late nights and early mornings; beers, and never asking anything when one of them let a little history slip. *Her* history was mostly out there. Her present – well, that took a lot longer.

She reached home and gratefully discarded shoes and jacket, turned to the Gaggia in the kitchen and moments later, changed to a soft t-shirt and casual pants, savoured the smell of excellent coffee. It had cost her a small fortune, judged by her income then, and she'd never regretted a cent of it. She threw a Thai ready meal in the microwave, sipped her coffee, and considered the revelations of the day.

Revelations were not what she needed, right now. She needed stability: an organised life where she knew that each working day would bring her shift and her team; a victim who needed justice. Not unknown randoms; photographers with a plan and, worse, photographers who had shaped her history.

And yet... unbidden, her memories came, as she ate her green curry on noodles.

Post-graduation, a party, all her many friends. They had been surprised that she was going for the Academy, when most of them had been intending to take the LSAT in the fall and then move on to law school, but they had accepted that she was dancing to a different drum from them. She was still in touch with some of them: some had drifted, which was no surprise: they'd mostly gone into commercial law, and, like vampires, they never saw daylight. That night, however, they'd all still been together, and they'd been having a ball. Then this guy – this *Carval* – had shown up, taking photos non-stop, claiming he was doing a photography elective. None of them had cared enough to argue. He hadn't really looked any older than the rest of them and anyway, the more the merrier.

She'd danced with him, briefly; spun and laughed and been right up close; and then he'd kissed her, very expertly – and she'd been spun away by another and the mass of happy, dancing graduates had closed around her. She'd never really thought about it again: sure, he'd been good looking, and he had kissed well, but so did lots of others. Probably if he'd kissed her again she'd have been seriously interested, but one kiss wasn't enough to find him again on that summer night.

Now he'd shown up with the photo that had made her life – no. It *hadn't* made her life hell. Sure, it hadn't been pleasant at all, but she'd come through. She'd won.

And all the scars healed, in time, leaving her tougher and better fitted to the job she did. So on balance – she'd take it.

Except that now she knew who'd taken the picture (she'd always known when). What she didn't know was how it had got to Marcol, or Birkett.

She bared her teeth at her empty apartment: in no way a smile. She was good at interrogation. If Carval managed to find them – and he'd have one hell of a problem with that – then he might find that he'd gotten more than he bargained for.

Right. He might have gotten photos. But *she* was going to get answers. She fell asleep on a tide of satisfaction.

***

"C'mon, O'Leary, road trip. Let's go toss Belvez's apartment. Landlord's expecting us this morning."

"Road trip?" O'Leary asked happily. He loved road trips. Casey had no idea why, because although he spent all his time pretending to be a Mid-Western hayseed, he – as far as she knew – had never been out of New York State in his life. She actually wasn't quite sure that he didn't regard the Bronx as dangerously foreign.

"Yep. Let's go."

Belvez's apartment was a two room walk-up, fortunately only on the second floor. When they opened the door, it was pretty neat: quite a contrast to his dress. CSU were summoned, in order to do a full sweep for any evidence, and while they were making their way over Casey issued instructions to Andy and Tyler relating to harassing all the various techs and warrant-granters about bank accounts, phone records, street cameras around the crime scene and all the other paraphernalia of investigation that should have arrived and hadn't.

She and O'Leary tugged on nitrile gloves and started to look around, cautiously, trying not to disturb the scene.

There was minimal mess, underneath which it was relatively clean, only a mug on the counter in the kitchen; a used bowl and cutlery, which looked like they might have been breakfast, were waiting to be washed up. On further exploration, the bed was semi-made, and the towel in the bathroom was dry.

"Looks like he never came back." She poked around a little. "You see any phone, laptop, anything like that?"

"Laptop's here," O'Leary said, pointing at a desk.

"Yeah. Well, CSU can take that in and try to strip it. If he'd had a phone on him at the scene we'd have found it. So it ought to be here too."

O'Leary looked around the desk, and began with its drawers. Casey started at one side of the room and worked methodically through each area.

"A-ha!" they said together, spotting an edge of phone peeking out from under a cushion.

Casey pulled it out, and swiped it. Naturally, it needed a passcode. She tapped in a sequence. It opened up.

"How'd you know the code?" O'Leary said with astonishment. She smirked, happy as always to have pulled off a trick that surprised him.

"Magic," she said, and wiggled her fingers. O'Leary grinned.

"C'mon," he rumbled.

Casey sighed. "Most people never change the initial code. I always try it first. Seven times out of ten, it works."

"Oh. That simple? Why've I never seen you do it before?"

"Yep, that simple. Usually CSU do it first." She glared at the phone. "We'll need to look at all these contacts properly. Soon's we get back." She bagged and tagged the phone, and they continued around the flat.

The desk was covered in papers. The papers were covered in meaningless diagrams and strings of letters and numbers. Memory heaved into action and found long-disused information in Casey's head, following which she made a very satisfied noise.

"Chemical formulae," she said smugly. "What's he doing with formulae in his apartment? He's got security clearances, so he shouldn't be doing that, surely?" She took some careful photos on her phone. CSU would want to bag, tag and then run the papers for prints.

"Apart from this here desk, it's all pretty tidy. Seems a bit strange that he's all neat an' his desk's like a bomb hit it."

"Yeah..." Casey agreed slowly.

"Your desk looks like you polish it every mornin', an' your apartment's the same. Most people are all tidy or all messy, not like this."

"What are you thinking?"

"I'm thinkin' that someone's been in here lookin' round before we got here, an' didn't tidy up the desk behind them. I'm thinkin' that it ain't burglary, 'cause the phone an' laptop are right here."

"If there's anything to find, CSU'll find it."

At which apposite moment CSU arrived.

"We think someone's been searching here before we got here."

"Okay. We'll find anything there is to find."

Casey and O'Leary had almost completed their search when they investigated the bathroom and its small cabinet, mostly to get out of CSU's way. CSU tended to get tetchy if ordinary cops messed up their careful procedures.

"This is weird, Casey."

"What?"

"He's got four unused cans of shaving foam."

"Why's that weird? He didn't have a beard, so he must shave. Maybe he bulk buys."

"They rattle. Shaving foam don't rattle."

Casey turned away from looking under the sink. O'Leary demonstrated.

"Okay, maybe you got something there. Leave them for CSU. In fact, let's get out of this room. CSU need to have a proper look."

"But Casey..." O'Leary rumbled.

"No buts." She glared at the bathroom, and incidentally at O'Leary, who was impervious. "CSU can sweep it. Come on. Let's go see what the others have found, and seeing as I'm feeling nice" – O'Leary blew her a raspberry – "we'll go on another trip this afternoon." She patted him on the shoulder, since she couldn't reach his head.

"Where we goin', Mommy?" he chortled.

"Don't make that noise, you'll wobble all CSU's readings."

He grinned. "Where we goin'?"

"I thought we'd go see this Mike Merowin. He sounded pretty interesting."

"Mebbe so."

"Let's get back, then."

When they got back, Andy and Tyler had found that street cameras around the university were useless, and so were Belvez's phone records. Occasional calls to the landlord, all more than two months ago; calls to the university, also all more than two months ago; and calls to his brother, back in Albuquerque. Belvez, it seemed, was not a chatty sort. Tyler approved. No-one else did.

"Okay, give me five, O'Leary, and then we'll grill Merowin."

As soon as Casey disappeared, O'Leary pulled out Carval's card and his phone. The others looked at him as if he was utterly insane.

"What are you *doing*?" Andy squawked.

"You're crazy. Totally batshit," Tyler added.

"Proximity," O'Leary said happily. "An' just think of us bein' stars of the show. Captain'll like that."

"Not when Casey's arrested for Murder One, he won't. That'll fuck up his stats, bigtime."

"Trust me. It's only proximity. No-one's gonna be shootin' anyone." He tapped in the number, saved it to contacts and assigned it a speed dial, and made the call. Andy and Tyler regarded him doubtfully.

"Carval," O'Leary rumbled. "You wanna take some of them photos, you can find me 'n' Casey at Havemeyer Hall, Columbia."

He blinked.

"Captain said we had to let you tag along." His tone was saintly. His expression was impish.

"Not my problem. Take your shots or don't. Don't make no never mind to me."

O'Leary cut the call.

"Waallll, that should do it," he grinned.

"I'm leaving," Andy said. "I hear they're looking for detectives down at the Twelfth. Less chance of getting shot."

"I'll come too," Tyler said. "This is a clusterfuck. I'm not helping you outta this one, Bigfoot."

O'Leary merely smiled, as happy as a lamb in spring.

***

Carval had started the day by calling Allan both to admire the board – which he had done, with more enthusiasm than expected, and to discuss finding cops. Allan was not helpful.

"It's not like you're trying to pick up the first call to the scene," he explained patiently. Carval didn't like patience. He liked answers, results, and instant gratification. (Or indeed long-drawn out gratification, in certain circumstances) "If you were, then we could just get a scanner with two taps on the keyboard, and monitor the channels. But you're not, because they're on a live case and so they won't be using the radio. There's no easy way of monitoring that. You might just have to hang out at the precinct door all day."

Allan had an expression of some considerable amusement at the thought. Carval scowled at him, which only made Allan more amused.

"I don't wanna sit like a stray dog outside the door."

"Maybe you should stop sniffing after the cops, then?"

Carval bridled, which was at least partly fuelled by the knowledge that it was true. "Look at the photos! You want me to do this exhibition, yeah? You see my centrepiece, yeah? Well, I need those cops. So if you want me in the Dechsin Gallery in six months, you damn well help me fix it."

Allan stared at him. "Cool it, Jamie. I was teasing you. It's going to be a great exhibition."

Carval acquired a slightly shamefaced expression. "I gotta do this one, Allan. It's going to be amazing. Even better than the last. But I've got to keep following them. Look at them." He gestured. "Look at the expressions, the force, the *dedication*. I'll make them the poster child for detecting. They'll be the epitome of how to do it. *Everyone* will see what they can do. You don't get it. They're absolutely one team, right at the top of the game. I wanna show that. I *gotta* show it."

Allan hadn't heard Jamie on this sort of run for nearly a year. He was alight with the need to take photos and make this theme work. Allan couldn't be happier, but he wasn't going to show Jamie that just yet.

"Mm," he hummed. "Sure you do. But how much is the team and how much is that woman?"

"My camera *adores* her." Which was absolutely not an answer, of which Allan was perfectly well aware. "She's the centre. The axis. They all spin around her." *So might you*, Allan thought very privately. *Oh God. Here you go.* "But I need them all. *Look*," he said again, pointing at Andy, looking round at Casey and then another. "Look at the *cohesion*. They're a unit. Almost a family, but closer. Don't you *see*? It's all of them."

"Okay. Okay. We'd better find a way for you, then."

Carval's phone rang. He frowned, and swiped on. "Jamie Carval." His jaw dropped. "O'Leary? Why're you calling?" Allan could hear a bass rumble, in which words were not particularly evident. Jamie looked like someone had slugged him. "You what now? Havemeyer Hall? Why are you telling me this?"

More quietly thundery rumbles. "You mean it? What – and if she didn't appreciate it?"

Carval stared at the cut call and the phone screen. "*That* was unexpected," he breathed.

"What?"

"The big guy. O'Leary. Him." He pointed.

"I'd guessed," Allan noted dryly.

"He just called. They're off to Columbia. If I hustle, I'll be there first. Then I can follow her all around. Take shots. She's been ordered to let me. They all were. I gotta go." He's tugging on a sweater and jacket as he's talking, words tumbling out. "Seeya later." He grabbed his camera bag and hurtled out of the door.

Allan was left looking at the empty space that a moment ago had been full of Jamie, and then surveyed the board. He wouldn't tell Jamie just yet, but even from these few, first photographs, unstructured and without any working up, he thought that this exhibition would be his crowning achievement. Now if only Jamie could manage not to ruin it by hitting on the woman – Casey – at least *before* he'd got what he needed, it would all work out just fine.

Allan went back to his office downstairs, much happier than a week ago, and started to call his extensive list of contacts to begin to make tentative arrangements for an exhibition. His life was so much easier when Jamie was happy, photographing – and out of the way. Jamie left a trail of impulsivity and chaos behind him when he was bored, and while Allan was well capable of fixing it, he'd rather arrange exhibitions.

***

"How did you get here?" Casey snapped.

Leaning on the stone pillar at West 120th was an already familiar, and annoying, figure. Annoyance was not alleviated by the contradictory feeling that he really did look rather good in chinos and a soft leather jacket. It was enhanced by the irritating knowledge that it was pretty clear that he'd been stealing photos again.

O'Leary was out of view. Specifically, he was behind Casey, where she couldn't see his face, which was dropping a very large wink at Carval, who managed with some considerable difficulty to preserve an unchanged mien as they all fell into step towards the Chemistry Department.

"On the subway," he smirked.

"How did you know we'd be here?"

"I'm very good at guessing. Chemists belong in chemistry departments."

Casey muttered darkly. It all seemed far too pat. However, dumb ideas like trackers on her car or coat were ridiculously paranoid. No-one was that dedicated to their art. She deflected, which had the happy coincidence that it stopped her analysing the rather too-warm smile and appreciative look in his eye.

"You can take photos of O'Leary, then. He wants to be a star. Though even the astronomy department doesn't need another gas giant." O'Leary rumbled chidingly. Casey glared back at him. Carval muffled a snicker. "I am going to meet our witness. You can stay and be snapped if you like."

"Snapped on film or snapped at. Ain't much of a choice you're givin' me." Both of them ignored Carval's insulted cough.

"Nope. Now let's go do our job."

"I'll just sit here in the sunshine till you finish." Carval smiled at O'Leary, and managed to avoid smiling at Casey. "How about coffee when you're done, and a few shots? There's a coffee shop over there." He gestured at the Joe café. That invitation excluded Casey as well. Of course she hadn't wanted to have coffee with Carval. She would have work to get on with. So would O'Leary, though it wasn't her place to micro-manage him, and they had been ordered (ugh) to co-operate. So it was a little dumb to feel mildly rejected.

"Sure," O'Leary drawled easily. "Sounds good. I'll see you here."

Casey was halfway to the door before he'd finished the last sentence. It only took O'Leary two strides to catch up, but Carval found that the view of her stiff spine was rather amusing. Of course, watching her irritated stalk was also amusing, but there was enough of a sway to be just a little arousing. That worked. He'd just play a little hard to get, and then when there was some possibility of *private* conversation, he'd explain.

CHAPTER 10

O'Leary caught up to Casey in short order. They slid into the back of the room in which Merowin was instructing a group of extremely bored-appearing young people, who Casey pegged as freshmen realising that chemistry was not their bag. Certainly the ill-concealed winces at their questions indicated that Merowin didn't think much of their knowledge and understanding. He breathed a long sigh of relief as they left, and then realised that there were two people, *not* students, striding up to him.

"Yeah?" he said.

"Detective Katrina Clement, NYPD."

"Detective Colm O'Leary, her partner."

"Are you Michael Merowin?"

"Yeah, I'm Dr Merowin. What's this about?"

"We'd like to ask you a few questions about Ricardo Belvez."

"Oh, John's new hotshot."

That sounded a little edged, already. Hm.

"I'm sorry to tell you that he was found dead."

"Dead?" Merowin's voice rose shakily. "Dead? What happened?"

"He was found in a back alley. Someone had hit him on the head."

"He was mugged?"

But there was an odd note in Merowin's voice, almost as if he hadn't been expecting that. Casey parked it, exchanged a swift glance with O'Leary, and went with the standard approach.

"Mm," Casey said, in a way O'Leary, at least, recognised. He was used to it, and didn't flicker so much as an eyelid. "Had you been working closely with him for a long time?"

"Nah. He came in from New Mexico, a few months ago, and I've been on the East Coast all the way. I was at Florida State before I came here."

"Were you friends?"

70

"We got along. We're pretty busy, so there hasn't been much time for socialising."

"How long have you been in Professor Terrison's group?"

"Since post-grad. Eight years, now. I'm the senior researcher."

"So Professor Terrison said." Merowin preened a little at the recognition. "Does that mean you get all the kudos and publicity?"

"We don't get *publicity*. We're not celebrities." Merowin cast a scathing glance at Casey. Clearly she'd hit a nerve, even if this Merowin was pretending it didn't matter. "We do much more important work than celebrities." It sounded like he'd have preferred to use a much nastier word. "Our formulae change lives, not that we get paid for it."

Casey and O'Leary exchanged glances. That would be worth a look. Dr Merowin's financials might repay some research of a very different nature from his. Some chemistry was much more lucrative than other types. Of course, those were often highly illegal, too. The mysteriously rattling shaving foam canisters loomed large in both their minds.

"Professor Terrison said you were the key contact with Telagon, and that they funded the group pretty well."

"Yeah. John isn't big on admin and organisation, so he leaves it to me. We need to keep them sweet. They're huge, and if we make compounds that they can use they keep funding us. They've got a lot of money."

"I heard that they were puttin' up a lot more money on account of Belvez joinin'," O'Leary drawled. "Musta been a tad hurtful when you'd been the top man."

"No." That denial came pretty fast. "If we get more money, we all benefit. No point pissing off the new blue-eyed boy. I thought we could get to be good pals, maybe, if the work ever died down, and anyway we have to work together" – he clearly remembered – "*were* working together – and it's not good to be on the outs when you're doing complex syntheses." He grinned, suddenly, turning his sharp face appealingly boyish. "A bad mental atmosphere doesn't really contaminate the experiment, but you sometimes wonder."

"Did he have any arguments with the rest of the group?"

"No, he was pretty easy-going. Worked hard, didn't brag. He was a good guy. Fitted right in."

"Did he mention any other friends, or girlfriends?"

"Or boyfriends?" O'Leary added, remembering the hostility of the landlord. Casey nudged his knee with hers without being obvious.

"Um..." Merowin flicked his eyes away, and back again.

"Boyfriend?" Casey followed up on O'Leary's question.

"Yeah..."

Merowin was clearly unhappy with the admission, but it wasn't at all clear whether that was because he disapproved of same-sex relationships or he thought that the cops would. He'd have been right about the latter, with certain cops. O'Leary, for all his size and reputation, could have provided chapter and verse on who. Even O'Leary had had to deal with some… issues. Once per idiot, but still not fun.

"Do you know his name? Address?"

There was a small but definite flicker of his eyes.

"You do, don't you?" O'Leary was sympathetic, but firm. "C'mon, Mike" – Casey wouldn't have done that, but man-to-man it seemed to work – "you said you were gettin' to be pals, an' since you'd been workin' together successfully you'd both benefited. Help me out here." It was O'Leary's best good cop drawl, not as down-home dumb as usual, but still, Merowin took it at friendly face value.

Merowin's eyes flickered around, and didn't find any help in the Periodic Table on the wall, nor in the stick-and-ball models in bright colours. Casey stayed absolutely quiet, and nudged O'Leary to keep him wordless too when it looked like he might fill the silence.

"He never said much, but sometimes he mentioned a Troy," Merowin eventually managed. "Troy Bolton."

O'Leary burst into booming laughter. "You're kidding, yeah?"

Casey looked entirely, and falsely, blank. Merowin looked much more sincerely blank.

"Guess you don't like musicals, or musical films, or have small kids?" Since when had O'Leary had small kids? On the other hand, he'd occasionally mentioned small nieces.

"No." There was a slight edge on that which made Casey wonder if Merowin even had a girlfriend. Or a boyfriend. "I'm single. What's the deal?"

"Troy Bolton is the star of High School Musical. For about five years, you couldn't get away from it if you knew any pre-teens anywhere. Set in New Mexico, too."

Casey wondered instantly if the name was a fake. It was just too coincidental. O'Leary was clearly thinking the same, and his eyes were sparkling. He so loved debunking mysteries and conspiracies.

"Did he mention any other names?"

"Not that I remember."

That was a relief. If there had been other names from stupid teen musicals (not that she'd *ever* admit that she'd gone to see it, one evening when she'd just needed something totally mindless, and anyway the songs were good) she would have had to go outside and scream. Or burst into song, perhaps.

"Do you know anything more about this Troy Bolton?"

"No."

"Okay. We'll need the names of your main contacts at Telagon, please, just so we can confirm. Standard practice."

Merowin scribbled a name on a pad and handed the torn-off sheet over. "Terence Brewman," he said. "He's the research evaluator. Decides whether to recommend they fund or not."

"Thanks. So he's pretty important?"

"Yeah. Reports straight into the board of directors."

"Okay. Thank you. If you remember anything else, call me. Anything at all." She paused. "We're interviewing the rest of the group, but I'd appreciate it if you keep it quiet for now."

"Sure, but... why?"

Casey decided on a bit of scary misdirection.

"Well, someone's gone after the latest guy pulling in big bucks for the group's funding" – Merowin went white and looked sick – "so someone's lost you millions of dollars if you can't replace Dr Belvez. Just in case someone's going after the key players in this group, we wouldn't want you to be the next one."

"Next one? Who'd – no-one would want to mess up our funding here. It pays our wages."

"You never know who's in competition for the money. So don't go talking about this, in case someone thinks you're taking too much of an interest."

"Okay. Not a word."

He watched them all the way out of the door.

"Back to the precinct, O'Leary. This is weird. Let's see if there's anything sensible back in the bullpen. And on the way you can explain your High School Musical kick to me."

"Nuthin' to explain. I got nieces. You know that. They were the right age. I got dragged along." He smiled. "More to the point, Pete's got nieces too. So we got dragged along a bit more. Five, or mebbe five hundred, times later, you pretty much got it locked in your head. Catchy tunes."

He hummed, sounding like a bass bumblebee.

"But I got an invitation to coffee, an' I'm thirsty."

***

Carval, under-caffeinated and hungry, watched the cops enter the building, wished very strongly that he could take photos of them when they were interviewing suspects, and took himself to the Joe café without hesitation, where he read a handy newspaper while attending to his stomach and watched the students come and go. Nothing particularly inspired him to point and shoot. He was, in fact, bored.

Being bored was not unusual. Carval's boredom threshold was extremely low, and frequently led him into trouble. Today was no exception. He spotted O'Leary, who appeared to be trailing a small Casey-shaped satellite, and bounced out of the cafe to try to find something a lot more interesting than the news.

"Hey," he said, mainly directed at O'Leary, with a deliberately minimal inclusion of Casey.

"I'm going back. See you later, O'Leary. Carval," Casey tacked on. His name was almost added soon enough not to be an afterthought.

"Don't you want to get a coffee?" O'Leary asked.

"No time. I need to be back."

Casey swung off, without further ado or farewell. There was a little space of silence around Carval, and a large one around O'Leary.

"I can't wait long," O'Leary said. "Got work. But iffen you get the coffee, you c'n walk up with me an' we'll have a little chat."

Carval took the brick-like hint without flinching, and led the way back to the café to order go-cups.

"Why did you tip me off about where Casey'll be?" Might as well tackle the elephant in the room.

"Waallll, I do like a good soap opera."

"*Soap opera?*" Carval hissed. "I'm not some entertainment show."

"Naw, but you are just a little bit interested in my pal Casey, an' she needs a distraction. New toy," he said provocatively. "Even if she just yells at you, it'll be good for her."

"*Toy?!*" came back with even more venom. "I'm not a distraction and I'm not a toy. You can just fuck right off." He started to move away, heedless that he hadn't got his coffee. O'Leary clamped one huge hand on his shoulder and Carval found that he wasn't going anywhere at all, until O'Leary decided to release him. He was a walking arrest warrant and Black Maria, all by himself.

"Stay put."

Perforce, Carval was already stationary, but the sheer menace in the amiable O'Leary's voice would have compelled him, not a compliant man, to obedience.

"We coulda done this the nice way, but if you ain't gonna play nice, waallll, neither will I. So. You fucked up Casey's life with that photo, which you know now, even if you didn't then, an' you owe her."

"I don't owe you or her anything at all. Some bastard steals my photo, that's not on me. You're not putting that at my door." He started to move again, and was prevented.

"You think?" Menace was magnified.

"Yeah, I do. I own *my* mistakes, but I'm not taking on other people's," Carval insisted, with possibly suicidal courage. Facing up to a man who could break him in two with one finger was less than sensible, but his temper, normally slow to rise, was taking over, and he wasn't being pushed around by O'Leary. Somewhere, in a tiny corner of his mind, he dimly realised that if he came across as a pushover, he'd have lost any chance of gaining their respect, and with that, any chance of good photos. "So if you think you're going to blackmail me into something, you can fuck right off. You're not doing that to me and" – he growled with sudden enlightenment – "there's no way you'd do that to *your pal Casey*. Not if you're actually friends. You" – he stopped. Calling a grizzly bear names was a short route to sudden death – "You've been *testing* me."

"Not dumb, are you? Sure. I wanted to work out what sort of guy you are. Anyways" – a slow smile reappeared – "you're interested. Can tell that a mile off."

They collected their coffees, and moved out.

Carval was not notably soothed by the smile. There were too many teeth in it for his comfort. "Why are you doing this?" he said combatively. "You don't know me from Adam. You have no idea what I'm like. And you have *no right at all* to act like some oversized Cupid. I thought you said you were Casey's friend? You don't sound much like a friend to me. I thought that sort of mean-girl manipulation stopped at age sixteen."

Astonishingly, O'Leary's grin had widened. It was now thoroughly approving. "I knew you were a good guy," he said happily.

· "You don't get it, do you? I'm not some patsy in your teen-girl drama."

"I get that," O'Leary drawled. "But you want your photos and you want a chance at Casey. An' I wanted to know if I should be lookin' out for her a bit more'n usual."

"You vet her dates?"

"Naw. That's up to her. We just… keep an eye out."

Carval didn't miss the 'we' in that. Hayseed-O'Leary was about as much of a hayseed as a space rocket. No doubt many criminals had been deceived. Carval was not. That had been a warning.

"Well, you don't have to keep an eye out on me, because she's not interested. I don't go where I'm not wanted."

"Good to know. We got ways of dealin' with that."

"You threatening me is old already. How about you save it for when it's justified?"

"You just told me I don't know anythin' about you, so mebbe it is justified."

"Oh, for Chrissake lose the imitation of a haystack. It isn't working and it's getting old real fast too. Let's just agree that you're smart and you could snap me like a twig and get past the preliminaries already. She's not interested and I want my next exhibition to be as big a success as the last one. If you guys co-operate, it will be. If you don't, well, I'll change the focus from your team to cops generally. Someone will want the PR for their precinct, if your captain doesn't."

Carval shrugged, mentally crossed his fingers and hoped that this would work. These cops – all of them – were far too smart for anyone's good. He might have concluded that they were a really mismatched team, but that certainly didn't mean that they were dumb. In fact, they might have been a mismatched team *because* they were collectively very smart, if, certainly if his current interactions were anything to go by, *difficult* to deal with.

"What's your story?" fell out of his mouth without the benefit of his brain intervening.

"We ain't got time for that now," O'Leary drawled. "But if you think you can stand a little more of my haystack company, we could have a drink later, an' I might feel inclined to tell you. Right now, I gotta get back to the precinct. I'll see you in the Abbey Pub, round about eight. Mine's a Guinness."

Carval didn't imagine, even on brief acquaintance, that his cops did sociable chit-chat when they were working. Banter, maybe – he'd seen some of that already – but not stories. That was obviously for after the day's work was done. With O'Leary's invitation, a small tendril of hope that he might be able to achieve some interaction with the team sprouted.

O'Leary entered the precinct and was gone in three huge strides. When he hurried, distance was eaten up most impressively.

Carval meditatively drank the remains of his coffee, and considered both what O'Leary had, and more interestingly had not, said, which *had-not-ness* had included a remarkable lack of comment on Carval's contention that Casey wasn't interested. He was still no clearer as to O'Leary's motives, though for a man who liked to imitate an ambulating haystack he was appallingly Machiavellian, so there was undoubtedly a plan being developed which he, Carval, would not like.

Of course, the reason he wouldn't like it was because he hadn't been involved in its development. He wasn't keen on people plotting around him, especially when he seemed to be crucial to the plot. If there was going to be plotting, he intended to be one of the conspirators.

Hm. Definitely a raised eyebrow, directed firmly at O'Leary. Previously, in Carval's experience, big brothers (which was how O'Leary came across) warned him off, they didn't encourage him. Therefore, there was something he didn't understand going on, and it wasn't just the fiasco of the photograph. He didn't think that Casey-the-cop would have a problem finding dates, if she wanted a date. Therefore, he worked out, she didn't want dates. Or she didn't tell O'Leary about them, of course.

He didn't like the second thought. That was ridiculous, because he'd only spotted her three days ago. Allan would quite definitely kill him: Allan was always very nervous when he'd found a new topic, which was totally unfair, because the photographs always came first. It was just that sometimes they took a long time to arrive.

Thinking of which, he'd better get back and talk to Allan. Make sure that he, Carval, would have enough time to get this show firmly on the road.

***

Unbeknownst to Carval, Casey had hustled back to her case with a slight feeling of irritation that she hadn't at least been asked to have a coffee. Albeit she hadn't had time, it would have been nice to have been asked. It would also have been nice to know what O'Leary was up to. He was about as subtle as a Boeing 747 rolling up next to her, and she was sure that he was on another of his big-brotherly kicks. No matter how often she told him to back off and leave her (currently non-existent) love-life alone, he just kept trying to play Cupid.

His efforts at being Cupid almost always coincided with one of her father's episodes. As if he thought she could do with a distraction: something (or someone) easy and fun. Usually, though, O'Leary confined himself to other cops, or firemen, or other law enforcement types – and usually, he simply suggested to her that one of his many, many acquaintances was single and looking for a date. His current behaviour, with no precipitating episode, was suggesting very strongly to Casey that he was taking a much more active role. She'd just have to ignore it.

She turned to her murder board. The so-called Troy Bolton was added. O'Leary, arriving not long after Casey despite his pause for coffee, expressed deep disappointment that the school in which Leon Belvez taught was not called East High, in which case, he'd have bet good green dollars that Leon was Troy.

"Though Troy was Zac Efron, y'know."

"So not cool," Andy said. "Bubble-gum entertainment. *So* not cool."

The team fell upon him with imprecations and commentary on his cultural pretentiousness, until Casey called them to order with the single warning that Kent might well appear at any moment.

"What about Merowin?" Tyler asked.

"I think there's something there."

"How'd you know?" Tyler asked.

"He opened his mouth," O'Leary flicked back, without needing to think. It was an old joke.

"*Doctor* Merowin," Casey said with considerable sarcastic emphasis on the title, "thought that he was cleverer than us."

"We. Cleverer than we are," Andy said mischievously.

"Leave your pedantry at home or apply it to Dumpster diving with the uniforms," Casey snarked. "Anyway, I didn't have enough to hit him hard." She paused. "Andy, d'you think you could get footage from any street cameras near Belvez's apartment?"

Andy was inscrutably but obviously smug. "Already on it. Waiting for it to come through."

"Nice work. Okay, let's get down to it."

As the time passed, the murder board received a little more decoration but the camera footage did not appear. Casey hated waiting, and waiting was what she had to do. The three men subtly did not enter her line of sight.

CHAPTER 11

Shortly, Captain Kent, emerging from his office and surveying his domain, found his little team of oddities hard at work, and was satisfied. In the four years he'd had them all, he'd been pretty pleased. Not that he told them that often, of course. They needed to have competition, and a target. He'd snapped the first two up when they became available. O'Leary, even then, could sort out any situation simply by ambling up and asking if there was a problem. Somehow, angry types never had a problem, and calmed down, just as soon as he stood up straight. Neat knack to have, Kent thought. Clement, well, who wouldn't want to have the top Academy graduate? Aiming for Homicide, and Detective, even then – he'd had a few misgivings, though. She was a bit too pretty, and there had been those rumours, but he'd taken Garrett at the Third's word on her and Garrett had been right. She'd never put a foot out of place.

In fact, she was almost – no, not *shy*, and certainly not timid, but, well, *reserved*. That was it. Reserved. Tight with the mountain, but though she was friendly she didn't make friends. Garrett had mentioned that, too. Kent, however, didn't care if she made friends as long as she solved cases, and the Clement-O'Leary team surely did that. Good cop-bad cop: they'd got that nailed – and because it was O'Leary who came off like everyone's best pal with that ridiculous hayseed drawl and *Clement* who went in for the kill, criminals and suspects and witnesses were so surprised that they tended to blurt out far more than they had intended.

So Captain Gareth Kent frankly, my dears, didn't give a damn about Clement being reserved as long as she delivered the goods. O'Leary was pals with everyone, and that was just fine. It wasn't like anyone gave Clement grief, or thought she couldn't do her job. They respected her, and sometimes they went along and watched her in the box and came back just a little nervous.

Kent noticed with some surprise that O'Leary had left his oversize chair (he'd broken two before the budget was amended to get a reinforced one) and was aiming for him. This was not quite unprecedented, but it was certainly not normal. That team stayed clear of him. They fixed their own issues, internally. They didn't bring them to anyone outside the four of them, which was also a little strange. However, anything that kept his to-do list shorter was good by him.

O'Leary sidled through the door, which was quite an achievement at his size.

"Sir, you got a minute?"

"Yes, Detective. *One* minute." Kent ran a tight ship. He wasn't their pal. He was in charge, and he was very well aware of the need to stay that way.

"Sir. Um... that photographer."

"Making trouble? I can't do anything about that."

"No, sir. Um..."

"Get on with it, Detective. You're not normally shy."

"He wants us to co-operate. Um..." – the big man cringed, and tried to look smaller – "um, I was thinkin' that mebbe you'd let him take some photos in here. Good PR."

Kent was so surprised by the statement that he didn't say anything for a moment. Good PR was always useful, but the suggestion came from such an unexpected source that he was left speechless. Also, he didn't like disruption. That photographer could be very disruptive. On the other hand, thanks to some very public PR disasters by other forces, good PR was vital, right now. 1PP was very keen on good PR.

"I'll take it under advisement. Don't mention it to anyone else. Dismissed, Detective."

O'Leary sidled out again.

Casey looked at her notes, and put in a call to Telagon, asking for Terence Brewman. When he eventually called back – office types being absent from their offices on Saturdays – she convinced him that he should help her out, and arranged an interview for Tuesday morning: Brewman being otherwise occupied until then.

The remainder of the afternoon passed in hard work and harder thinking. Many pages of notes later, some discarded, some retained; Casey stretched largely, winced, and looked at her watch.

"Time to go," she said wearily.

"It's only an hour past end of shift," Tyler pointed out, with a grin. "You slacking?" She growled.

"I'll be in the Abbey Pub, iffen anyone else wants to come along," O'Leary invited. "Likely I'll have dinner there. Pete's outta town, and I'm all on my lonesome."

"Nah," Andy declined, with a slight smile. "Busy."

"I could use a beer," Tyler said.

"'Kay then. Seeya Monday, guys."

O'Leary's bulk lumbered for the door, followed by Tyler's strides. Casey tidied up her desk, slowly, collected her purse, and noticed Andy's curious eye. She deflected.

"Come on. Time to go. Where are you off to? Theatre?"

"Some experimental show down at La Mama."

"Enjoy. Can't say I would. What's wrong with a nice hit musical?"

"Apart from the ticket price?"

They wandered out in friendly argument about Casey's lack of broadmindedness and Andy's pretensions to culture, and divided at their respective vehicles.

***

"Why're you in the bar?"

"Told you, Pete's outta town, an' I'm bored of lookin' at my walls. He cooks better 'n me, too."

"Huh."

O'Leary, unusually, got the beers in without being prompted. Tyler looked at the bottle, and downed a fair amount in one.

"Bad day?"

"My eyes are bleeding. Too many databases."

"Quicker than it used to be."

"Yeah." Tyler swigged again, and then sat bolt upright. "Why's he here?"

"I asked him," O'Leary replied.

"What are you playing at, man? D'you want shot?"

"I like him," O'Leary rumbled. "Got some balls. Faced me down, earlier."

Tyler stared. "Shit." He regrouped. "You like everyone, Bigfoot."

"Everyone likes me."

"Till they know you."

"Very mean." O'Leary protruded the ice-shelf of his lower lip. "Mebbe I'll make an exception for you."

"Bring it. When I put you on the mats" –

"You can't take me, Tyler. I win five times outta six."

"So tomorrow'll be the sixth," he said, a little aggressively. O'Leary merely grinned amiably.

"That this side of never? 'Cause you ain't done it in months."

"I'll put you down next time."

O'Leary grinned, irritatingly. Carval finally sat down, one bottle of beer and fifteen photos to the good.

"Is this a fight anyone can join?" he asked.

"Can you spar?"

"A bit," Carval said, cautiously.

"Then you can join. Tyler here can't match me" – there was a noise of utmost disagreement – "so you can have a go. I guess you'll see plenty of the mat."

Carval shrugged. "Maybe." Tyler gave him an odd glance.

"Anyways, you came."

"Yeah. Why are you here?" Tyler jabbed.

"I asked him."

"Why? You never said why a minute ago."

"Did. Said I liked him."

"*He* is right here, but I can go if you wanna have a private fight."

"Naw, don't do that. You wanted to know my story."

Tyler goggled.

"Thought I'd be a footballer, didn't have the talent beyond high school, went to college – majored in criminal justice" – it was Carval's turn to goggle – "joined the Academy."

"That's not all of it," Carval said, and didn't allow his brain to intervene to stop his thoughts falling out of his mouth. "There's something about each of you. You're the odd ones out. None of you play well with anyone else. You fit with each other but no-one else does. So what's the rest of it?"

"How'd you work that out?" O'Leary asked sharply.

"Boy's got a brain," Tyler noted, not approvingly. "We're not misfits, though."

"Just a li'l different." The lazy, dumb-sounding drawl was back.

"So how'd you work it out?"

"Just looking at you all. You've nothing in common, but there's something about every one of you that shows in my photos. And there's four of you. I thought cops came in pairs, like the animals going into the Ark. So what's the story?"

"Why's that your business?"

"It's not, if you don't want to tell me," Carval said disarmingly. "But I take better photos when I know the story."

Tyler's scowl didn't soften. "You don't know me, and I don't know you. You don't get to know."

O'Leary shrugged. "Naw, that's not all of it." Tyler stared at him. "But like the man said, you don't know me. I think we might be seein' a lot of you, but you ain't one of us. So no, you don't get the story. You get enough not to do or say somethin' dumb."

"Do I get any stories?"

"He could get the one about the weightlifting," Tyler smirked.

O'Leary grinned. "Sure. That story's no secret."

Tyler was snickering gently. Clearly he knew the tale.

"When I was in the Academy, year before Tyler here" –

Tyler looked a bit older than that timeline indicated. Carval thought for a second, and blurted out his conclusion without a pause. "You're military."

"Army," he confirmed, and said no more, though the scowl lifted fractionally.

"When I was in the Academy, we thought we'd have ourselves a little competition. Weightlifting. Handicapped, 'cause otherwise it wouldn't've been fair." Carval guessed not. Surely there couldn't have been more than one mountain in the class? "Anyways, we…er… couldn't get into the gym that late, an', waalll, there might have been some beer drunk" – his moon-face turned pink, and Tyler snickered more loudly – "an' the upshot was, we thought we'd do it with the recruits."

Carval snorted, and then collapsed with laughter. "I wish I'd seen that," he managed. "That would be spectacular. Like the circus strongman, only in uniform."

"Yeah," Tyler said. "Tale was still told when I got there."

"I guess it's still told now?"

"Prob'ly."

"So you got my story, and you've worked out Tyler was Army – who're you?"

"Finished high school, went to college, bummed around with a camera for a few years. Did some glamour shots to get started" – might as well put the truth out there: keeping that secret wouldn't last five seconds if they Googled him and hiding it wouldn't impress anyone – "then did some reality exhibitions. Last one was the panhandlers of New York."

"You got a bit of a reputation."

"Yeah. My shows do well." He rode over the opening mouth of O'Leary. "And I'm thirty three and I'm not a blushing virgin." No point hiding that either. It was all over the search results. "So shoot me. I don't guess you pair are pure as driven snow either."

Tyler raised eyebrows and fixed Carval with a pinpoint stare. "We're a team," he said flatly.

"I've already had the intimidation bit from O'Leary. Let's not, and say you did." Carval glared back.

"You were right. He does have some balls. I still think you're batshit crazy, though."

Tyler downed some beer in a very non-conversational way. It seemed that he'd found out whatever he wanted to know, for now.

"Seven years in the Army," he suddenly said. Quit after my unit got withdrawn from the sandpit after they got themselves a prime minister. Same year, finished the Academy, went to the Fifteenth precinct, stayed there a bit. Looked for a new place, ended up with Bigfoot here and Casey." He paused. It appeared to Carval, mostly from O'Leary's surprised expression, that that might be more words than Tyler had emitted all week. "Worked for me."

"Didn't know you knew that many words."

"Don't waste them. Not like you."

"So now we're all pals," O'Leary said on a satisfied note. "Let's have another beer an' talk about sport, like men do. All this touchy-feely stuff is for the girls." Tyler cast him a cynical glance. "'Cept Casey. She don't do talking."

"I already noticed," Carval put in dryly.

"She let you sit with her in a coffee bar, so I reckon you're already plenty of words ahead of where you should be, an' she hasn't shot you yet. Doin' good, photographer."

"Not that I don't appreciate the cheerleading, but how about you give me a proper answer to why you tipped me off about where she is, because that didn't figure in the earlier intimidation party."

"I told you, she needs a distraction."

"And I guess you're not going to tell me why because surprise, surprise," Carval bit out, "you don't know me."

"Exactly so," O'Leary drawled. "An' besides, she might be tiny but she packs a mean punch. I like my nose the shape it is right now."

"And if I don't play along with your game?"

"You don't get any photos."

"Like I said earlier, I don't give in to blackmail. There are plenty of cops in Manhattan. I don't need it to be you four."

"Yeah, you do," O'Leary said bluntly. "You got a vision. I c'n see it already. You need it to be us. Whatever you caught, you ain't gonna get it from the others. So you need us."

"I can do something completely different. I don't have to do cops. I can go off to some hick town and do small town America. You don't have any leverage here."

"Nor do you."

"Stop," Tyler said, with a note of command. "Had enough. Stop playing whose-is-bigger. You both want something. I think you're both crazy, but it's up to you. Leave the butting heads and pal up. You already agreed you liked each other. Play nice."

The other two men regarded him as if he had grown a second head.

"Play nice," he said again, firmly. He turned to Carval. "You don't scare easy, do you? Bigfoot's got it right. Casey could use a distraction." He punched Carval's shoulder, not quite gently. "Tag. You're it."

Carval boggled at them both.

"We don't want shot. You... not our problem. You're interested, so you make it work. Or not."

"You guys are something else," Carval breathed. "What if I just tell Casey you gave me a free pass and encouragement?"

"She can't do much about it. Can't spar better'n us, won't shoot us. Likely she'll sulk for a bit." They shrugged in unison. "We'll live. You might not," O'Leary added happily.

"Beer?" Carval asked. Clearly he wasn't going to get any more details from these guys. Equally clearly, there was some level of acceptance, which he wasn't inclined to turn down. Some time later, male bonding had occurred over sport and beer. Carval left with a slight hesitancy in his walk. O'Leary remained as stable as the Alp he resembled, and Tyler clearly had the hardest head in creation.

He was still as confused by O'Leary's actions as he had been from the beginning. Obviously there was something going on with Casey, but there was no reason at all why he should be recruited to solve it. He hadn't been *that* blatant, had he? It couldn't just be the past photo. Casey's stance, walk and air of being firmly in charge didn't argue for her being less than confident in her own skin. Something else was going on.

Carval's curiosity, never normally applied to the women who were happy to surround him, woke up. He wasn't arrogant (really not) but he'd never had a problem attracting women; and he'd been just a little piqued that Casey was unfriendly. She ought to be a little friendlier. He'd become complacent, he realised, hard upon that wish. Ugh, he thought. That wasn't good.

On the other hand, he'd got both proximity and encouragement from the other two. That just left Andy. Maybe he should get to know Andy. He might talk, Carval supposed, though he wasn't betting his life savings, or indeed a nickel, on it.

All those men – all four of this team, not just the men – had secrets. *That's* why they were the oddball team. They knew each other's secrets, and they kept them. He sat down, a little fuzzed by the beer, and tried to think.

Tyler was ex-military. The focused stare reminded Carval of something, but he couldn't pin it down. O'Leary – could be anything: for a man who seemed so open he was pretty shut down. Andy – another mystery, but his eyes were old, and that meant pain. Carval had seen that look on some of the panhandlers, the ones who expected a blow or a curse or a kick – and some of the boozed up boys from the universities or Wall Street would supply it. Could Andy have been beaten up badly, some time long ago?

And then there was Casey. Cool, cold, reserved Casey-the-cop. There was the photo, and the men had said enough for him to work through that tale. Someone hadn't liked being beaten to the top, and had tried some pretty underhand tactics – pulling his photo would have taken *work* – to bring her down.

A tendril of bleary thought wriggled into his head: beer allowing connections. He could find out who had stolen his photo. He could also find out how Casey had done at the Academy – and who had come second. Surely there had to have been records somewhere.

Nobody got to misuse his photos like that. Nobody.

CHAPTER 12

"The cops were back today. Interviewing me, and everyone else in the group." His voice shook.

"So? I told you what to do."

"I didn't give anything away," he whined. "But what if they suspect?"

"What did they say?"

"Said he got hit on the head. Nothing else."

"If he was hit hard enough, they won't look further. If it looks like a mugging, they'll think it is a mugging."

"But if they do tests…"

"If they had anything, they'd go in harder. Stop pussying around and man up."

"Did they ask about the chemistry?" A less confrontational voice, previously silent.

"No…"

"Well then. No problem."

"But it was the same two as spoke to John. Big guy – massive, and a woman."

"What're you worried about? Big guy'll be a meathead, and women don't get science. Nothing to worry about."

"They think I was jealous of Ricky. They'll go after that."

"You were." It was a callously throw-away comment. "But they'll expect that. They'll see the obvious."

"What if they find out about her?"

"How are they going to do that, if they can't even spot the gas? Anyway, you got her wrapped around your little finger. Just keep her happy. Nice meals, pretty presents. It's easy to keep her happy and quiet."

"And if the cops find more?"

"We'll deal with that. The money we've made, that'll buy a lot of problem-solving." A menacing pause. "Don't be a problem."

CHAPTER 13

Casey drove home to her neat, small apartment with its high ceiling and tall windows, surveying it approvingly. The wooden flooring gleamed softly under the light, her cosy, warm-toned rugs kept her toes from getting cold, and the clean lines of her desk and bookcase blended happily with her comfortable couch and chairs. She changed into sweats, made herself dinner, chased it with coffee, and settled down with some easy-watching soaps and a good book. She had a secret – *very* secret – fondness for the better paranormal stories, and right now she was some way into the deeds of Kate Daniels. Of course, she'd never have let the team know that, though she thought that if paranormal had been real, O'Leary would certainly have been a bear. Andy would have been a coyote: smart and sassy; and Tyler a lone wolf. She read happily for a few pages, until her phone rang.

"Hello?"

"Miss Clement? This is Sergeant Dawes of the Eighth precinct." She knew what the next sentence would be. Just the same as it always had been.

"Detective Clement here, Sergeant Dawes. Homicide, out the Thirty-Sixth." His tone changed, cop to cop.

"Detective. We have a David Clement in here. He asked us to call you."

"Drunk?" asked Casey wearily. Drunk, open container: just like before, just like always. *Oh, Dad. Why?*

"'Fraid so, detective. You'll need to come get him, get him out. He's a pretty quiet drunk. We've not processed him yet, and seeing as you're another cop..." He tailed off. They both understood. It was very unofficial, but sometimes it happened.

"Thank you," she said, heartfelt. "Okay. It'll take me less than an hour to get there. Be there as fast as I can, Sergeant."

She raced through dressing more professionally, slung on her shield and gun – she had to look like a cop, to deal with other cops – and departed at some speed.

The desk sergeant assessed her cop status in one smooth, sympathetic glance.

"Detective Clement. Sergeant Dawes?" The stocky man at the desk nodded. "I've come to get my father. Anything you can tell me?"

"Picked him up – brought in around four this afternoon, dead drunk. Tossed him into Holding till he woke up" – she winced – "and when he did, he asked for you. So I called you. Didn't know you were a cop. He never said."

"Thanks," she said again, equally grateful. Dawes gave her a look of comradeship. "Can we get my dad up?"

Dawes started on the routine and Casey dutifully signed for all the right things in all the right places. She knew exactly what to do and where to sign. She'd done it all before. When she'd finished, Dawes arranged for her father to be released to her, and he was brought up a few moments later, looking filthy, guilty, and most of all, still drunk.

"Catkin," he slurred, and nothing more.

"C'mon, Dad," she said calmly. "Let's get you home to bed." She put an arm around his shoulders to steer him in a straight line, and escorted him to her car. There was already a sheet over the passenger seat, and once she'd installed him she handed him, without comment, a bowl. Usually it wasn't necessary. Usually.

She also rolled the windows down, which was always necessary, and took her father home, again. He did this every couple of months, now. The episodes were getting closer together, more intense. She didn't ask why: she didn't need to.

By the time she was done with him, had coaxed him into a shower, cajoled him into eating something, even if it was only a grilled cheese sandwich, cozened him into drinking enough water that he might not suffer too badly in the morning; by the time all that was done, it was close on midnight. She stowed the sheet and unused bowl back in the trunk, and went home to her own bed. Tomorrow would arrive soon enough, and she could bury her family's issues in the satisfaction of her work.

But still, she didn't sleep well. One day, it wouldn't be as easy as persuading her father to wash, eat and rest. One day, and maybe that would be soon, it wouldn't just be a bender every couple of months, when his pain was too much. One day, but pray God it wouldn't be soon – pray God it would be *never*, but she knew that was in vain – it wouldn't be a phone call, it would be a knock, and *I'm sorry to tell you, Miss Clement.* She could feel it coming closer, day by day.

One day.

***

"Not looking so fine there," O'Leary rumbled on Monday morning. Casey glared at him, spoiled by a yawn. "You okay? That's a pile of coffee cups." Okay, so there were two. But she'd been here forty minutes so that was reasonable.

"I'm okay." She shrugged, uncomfortably. "Just…. Dad."

"Ah." O'Leary said nothing more.

Casey regarded her e-mail balefully until, possibly as intimidated as her suspects usually were, it pinged. ME McDonald's report popped up in her e-mail.

Now that was truly weird. Their boy Belvez had indeed been suffocated with carbon monoxide. However, there were no soot particles, and no other gases. It looked, said McDonald's report, as if it was pure carbon monoxide. Not a contaminant in sight. Or in spectroscopy, for that matter. Where on earth did you…

"In a lab!" Casey said out loud.

"What?" said O'Leary.

Casey dropped her pen. O'Leary did not drop his barrel of coffee or his breakfast McMuffin – just.

She dialled McDonald.

"Dr McDonald?"

"What do you want, Detective Clement? I am busy."

"The carbon monoxide. In your professional opinion, is that lab-grade?"

"Yes. Did you not read the report? I said it was pure. Uncontaminated. Of course it is lab-grade."

He cut the call. Casey scowled at the phone, but ticked off the potential loose end as tied up.

"He was suffocated with pure carbon monoxide. It must have come from a lab. Matches up with him being a chemist. "

"Or a supplier who supplies labs," O'Leary offered up.

"Yeah, that too. Okay. Andy!"

"Yes?"

"Can you move on to running all the possible suppliers of gases to labs? We're looking for carbon monoxide suppliers."

Casey's well-developed antennae for the weird and complicated were not so much twitching as whipping. She chewed the end of her pen and pondered. Pondering was not improved by the dearth of information, but Andy and Tyler were head down in their work. She quit pondering in favour of caffeinating, and made herself a coffee with which to finish reading McDonald's report.

The report was as thorough as McDonald always was. "Ah-ha. He was bashed on the head with a rock. McDonald found earth and stone chips."

"He wasn't killed where we found him."

"Guess not. You don't get lab gas or rocks in a back alley."

"Unless they took them out a handy flowerpot."

"Not very likely."

"No – but you do get gas in the labs at Columbia. You must do. I mean, there's really only Columbia and NYU, and why cart a corpse up from NYU to Columbia?"

"I do hear those frat boys get up to some rivalry," O'Leary pointed out.

"Not murder, though. That's going a little too far."

Casey paused. "Okay, so it's likely Columbia. But we need to consider that it might be some other facility – do they use carbon monoxide for anything at CSU or in the morgue?"

Everyone looked solidly blank. So did Casey. "Volunteer to find out?"

Everyone tried to hide. "Guess it's me, then." She pouted. "McDonald hates me."

"McDonald hates everyone, so bat your eyelashes and suck it up, buttercup. You had the idea, you go follow up." Casey threw a pen at O'Leary, who caught it without difficulty and snickered.

"Ain't gonna work. No-one's gonna come see McDonald with you."

"Okay, I'll go see the morgue and then I can harass CSU in person."

Casey swung out of the door on her new trail. Behind her, O'Leary tapped out a text.

***

Casey arrived at the morgue in short order, and, focused on her investigative trail and need to reduce the possible options for monoxide-murder, completely missed Carval's broad figure, leaning on a lamppost near the door with camera to face, whipping off shots by the dozen: long shots and close-ups.

"Hey," she greeted the techs that she passed. "McDonald in?"

"Yeah," one drooped. "He's in as fine a mood as ever." Casey translated that to mean that the tech had been reamed out for some misdemeanour such as blinking or breathing, and drooped a little herself as she passed along the sterile-smelling corridors to the ME's domain, where she knocked. Politeness cost her nothing, and it might soothe the savage beast of McDonald's irascible temper.

"Yes?"

It hadn't. McDonald sounded hugely irritated and it wasn't even nine-thirty yet.

"What do you want?"

"I need your help," Casey said. "I've read your report, and you noted that Belvez was hit. I guess that was likely hard enough to leave him unable to resist the suffocation."

"Yes? I know this, Detective. I do not need a recitation of my own words."

"I need to know if there is any reason that you would use pure carbon monoxide here in the morgue," Casey said baldly. "I need to eliminate everywhere I can that might use it. I'm starting with the places where" – her tone held a slight warning – "I can get immediate co-operation."

"I do not," McDonald stated. "I have no reason at all to use any form of carbon monoxide." He paused, and his lips twisted. "In the spirit of assistance" – strangely, Casey heard *and getting you out of my way as fast as I can* – "I suggest that you would achieve most in the least time by talking to the administrative office, and specifically the purchasing staff. They would be able to tell you if we have ever purchased pure carbon monoxide."

Casey, for possibly the first time ever, favoured McDonald with a brilliant, full-hearted smile. "That's a really good idea. Thank you," she said with sincerity. "That'll save me hours. Much appreciated, Dr McDonald." She made for the door at some speed, anxious to get started, and therefore missed McDonald's stunned reaction to a detective actually smiling at him. Fortunately, she also missed his mutter of *shouldn't a detective have thought of that*, which would have quite ruined her excellent mood.

She swung through the morgue to the admin department and was shortly in happy and productive conversation with the purchasing clerk, one Duval Carter, who was utterly delighted to take actions directly relevant to her investigation and promised her results by the end of the day at the very latest.

Casey almost danced out of the morgue, which was not her normal reaction to its grisly function, with a broad smile. Next up, CSU, both for carbon monoxide questions and to see if there were some more results.

"Hey."

What the actual fuck? Her broad smile disappeared instantly, as did any desire to dance.

"What are you doing here?"

"Tagging along," Nemesis in the form of Carval said smugly. "I found you, so now you have to let me tag along and take shots in public places. Where are we going next?"

Casey emitted a noise that wouldn't have disgraced an infuriated falcon. That rat *bastard*. How did he *find* her? This was unfair. Ridiculous. Unbelievable. Flattering – *what?*

"How did you find me?"

"Probability," he said airily. "Detectives visit the morgue. So I took a chance." He didn't think that dropping O'Leary in it would really help him here. Or O'Leary, of course, though that was pretty secondary to keeping his own skin intact. He took a couple of shots over her car roof. She looked totally adorable when furiously flustered. Another excellent contrast. Her hair was pulled back in the same tight, controlled clip as previously: must be a work thing. He'd have liked to see it loose.

Casey was frantically trying to resist the urge to shoot this annoying photographer. Jumping up and down and screaming was for toddler tantrums, and certainly not for mature, sensible women. It was just very, very tempting. Worse, he was right. She did have to let him tag along, and indeed take shots.

"CSU labs," she growled, and got in. Carval disposed himself in the passenger seat. "What're you doing?"

"I found you, so you have to let me follow you."

She had to put up with him actually in her actual car? What fresh hell was this?

"You don't touch anything. You don't say anything. Make yourself invisible."

"I'm going to take some shots." That statement did not go down well, from the infuriated noise she made. The engine started with an over-revved screech which was entirely in accordance with the expression on her face. Carval took a shot of her hands on the wheel, and then ceased shooting until she'd pulled out into the traffic and was concentrating on the road not on him. She didn't look at him once, which allowed him to take more shots of her competent, elegant hands and her excellent profile.

Casey didn't use the ride to interrogate Carval about the photo that had infested her Academy months with rumour. She would save that for a time when she wasn't so intent on a different trail. When she had time; when she was cool and cold and reserved and forensic. She wanted answers, not emotions. Emotions were not required.

By the time she'd reached the CSU facility in Queens, she still hadn't said a word to him, which didn't worry Carval in the slightest, lost in photographic heaven and with the memory card half full. His reverie was interrupted when the car came to a smooth halt, and he scrambled out in order not to be left behind.

"You can't come in," Casey informed him with quite unnecessary satisfaction. "The lab isn't a public place. You'll have to stay outside."

There was a park opposite the sand-coloured, stone-faced building, though Carval couldn't see any unoccupied benches which weren't far enough away that Casey could depart without him. He expected that she would try.

"There's a coffee shop down the street," she added reluctantly.

"If you don't leave without me" – she flushed slightly – "I'll get you one too. Double espresso do?" She nodded, tersely. "How long will you be?"

Casey consulted her slim watch. "Twenty minutes. If you're not here then I leave." She was completely uncompromising.

"Promise you won't go without me?"

"You sound like you're five. Not attractive."

Carval bit his tongue in order not to say *what would be attractive?* He looked down at her angrily sparking eyes and set mouth. "Please?"

"O-*kay*," she said with exasperation.

"And I want a couple of shots now."

"What? No."

"You were told to let me." He smiled beautifully. Casey was very obviously unimpressed, though – well, now, *that* was interesting – there was a very small line of colour on her high cheekbones. He couldn't tell a single thing from her brown eyes, though. He supposed that a good poker face was an advantage for a cop.

"Get on with it, then," she capitulated, with poor grace.

"Just let me come round the car, and get focused, and then walk in."

She gaped. "That's it?"

"Yep."

"No" – he heard *dumb* – "poses?"

"Nope. Just walk in like you normally would. I don't want poses, I want natural." She flicked a quick, uncertain glance at him, waited until he was ready, and on his brief gesture moved off. It took her three or four strides to relax and walk normally, which Carval confidently expected was how long it took her to forget his annoying existence completely. He kept shooting till the door closed behind her, and then strolled down the street towards the row of low-rise buildings, odd little shops and interesting restaurants until he located the coffee shop.

An Americano for himself drunk, and another, with a double espresso, purchased to go, Carval sauntered back to the Crime Lab with a comfortable five minutes to spare. Casey wasn't there, so he sat on the hood of her car and enjoyed the September sunshine, idly snapping the play of light and the way in which the leaves glinted differently as the wind moved them on the trees of the park, and sipping his coffee, which was really rather good.

Life was pretty swell, right now.

***

Casey was uncomfortably conscious of Carval's lens focusing on her – for all of three steps. Then she forgot him. She started with the purchasing department, and received the same delighted co-operation as Duval had provided. Clearly even the admin staff were keen on being directly involved in crime solving. That disposed of, she strode briskly along to find the CSU team, who were not as glossy as the TV show but were just as brilliant.

"Hey, guys," she announced happily. "I was over here so I thought I'd say hi."

The team regarded her a little sceptically. "What do you want?"

"You always say that. Why can't I just be sociable?"

"Because you're never just sociable. You've always got an ulterior motive. This is about your vic, isn't it? We sent you prints straight away, with the clearances. ME's sent you his report. What more d'you want?"

"I want some more," Casey said. "Please, CSU, I want some more." Everyone sniggered. "Was there anything interesting at the scene?"

"Nope. Some drag marks, which I guess you expected since people don't get suffocated with pure gases in back alleys; and nothing else. No unknown prints, or known ones."

Casey made a horrible face. "Anyone with half a brain knows to wear gloves and then bleach them."

The tech nodded sympathetically.

"What about his apartment?"

"That's what we're working on. A lot of prints, but nothing's popping up yet. Soon as it does, you know we'll ping you."

"What was in the shaving foam containers?"

"Ah. Well," the tech said enticingly, "that was interesting. It's on your e-mail."

"Just tell me, hmm? I wanna know."

"It looks like lens cases."

Casey boggled. "Lens cases?" she repeated. "Why on earth lens cases?"

"We don't know. We haven't opened them yet, in case it's something sensitive. Don't want to damage them." She lifted an eyebrow. "Could be light sensitive, and opening them will mess them up."

"Okay," she agreed slowly. "Um… we might have a chemist on tap. Professor from Columbia. Can you leave them shut till I make sure he's not a suspect, and then we might get him to take a look under controlled conditions – with you guys?"

"Sure," the tech assented, equably. "Anything to keep the to-do list shorter."

"Thanks. Guess I'd better get back. Let me know about anything else, yeah?"

"Sure, Casey," the tech groused. "We always do."

She grinned mischievously. "Gotcha. See you."

Now that was very interesting. Lens cases? Weird. Definitely weird. Who kept contact lenses hidden like that? Answer, nobody sane. Ergo, not contact lenses, and further, likely something Belvez shouldn't have had. That was a thread that would repay some serious tugging. She could see a discussion with Terrison arriving at full speed on Track One, which made her happy. Progress on cases always made her happy.

Outside, the sun was shining, and Casey, buoyed up on a tide of case-related possibilities, hustled to her car, ready to roll again. Lunch had not figured in her thinking – it often didn't, which was why she had a desk drawer full of candy bars which the boys didn't raid on pain of broken fingers.

"Coffee?"

Oh. He was *still* here. Dammit. Oh, well. She could drop him off somewhere. The East River sprang to mind. From the Robert F. Kennedy Bridge.

"Coffee?" he said again, and shoved a small go-cup under her nose. She blinked.

"What's this?"

"Coffee."

"I got that."

"Oh. Double espresso, though likely it's a bit cold by now."

Casey took the lid off and poured it down her throat without any concern for the temperature. "Yep," she said, and then, remembering her manners, "Thank you." Her mother had maintained her manners, whatever else she'd been forgetting.

"Woohoo," Carval said smugly. "I managed something you actually liked. Mark the calendar."

"Don't worry," Casey snipped straight back. "I'm sure it won't happen again."

"Oh, I'm sure it will," he drawled. "Right when you least expect it."

She positively flounced into her car. Carval hastened to take shotgun, before she scorched off without him. He spent the first few moments taking a few more photos, and certainly didn't mention that he'd taken six in the few strides she'd taken from the door of the Crime Lab to the car, four more as she was downing her coffee, and two while she was storming into the car. One of them would surely be useful.

CHAPTER 14

Casey's good mood had dissolved in an instant at Carval's smug response to her thanks, and she'd bitten straight back. She'd *almost* been prepared to accept that he had a good point – after all, he'd provided her with the right sort of coffee – but then he'd spoilt it. Well, the hell with it.

She didn't bother with conversation. Her behaviour was not a sulk, because she didn't ever sulk. She was pondering her case, which took up all of the headspace that wasn't needed for negotiating the New York traffic.

"Did you get what you wanted?" he asked, halfway back to the precinct.

"Yeah." She meant it as a shut-down. She didn't want to talk.

"Who was he?"

"Why do you care?"

Carval gasped. "Because I'm human." And then, astonishingly, he quoted: "*Any man's death diminishes me/Because I am involved in mankind/And therefore never send to know for whom the bell tolls/It tolls for thee.* So of course I care. Not personally," he said hurriedly, "that would be silly, but in the same way that I" – he faltered, searching out a word – "cared, um, respected those panhandlers that I shot last year."

"Oh," Casey murmured, and for the first time it wasn't tinged with anger or irritation, nor was it that heavy misery of the café. She was marginally intrigued, and the knowledge that he could quote poetry was surprising. The irritated atmosphere softened slightly.

"So who was he? Why would anyone want to kill him?"

"We don't know the second. That's what we're trying to find out. When you know why, you usually know who. Oftentimes, it's money or sex. They call it love but it isn't. If it was love they wouldn't kill each other…"

She trailed off, a thought twisting her face and her gut. If Mom hadn't had the accident, she wondered if she might have thought differently, later.

She refocused. They'd never had to make that ghastly choice.

"His name was Ricardo Belvez. Researcher. Chemist."

"Mm?" He didn't mention that O'Leary had already told him that he had been a chemist.

"He was hit on the head, suffocated, and dumped where we found him." She could sense Carval's cringe. "There are some odd features, but that's the basic story."

Astoundingly, Carval took the hint.

"So your team," he said, instead of asking more about Belvez. Casey made a slightly surprised noise. "What?"

"Most people are interested in the death. Ghouls," she added, disparagingly.

"I'm not. I'm interested in the living. Death is dead. There isn't anything much to shoot in a corpse. I'm interested in life. People. Expression and movement and interaction." He sounded thoroughly enthusiastic, almost boyish. Casey flicked a glance towards him and back to the road. "Catching the moment and the fleeting emotions. Like – you know that really famous VJ Day shot of the sailor kissing the nurse? Like that. Spontaneity. You only get that with real people, doing normal – well, maybe not normal, but, um, *unplanned*, things." He frowned. "That's not right. Um, people who don't think they're being watched. Not posing models and that sort of thing. You can tell it's fake from a mile away."

He paused. Casey didn't say anything. Truth to tell, she was too surprised to say anything. His patent sincerity had displaced her angry upset. Maybe he did have a good point. She arrived at civility, if not necessarily liking. He was really quite attractive when he was talking about photography – *what?*

"So I shoot real people just going about their business."

"Panhandlers have a business?"

"They've got a life, just like you or me. So I shot it."

"I saw the exhibition," Casey offered.

She had. It had been brilliant (not that she would say so here and now) – and then she'd gone home and wept her heart out, because the expressions on the faces of the panhandlers had been just like the expression on her father's face ever since her mother passed, beaten down and hopeless, and she couldn't bear the similarity.

"You did?" He was on that in an instant.

"Yeah." Another close-down, and again he took the hint, though there was a smidge of hurt on his face.

"So," he said again, after a silent, awkward beat, "your team. I thought cops came in pairs?"

Casey seized on the neutral topic, and completely forgot that Carval was an irritating nuisance who she didn't want to help. Anything to stay well away from anything personal. Even her burning desire to interrogate hell out of him was tamped down – anyway, interrogating him where *she* couldn't walk out would be bad tactics.

"Uniforms patrol in pairs, however the boss assigns them. That's where O'Leary and I started out."

"You were uniforms together?"

"Sort of. He was already there." She didn't mention the arrest. That would just have been embarrassing. "I guess they thought we'd average out to two ordinary uniforms."

He grinned, and the atmosphere in the cruiser became a little more comfortable. "Guess so. He's pretty big."

"Oh, yeah." Casey spotted an opportunity for a little revenge for O'Leary's ragging her. "Get him to tell you about the weightlifting competition in the Academy."

"Okay," Carval said, and absolutely did not mention that O'Leary already had. To tell her that would tip her off that he'd already been sociable with parts of the team.

"So we were uniforms together, and then when we made detective – same time, five years ago – we just stayed paired up. We moved precinct, though. Captain Kent needed a new pair – retirements, transfers, you know, people are always moving around."

"Lucky that you stayed together?"

"Yep. But… if you've got a good pair you try not to break it up. Some people work better together than others, and you don't want personality clashes."

Carval detected an interesting evasion and hitch there. Clearly there was a story behind that. He put it together with the story the three male cops had told him on their first meeting, and O'Leary and Tyler's conversation the second time, and allowed two and two to make four. He wondered very strongly why O'Leary had been so keen to work with her, and what his story was. He didn't ask. He hadn't expected that Casey would actually talk about her own team, and he wasn't going to disturb this amazing fit of speech.

"Okay," was all he actually *said*. "But there are four of you."

"Yes. O'Leary and I were teamed up, and not long after we got there Tyler transferred in, and, well, we liked him."

Another evasion. *We liked him* implied that a lot of others – maybe everyone – hadn't. Tyler had seemed pretty hard-core macho to Carval, and maybe only O'Leary could deal with that.

"Anyways, we kept him. It works. And then there was another shift-around and Andy joined, and four's a better number than three, and he fit." And three times was the charm, Casey-Cop. That was a third evasion. Definitely the Misfits team. "So we kept him, too, and the Captain was cool with that."

"Why didn't any of them come with you today, if you work in pairs?"

Casey acquired a mischievous and stunningly attractive smile. "Because nobody likes going to see ME McDonald, and I drew the short straw. He gets antsy if more than one of us goes to the morgue. He's not a people person." She smirked. "He's nearly as sociable as his corpses."

Carval guffawed.

Before he could ask anything more, the car pulled up outside the precinct, and conversation ceased. Casey's calm professional face slid on.

"We're done," she said briskly. "Bye."

He put a hand over hers, swamping it, as she went to unlock her seatbelt. "Don't be like that. I'll be back photographing. Wouldn't it be much nicer to be friends?"

"I don't think that's necessary. You know about the team. It's plenty." Hell. He'd moved too fast and she was spooking. She tugged her hand away, and opened the door to vacate the car. Double or nothing, he thought, and hurled the truth out there.

"I never sold that shot," he bit out. She stopped. "Whoever stole it, that's on them. Not me."

"Whatever. You took it, so it was there to be used." She got out, suddenly tightly caught into herself. "Might not have been your intention, but if you'd never taken it, it couldn't have happened."

He was there in front of her. "You can't blame me for someone stealing it. That's like saying your victim deserved to get dead."

"Whatever," she said again. "Take your pictures and let me be. Be pals with the others." It was a concession he didn't expect, but it wasn't enough.

"All of you," he said obstinately.

"I have work to do. You're in my way."

"No," he said.

She suddenly realised just how much bigger than her he was. Bigger than Tyler, who was not a small man. Up close, he wasn't just tall, but broad. Broad enough to envelop her – *what?* No. She hadn't time for that. He was still arguing.

"No. We're going to deal with this. I don't care if you don't want to talk, but I'm not letting you go on thinking I screwed you up when I had nothing to do with it. Some bastard stole *my shot* but that's not my fault."

"Fine. It wasn't you. I get it." She slid sideways. He stepped in front of her again. "You're obstructing me," she said, warningly.

"That's a cop-out. Okay, I'm out of your way. But this conversation is not done. I'm not gonna be blamed for something that's not my fault."

"Why should you care anyway? Take your pictures and leave."

"You won't react right. You won't be you if you're all cross and blaming me. Your reactions to me aren't what I want. I want your reactions to your day."

"So it's all about the photos."

He couldn't tell if that was good or bad from her voice.

"Yes."

It was…well, not the wrong answer. It might not have been entirely true, but it wasn't the wrong answer. She eased slightly.

"Fine. I'll think about it."

He smiled down at her. "That'll do. Shake on it?" He extended a large hand. She hesitated for a second, and then took it and shook once, firmly, then let go.

It was just as well she had let go quickly, because Carval was not inclined to let go at all. The sudden shock of voluntary contact had burned through his arm. He stared after her, too rattled even to pull out his camera.

And then he turned away and went home, where he intended to work out what the *hell* that was all about.

***

Casey stalked back into the bullpen with blood and murder in her eye, which at least stopped her thinking about the sparks that had run right up her arm when Carval had put his hand over hers, and then again when she'd shaken his hand. Suddenly, a lot of things were becoming clear. O'Leary was a *rat*, and when she got a chance to speak to him in private, there would be *many* words had with him. He knew perfectly well that she didn't want followed around and photographed, and why.

"Which of you told that photographer about the photos?" she hissed at the others.

"We put the hard word on him," O'Leary said. "Somewheres in there we – and he – worked it out. He wasn't tellin', an' he wasn't very happy, neither. Swore worse 'n' Tyler when I put him on the mats again."

Tyler nodded, not seeing the point of words.

"An' then he stalked out. So we had a few more beers." O'Leary looked her in the still-fulminating eye, and notably failed to mention the *second* evening of beers. "So no call to be raisin' Cain on us. Anyways, what'd you find out?"

"McDonald had a helpful idea," she said, to general astonishment and, in Andy's case, fake fainting. Tyler poked him with a pencil. "He said if I wanted to know about carbon monoxide orders, to go to the purchases department. So I did, at the morgue and the Crime Lab, and they promised me it by the end of today. So maybe we can do the same with the colleges and universities?"

"I was looking at that," Tyler said. "Got bored waiting for the phone records. I got a list of all the schools that might use it, and I called the city department of education to make sure the high schools don't use it. They don't," he added, forestalling the question. "Andy was looking at suppliers."

"Great. How many schools do we need to look at?"

"Seventy seven."

Casey choked. "How many?" she squeaked, horrified.

"I got a coupla uniforms wiping out the ones that won't count. Like Juillard. Law schools. Business schools. Won't be so many when that's done. And then I'll get them to do the calling round. No point us doing grunt work like that. We got enough to do."

There was a very relieved sigh from Casey.

"Don't you love me no more?" O'Leary asked plaintively.

"Uh?"

"You went on a road trip an' didn't take me. You went to the Crime Lab without me. I love that place."

"You just want to be on TV. In the back of a CSI episode."

"Why not?"

"You wouldn't fit in shot. They'd chop your head off."

O'Leary pouted pathetically, which had no impact at all on Casey.

"Did the lab have anything new?"

"Yes. Remember those rattling shaving foam canisters?"

"Yeah? What was the rattle?" O'Leary asked hopefully. "I wanna know. I found they rattled, so I should get to find out why."

"Hmm," said Casey, pretending to read the e-mail and hiding her smile. "Verrrry interesting."

"What, Casey?"

"Mm. I didn't expect *that*."

"Casey," O'Leary rumbled warningly.

"I see. Yes. That's really useful. Hmmm."

"*Casey!* Stop it and tell us what CSU found."

"Hmmm," she said again, mischievously. They collectively surrounded her, and growled. She wasn't noticeably intimidated.

"C'mon. Spill."

"The rattle was lens cases."

She smiled at the stunned expression on three faces.

Andy whistled sharply. "Really? That is *so* not what I thought. I thought it would be pills."

"So did I. Chemist, rattles, gotta be pills, really."

"But... why on God's green earth would he have lens cases hidden *anywhere*?" O'Leary asked. There was a short silence.

"Lenses? Who keeps their contacts in shaving foam?" Andy said. "That's weird."

"Yep. So I don't guess it is contact lenses. What I think we're going to do is try and clear Terrison out of the way, and if he's not a suspect we can get him properly involved and some answers." She made a note. "I brought back proper copies of the papers we found in Belvez's apartment, too. I'd like his take on them, if we can get comfortable that he's out of the frame." She gazed around at the others. "Andy, anything new?"

"No. Nothing on cameras round the landlord yet, but I've requested more footage from around both NYU and Columbia: wider time gap. If Tyler's guys can narrow down the list of other colleges, I'll get footage from them too. I don't guess that the Theological Seminary is gonna be high up my list, and I'd rather save my eyes for something likelier."

"Don't think God needs carbon monoxide," O'Leary rumbled.

"Lightning works just fine, the preachers say."

"Suppliers?"

"Twenty seven within a hundred miles of Columbia."

"Ow. Well, that kills that idea."

"Yeah?"

"If there had just been one, then we could have got their customer list, maybe. With twenty-seven, they'll all supply everyone, likely. No mileage more in that idea." She shrugged. "One thing less to worry about."

Suddenly Andy yelped happily. "CSU got into the laptop. Finally."

"What've they found?"

"A lot of stuff that means nothing to me. Formulae like the ones you found in his apartment."

"Wow. Right, we really need to decide about Terrison. Lens cases, papers with chemical formulae on them, and a computer full of chemistry – we need him. What do we know?"

"Nothing's come up on him. Lots of published work, seems like he's pretty respected."

"Street cameras show him leaving the university around seven Wednesday, and I don't see him coming back. As far as I can tell, he went to the subway."

"Do they have security passes for out of hours work?"

Andy grinned. "They sure do. And Terrison's didn't trip all that night. Belvez tapped his out at about nine, back in around eleven, out again at eleven forty-five."

"Terrison's not looking likely, is he?"

"Last thing, Terrison's subway pass put him at Penn Station at seven forty. Cameras from there – they come back quicker than anyone – show him getting on the New Jersey train. He got off at Clifton at eight fifteen, according to his pass. There's nothing to show he came back."

"I think he's out of it. I'll go check with the Captain, but I don't think he'll disagree."

Casey collected up the evidence that she was pretty certain eliminated Terrison, and strode off to beard Captain Kent in his den. Shortly she reappeared.

"He agrees. We can use Terrison as an expert consultant. We're good to go." She was dialling almost before she sat down.

"Professor Terrison, please." A short pause.

"Professor, it's Detective Clement."

"Detective? Have you found out something about Ricky?"

"We're working on it full time. But we need your help."

"Sure, anything."

"We found some chemical diagrams at his apartment, and we need someone to take a look at them. There are some papers and a laptop."

Terrison sucked in his breath. "At his apartment? But... he shouldn't have taken them home. I'd better see them."

"Thanks. Could you come here to look at them? Chain of evidence, you know. I can give you copies of the papers, but the laptop needs to stay here."

"Okay. Anything to help."

"There's one more thing you can do. We found some lens cases in his apartment. We haven't opened them. I'd like you to come with me to the crime lab and do it properly – we don't want to damage the evidence."

Terrison gasped, as if someone had punched him. "Lens cases? I don't... I can't believe that. Ricky might have taken stuff home to work on – though it's an absolute no-no – but..."

"But what?"

"But the only reason for lens cases is to take the synthesis home," Terrison said miserably. "I can't believe he would be stealing one of the compounds."

"Stealing?"

"I said if there was a big breakthrough it was worth a lot. It would be worth a lot to a competitor of Telagon too."

"You mean industrial espionage?"

"Yes." Terrison sounded like he was about to cry. "I just can't believe that Ricky would do that."

There was nothing Casey could say to that. She rang off, with Terrison's agreement that he would come to the precinct tomorrow afternoon. She would have finished with Brewman by then.

CHAPTER 15

Carval attained his studio and automatically downloaded his camera. It had become habit, after an ill-advised evening some years ago had resulted in a loss of several shots he would rather have kept. Now, he downloaded every night – and in between, too, if he was back in the studio. He'd sooner have forgotten to brush his teeth or shave than forgotten to download and then back up.

He flicked through his latest shots, removed several instantly, but then leaned on his desk and, instead of considering his exhibition (though he had some inchoate thoughts on how to use the pictures of her hands) allowed himself to consider the shock of actual contact with Casey-the-cop.

Until he was looming over her, he hadn't realised just how much smaller than he she was. She wasn't tiny, but she also wasn't very tall, so the impression of size he'd previously had was simply her presence. Even in her shoes, she'd barely sneaked over his shoulder. He'd envelop her, enfold those very enticing curves.

Except that she wasn't exactly receptive. She'd barely made it to civility. Except going the other way, though, there had been that interesting line of colour on her cheeks on the way into the Crime Lab.

He sat back and decided that he was quite definitely interested in Casey-the-too-cool-for-school-cop. He looked at his shots, and though the single attempt at capturing her uncontrolled, mischievous smile had emphatically failed, it was enough to remind him that when she relaxed and wasn't angry, she was stunning. At least until he had spooked her.

His mind wandered off down a different path. What was the massive O'Leary playing at? Casey's team had put the very hard word on him, including O'Leary, and the very next morning he was being tipped off about where she'll be? What was the man doing? Granted, he was so enormous that short of an automatic weapon nothing would stop him, but it still seemed like a pretty dangerous game. And then, after that, Tyler had weighed in, too. That was utterly weird. On the other hand, it had gotten Carval what he wanted, which was photographs and proximity to Casey. He decided, callously, that O'Leary's actions were O'Leary's problem, and returned to contemplating Casey.

Half a day's proximity had been interesting. She wasn't keen on make-up – there had been a slick of mascara, a touch of eye-liner and possibly a smear of lip gloss, but she certainly hadn't spent much time on it. Hair, as previously noted, pulled back in a clip. It might have taken her five minutes, at most. Dress: functional. Dress pants, mid-heeled shoes, silky tee, blazer. Strong colours. No rings, one slim watch, no earrings, no necklace. No adornment. Nicely curvy, but she was fit and honed.

Oh. Of *course* no adornment. Not after that photo. He growled. He was exceedingly pissed that anyone would, first, *steal* his work and, second, use it to slut-shame anyone, let alone someone who hadn't deserved it. On less than a week's acquaintance, he was already quite certain that casual hook-ups were not Casey's style. Conceited it might have been, but anyone interested in casual hook-ups would have given him the eye, or the come-on. He didn't have a problem attracting pretty women.

Oh, oh, oh. That interesting little line of blush-colour had been when he gave her the full smile. She *had* liked it. Mmmmm. That was interesting, too. Well, well. Maybe his cool cop wasn't quite ice-cold.

It took him a while to remember that he'd had an idea. He'd track down the thieving bastard who stole his photo and misused it: that was his plan. He had intended, he finally remembered over a very strong latte, to start with the Academy and Casey's history there. He pulled his laptop on to his knee and tried that fount of all knowledge, Google.

There were, regrettably, thousands upon thousands of Clements. Even after his Casey-confused brain told him that he should limit it to the USA, and then to New York, there were still an awful lot of Clements, and not one of them was called Casey. The lack of results was irritating: Carval liked speedy results, and he wasn't finding them. He kept refining his search terms: unusually persistent, and eventually managed to locate a list of graduating Academy recruits in 2008 which included a K Clement. There were no images, so he had no idea if this was *his* Detective Clement or not.

He really shouldn't have been thinking like that. *His* Detective Clement-Casey? Uh-nuh-huh. She was definitely not his: she'd made that perfectly clear.

He simply wanted her to be his. Well, wanted her. Full stop. He'd always got what he wanted, eventually. He'd had to. Since his parents passed, nobody else had helped him do it, and professional photography was a cutthroat game, in which you didn't make good by being unselfish and nice. Still, he'd never wittingly hurt anyone, his models were well used to the game, and he didn't plagiarise (or whatever the word might be when it was pictures). All in all, he wasn't a bad person, he concluded comfortably. Nothing that should put a cop off him. He would catch his Casey.

First stop to catching his Casey: getting into the Academy. Carval made himself another coffee, and Googled some more. Google was as equally unhelpful on the subject of tours as it was on the subject of Clements, which was decidedly unfair. Other measures were clearly required. He tapped out an e-mail to Allan, which Allan would act upon on tomorrow morning – he wouldn't disturb Allan late at night. Allan had many subtle ways of ensuring his displeasure was known, and his time off was sacrosanct.

A. Pls fix me a tour of the NY Police Academy. JC.

There. That would be enough for Allan. He'd sort all the boring stuff, like permission and tour guides. And, Carval thought very happily, he might even get a few background photos. He e-mailed again.

A. I wanna take shots, too. Pls fix. JC.

All fixed.

He ambled off quite happy with life. He set his alarm, slid into his very comfortable king size bed, and slept like a happy child. His dreams were rather explicitly adult.

***

Casey went home before she had to go see her father; to shower and change, remove the reminders that she was a cop. Her father didn't need to be reminded about cops. After all, he saw them from the wrong side every couple of months. And yet she couldn't just leave him to drown, because it was still *only* every couple of months. For now.

She put on a soft skirt and pretty top, brushed out her just-past the shoulder waves and clipped them up again, more softly than she would for work, a few dark tendrils curling cheerfully at her nape and ears, and departed, steeled against the apologies and memories and misery. Five years of apologies, though fewer of those, dropping to none at all, lately. Nearly seven of memories, now. And always a little worry that it might, later, be her, that genetics would come back to bite her, though the doctors said that it was very unlikely.

She drove out to Brooklyn, to her father's small apartment: assessing it as she entered. Clean – she paid for his cleaning service; tidy. Soda on the table: a small relief. Too often, it was a stronger drink, but she didn't comment. He had his coping mechanisms. She had hers. It wasn't for her to call him out, and anyway, it didn't work. She used to try. She didn't try any more.

He wasn't much taller than her, stooped now, grey-haired, bent around a small pot-belly that hadn't come from overeating. His eyes didn't hold the personality they used to, but he was happy to see her, and his smile was as gamin and warm as ever it had been.

"Catkin," he said happily. "Come to tell your old dad tales of the big city?"

Carefully censored tales, yes.

"Sure, Dad. We caught a weird one this week."

"You often do. Are you sure they don't just lie in wait for you?"

Casey was already sure he remembered nothing of Saturday night: not going out, not drinking, not being taken home. That was not new news. He hadn't remembered any of the previous six, eight, ten times. She wasn't going to remind him.

He used to remember. And then he drank more, to forget. Now he forgot why he was drinking at all, but when he was sober, he still remembered. She wondered, now, if he'd suspected. She hadn't. The little lapses, the occasional stumbles, the headaches – that was just Mom.

Until the autopsy showed that it wasn't *just Mom* at all.

She turned away from the thought.

"I don't think so. We get just as many pop-and-drops as weird ones."

"So what's this one?" He was always interested. Even though he used to be an architect, he was always interested in the crimes. He used to love cop shows, though after she went to the Academy her dad never let her watch with him. He said it spoiled it, hearing about the reality.

When reality had intruded, he'd stopped watching. Once his wife had been autopsied, he kind of lost the taste for CSI, or Bones. Even if there'd been no crime, only the disease.

"A research chemist, who was bopped on the head and then suffocated with lab gas. We're not far enough along to have a good reason, yet. I'm leaning to professional jealousy, because his boss said he was a rising star."

"Sounds interesting. You'll tell me how it pans out?"

"Sure I will. Don't I always?"

"You're a good kid, Catkin. Keeping me entertained."

If only I could keep you sober, but no-one can do that except you.

Conversation, over a simple dinner, turned to the construction of the National Museum of African-American History and Culture. Her father was, for once, fully engaged in the architectural niceties of the building.

"And, you know, it's due to open in a couple of weeks. Maybe I'll take a trip down to DC and see it."

"I'd give it a month or two. It's bound to be popular, even when the schools are in. Let it settle down, or you won't be able to see a single exhibit through the crowds. It would be a shame to go down specially and then not get a good view."

"Maybe." He smiled. "We could both go. Stay somewhere near the Smithsonians, visit the museums, see this one."

"That would be nice," Casey agreed, and let her heart break a little more, because she knew it would never happen. He'd forget, the next time he remembered her mom. She preserved a bland, enthusiastic demeanour, and kept the conversation on architecture and museums until it was time to go home.

"Bedtime for me, Dad. Let me know about DC. We'd have a great time."

Her father smiled widely and affectionately, and was obviously made happy. "Night, Catkin." She hugged him tightly, kissed his broken-veined cheek, and left.

She didn't weep till she was safely home, and then she did, again. Not that crying would do any good, or make her feel better. She'd have stopped the tears, if only she could. Still, even though she was on shift tomorrow, her eyes wouldn't be red. Even if they were, no-one would comment unless she did. They'd simply buy her a beer some time, and let her tell them as much or as little as she chose, same as she'd do for them.

Even so, Casey knew she wouldn't find sleep for hours, which was considerably later than she'd have liked on a work day. She dealt with her insomnia with a good book. At least, she read the book in between her extensive searches on Google. Late into the night, she'd read several chapters (and enjoyed all of the snarky, sassy, kick-ass Kate Daniels actions) but she had also formed a very interesting picture of Jamie Carval, professional photographer and world-class pain-in-the-ass. She couldn't run him through the police databases – it would have been unprofessional and, more importantly, Captain Kent would have had her ass for it – but Google was very comprehensive, as was Twitter. Jamie Carval was a very popular man with celebutantes and wannabe-famous Z-listers. On the other hand, the photos were astonishing. He had talent, much as she hated to admit it.

Admitting it meant that she had to admit that the original photo of her at Stanford was also brilliant. If it hadn't been used against her, she wouldn't have cared. She might even have been rather flattered. She would certainly not have been upset.

She might even have wondered what he'd thought of the girl she'd been then. Because he'd been pretty keen to be pals with the woman she was now.

That was a dangerous line of thought. Just the same as the feeling of his hand over hers had led her down a dangerous line of thought, and now that she'd remembered that feeling, and the original kiss, it was an even more dangerous line of thought. Jamie Carval was far too sexy for anyone's good, and she wasn't usually up for a brief affair, which seemed to be his style.

On the other hand, a no-strings affair would have been a useful distraction. She steered well clear of the cops and similar types that O'Leary sent her way, but someone who wasn't part of her world – and wouldn't become so – didn't carry the same risk of gossip, or the same difficulties when it inevitably ended.

And, well, she'd felt the zing. Not only that, but she liked big men: liked to feel safe and enclosed. It would be a nice change from her daily life, where she was the one with the gun. Carval was certainly a big man: broad and tall. Much taller than she: she was only just above his shoulder in her moderate heels.

She forcibly turned her mind away from Carval back to her book. She didn't need complications.

But a nice simple uncomplicated affair could have been good...

But again, she didn't *like* having her photo taken, and even the photos she'd already seen had far too much of her in them for her taste. Although too much would have been anything more than a blurred edge of shoulder, unidentifiable to anyone, of course. *But* she didn't like it, talented or not. And that was a major complication.

She went back to the book, again, and successfully managed to avoid thinking about Carval at all, even when she was tucked up in her bed and trying to find restless, tossing sleep.

***

"Jamie, what the hell is this about?"

Allan came bursting in first thing in the morning, clearly upset by something.

"What is it?"

"Touring the Police Academy? What's that all about?"

"I wanna."

"You want to do lots of things, but why this? You're chasing after that cop, aren't you? We've talked about this. If you want to show in six months, you need to concentrate on the photos, not the skirt."

"She doesn't wear a skirt," Carval pointed out annoyingly.

"Not relevant. I thought you wanted to take shots?"

"I do. And if you read my *second* text, you'd have seen I wanted that."

Allan stopped in his tracks. Sadly, not for long. "Yeah – as an afterthought. If you were thinking about the photos, you'd have put that first."

"Stop nagging me. If I wanted nagged, I'd get married."

Allan snorted. "You? Married? May I live to see the day."

Carval scowled at him. "What's that meant to mean?"

"Well, the family photo album would be great, but you're not exactly peaceful or organised."

"Nope. Since I'm not getting married, though, you'll be stuck with me for a while yet. Now, will you arrange a visit to the Academy or do I have

111

to?"

"I'll do it. But you need to get this show on the road, Jamie. It'll have been a year by the time it's ready. You don't want to fall out of view."

"I got the royalties."

"They don't last for ever."

Carval muttered. Allan departed, satisfied that his point was made, but deeply worried that Jamie was definitely off on one of his pursuits.

A while later, Allan returned.

"Okay, you can go see the Academy later today. Someone will escort you round. You can take photos, but not of any identifiable subjects. No clear faces, Jamie!"

Carval pouted. "That's no fun."

"And they *will* check, at the end."

"What?"

"They will check. So just for once, play by the rules, okay?"

"I don't like rules," Carval grumbled, sounding like a five-year old. "They get in the way."

"It's that or no visit."

"Okay, *okay*. I'll behave."

"Good. Be there at two. You know where you're going?"

"Yeah. Out to Queens."

Allan tip-tapped off, satisfied that Jamie would not cause mayhem – that time. And it would keep him away from the cop he was chasing after, for a day, which might just have cooled his jets a little. If only he wasn't so…single-minded. It was great when it was photographs – the panhandlers had been brilliant – but the possibilities for trouble were almost endless, and Allan's imagination (and Carval's history of chaos) didn't do anything except feed his paranoia that he'd shortly be bailing Jamie out.

Allan smiled mischievously. That wasn't a bad idea. Put Jamie in the cells for a night or two, with his camera, naturally, and see what came of it. Knowing Jamie, some interesting stories, a lot of good shots, and some very dubious friends to add to his extensive collection of odd people whose acquaintance he had made. He smirked at his neatly polished shoes. He'd keep that plan in reserve.

CHAPTER 16

The bullpen was still nicely quiet when Casey arrived, yawning: far too early, but she hadn't slept well: worried about her father. Easier just to work.

She wanted a head start on Terence Brewman, and a chance to clear her thoughts of annoyingly attractive photographers before she put the frighteners on the research evaluator. Of course, she was still irritated that O'Leary was meddling, but she'd deal with him when she had time. Right now, she'd deal with all of it with a round with the speed bag, and then a double espresso. Hitting the bag always helped her to think. She didn't always want to run, especially if it was dark, and if she wanted heavier endurance work she'd use the rowing machine, but thumping the bag allowed her to work off a lot of frustration. She always had a lot of frustration to work off after she'd dealt with her father.

Making her coffee, from the small machine they'd clubbed together to buy when they'd collectively decided that the machine sludge was undrinkable (it wasn't a patch on her Gaggia, but it was better than dishwater), Casey was ready to face the day. Whether the day, and specifically Brewman, was ready to face her remained an open question.

She remembered, dispiritedly, that she couldn't go to Telagon before nine. It was really not fair: some nice intimidating interviewing was just what she needed.

On the other hand, she could always interview O'Leary. Not nearly as likely to be satisfying, because he was completely, imperturbably amiable no matter what, and he could, if he wanted, simply pick her up, hold her out at arms' length and watch her complain, but letting him know that she'd sussed out his plan wouldn't be a bad idea. She certainly wouldn't be telling him she was considering it, though. He'd be smug for weeks, and O'Leary being smug was profoundly annoying, the more so as he was far too big for her to do anything about it, such as dumping him on the mats.

She couldn't even *try* to spar with him, or with Tyler. She liked all her limbs in one place, and all her ribs in one piece. She could be the women's world champion sparrer and she'd still be turned into ground beef by either of them. She and Andy practiced together, which suited them fine. They were still really good, for their respective sizes and weights, but there was no way on this earth that either of them would ever come out of a session with Tyler or O'Leary uninjured, and Captain Kent had a blistering attitude to stupidly incurred injuries. Unpaid leave and black marks were not Casey's style. No, thank you.

At that happy moment, O'Leary ambled in, smiling cheerfully at the day.

"Hey," he said. The smile started to wash off his face as Casey turned to him and he recognised her expression.

"Morning," she said, and bared her teeth in a distant cousin to a smile. O'Leary scented the danger, but not an escape route. "Can we have a word? Privately?"

"Sure," O'Leary reverberated. They attained a conference room, where Casey shut the door firmly.

"Why are you tipping off the photographer about where to find me, O'Leary?"

"Me?" he said plaintively, which they both knew was anything but a denial.

"You."

"Would I do a thin' like that?" He protruded the shelf of his lower lip, which had no effect on Casey. O'Leary trying to be cute never worked on her. They'd been friends too long for that. She couldn't pull that trick on him either, of course.

"Yes."

"Mean."

"I didn't ask *if* you did it, I asked *why*? Are you trying to match make again? Because I already told you that playing Cupid isn't needed."

O'Leary regarded her from under his twig-like eyelashes. "I reckon you could do with a distraction, an' since you don't like any of the pals I suggested to you, leastways this one you c'n always yell at. Or kiss him. Your choice."

Casey made an indeterminately aggravated noise.

"See, you're cross already," O'Leary said placidly. "You need someone to fuss at – that ain't us. We don't like you fussin' and makin' life troublesome."

"So you think you need to *match make*?"

"Wouldn't call it that. Just… options. That's it. Options. An' if you're yellin' at that Carval guy, you ain't yellin' at us." His face turned serious. "We c'n see your dad ain't gettin' any better, an' you're pickin' him up a little more reg'lar. So iffen you need a little distraction, I don't reckon as that's a bad thing. 'Sides which, he's no patsy." The amiable, dumb grin reappeared. "Might even stand up to you. That'd be fun to watch."

Casey growled wordlessly, threw open the door and stomped out. O'Leary smirked at her offended back. Somewheres in there, she'd forgotten to tell him she wasn't interested. She'd also forgotten to tell him to stop calling Carval and tipping him off. Now wasn't that peculiar?

He ambled to the coffee machine and then back to his desk, pondering. He was more than a tad worried about his pal Casey. Her dad hadn't got over her mom's death, and he'd gradually been getting worse. Used to be, it was occasional. Now, seemed like it was getting to be frequent. The three of them would hold her up if they had to, but she could use a friend who wasn't one of them. Since she'd turned down everyone he'd suggested, mebbe she needed something different. Still, he'd just leave Carval alone today. It'd be interesting to see what Carval would do if he wasn't contacted. And Telagon was a whole different ball game from meetin' at Columbia. Not discreet to invite Carval along. No, sirree.

"Andy," Casey called, "You want to come to Telagon – you said you knew a bit of chemistry?"

"Okay."

"What 'bout me?" O'Leary grumbled.

"Andy speaks chemistry, so he said. You don't. You can help Tyler on the gases. Let's find out who orders them at Columbia."

O'Leary scowled and growled at Casey's smugly retreating back, which achieved nothing.

Telagon occupied a very swish, modern building in Midtown. They were shown up to a cleanly corporate boardroom, where there was coffee, but no Brewman. He arrived a few moments later, without any apology for his tardiness. It didn't endear him to either cop.

"Detectives Clement and Chee," Casey said briskly, extending her hand. Brewman had to make a rapid realignment, since he was rather obviously aiming for Andy. Casey instantly concluded that he was the sort of idiot who would always assume that the male partner was senior. Now she really didn't like him. She examined him, slowly. High, slightly whining voice; mid-height, a little overweight – enough to notice; business dress, no tie, but shirt and dress pants, good jacket, brogues. He hadn't any jewellery, so chances were he was unmarried. Neatly trimmed dark hair, which didn't disguise the balding at his crown, blue eyes. He was a typical middle-management drone.

On the other hand, he was in charge of doling out a huge budget – millions of dollars to just one group – every year, so he must have had some smarts somewhere. Better not underestimate this guy.

"Thank you for seeing us, Mr Brewman," she started. "I understand that Telagon funds Professor Terrison's opto-electronics group at Columbia University?"

"Yes," Brewman said cautiously. "Why are you here?"

"We're investigating the research group." It wasn't a lie. But just for an instant, there was a flash of worry across Brewman's face, which cleared on her next words. "Dr Belvez was found dead last Wednesday."

"That's terrible," Brewman said. "We'd just poured money into that group because he joined. Another five million, to go with the twenty we'd already laid out."

"Wow. That's big bucks." Casey encouraged.

"He was supposed to be the next big star. But..." Brewman paused. Casey thought it was just a little too pat. "He wasn't doing as well as Dr Merowin. I guess he needed a little time to settle in." He acquired a mournful look. "Now he won't get the chance. Tragic. It's a major loss to science."

Andy tapped Casey's foot. To Brewman, his face was inscrutable. To Casey, it said as clear as day that Brewman was laying it on too thick.

"Could you explain how you decide to fund?"

"Why is this relevant?" Brewman was instantly tense.

"You're a very generous funder. I'm sure that Terrison's group appreciate it – but I have to consider whether other groups might be jealous."

Now *that* was interesting. Brewman had relaxed. Whatever the issue with decisions on funding – and there was one: he'd tensed right up – it wasn't about competition.

He explained, in considerable detail.

"Thank you. So as long as the results keep coming, you fund."

"That's right." He smiled patronisingly. "We need new compounds to keep progressing. No new compounds, we start to lose money, our stock price falls, and a lot of ordinary people lose out."

"How's that?" Andy asked, feigning naivety.

"Our stock is a key component of the Dow-Jones index. Retirement funds and investments – people's savings – rely on it."

"I get it."

"So it's really important that your profits stay up?" Casey asked blandly.

"Of course."

"Dr Belvez's death must be a blow to that."

"If he'd been delivering, it would have. But Dr Merowin is producing much better results, so although it's a blow, it's not that critical."

"I see," she said, and faked a moment's thought. "Do Telagon's employees have an interest in the profits?"

"Of course. We have an employee share option program and a 401(K) retirement plan. Everyone is wholly committed to our success."

"But you're the one who decides if the research is worthwhile?"

"Yes. I report directly to the Chief Research Officer, who's on the board. He reviews everything. Two pairs of eyes."

"Mm. How do you make sure it all stays secret?"

"Corporate espionage, you mean? It's need to know only here – me and Carl" – she raised an eyebrow – "Carl Sackson, the Chief Research Officer. All the research group is under confidentiality restrictions, and the penalties are huge."

"Pretty secure, then?"

"Yes. Money always talks, but anyone trying to cheat us would end up on the wrong end of that conversation."

Yes, money surely does talk. So why would anyone kill Belvez, rather than sue the hell out of him?

Casey wrapped up the interview with thanks, and she and Andy left. They didn't discuss anything till they were safely back in the bullpen.

"Useful?" Tyler asked.

"Interesting," Andy got in first, and gave the download.

"Weird."

"If they've got such big penalties for leaking, why would Belvez have tried to steal the info – and why would anyone have killed him over it, rather than just sue him?"

"Mebbe penalties would be on the whole group, not just Belvez?"

"Maybe. We'd better ask Terrison."

"Or maybe someone's running a bluff," Andy said.

"Huh?"

"I know a bit about the money side." He did. Andy day traded, and made a bit from it. "If the profits depend on the results, then if Brewman and that Sackson guy are the only two that know them, it's going to be pretty easy to fake it if things aren't going so good. Cover it up."

The others stared at him. "Fraud?"

"It's a possibility."

"That's going to change the game a bit."

"Sure is."

Another possible motive went up on the board.

"I got the name at Columbia," O'Leary rumbled.

"Uh?"

"Person who signs for gas orders."

"Who?"

"Woman called Karlen Petersen. Lab tech. Ran her, nothin' popped, but I got a picture of her from Facebook."

"What's her connection?" Casey's eyes were sparking with the knowledge of another trail to follow.

"None yet. Just a lab tech. But it's worth a follow up, isn't it?"

"Sure is. Let's stick her up on the board too. Got a photo?"

O'Leary messed around for a bare moment and produced a rather dolled up photo of a statuesque blonde in somewhat revealing clothing, brandishing a glass. "Ain't Facebook wonderful?" he asked rhetorically.

"Yep." They collectively grinned at each other.

"Lunchtime," Tyler noted.

"Terrison's coming at two. We'll need to hustle."

They barely had time to gulp down their lunches before he arrived.

Terrison shuffled in, appearing old and tired, as if he'd barely slept.

"Professor," Casey said gently, sympathetic to his suffering, "I know this is hard for you, but we really need your help to find the truth. Even if Dr Belvez was taking the results without permission, he didn't deserve to be murdered for it."

He simply nodded, heavy headed.

"I've got copies of the papers that were found in Dr Belvez's apartment here, and I'd like you to take a look at them." She passed them across. Terrison began to peruse them, carefully. "Would you like some time?"

"Yes," he said, frowning. "Could I have some water, please?"

"Sure."

Casey took her time getting the water. When she returned, Terrison was frowning even harder at the papers.

"This can't be," he said.

"What's wrong?"

"These are Mike's papers, not Ricky's."

"Mm?"

"From the results Ricky was getting before I recruited him, I'd have expected his results to be much better than Mike's. If he was going to steal" – he winced painfully – "anything, he should be stealing his own work. It was truly brilliant."

"Telagon told us that Mike's results were better than Ricky's."

Terrison's head flicked up. "Really? That's astonishing. Mike must finally have come through, because that certainly wasn't the case when I reviewed Ricky's papers. Mind you, that was six months and more ago. It takes a long time to move someone, and I've been busy supervising my doctoral candidates, so I haven't really been paying attention to those two because they're both able to get on without me."

He stared at the formulae some more. "Something doesn't feel right," he said vaguely. "The optical tests are giving much better results than I'd expect." He stared and frowned some more. "I need to run through this synthesis."

"Can you do that without tipping off anyone in the group – anyone at all?"

"Yes. It'll take me a couple of days to review, though. But if I could have help it might be quicker."

"No," Casey said. "Someone's trying to get your group into trouble." *Mike Merowin, for preference, but let's leave Terrison his illusions for now.* "You've lost Ricky. They can't afford to lose you or Mike too."

Terrison's colour shifted to a pallid greenish-white as that comment sank in.

"Can I see the laptop?"

Casey brought it in, but it didn't tell Terrison anything different.

"Okay. I'll need you to be present when we start on the lens cases. When's going to be a good time for you to take a break from reviewing?"

Terrison peered at her. "It might be better if I looked at the lens cases first. If they've got the compound in them, I can repeat the optical testing and confirm the results. I have access to copies of the results for all our work."

"How about tomorrow? O'Leary and I will meet you at the CSU lab" – she gave him the address – "at nine?"

"Yes," he said, distractedly.

"At nine, tomorrow."

He focused. "Yes. Nine tomorrow, CSU labs."

***

Later on, after Terrison had left, Captain Kent poked his nose out of his office, spotted O'Leary, and summoned him brusquely.

"Detective O'Leary, a word."

O'Leary's massive shoulders cringed. He trudged off as if he were going to his own execution. Summonses by the Captain were never a good start. The door shut behind him: a soft thud of impending doom. The bullpen turned away out of respect (and terror that it might be another of them next).

"Detective O'Leary," Captain Kent said coldly. "You suggested that I might allow Mr Carval to photograph in here. I said that I would consider it. I have done so, but it occurs to me that your suggestion was unorthodox. I presume you had a reason for that suggestion. What was it?" He paused. "Before you answer, be aware that I do not consider good PR the whole reason that was in your mind."

O'Leary cringed some more, and tried, without success, to disappear. Captain Kent in full superior mode was scary, even if O'Leary was six-ten and could snap the Captain in two without noticing.

Kent changed tack, since all that intimidation was achieving was silence. "Look, O'Leary, I know you four deal with your own issues, and I've never asked about it because it works. Your issues aren't my business unless they affect my precinct, and so far they never have. But you wanting this photographer in: that is affecting my precinct and so it is my business. Something's going on, and you need to spill the beans so I can make a

119

proper decision. Right now, I'm inclining to *no*, and I'm going to need a damn good reason to change that to *yes*."

O'Leary squirmed, rather like an embarrassed anaconda. Kent, a man who knew the value of silence as an intimidation tactic and who was not afraid to use it, waited. And waited. The atmosphere did not lighten. O'Leary continued to squirm. Just as Kent was about to evict him, his sub-sonic bass emerged.

"Casey's pa ain't well," he muttered. "Been a little fond of the bottle for a while. Um… this Carval's a distraction."

"He's a photographer. Even I, O'Leary, am aware of Clement's dislike for photographs."

"If she's arguin' with him, she's not frettin' 'bout her pa."

"If she's working, she isn't fretting about her father either."

"I guess," O'Leary said rather doubtfully.

"On the other hand, I have no desire for any of my detectives to become ill through overwork. Okay. Thank you for telling me the truth," Kent said with some bite. O'Leary winced. "I'll consider. It's not *no* yet. Dismissed."

Kent watched O'Leary droop out, and considered. He was not a counselling service, nor was he interested in his detectives' personal lives. He'd put the four together because, in his view, they fit. Clement and O'Leary came as a team, and, well, he hated to admit it but it was always difficult to pair a good-looking girl with someone. Got messy. So they were already a team and it was easier to keep it that way. Tyler, well, he was about as macho as they came. Ex-Army, and boy oh boy did it show. Again, he was difficult, because everyone wanted to prove they were tougher than the Army man. Unfortunately, they were wrong. So when O'Reilly at the Fifteenth wanted him moved out, Kent had thought that putting him with the woman and the big man might work, especially as O'Reilly had mentioned that sometimes he got a bit tense. Kent had thought he meant with the constant push of competition. And it did gel, but three was an odd number, so when Chee came up, with a stellar record but an inability to work closely with anyone, Kent had another management hunch, those three needed a techno-geek, and it worked.

But maybe he should have done a little more digging into each of their backgrounds. He hadn't known anything about Clement's father, and that was the sort of big thing that might make a difference, down the line. He didn't cut anyone any slack, but that wasn't the same as taking account of circumstances. And if Clement had that sort of a secret – which the team knew – what else were they hiding from him? They were very tight. *Very* tight indeed.

Kent's investigative instincts were aroused, which would have horrified any of his four detectives. He might not have been a pally, all-chums-together Captain, but he liked to be closer to what was going on than they'd think. There was no problem with that team – but he didn't want to find a problem arising when he could head it off at the pass.

He shut the door that O'Leary had left open, and began to run a few searches of his own.

***

"What did he want?" Casey asked.

"A report," O'Leary said.

"Ugh."

Casey didn't ask anything more. Reports to Kent were something she generally liked to avoid, until her case had been solved. O'Leary breathed an unseen sigh of relief, and went back to investigating. Along the way, he quietly tapped out a message to Carval, suggesting that he might want to turn up at the CSU lab at around eight-forty-five the next morning.

Much to everyone's disgust, Kent noticed them all still working long after shift end, and objected. He was strict on overtime, expecting them to work their collective asses off in normal shifts, not do extra hours with no reason. But when they were on the trail, it was irritating.

Casey hit the elevator with a distinctly disgruntled flip of her hair. She could feel linkages idling just outside her knowledge, and she wanted to push on till they fell into place. However, Kent was frowning at her and even as she stepped into the elevator she could feel his beady eye ensuring that she was really leaving.

CHAPTER 17

Carval was bored by eleven a.m. on Tuesday. No-one had texted or called him to tell him where to find any of the cops; he was fed up of messing around with his photos and corkboard; and trying out filters, colour washes, black-and-white and sepia tints had long palled. He thought about wandering back out to the Thirty-Sixth, and parking himself outside the door to take shots of a further wash and wave of humanity, but he couldn't really muster the enthusiasm. He wanted it to be lunchtime already, so he could go to the Academy and start his investigations into the sonofabitch who stole his photo.

Actually, there was a point.

"Allan," he called down into the office, before he was halfway down the stairs, "Allan, I need you."

"What?"

"I didn't tell you. Someone stole one of my photos."

"You what now? Why didn't you tell me? We need to fix that right now. You've got copyright. Who is it? Where is it? What did they do?"

Allan's law-abiding soul was outraged – and his diligence in maintaining Jamie's rights even more so. No-one stole Jamie's stuff on his watch. No-one. He, Allan Penrith, was staunch in his client's defence.

"We'll fix that ASAP," he said briskly. "Tell me what you know and how you found out."

Jamie cringed, which was surprising. Normally, he was pretty keen on his rights – and royalties – and on pursuing them with considerable force, if required. Allan was good at considerable force, in defence of intellectual property rights. His legal background came in very handy in times like that.

"Um... I found out on Thursday."

"*Thursday?*" Allan screeched. "Why are you only telling me *now*? That's *days* I've lost. That could be critical. When did you take this photo?"

"Um... nine years ago?"

Allan emitted an infuriated noise which contained no intelligible syllables at all. "When was it stolen?"

"I don't quite know. Eight years ago, maybe? Early 2008?"

"Tell me you at least know which photo it was? Not that this will help me much. I only started representing you five years ago" –

Jamie intervened. "And I've been trouble ever since. Yeah, yeah. C'mon, Allan. Help me out here."

"How about you start by helping me out? Show me the photo."

Jamie hunted it out on the computer. Allan simply stared at the photo, Jamie, the corkboard, the photo, Jamie, the corkboard... There was a long moment of stunned silence, in which Allan achieved only a very accurate impression of a stranded codfish.

"You... you... that's *her*!" Jamie nodded. "You shot her *before* you got on this cop kick?" Jamie nodded again. "*Please* tell me you didn't sleep with her, or date her, then? I don't want to know that you've complicated this with a vengeful ex."

"No. I kissed her." Allan howled like a dying dog. "No, no. Once. At the graduation party. I was taking shots – remember that college recruitment poster?"

Allan looked utterly blank. "No. *Five* years working with you – but right now I feel like it's *fifty*. How do you *always* create chaos?"

Jamie glowered. "This isn't my fault! Some bastard stole that photo or cut it out the poster or something and I want them *crucified*!"

Dead quiet hung between the two men.

"Let's have a coffee and you can tell me the whole story," Allan soothed. "Sounds like there's a lot more to this than I know."

Shortly, his small, neat fingers had produced two excellent cups of coffee and Jamie had, in consequence, calmed down slightly.

"Now, tell me everything."

"I didn't know it was Casey-the-cop until I kept thinking that that one" – he pointed to the centrepiece – "looked familiar. I was worried I was copying someone else, and we don't need that" –

"No, indeed" –

"So I kept thinking and suddenly I thought it was another of *my* photos so I searched through them all and found it. That was Wednesday night – well, Thursday morning really" – Allan sighed heavily and reprovingly – "you're not my mom, don't start on the *go-to-bed-earlier-bit*, and anyway I was in bed but I woke up – and then when I went to their precinct to see if I could follow them I took that one too. I took all the shots I'd taken back then." He swigged his coffee. "But it was this one that rattled her. She was really shocked and then she said 'You?' and just stormed off."

"Okaaaayyyy," Allan stretched out. "And?"

Jamie wriggled uncomfortably. "Well-er-um," he mumbled. "I – er – convinced her to meet me that evening."

"How? Please tell me I don't have to bail you out of harassment charges?"

"No. I – um – said it was that or I'd go to the precinct." Allan howled despairingly again. "So she showed up. With the rest of the team," he said very indignantly, "which was absolutely *not* the plan." Allan raised his eyebrows with a considerable dose of cynical amusement, which didn't improve Jamie's mood at all. "She said they'd been ordered to let me take photos – she called them *snaps*" – more high indignation – "and then she said that she wouldn't tell me where she – they," he hurriedly corrected, to more amusement, "would be. And then she stalked off again and the rest of her team decided to put the hard word on me."

"Sounds like she'd got you sussed. Down to a T."

"You're supposed to be on my side."

"Won't hurt you to be treated a little less like a rock star occasionally," Allan said callously. Jamie huffed at him.

"Anyway, they said this photo got spread around to slut-shame her at the Academy."

Allan's mouth dropped open and his eyes goggled from their sockets. His lips flapped a few times, but no words emerged.

"So some sonofabitch went looking for it and found it and I want them *punished*."

"Why?"

"It's *my shot*. No-one gets to misuse my shots like that."

"But *you* weren't hurt. And it wasn't used for profit so you can't sue them for that. This isn't your fight, Jamie. It's hers, if it's anyone's."

Jamie stared mutinously back at Allan. "I'm not letting this go. I wanna find that bastard and scare the shit out of him. Make it happen, Allan." He hunched, and suddenly seemed far more aggressive than usual. "I *want* this guy."

Allan trudged unhappily out of the office. Jamie was already in far, far too deep, and that had *nothing* to do with the cops as a team and *everything* to do with the woman. Oh God. He thought hopefully of putting Jamie into a jail for a couple of nights, as previously considered – but this time to give himself, Allan, some peace. This was turning into not just one of Jamie's pursuits, but one of his crusades. Oh, God.

Still, Allan prided himself on his ability to achieve anything, and if he were totally honest he'd agree that whoever stole the photo needed – well, *corrected*. He attained his comfortable chair and polished wooden desk, and started to think about methods of correction.

***

Carval managed, with some difficulty, to occupy himself until twelve thirty sharp. He swiftly assembled himself, washed, brushed and tidy, with his camera, ready to go see the Academy. He also slid his list of questions into the inside pocket of his jacket. Simply to remind himself of his purposes, he thought. On a sudden whim, he also included the photo of Casey surrounded by her team as they'd come into the Starbucks by the Thirty-Sixth.

The drive was relatively quick, which he hadn't expected, and he found himself on 28th Avenue in Queens at one-thirty. There wasn't a coffee bar in sight. That was pretty grim. Cops drank coffee, didn't they? He looked at the car's clock, and took a loop around. Finally he found something called Sparky's Deli, which sold him adequate coffee and a pastry. He ate and drank leaning on the car, and then drove back round to the shiny, new building, with reflective glass in grey cladding.

From across the street, he took a series of photos as the sun slipped in and out of the clouds, trying to catch the moods of the weather as reflected in the building. He loved digital cameras. He could just keep shooting and select later.

At a precise five minutes to two – regardless of Allan's admonitions, he did actually appreciate that the Academy didn't have to let him in and he was genuinely grateful – he went to a reception desk and notified the desk officer of his presence.

Not long later, a clean cut, tall mixed-race man with bright, intelligent eyes and an impressive demeanour appeared.

"Hello," he said. "Mr Carval? Welcome to the Police Academy. I'm Sergeant Carter, one of the instructors here." He didn't sound wholly convinced that Carval should be allowed in.

"Hey," Carval said. "Nice to meet you." He extended a hand, and exchanged a firm handshake, one male grip-unit short of a challenge.

"I've been told you want to look around. Take some photos. You've been told there are to be no identifiable faces, and at the end of the tour I will check."

"That's fine. Did anyone tell you why I wanted to come here?"

"No." Carval heard *should I care? Is it in any way relevant?*

"My next exhibition is around New York's Finest. Looking round here is part of that." He smiled. "This is where you make them."

"Mm," Carter hummed, not convinced.

"Like this," Carval said, a little offended by the lack of interest, and stopped Carter, pushing the photo of Casey's team under his nose. "This is what the Academy creates."

Carter stared at the photo. "*You* took this?"

"Uh-huh. That's what I do. Catch the truth in the moment."

"Oh," Carter emitted, sounding utterly shocked.

"So these four, they're a team. You can see it in every line. That's what you produce. That's why I wanna look round. No faces, but I don't need the faces."

"How did you get these four on film?" Carter's surprise was palpable.

Carval spotted an opening. "Ran across them when they caught a case. Their captain said I could take photos in public."

"They're co-operating? *They're* a *team?*"

Carval was sure he hadn't been meant to hear the last sentence.

"Sure they are," he said blandly. "Why not?"

Carter started down the wide corridor. "Come look at this," he said, which was not informative. Carval trotted along behind him, till they reached a large glass cabinet. "Trophy cabinet."

"Can I take some shots?"

"Sure. But first, take a good look inside."

Carter stepped back, and stood, very much at ease, out of the way, while Carval peered in.

He was still staring round the cabinet five full minutes later. In summary: top range scores: Recruit-Officer J. Tyler, with a perfect score; top technology score, Recruit-Officer A-C. Chee; weightlifting and sparring records (that was absolutely no surprise) Recruit-Officer C. O'Leary. And then there were the rest. If it was in there, as far as he could see, she had won it. Recruit-Officer K. Clement. Everything else. Top of that class, by some margin. He noted, too, that the four of them had all been in different classes.

He turned back to Carter. "Wow."

"Yeah."

Strangely, Carter didn't sound one hundred percent happy.

"What's the problem? They're clearly really good, and they're an amazing team. You can see it a mile off."

"Yeah. But" – Carter stopped.

"Mm?" Carval hummed confidentially.

"They got issues. All of 'em."

Carval said nothing about that. "Can I take a few shots of the corridors and cabinet?" he asked instead, in a very non-enquiring, non-threatening way which he *also* hoped would lead Carter to keep talking. People usually talked to him, if he seemed interested – and he was almost always interested in the people around him. It was what made his shots great.

"Yeah." Carter took a step back along the corridor, and then, unexpectedly, almost immediately started to talk again.

"O'Leary, he was okay. Pretty amiable, unless someone started in with the anti-gay. Didn't work out till a long time after that it was because he *is* gay."

Carval was studiously unreactive to that, though it certainly did explain a lot about why O'Leary was so closed off.

"Guess it's easy enough to be amiable if you're that size and that strong. No-one was going to come out on top in a fight except him."

"Mm?"

"Tyler, he was pretty quiet. Bit older than most, ex-Army. You know that military get automatic exemption from the college credits part of the entry requirement, and there's some leeway on their age?"

Carval shook his head.

"Well, they do. But oftentimes some of the others take them as a challenge. Want to show the military that they're no better than the rest. Tyler, he never lost his temper about that, but he played to win whenever they tried it, and he didn't like to take long about it."

"His shooting? Isn't a perfect score pretty unusual?"

"Yep. He was a marksman. I reckoned he might have been a sniper, but he never said squat about it, and I didn't look in his personnel file. Only I saw him spook once, when a truck backfired when they were out on the track. Just for a second, he froze. No-one else really noticed."

Again, Carval stayed bland-faced, but the expression on Tyler's eyes that he thought he'd recognised fell into place. It was the expression he might have had when he focused the camera shot – which Tyler would have had when focusing a rifle. He thought Carter might have been closer than he knew to the truth. He'd think about the spooking point later.

"Chee was just quiet. Played along, but didn't get close to anyone. Most of the recruits, they team up, make friends. Chee never did. Part of the team when it was needed, but when the job was done he slid away. Good at hiding from the socialising."

Carval waited. Andy's secret was still secret, and he wondered what it was. Before the Academy, clearly. "And Clement?"

Carter stopped talking. A few more steps were taken down the corridor, and they exited into a large gymnasium where a class of red-faced, puffing recruits (all of whom were in good physical condition but working out very, very hard) was present.

"Can I shoot?"

"Yes, but no faces in focus."

Carter took a breath, about to announce their attendance. Carval stopped him. "Don't. Please. I don't want posed. I want natural. Don't draw attention to me. The camera isn't large and in a minute they'll forget I'm here." Carter made a tiny signal to the instructor, who took the hint and ignored them.

He waited a few beats till the class was in full agony and then started: pointed and kept clicking and would sort it out later, careful to avoid any faces in focus. It wasn't hard, when everyone was moving. He adjusted his settings to take long exposures to try to capture the sense of movement: flex and burn; and then massive close-ups of the sweat patches on backs and under arms; the droplets on an unidentifiable patch of forehead and cheek. Carter was quiet and motionless by the door as Carval slipped soundlessly around, trying to stay out of view of the recruits. When he had shot enough, and before he could be in any way inadvertently disruptive, he slid back to Carter.

"Thanks," he said very softly. "I'm done in here. Wanna see, outside?"

Carter's response was to usher him out the door. "Okay," he said when the door was closed. "Let's see what you got."

Carval brought up the pictures, and let Carter flick through.

"Not bad, man. Not bad at all. No need to delete any of these."

"What else can I see?"

"Let's go to one of the classrooms. They're doing some interviewing practice there." Carter had relaxed completely. Carval had clearly gotten something right.

"Clement," he said out of the blue as they march towards the classroom. "There's a thing. Came in all uptown and pretty, and frankly I thought she'd wash out in a week. But she didn't. Worked hard, really hard, and suddenly she was at the top of the standings."

"Must have been hard for some of the others," Carval probed, on a hunch and a prayer.

"Yeah. We had a couple of guys from cop backgrounds: runs in families, you know. They weren't too impressed."

"No?"

"Well, you know, if you've been immersed in it all your life then you expect to do well. You get what's coming, you've probably been practicing for months, maybe years – and you've got a lot of tradition to live up to."

"Basically, you expect to be top. Set the standard."

"You got it. So Marcol, he expected to be top, and when he wasn't, he worked harder, but so did Clement, and in the end, they were fighting it out. Something was going on, though, because about halfway through Clement switched on the afterburners, shut down, and after that there was no way back."

Carval clocked the name. Marcol. He'd look that up later. "Mm?"

"Yeah. I did wonder if he'd made a move on her, but it was really unlikely, and we don't encourage fraternisation between the recruits. It doesn't help. Anyway. She came top, and that was that. But she didn't make any friends – a bit like Chee, really. Played with the team just as long as it was needed, worked her ass off, and then slipped away as soon as it was over." He shook his head. "None of those four played well with others. Can't believe that they gelled into a team like in that photo. That's amazing."

"So you do class lists?"

"Yeah. But after graduation, it's not relevant. It's how you do on the job that counts then."

"For sure."

He stopped at a door. "Here's the class that's doing interview practice. I'll go in first, talk to the instructor, and when they settle again you can take your shots. No faces," he reminded Carval.

By four, Carval had seen everything, photographed all of it, and established a very easy relationship with Sergeant Carter, though disappointingly Carter refused to be photographed. Carval didn't (for once) push his luck. He was in a pretty good place right now with the shots, and he didn't want deletions because he'd irritated Carter.

"Thanks," he said, very sincerely. "That's been great. You do a tremendous role here. I never realised how hard it was to become a police officer."

"You're welcome," Carter said, and escorted him out.

***

Back in his studio, photos downloaded and Marcol's name scrawled on a post-it stuck to his screen, Carval was just a little ticked off that no-one was telling him where to find Casey. No contact at all today: it wasn't fair. Even if he had been out all afternoon, it was still not fair. He grumped downstairs.

"Allan," he called through the office, "Allan, can you find this guy for me? He's a cop. Marcol."

Allan emerged. "Does he have any more of a name?"

"I don't know. He went through the Academy here in 2008, though. Cop family, so there might be a few of them."

"Why don't you just say 'Allan, please find me a needle in this skyscraper sized haystack'? It would be easier."

"He's the guy who had something to do with stealing my photo."

Allan flicked him a sharp glance. "How did you get his name?"

"The sergeant showing me round the Academy let it slip."

Allan's eyebrows rose, though he didn't say anything. "I'll see what I can do," he said, thinking that, much as he disliked all of this and much as he was sure that it was all going to go catastrophically wrong, he'd be better off keeping Jamie happy. The backwash of a miserable Jamie was very unpleasant and it would certainly mean that the exhibition would be delayed. Somewhere in Allan's capacious contacts list he had a reliable and discreet PI.

Fortunately, before Allan's calm, controlled life could be further disrupted by Jamie's whims and demands, Jamie received a text, his face lit up, and he beamed.

"Gotta go deal with my photos. I'll be out tomorrow following the cops. See you later," he said, through the opening door. "Lock up the office for me? Thanks." And he was gone, leaping upstairs to the studio.

129

Allan flicked through the contacts till he found the one he was looking for, and dialled.

"Hey, Greg. Long time no speak. I've got a job for you, have you got time to do it? It should be pretty simple."

"Yeah? That's a nice change. Tell me it doesn't involve divorce, drugs or guns?"

"No, just some easy information gathering. "

"I like it already."

"I want you to find out everything you can about a cop named Marcol. Likely there are a few of them, but this one graduated the NYPD Academy in 2008. That's all I know."

"Okay," Greg hummed. "Not quite so easy, but no-one's likely to shoot me. When d'you wanna know?"

"As soon as you can – just let me have whatever you can get when you've got it."

"Sure. I'll send you an estimate when I've had a look-see. Usual rates."

"You're a shark," Allan said almost affectionately.

"And I get results. All legally."

"I know. Thanks, Greg."

"Bye."

Allan returned to his job of managing Jamie's life for him, not without a nagging feeling that something was about to explode in his face.

CHAPTER 18

Captain Kent had spent a large portion of the afternoon, during which he had expected to review staffing and overtime schedules, in the much more interesting task of researching his best team's background. He'd found it rather intriguing. He knew about Clement's professional history. He hadn't known that her mother was dead, nor that her father was being picked up drunk on an increasingly frequent basis. Similarly, he hadn't known that O'Leary was actually married to his partner. He'd kept that one very quiet – which was undoubtedly explained by a few comments in O'Leary's record on the subject of sparring with some names which Kent recognised as the subject of civilian complaints. It appeared, reading between the lines, that those guys had hit the mats a little harder than usual, coinciding with some non-banter on the subject of same-sex relationships. Mm. Two oddballs teaming up against the odds.

Tyler had been more difficult, but a call to O'Reilly had uncovered the interesting fact that his top shooter occasionally spooked at loud bangs. Mm, again. Tyler's honourable discharge and decorations hadn't covered the possibility of a remnant of PTSD. He'd got through psych, though. And then there was Chee. Nothing at all in his personnel record to explain why *he* didn't make friends. Kent, by now thoroughly intrigued, dug back a bit, and found a rather interestingly extensive medical history, which to the trained eye should have – but had not – triggered a CPS referral.

Well, well, well. Secrets and not-quite lies. No wonder they didn't play well with others. Kent frowned at his findings. They were not entirely good news. There were a lot of possible fractures in this team, and it was quite astonishing that they hung together as well as they did. It was not astonishing that they didn't talk to anyone. Any of this would have been grounds for watching them very closely, and the team were not keen on micro-management or, it appeared, poke-noses in the bullpen.

He sat back in his office chair and thought. He had no good reason to interview his team. He didn't have one yesterday and he hadn't got one today. What he *did* have was a slight problem. Now he had the information, he could see what O'Leary had been trying to do. The man had said *distraction*. That was all very well, but Kent didn't want his detectives distracted from solving cases. By anything.

He contemplated his results again, and then quietly filed them away where he could find them if he needed them. He wouldn't do anything precipitate. He hadn't become a Captain by making hasty decisions. He began to think carefully, without any *distractions*, about the pros and cons of O'Leary's suggestion.

Top of his cons list was that he didn't like blow-ins in his precinct. He didn't encourage frequent, or indeed any, visits by families: the bullpen was not a day-care facility. He had no desire to have outsiders popping in. Not only that, but it was uncomfortable to have non-cops present when witnesses or suspects were being questioned – except their lawyers, of course.

Top of the pros list was that he would neither allow 24-7 presence in the precinct nor would he approve the overtime. If Clement really had no other distraction, then that was her problem, but he would not permit her to use the bullpen as a second home. If O'Leary thought he could trail a *distraction* in front of her, then maybe Kent would be wrong to raise too many obstacles – as long as it was O'Leary who took the pain when it inevitably caused ructions.

He pondered, and abruptly thought of one other matter. He loved his wife very dearly, but culture – not so much. And she was very keen on culture. Now, it was a little sneaky, but… he would win an awful lot of domestic brownie points if he could tell Darla that Jamie Carval – yes, *that* Jamie Carval – was photographing in his precinct. The photos had been quite good, too, though he'd still rather not have paid to see them.

He sat bolt upright. That was what he'd do. If Jamie Carval wanted to take photos in Kent's bullpen, he could – as long as Carval would agree to an introduction to his wife and possibly a private view of the photos he was currently taking. Kent was exceedingly pleased with his idea. His wife would be absolutely delighted. Carval would get his – prearranged, there would be no random wandering in and out here – shots in the bullpen, and Kent would be in domestic heaven for *years* to come. Even better, it didn't require any real effort from him (apart from thinking it up). All the effort and suffering would come from his oddball foursome: not that he expected there to be any effort or suffering.

Perfect. Just plain perfect. He'd speak to O'Leary tomorrow. For now, it was time to go home – and the team was going home too, if he had to order them out, which he probably would.

Ah. His motley crew were discussing going home. Perfect. "I agree," Kent said from behind them. There was a collective jump. "The overtime bill is rising for no reason. Head home for the night and look at it fresh tomorrow." He flapped his hands at them, shooing them towards the exit. "That means you too, Clement. Out."

***

"Mornin', Casey," O'Leary reverberated, smiling at the day.

"Hey."

"Fancy meeting you here," came smugly from behind them both. Casey smothered a yelp.

"You!" Swiftly followed by, "O'Leary!"

"Yeah?"

Casey abruptly realised that this wasn't a discussion she wanted to have in front of Carval. Equally abruptly, she realised with some dismay that she was *almost* pleased to see him. She covered it with a glare, and received in return a smile that conveyed rather more *I-know-you-don't-mean-that-glare* than she would have liked.

"What's happening today?" Carval asked.

"Cop work," she answered briskly. "Seeing as this is the Crime Lab, and all."

O'Leary growled chidingly at her. "We're doin' a little research," he explained. "Got some int'resting stuff – an' here's our expert, right on time."

"Hello."

"Hey," Carval offered to the new man, and extended a hand. "I'm Jamie Carval."

"Oh," he said, dully. "The photographer? Er, hello."

Carval was exceedingly gratified to be recognised. "Yes. You?" He ignored O'Leary's growl. This neat little man looked interesting, in the same way that most things looked interesting when he was bored.

"John Terrison. Professor of chemistry at Columbia."

"Yes?" Carval asked, managing to confine his interested demeanour to Terrison and O'Leary. "I did a chemistry elective but apart from some interesting stuff on darkroom developing I didn't retain much."

Terrison smiled in a patient way which implied that that didn't surprise him. "I'd have thought you'd be a little more interested than that," he said, a spark of enthusiasm lightening his gloom. "The work I do is all around optics."

"I thought that was physics?"

"New compounds for specialist lens construction. We're hoping for better performance in tough conditions," he simplified.

"I see," Carval said, though he didn't, really. Lenses were what he went to very specialist shops to purchase, and though he took considerable care

133

to ensure the lenses were technically precisely what he needed, the compounds and chemistry involved in making them were entirely irrelevant to him. He wanted performance, and he'd pay pretty much whatever that took, but how that performance was achieved didn't matter.

"Professor, it's time we went to see the techs."

Terrison turned to trudge alongside Casey. Carval, wondering why Terrison was so depressed, took a set of shots of their respective backs, walking away.

"Good you left his face out," O'Leary's bass approved. "Makes it easier. Now, iffen you cared to sit around a spell, there's a coffee shop just down the street thataway" – he gestured – "an' if we're goin' to be all day here, I'll let you know so you c'n do somethin' diff'rent an' not waste time."

"I know the coffee shop. I went there last time. Okay. I got nothing much else to do today, anyway."

"Must be nice not to have a schedule."

Carval grinned. "Early on, it would've been nice to have a regular pay check."

O'Leary raised a hand in recognition of the point, and strode off after Casey and Terrison, catching them at the door. Naturally, Carval shot that, too.

***

"Hey, guys," Casey greeted the CSU techs generically, smiling happily around. She could feel lines of enquiry consolidating into the hope that Terrison would provide a breakthrough. She was sure that Merowin was less of a good guy than Terrison thought, but that didn't mean that Belvez was squeaky clean either. They could easily both have been bad. They could have been working together, and fallen out, and she surely was not ruling that out for a moment.

"Hey, Casey."

"This is Professor Terrison from Columbia's Faculty of Chemistry. He's come to have a look at those lens cases of mine."

Both the techs and Terrison blinked. Neither of them said *yours?* but it was quite clearly written on their faces.

"What do you need to do?" she turned to ask Terrison.

"It depends what tech you've got here," he started, and then descended into a very technical discussion with the Crime Lab staff of which Casey understood not one single word. When they paused for breath, during which wait she and O'Leary had traded the bemusement-confusion title between themselves several times, she intervened.

"What can you do?"

"I can run some of the optical performance tests here: enough to give me an idea of what this is. If I need to do more, I'll need my own equipment."

"How long will the work here take?"

"Not too long. Maybe an hour?"

"C'n we do anythin' to help?"

"No," Terrison stated bluntly.

"Okay," O'Leary accepted. "Then I guess the tech'll stay with you – chain of evidence" – the tech looked quite happy with this plan – "an' Casey an' me'll go get some coffee an' think about how to do it if you need your own lab."

"I'm happy to go to Columbia," the tech enthused. Clearly he didn't get to go out much.

Casey regarded O'Leary very cynically, but didn't argue.

"Okay, back in an hour. C'mon. I want coffee, an' you need it." He swept them out of the door. Behind them, the tech was happily offering assistance, note-taking, and general worshipfulness at being faced with a world-class chemist. This was entirely unusual: the Crime Lab techs were pretty damn brilliant in their own right, and while they were not precisely arrogant they were (rightly) aware of their own worth.

"What're you doing?" Casey asked crossly. "I wanted to" –

"Wanted to what? You di'n't understand any more words than I did. Let them get on with it without us makin' dumb comments an' askin' dumb questions. It'll be quicker that way."

"What if I don't want coffee?"

O'Leary stopped dead and pulled out his phone.

"Huh?"

"I'm callin' 9-1-1. If you don't want coffee you're dead. Better get you to the morgue. McDonald'll find out how you're still walkin' an' talkin' even though you're dead. Scientific miracle."

"Shut up. I'm not dead."

"Waallll, let's go get coffee. 'Less you got a diff'rent reason not to."

Casey glared. O'Leary grinned amiably. She did want coffee. She didn't want interminable and incomprehensible technical terms – but she didn't want O'Leary playing Cupid either. She could almost see the teeny white wings poking out from his wide back. She growled.

"C'mon. You ain't scared, are you?"

No, she was not. "No!" she said indignantly. "What would I be scared of?"

O'Leary acquired a saintly expression and didn't speak.

"I am *not* scared of any dumb photographer."

Still no comment, and a widening of the intensely irritating smile, accompanied by a big-brotherly air which was equally irritating.

"I'm *not*." She grumped off down the street towards the coffee bar. O'Leary followed, smiling contentedly at her stiff spine. Proximity, that was what Casey needed. He knew that because he hadn't missed her reaction to

Carval arriving, and if she'd just loosen up a little he'd probably be an interesting pal for her. Might even cancel her pathological hatred of photos, though that was likely wishful thinking.

"Double espresso," Casey said to O'Leary, who grimaced at her. "You wanted to come here, you buy." He made an even uglier face, but complied. He waved at Carval, who was regarding them with interest.

"Didn't expect to see you here," Carval queried. A hint of a smirk played at his lips. Casey flicked her glance away from them, rather too quickly, and scowled.

"They're talkin' chemistry. We don't speak science," O'Leary drawled. Casey didn't comment.

They collected their coffees, and O'Leary waited for Casey to sit down. She was, not so unobtrusively, trying to ensure that he sat down first.

"What are you waiting for?"

"My mom always told me to let ladies sit down first," he pointed out comfortably. "An' I'm scared of my mom." Casey made a rude noise at him. "I am!"

"Your mom is five foot nothing."

"Yeah, but she's my *mom*. An' she's got this look…"

"Coward," Casey teased affectionately, and sat.

"Don't you do what your mom tells you?" Carval put in.

There was a very unpleasant moment of silence.

"My mom passed a few years ago," Casey bit out, each word snapped off short. "Cancer." O'Leary winced. Her eyes fell to the table, and she buried her face in her coffee cup.

"I'm sorry," Carval said very awkwardly and uncomfortably.

"Thank you," she said automatically, coolly, face and voice utterly closed down. She made no effort whatsoever to restart conversation, and if O'Leary hadn't been between her and the door it was pretty obvious that she'd have been running out of it without ceremony or farewell.

"I'd have thought you had to stay with Professor Terrison," Carval tried, a little desperately.

"Naw. CSU are fine. They'll keep everythin' on the straight an' narrow. We got most of an hour to wait, an' there's nothin' we c'n do. Tyler an' Andy got everythin' under control back home, an' we don't have time to go see anyone else in between." He grinned. "Don't usually get time to take a break."

Casey curled into the corner and didn't talk: the men didn't try to include her.

"Is it pretty intense?"

"Can be. New case, the first twenty four hours are critical, and we'll be hard at it right through. Depends on the labs and the databases, though. We can't work on nothin'. Need ID's, need somethin' to go on. If we get that, then yeah, pretty intense." He gulped at his coffee, the cup tiny in his meaty paws. "Captain keeps an eye on it, though. He's not keen on overtime for no reason. Iffen we're doin' overtime, we better have a good reason. So we always do."

"What's the story with this one? Casey said he was a chemist, got suffocated."

O'Leary flicked a glance to Casey, who made a weary, don't-care-if-you-do gesture.

"We don't rightly know yet. Sure he was a chemist, got hit on the head an' then suffocated" – he paused, clearly choosing his words – "in an unusual way; but we don't know why. So Prof back there's lookin' at some work he had, in case there's somethin' helpful."

Carval, in a severe attack of discretion, didn't ask for details. If they wanted to tell him, they would, if they could. Either way, asking wouldn't get answers.

"I see."

Conversation lapsed. Casey seemed to have disappeared inside her own head, and might as well not have been present, and O'Leary wasn't talkative any more. Carval drank his coffee, and didn't break the peace.

"Time we went back," Casey said. She looked towards Carval. "This might take a while. No point you waiting for us."

O'Leary looked as if he was about to say something, stopped, and then said it anyway. "It won't be that long, Casey. He'll either know, or he won't, an' he'll want to go back to his own lab. I'll take him back to Columbia. You go on back to the precinct an' see what the other two have found."

Carval didn't understand that intervention.

"I'll see what he said. Then yeah, if you wanna take him to Columbia, that's fine. Chain of custody, and all that. You can listen to the chemistry on the way. Give me a call when you get him there, and I'll send a uniform down. No point you doing nothing there when we've got plenty to do." Her lips closed tightly.

"Okay. Let's go."

Carval simply followed along with them, without asking permission. He wouldn't be asking forgiveness, either, for that matter. He was exceedingly interested in O'Leary's intervention and Casey's state of semi-fugue. Sure, losing one's parents was hard – he knew exactly how hard it had been for him; and his parents had been older, frail. He'd been a late, surprise baby – but she'd reacted very strongly, for a few years on from the event. That's...odd. O'Leary effectively telling Casey what to do was odd, too. He hadn't had the impression that O'Leary was the leader in that pair. Of course, he wasn't precisely a follower, either.

O'Leary had told him that Casey needed a distraction, and then Tyler had agreed, and tagged him. But he hadn't said why, and if it were only the photographs they wouldn't have been putting him in proximity. They wouldn't tell him the story because they didn't know him, so if he wanted to work out what he'd be getting into then he'd need to do it himself. Or not. He didn't have to. He could simply…well, have a casual liaison. Or a longer, but still shallow, liaison.

Carval concluded, for later consideration, that whatever was up was connected to Casey's mother's death, somehow. Which was just plain dumb, but he couldn't shake the feeling as they strode briskly along the sidewalk back to the Crime Lab, during which short time she was no more communicative than she had been in the last quarter hour, nor did she in any way touch either man, even a brush of jackets.

"I'll wait in the park across the street," he said. O'Leary nodded. Casey bobbed her head once only, and turned straight for the door.

"Seeya in a bit," O'Leary cast backwards at Carval as he and Casey entered.

***

"You okay?"

"Yeah. It just hit a bit hard. It's the time of year." Her face twisted. "I should be over it, really."

"If only your pa was." O'Leary's bass came softly.

"I guess. Thanks," she said, and O'Leary didn't ask why. The solo journey back to the Thirty-Sixth would give her the time she needed to recover, and both of them knew it. It was what partners did.

In the lab, Terrison had a frown carved into his forehead. The tech was regarding him worriedly, as Terrison read and reread, checked his measurements and frowned yet harder. The cops didn't break his concentration. After a few more minutes of hard-thinking silence, he looked up.

"This makes no sense at all," he fretted. "The results of the optical testing that I can do here" – the tech made a small noise – "It's not your fault," he added reassuringly, "but my equipment does more – the results make no sense. These gels in cases 1 and 2 are giving me results that are as good as Ricky's, but the ones in 3 and 4 aren't. They're about where Mike's were. But you said Telagon said that Mike's synthesis was better than Ricky's, so maybe 1 and 2 are Mike's." He raised bewildered eyes. "I'll have to make both of them, from scratch, to check this. If Ricky's was better, then why did Telagon think it wasn't?"

Now *that*, both detectives thought, was the key question. They exchanged a glance of complete agreement.

"Do you need to take the gels back with you?" Casey asked.

"No. Not now. As long as you keep them safe here," he said, in unwitting insult: of course they would. However, it meant that there was no need for chain of custody on the lens cases, which was helpful. "I need to make these. End to end. This makes *no sense*," he almost wailed.

"Okay. Look, Detective O'Leary will give you a ride back to Columbia."

"That would be good. I came straight from Penn Station."

"Thank you for your help, Professor." She thought. "How long will the syntheses take?"

"Oh, not that long. Maybe a couple of days. If it's longer I'll let you know."

"Thanks. Okay, O'Leary, let's get going. I'll see you back at the precinct."

She swung out. O'Leary gazed down at Terrison. "You ready to go?" he drawled.

"I guess so." He seemed to realise something. "Um... where are the restrooms? And" – he blinked uncertainly – "I'd really, really like a coffee. I – er – got a bit caught up in the tests and, er..."

"Sure," O'Leary rumbled reassuringly. "We c'n manage that. I'll just drive a little faster. Don't make no never mind to me."

He steered Terrison in the right direction and, after a moment of his own, told him he'd meet him outside, which would give him a couple of minutes to collect Carval and see if he needed a ride too.

Shortly, the three men were walking back to the coffee bar. Terrison, being small, bore an amusing resemblance to an arrested criminal between them. It hadn't affected his mutterings. He was talking, largely to himself since neither other man understood it, about optical compounds.

Carval paid for the coffees as Terrison continued to expound on the potential for new optical breakthroughs. Sadly, he understood approximately one word in six – usually *and*, or *or*. He was somewhat soothed by O'Leary's equal confuddlement. They wandered back, swigging from their go-cups, and letting Terrison mutter miserably.

"Anyways," Terrison said, "thanks for the coffee. There must have been a mistake," he repeated for the third or fourth time, and wandered dismally with them towards O'Leary's car, shoulders stooped.

"He's not happy." Carval said, conveniently a stride behind, and very quietly.

"His magic money tree got dead," O'Leary rumbled cynically.

"I think he's genuinely upset. What's the connection to your victim? Money tree?"

"Belvez" – Carval noted the name – "had just joined his group. Pullin' in even more research cash. Prof there really seemed to rate him."

"Oh."

The discussion ceased as they all enter O'Leary's large SUV. Carval assumed that no smaller car would fit him, and looking at the lack of roof clearance was confirmed in that belief. He courteously allowed Terrison to take shotgun, and disposed himself in the back. The ride back was quiet, broken only by further mutters from Terrison, who was deposited at the Columbia entrance.

"Professor," O'Leary said, "c'n you do me a favour?"

"Sure?"

"Don't tell anyone in the group you're makin' these things. Someone" – he was repeating Casey's warning – "has it in for you an' the group, an' we don't want you gettin' hurt. So keep it under your hat, 'kay?"

"Okay," Terrison acceded, "but I'm sure it can't be anyone in my group. It's just not like that."

"Mebbe not, but let's not take any chances. We don't like our experts gettin' hurt."

"Okay." Terrison didn't look as if he agreed with the thesis, but as long as he agreed with the action that would be fine.

CHAPTER 19

"What've we got, guys?" Casey asked as she strode back in, composure restored by the solitary drive back from Queens. She'd needed the space, and O'Leary, annoyingly playing Cupid or not, had, as ever, had her back and given her it.

"Been running Petersen for you. Nothing special. Where's Bigfoot?"

"Taking Terrison back. He'll be here shortly. I want a go at Petersen, on home ground. Keep her all fat and happy till we know what's really happening here."

"What did Terrison say?"

Casey's brow wrinkled. "It's weird."

"That what he said or what you think?"

"Both." She scrawled on the whiteboard. "He didn't like the results. From what he was saying, Merowin's results aren't as good as Belvez's, but that's not what Telagon were telling us." She developed a nastily feral smile. "What did you think of Telagon, Andy?"

"I thought they had a lot riding on the results." Andy smiled, equally nastily. "If Belvez's results were better than Merowin's, you'd think they'd change horses. But if they've been – hmm – *massaging* their results, Belvez having replicable results might put a big spoke in their wheel."

"I think you're thinking what I'm thinking," Casey agreed. "I think this is all tied up with Telagon too." She drew a few connecting lines. "There's a lot of money – and jail time – at stake here."

"Need to be careful," Tyler said. "Big companies can pull strings."

"Yeah. Anyway, Terrison's gone back to run both syntheses. He's really not happy. Deep down, I guess he's suspicious too." She smiled. "After lunch, I think O'Leary and I'll go talk to this Karlen Petersen."

"Sounds like we get to stay here again," Andy groused. "Even Tyler's going to be as pale as a vampire if we don't get to go out soon. I'll get

Vitamin D deficiency."

"What happened to 6 a.m. tai-chi in the park? Don't you get sunlight then?"

"If you ever woke up that early you'd know it's before sunrise."

"Then it's night time, and that's for sleeping," she flipped back. "Anyway, we'll go out and get lunch. Wouldn't want you to have bandy legs. I'm sure that wouldn't be good for tai-chi."

Tyler snickered at Andy's offended glare.

"Next time we spar, Casey, I'll show you what tai-chi's good for."

"Bring it, Andy. I need the practice."

"Soon as we get a slow-down in the case" –

"Or solve it" –

"We'll have a go-around."

"Sure."

O'Leary wandered back in just in time to hear the end of the teasing, and breathed an unseen sigh of relief. Casey seemed to have pulled herself together again. It was just as well, because it meant she probably wouldn't kill him for telling Carval they'd likely be wandering back down to Columbia that afternoon. His stomach rumbled, vibrating the desk.

"I'm hungry," he said plaintively, and had another brilliant idea. Today had made him totally sure that Casey needed distraction, so he was going to make sure distraction happened. "Let's go out an' get some lunch."

"We already agreed that, Bigfoot. It's not feeding time at the Zoo just yet."

"Give it time. Let's try and tie some of these loose ends off. What did we get from the rest of the research group?"

The next hour passed in efficient analysis and general tidying up to reduce the mass of data to useful information. Finally Tyler stood and stretched.

"Lunch," he said tersely.

O'Leary bounced up, rattling the window by his desk. "Where are we goin'? I'm starvin'. Even Andy's skinny ribs look good right now."

"El Nuevo Tina," Tyler decided for all of them, and off they went. At the back of the group, O'Leary sent a surreptitious message.

***

"O'Leary!" Casey hissed, after they were all sitting down with various lunches. "Was this you?"

O'Leary grinned widely. Tyler and Andy shuffled backwards, out of the line of probable fire. Carval took a couple of steps forward. "Hey, all."

"My pal's come to lunch," O'Leary lilted. "Get yourself somethin' to eat, an' come join us."

When Carval reappeared at the table, O'Leary tugged up another chair and, to Casey's horrified look, put it next to her. Admittedly this was because they were at a rectangular table and Carval was now perched at the end, sticking out into the aisle, but still, it was *not fair*. She glared viciously at O'Leary. The glare was not at all lessened by the knowledge that Carval's knee was, he being keen to avoid O'Leary's redwood legs, gently pressing on hers, which was having a rather peculiar effect on her. She put the fluttering of her stomach down to the dubious hygiene of the lunch bar, rather than the quite ridiculous idea that it was a flutter of attraction.

"Where are you going this afternoon?"

"Right now, back to the bullpen," Casey said, with satisfaction. There was absolutely no hint of any disappointment in her words or face, she was quite sure. So O'Leary should not be giving her that knowing glance. She was quite certain that she wasn't blushing. Not at all.

"I could use a walk," Carval said, without turning an eyelash. Casey turned her scalding glare on him, and therefore missed the identically evil smirks on the faces of the rest of the team. He smiled suavely. "I could talk to Tyler here, seeing as he was such a brilliant conversationalist in the bar the other night."

Andy choked on his soda, and O'Leary guffawed fit to shudder the table. Tyler just grinned, without words. Even Casey raised a grin, though it looked as if it sneaked on to her face without her permission. Carval thought there was just a tiny, almost imperceptible hint of a pout. It was almost cute.

It was *definitely* sexy. He'd have killed to shoot it, but then she'd kill him, which would be undesirable.

He brought his chair closer to the table, and resisted, with considerable effort, his desire to put a hand over Casey's knee. Or higher. Or a lot higher on her leg. He attached one hand to his sandwich and the other to his soda, and tried very hard not to watch Casey sucking her drink through a straw. He was under enough strain, so to speak, right now. He had a nasty feeling that the other men were secretly snickering.

They finished up their lunches and made to leave. Somehow – she strongly suspected O'Leary, but Tyler seemed to be involved too, which was odd – Casey ended up walking beside Carval. O'Leary ambled along alone, because there wasn't room for anyone else to fit on the sidewalk beside him, and Tyler and Andy appeared to be having an intense discussion. *Appeared* was the operative word. They were discussing basketball, the *rats*. Andy did not like discussing basketball, or baseball, or football. Andy liked discussing tai-chi and the theatre, at considerable and excruciating length, with comparative references to other productions.

She was therefore forced to walk next to the tall, broad, sexy – *no!* – totally irritating and oversized *photographer*. In her head, she'd have used that same intonation for *sewer rat*. He was too big. Every time he took a step his hand brushed hers. She was *almost* sure it was accidental. If she moved away, she'd be walking into the side of the building. She couldn't go faster, because O'Leary was in the way. She couldn't go slower, because Tyler would be treading on her heels, which would have been painful. In fact, they'd surrounded her. This was *not fair*. She smelt a co-ordinated plan.

Unfortunately, she could also smell Carval's cologne, and it was rather enticing. Coupled with the hand-brushing and the earlier knee-touching, it was all doing very strange things to her nerves and her normally cool and sensible brain. She was remembering how nice it was to have a large warm man surrounding her. Which was utterly ridiculous and not at all what she should have been thinking.

But she didn't take any steps at all to stop the brushing of their hands.

Carval, unlike Casey, was quite sure that O'Leary and, to a lesser extent, Tyler, had co-ordinated a plan, though it was clear that forcing Andy into a conversation about sport, about which even the audible snippets showed that Andy knew nothing, was very amusing for Tyler. It got him what he wanted, which was proximity to Casey. Sitting next to her with a certain amount of contact had left him with a very deep desire to *take* her hand and keep it, not to mention wrapping an arm round her and tucking her in: he was sure that she would fit just perfectly. However, he contented himself with ensuring that with every stride he brushed against her hand. Only her hand. Next time, it might include her swaying hip.

He glanced down at her dark brown head, and thought he spotted a tiny blush of pink at the edge of her cheekbone. And of course, she wasn't stuffing her hands in her pockets to avoid his touch entirely. He smiled rakishly into the air above her. Cool-cop Casey *was* interested. Just a little.

Just enough.

He walked with her, perfectly happy, all the way back to the bullpen with the gang. He didn't try to start a conversation – it wasn't like she gabbled, but in the right circumstances, silence said plenty – and hoped that he was creating a certain sense of comfort in his company.

He turned away from the precinct doors, when to his utmost astonishment Casey turned to him and said, "We'll be going back to Columbia again in about ten minutes."

He gaped. She glared.

"O'Leary'll tell you anyway. Might as well short-circuit that. He'll text you if it changes."

"I'll just wait here, then?" Carval offered. There was a pause.

"If you must."

An instant later she was gone. The others looked at him with approving smiles, and then they were gone too.

Full of the joys of life, Carval parked himself a little away from the doors and started to take a whole series of reality shots of everything that passed his eye until Casey and O'Leary re-emerged.

The team piled into the precinct stairwell. Or, at least, three of them piled, and O'Leary simply stepped. He was a pile all on his very large ownsome.

"That was cute," Andy chirped evilly.

"Since our oversized tattle-tale second-grader" – O'Leary yelped in disgust – "here is going to tell him every time I walk out the door anyway, I guess I have to play nice. But O'Leary, I'm going to get you back for this. Just you wait."

"Aw, Casey. Don't be like that. I'm your pal."

"Not this week, you're not," she huffed. "This week you're Yente." Andy snorted.

"Uh?" O'Leary emitted.

"Matchmaker from Fiddler on the Roof. And an old woman, which is what you're acting like."

"Tradition," O'Leary sang in a fine bass. "Tradition!" He stopped. "Dunno any more than that."

"Oh, not you *too*," Andy wailed. "Isn't it bad enough that Casey likes musicals? Now I have to put up with you too? There is no appreciation of culture in this team. None. I'm going to buy you all tickets for *real* theatre for Christmas."

"You recognised the name," Casey pointed out.

"I'm educated. That doesn't mean it's culture!"

He continued his cultural wailing all the way back into the bullpen, ignored by the other three. He had these fits of intellectualism once every few months, and it was good live entertainment.

Casey glared ferociously at O'Leary, which achieved nothing, and collected the pen and notebook which was all she'd need for Petersen. "Let's go," she growled.

Carval, mildly bored of waiting, picked up the titanic tread of O'Leary and attached himself to the asymmetric pair as they orient down the street towards Columbia. As earlier, he didn't try to open conversation, but ambled along beside Casey in perfect contentment, brushing her hand just often enough to make sure that the previous lack of distance hadn't been a one-off insanity. It hadn't. She allowed it to continue.

"I could get you both coffee, if you want? Tell me how long you'll be, and I'll have it when you're ready to leave."

"We won't know," Casey pointed out. "It depends how talkative our witness is." She paused. Her mouth twisted, as if she wasn't sure of her next words. "We could meet you in the café, after."

O'Leary's whale-sized jaw dropped open.

"Okay," Carval said amiably, as if it were no big deal. Subtly, he moved a scant inch closer, so that their hands were very definitely brushing, a little more than a moment ago. Her fingers were cool; the skin of the back of her hand unexpectedly soft.

"We might be a while," she said defensively. "You don't have to wait." As if she were trying to take it back without it seeming that she was doing it because she was... not scared, exactly, but nervous. She didn't want to show that she was nervous around him; about him. He let his fingers linger fractionally where they ran over and past hers, all the way down to Columbia. She didn't shoot, punch, slap or shove him, which was a considerable win.

"Okay. We have work to do," Casey clipped, as they arrived.

"See you in the café," O'Leary drawled. Casey flicked a fast, irritated glance at him. It appeared that she'd conveniently been forgetting her own commentary. Carval wandered off, and the two cops progressed towards Havemeyer Hall.

"C'mon, Bigfoot. Let's go talk to Petersen."

"D'you think she'll be there?"

"She's supposed to be on shift. They couldn't confirm if she was in, but it's worth a go. If not, we'll try her apartment again. After that, we'll start thinking about how to find her."

"You think she's avoidin' us? That ain't friendly, now, is it?"

"It's a possibility. If she is, that's pretty suggestive."

This time they went straight to the small office where lab techs apparently lived when they were not taking care of labs and the scientists who worked in them. A tall, nearly blonde woman of middle age was cleaning up glassware in a large sink. It was clear that she had once been fit. Her greyish lab coat had a number of dubious stains; she was in beat-up sneakers. She looked very little like her glammed-up Facebook photo.

"Karlen Petersen?"

"Who's asking?"

"Detective Clement."

"And Detective O'Leary."

She ran an uninterested gaze up and down them. "Yeah. What'dya want?"

"We want to talk to you about Ricky Belvez. People say you knew him."

"Sure I know him," arrived in a Minneapolis accent. "He's part of the group here."

Now, that was interesting already. From her choice of tenses, Petersen either hadn't heard about the death or was pretending she hadn't. Casey was tending to the latter, quite firmly. The big clue was that Petersen hadn't asked them why they were here. That was a big, big mistake.

"Do you deal with him a lot?"

"No more than anyone else. He lives in his own head all the time."

"Mm?" Casey encouraged.

"Always in here. Guess he didn't have a girlfriend 'cause he never seemed to go home, 'specially lately. First in, last to leave. Made it a real pain to finish our work. 'Least Mike leaves at a sensible time, most days."

O'Leary tapped Casey's toe, unseen. She tapped back. They'd both noticed that slip, and the mix of tenses. There was only one Mike in the group. Merowin. And... no *friend*? Girl or, per Merowin, boy. That didn't tie up either.

"Yes?"

"Yeah. Why're you here anyway?" she finally asked. "What's all this about?"

"Ricardo Belvez was found dead. We're investigating."

"Dead?" Petersen managed a semi-creditable tone of surprised horror. "What happened?" It was too late for her to cover that that was no real surprise to her.

"He was hit on the head, but there are some unusual circumstances. We need to close off all the angles."

Petersen simply stared at them, but there was a flicker of worry on her face.

"D'you know what he was workin' on?"

"No. But I don't think it was going so good, because if it was he wouldn't have been here so late."

"What was the group like?"

"Huh?"

"Did you all go out together for a drink, dinner, anythin' like that?"

"No."

"So you didn't know where Belvez lived?"

"Oh, yeah. Before he got here he was asking Mike where to live, and Mike said to me, and I got a pal who had an apartment out in Brooklyn, so I told Mike and Mike told Ricky."

"Who was the friend?"

"Mike."

"Mike? Michael Merowin?"

"No, not him. Mike Ahlbrechtssen."

"He's a friend of yours?"

"Yeah."

"How'd you know him?"

"I used to rent an apartment from him, back in Minneapolis," Petersen said reluctantly.

"Really? He wasn't keen on Ricky, seemed to me. What was his problem?" Casey asked, innocently. Petersen fell right into the trap.

"That guy who was staying over with him. 'S not right."

"Which guy?"

"Mike said Ricky called him Troy." O'Leary spluttered, and grinned widely. "He was there all the freakin' time. Mike didn't think it was right. An' Ricky wasn't allowed to sublet. No extras. So whatever was goin' on, this Troy dude shouldn't've been stayin' there."

Which certainly didn't tie up with Belvez not having had a friend and always being in the lab. Hmmm.

"Which Mike?"

"Merowin. He's big on rules."

"Did you ever see Troy?" O'Leary asked, evading Casey's toes.

"Naw. Mike told me 'bout him. An' anyway, Mike's got cameras in the hallway an' on the door. Stops trouble." She suddenly looked as if she hadn't meant to say that.

Now that was something good to know. *And* Casey now had enough for a warrant for the footage if she needed one, because this Troy was definitely a person of interest. Considerable interest. Still, her instincts were telling her that there was more to come from Petersen. It might be very interesting to get Andy to run a search for Petersen – and indeed Ahlbrechtssen, though that seemed a little less likely – through that footage he'd asked for around the Columbia chemistry labs, particularly the loading bays, and around the apartment in Brooklyn. In fact, a general search. See who was where, when. Then she could find out why.

"Okay," she said briskly. "Thank you for your time. If you think of anything else, give me a call on this number. We might want to talk to you again, so if you're thinking of going away," –

"Don't," O'Leary said, ominously. Casey poked him with her foot again.

"– tell me first."

Petersen looked disconcerted by that last statement. Good. A little disconcertment on the part of her witness-suspects was just what Casey liked. Nervous people tended to fret, and get careless, and then babble when she brought them back in.

"I got bruises," O'Leary said plaintively when they were leaving the lab and crossing the campus to Joe's Café. "Why'd you keep kickin' me?"

"I didn't kick you. I poked you with my foot to keep you quiet. She was nervous before we even started, and you joking would've relaxed her. I didn't want her relaxed. The more she frets the more she'll spill later. You know that. We always do that."

"You had an idea, din't you?" he said. "You weren't much surprised when she said she knew that landlord."

"Names."

"Names?"

"Both their names are Nordic. It was worth a look. Anything might be a lead right now, seeing as all we've got is confusion."

"You c'n say that again," O'Leary grumbled. "I'd rather haul her in an' ask about gas cylinders." He pushed the café door open and let Casey precede him.

"I don't want to do that till Tyler and Andy are done. Didn't you notice she was lying about knowing Belvez was dead?"

"A'course I did."

Casey grinned. "So we're going to get the evidence and then every time she lies we'll call her on it. C'mon. You know you love it when we do it this way." Her smile was brilliant and her face alight with the joy of the hunt.

"I guess, but you got all the fun in there an' all I got was bruises."

"Aw, poor baby," Casey said, and darted away from O'Leary's immense paw, snickering at his disgruntlement.

She ran straight into a solid chest, which proved, on looking up, to be Carval, who caught her as she lost her balance while bouncing off.

"Nice catch, man," O'Leary smirked at Carval. "Were you intendin' to let go of her?"

Did he have to? That was definitely not fair. There should have been a rule about catchers' keepers, or something similar. He didn't want to let go. Casey-the-cop fit him just right.

The point was made moot by Casey, luridly scarlet, detaching herself with a decided huffing sound. Carval met O'Leary's saucer-sized eye, and was not amused by the dancing mischief and knowing expression therein. Casey was refusing to catch the eye of either man, and was dusting herself down in a very *don't-you-dare-mention-it* way.

"Coffee?" Carval asked. There was a short silence.

"To go," Casey said briskly. "We need to get back."

"Fine," Carval said. "What's your poison, O'Leary?"

"White Americano."

Carval wandered off to the counter.

"He din't ask you," O'Leary noted innocently. Casey growled. "You been sharin' cosy coffee mornin's?" She growled more blackly.

"No."

O'Leary regarded her.

"No!"

More regarding.

"He bought me a coffee when *you* told him he could find me at the morgue."

"Mm."

"What?" she snapped.

"He's got a good memory."

O'Leary smiled knowingly. Casey scowled. Carval returned with three cups of coffee and distributed them without comment on the atmosphere, receiving automatic thanks which didn't exactly alleviate the strain.

"Let's go," he said cheerfully. He was already halfway to the street.

Part of his hurry was because he needed a little physical space from Casey. She'd come in, laughing and glorious; coruscatingly alive; and he might as well have been punched in the gut because he'd been left flattened and gasping for breath. Fortunately he'd captured it all on film. And then she'd tripped or failed to look or something and fallen into him and catching her – well, who was going to *not* catch someone who was falling? But catching her had tucked her into him and she ought to have been there more. She should have been there a lot more. Right then, and all night. And the next night. And the next.

And now he *definitely* needed some space, and some time to calm himself down, because diverting Casey into that convenient alley right over there and simply kissing her hard – would have been a *very* bad idea. He resolutely concentrated on the various techniques he had used for shooting the panhandlers without having to deal with the smell, all the way to the precinct. It didn't really help.

Casey didn't say a word to O'Leary all the way back, being – she told herself – engaged in drinking her coffee and not falling over her own feet. She steered well clear of the reasons why she might fall over her own feet, because the major – indeed, only – reason was two long strides in front of her, and his rear view – or the view of his rear – was very easy on the eye.

Of course, the excellence of the view was not the only thought skittering round her scrambled brain. There was another thought. *That* thought said wow. When it had finished squealing like a crazed teen inside her head, it morphed into *that felt really good*, which morphed in its turn into *it might be nice to do it again*. None of which were helpful thoughts, and certainly did not help her concentration for the rest of the day, or indeed the evening.

CHAPTER 20

The bullpen was bustling busily the next morning: the team were happily getting on with their work without anything – or anyone – to distract them. They needed to spend some quality time with the data, the matching, and the warrant requests – top of the list, bank and camera footage. Then she'd go see the landlord again. Some pleasant intimidating of suspects would improve Casey's conflicted mood immensely.

"Detective O'Leary!" Kent emerged from his office. "A word, please."

Please was better than no please. But it was still not good.

"And Detective Clement."

She hadn't done anything. This was definitely not good. She put her pen down and trailed after O'Leary, who was drooping his way into the office.

"I have been considering Detective O'Leary's suggestion that your photographer" – *whose* photographer? It wasn't *her* photographer. And what *suggestion*? O'Leary hadn't been suggesting anything to her – "be allowed to photograph in the precinct, by prior arrangement, on an occasional basis." Casey started to pray fervently and hopelessly. She'd never have been dragged in here if Kent wasn't going to consent.

"I intend to allow it. Mr Carval will be allowed to take pictures of the four of you at your daily work. You will devise a system that means that he doesn't disrupt your real job of solving crime. I don't expect him to be in your company for more than a minimal time in any given week. He will be permitted to take shots from the observation facilities of the interrogation rooms, as long as no suspects are identifiable in any way – or their lawyers, come to think of it. He is not allowed to be in the interrogation rooms with you. This isn't a TV show."

Casey was stunned into silence. Even O'Leary was dumbfounded.

"I will call him to let him know. Please let me have his contact details."

151

That meant – right then. Kent didn't tolerate delay or dissent.

"How long will this last?" she asked.

"The moment it disrupts you, it stops. I'll judge what's disruptive." *Dammit.* "Open-ended, but why would he need more than an hour a week?"

Because he's a freaking irritation who's trying to get up close and personal, never mind his freaking photographs, Casey thought bitterly. She rammed back down the naughty little thought that said *but now you'll see a lot more of a large, sexy man who's interested in you, so you could have some fun.* He was a *photographer.* She hated photographs.

"Dismissed," Kent rapped. They left.

O'Leary dug a card from his desk drawer, looked at it rather hopelessly, tried to straighten it out and dust it off, which didn't really improve matters, and trudged back to Kent's office to deliver it. He trudged back, to find Casey sitting on his desk, having cleared a corner of the chaos (O'Leary believed in the volcano method of paperwork management, or possibly in creating his own primordial coal strata) by shoving it across by eight inches and perching unstably on the corner thus revealed. She didn't look happy.

"What did you do?" she hissed furiously. "Stop playing freaking Cupid, you overgrown haystack."

O'Leary was not noticeably intimidated. "Told you, you need a distraction. Time was, you wouldn't be yellin' at me, you'd be tellin' me you'd booked me a slot down at the drag club to get me back an' laughin' at my expression. No-one said you gotta marry the guy, or even go to bed with him, just have some fun."

Casey thumped off the desk and stalked back to her own without a single word. O'Leary's massive brow wrinkled as he worriedly watched her. Six months or so ago, even, she'd have made a joke of it.

***

Captain Kent regarded the crumpled piece of card in his hand with some distaste, both for its state and its content. He was not at all convinced of the wisdom of his decision. On the other hand, he had a guaranteed get-out at any point, simply by declaring it disruptive and throwing the man out, and he was going to make his wife very happy. It'd all be fine.

He dialled the number on the card.

"Carval Studios," a disembodied voice said. It didn't exactly sound as Kent had expected. The voice was – well – *prissy.* The photo exhibitions hadn't suggested prissiness.

"Mr Carval? This is Captain Kent of the Thirty-Sixth Precinct."

"This is Allan Penrith, Mr Carval's agent and business manager," the prissy voice said, enunciating each word very precisely. "How can I help you?" There was a tinge of worry behind the clipped consonants.

Kent considered suggesting that Carval was a person of interest, simply to see what would happen, and rejected it as unworthy of a senior and respectable Captain. Just because he didn't like the voice was no reason to be difficult.

"Mr Carval is photographing my detectives," he said. "I wish to discuss that with him."

"Those photos are genius," Penrith stated. "You have no grounds to prevent him showing them."

"On the contrary, Mr Penrith, I wish to assist him."

There was a very strange noise on the end of the phone. It might have been *not you too*. Kent was offended.

"There are stringent conditions."

Now it was a noise of some relief, and possibly *thank God, there's someone else sane.*

"Who did you say you were?"

"Captain Kent, of the Thirty-Sixth Precinct. The detectives Mr Carval has been photographing are mine."

"Okay. I see. Why don't you tell me what the conditions are and, as long as they're reasonable, I'll make sure Jamie complies."

Well, now, this was better, Kent thought. Someone sensible, even if the voice was irritating. "He'll be allowed to take photos in the bullpen, but only of these four detectives unless he has explicit permission from the others. He can watch interrogations from Observation, and take photos from there as long as no suspects' or witnesses' faces, or their lawyers' faces, are identifiable in any way at all when the photos are used."

"He can pixelate or blur them, that's fine. I'll make sure he does."

"He can't just show up. He needs to arrange it with the team. He is not to disrupt their work – and if he does, he'll be out. No second chances, my decision is final."

"Fair enough."

Kent was beginning to like this prissy-voiced Penrith. "And one last thing. My wife is a considerable admirer of Mr Carval's work. If he wants me to allow him in, he is to provide my wife with a private showing of the exhibition, in which he, personally, will discuss it with her and explain anything she wants to know about his work."

Penrith squeaked.

"That's not negotiable, Mr Penrith."

"Okay. I'll agree to all of that provisionally, but I'll have to get Jamie's agreement too."

"Fine. As soon as you've got it all documented, we'll make it happen."

"I'll need your e-mail to send you it."

Kent provided an e-mail address, and thought delightedly of how happy his wife would be as the call closed. Penrith sounded like a sensible guy.

153

He'd hang on to his contact details, and deal with him unless he absolutely had to deal with Carval. Creative types were not his thing.

***

Allan put the phone down, stared at it in case anything else astonishing happened, such as an alien life-form appearing from it – and then dashed up the stairs.

"Jamie, *Jamie!*"

"Uh?"

"*Jamie!*"

It dawned on Carval that Allan was shouting. Allan almost never shouted. Screeched, when he thought Carval had messed up, but not shouted. "What's wrong?"

"Jamie, what have you done?"

"It's not my fault," Carval said reflexively. "I didn't do anything. I behaved myself perfectly at the Academy. Sergeant Carter liked me. I got some good shots, too. Look."

Allan didn't look. "Jamie, I just got a call – well, you did, but you never pick the phone up" –

"That's what you're for" –

"From Captain Kent of the Thirty-Sixth Precinct."

Carval snapped his brain into gear. "Captain? Thirty-Sixth Precinct? *Casey's* precinct? What'd he say? Why'd he call? What's going on? Tell me he isn't stopping me?"

"Calm down," Allan said.

"*Calm down?* This could *ruin* my exhibition. My photos. He can't stop me. I won't let him."

"Calm. Down."

"No! Look at my shots. I'm not letting some power-tripping proto-military desk driver stop me taking my shots" –

"Jamie, he's agreed to let you in."

Carval's mouth dropped unattractively open. "Say *what?*"

"He's going to allow you inside the precinct."

"You're kidding. I take it all back. He's a man of excellent taste and judgement."

"I think it might be his wife who has excellent taste and judgement," Allan said dryly. "Apparently she's a considerable fan."

"So I can go in and out as I please? Great."

"No."

Carval pouted. "What can I do?"

"You can take shots inside the precinct, of the team. If the other cops allow you, you can take shots of them. You can also go into something called Observation, and as long as you blur the faces of the witness, suspect and/or their lawyer, you can take shots of the interview."

154

"I can?"

"You have to arrange it in advance with the team."

Carval's face fell. "Casey'll find some way to bollix it up for me. Did I tell you what she did?" He was still indignant. "She was told to let me tag along and then she wouldn't tell me where she was going and said I'd have to find them."

Allan sniggered. Carval glowered at him.

"She'll do something to spite me."

"It's good for you not to get your own way," Allan said sententiously.

"I hate you."

"Stop being five. You're getting into the precinct. Anyway, that big guy" –

"O'Leary" –

"He seems to be on your side. He'll make sure it happens."

Carval smiled beautifully. "So he will," he said with satisfaction, and his smile acquired a wolfish edge. "So he will."

"There's one more condition."

"Yeah?"

"You have to give the Captain's wife a private exhibition of the photos and answer all her questions about your work."

"I can do that, I guess," Carval said absently.

Allan stared at him. Carval remained in a contented dream of considerable proximity to Casey, and didn't mind the private viewing at all. Normally he hated them, and wasn't shy about saying so. Right then, however, he was pondering all the ways that he could use this to take brilliant shots and to get metaphorically cuddled up to Casey, which should lead to some very physically cuddling up to Casey.

He was still shocked by the effect she had on him. Sure, he was pretty keen on pretty women, but the instant spark was new. Maybe it was because she wasn't flirting – she wasn't even playing hard to get. She was attracted, though. She might not admit it, but there was something on her side.

There was a hell of a lot of something on his side, and it wasn't only the way his camera loved her. He descended back into a contented reverie centred around how walking next to her, she'd been just the perfect height if only he'd been able to tuck her in; she'd be the perfect height to kiss him if she were above him…

That was not a clever thought. Flickers of interest or not, she was antsy and spooking. *Take it easy*, he thought. *Take it easy.*

***

Back in the bullpen, there was a Force Twelve thunderstorm circling around Casey's desk. Her head was firmly down, and she'd undone her clip so that her curls were hiding her face. Everyone got on with their own

155

work, as planned earlier, and no-one disturbed her. She'd get over it, or she wouldn't, by shift end.

She didn't, really. She'd spoken to all of them: her usual competently efficient self, but there was no banter and no indication that she'd welcome any.

She stood up to leave.

"I'm out," she announced. "It's late" – it was, in fact, rising seven p.m. – "and I'm going home. See you all tomorrow."

"Night," chorused from three desks, in pleasant harmony – tenor, baritone and bass.

"Night," she gave back, and was gone upon the word.

The stairwell door had barely closed behind her when O'Leary's mile-wide smirk appeared.

"She's not happy with you."

"Aw, she'll be happy tomorrow."

"Not," Tyler muttered.

"What are you two doing?" Andy asked.

"Waalll, when you were out bein' cultured an' all, me 'n' Tyler had a beer with Carval, an' we pushed him a little" –

"Lot" –

"An' he stood up to us pretty fine, so we" –

"You" –

"You did too. Anyways, we thought we should give him a chance, an' Casey a distraction."

"So why's she giving you the evil eye?"

"'Cause Bigfoot here's playing Cupid."

Andy smirked. "How's that working out for you right now?"

"Look," O'Leary said, suddenly serious, "she's worried about her dad, an' she's not having as much fun." His drawl had dropped away, which was always a sign of real importance. "Time was, she'd have suggested we double date, or something. Today she just hid, an' glowered."

"But what did you *do*, you big lunk?" Andy asked with some exasperation.

"Captain's gonna let him in the precinct, every so often. I suggested it."

Andy gleeped frantically. "You're crazy," he said. "You need some pills, cure that lunatic streak in you. I got some Chinese herbs that'll calm you down."

"It'll be fine. Didn't I hear you sayin' that it was cute?"

"Right up till you make like a colander, full of holes," Andy pointed out dryly. "Maybe she can't shoot like Tyler, but you're the size of a barn door so she can't miss."

"It'll be fine," O'Leary said optimistically. "No problem." He grinned. "Like I just said, she didn't shove him under a truck. So I'm just gonna let him know that he c'n come by early tomorrow, an' start." He pulled out his phone and did so, before he could forget.

"I'm going home," Andy said. "I'm going to update my will. I think you'd both better do the same."

***

Tucked up on her comfortable couch, showered and wrapped in an old, soft and comforting robe, Casey tried to read her book. On balance, reading about Kate Daniels had been a bad plan, if only because she seemed to have a large, strong man on tap, and Casey didn't. She humphed at her cosy apartment.

Casey liked big men. They were very comforting, she thought. She could do any protecting of herself she needed to do, but it was nice to be cuddled and cosseted into a big, broad frame. Cosy. She liked to be cuddled in and kept cosy, even if no-one who had seen her professionally would ever have believed that at home she was happy to be snuggly.

Which thought led her straight to the big, broad man who was both her current Nemesis and the easiest available option for snuggling. O'Leary's occasional suggestions were either too close to home – there was no *way* she was getting involved with another cop – or their shifts would be incompatible, or they just didn't have a brain. She might not have been going to out think Einstein (if he were alive) but she was certainly not dumb, and she would really rather have liked more from a partner than the physical.

Carval must be interesting, a little voice murmured at the back of her head. *You don't take photos like that if you're not informed.* She ignored it. *He's the right height.* She ignored that, too. Just because he would have been the perfect size for her to be tucked in under his arm when they were walking, didn't mean she had to do it. *He's lovely and broad. Think of being cuddled in.* She didn't. And then she did. And then she made a very cross noise into the unreceptive air and stomped off to make herself coffee and *not*, not, not, *not*, think about Carval. Not at all.

Ten minutes later she was thinking about Carval again. It was like freaking pink elephants. Tell herself not to think about pink elephants and they were the only thing she could think of. He was good looking in a slightly man-next-door way; not too pretty-pretty. Clean-shaven (good: she didn't really appreciate stubble burn – *what?*); nice cologne.

Freaking pink elephants.

She defiantly read her book. She'd found something different. Not Kate Daniels. Not, in fact, any of her extensive (and well-concealed) collection of paranormal urban fantasy, all of which involved big strong men – and intelligent, kick-ass women. She was not going to read anything that involved big strong men.

Right at the back of her bookshelves she'd found a dated, funny little

157

book called Don Camillo. She hadn't even known she had it, she didn't remember ever reading it before, but it was different: old and gentle, and almost philosophical. It was very soothing. She buried herself in the tales of the rural Italian priest and mayor, and didn't think of Carval, or indeed any pink elephants, for the rest of the evening.

In her pre-bedtime shower, however, he tried to sneak back into her thoughts. She ignored him, just as she would have done in reality. She slid into bed and snuggled down, nestled in her pillows and soft quilt – she had been extravagant in buying the best bedlinen she could afford: her sleep was fractured enough without uncomfortable bedding – all patterned in a gentle lilac: flowers and foliage swirling impressionistically on an ivory background. She liked soft hues in her bedroom; though she wore strong shades, towards the cool side of the palette: sea-greens, steel-blues, crimson or indigo.

It was the same throughout her apartment: all her furnishings soft and delicately hued; toning with the golden wood floor and warm rugs. No need to let the sharp edges of her daily life disturb her home: here, she could enjoy the softness and complete contrast to her job. She knew she needed a haven: a safe place in which to switch off.

To switch off from her job – and her father. No matter how she told herself that it was his choice, and she couldn't change it, she worried; and the closer together his binges were becoming, the more that her worry was turning to fear.

Of course, her team would stand with her: support her as she would them. (And she had: they all had. Closed ranks around each other when it had all gotten too much; when one of them had needed it; poured the beers and kept the harder stuff coming; taken them home afterwards and never mentioned it again. They fixed their own issues.)

But her father was beginning to be an issue bigger than she could handle; bigger than they could support her with; bigger than she could hide. She'd been set off balance when Carval mentioned mothers, and she was getting snippy with O'Leary, which he really didn't deserve, even if he shouldn't have been matchmaking.

Her dreams were uncomfortably realistic: the calls, the precincts, the pitying looks – in dreams, those were on the faces of her team, her precinct, her Captain; but they were taken straight from the expression shown by Dawes at the Eighth.

CHAPTER 21

"The cops were talking to me too. Why do they want to talk to me? I didn't have nothing to do with Ricky."

"Don't worry. They're never going to work out about the results. Just keep quiet and we'll be fine."

"But what if they get Mike's footage? What if Ricky managed to keep records? How did he die – did you do anything?"

"No! He was mugged in an alley. Tragic, but nothing to do with us. Look, no-one's ever going to find out about the results, and no-one's ever going to look at you. Just keep calm."

"I'm scared."

"Just come here. I'll make you feel better, just like always. Isn't that better?"

"Yessss. Ohhh, do that again. Come here."

"Don't talk about anything. Don't think about it. We'll be fine. We're going to have a great life."

***

"Yeah, she's gone."

"Will she say anything?"

"No. She's fine. All loved-up and calmed down."

"I don't want problems."

"She won't be."

"Make sure of it. Like last time."

"She won't be a problem. She likes the good things too much to rock the boat. She thinks it's about the results."

"So it is." There was a dark laugh.

"Those cops are really working, though."

"You're worried about a bunch of dumb cops? No way they'll understand. No-one else has, either. Even Terrison hasn't suspected, and if he can't see it, the cops won't." Menace shone through. "But make sure he doesn't. If we go down, you'll be going down harder." Pause. "With more reason."

"He won't suspect."

"Good. Remember. No problems. Problems need to get fixed, before they're too big to fix. So make sure there aren't any."

"If she's a problem I'll deal with it."

"Good. Make sure you do. Before I have to."

CHAPTER 22

Carval checked his phone when it cheeped brightly to see who was interrupting his evening, which he was peacefully spending daydreaming about the feeling of Casey caught in his arms and the feeling of her hand brushing his. She was definitely interested. He couldn't decide, however, whether to push a little, carefully, or to let her come to him. He wasn't exactly convinced that she would come to him, though. Okay, so he'd push a little.

He opened the text, and goggled. O'Leary must be the largest putto ever seen. What was his game? What was Tyler's? Tyler wasn't exactly a pushover, but he wasn't stopping anything. They were a tight team, so clearly they thought that this – he – would fix something, but they wouldn't tell him what it was and Carval was still dead certain sure that it wasn't *just* the photo: that there was something about her mother's early death that was still hurting her. Cancer… not pleasant, for anyone involved.

However, O'Leary had prearranged a time – oops, better just reply: he quickly texted back *ok, there just after 8, will ask for you* – so he was complying with the instructions. If Casey wouldn't talk to him, O'Leary would. One of them might even tell him how the case was going, which would be interesting and help him fit a storyline into his photos. All he really knew was that some high-flying chemist got dead. A little more information would at least ground any shots he took from – what had it been called? Observation? Anyway, maybe Tyler or O'Leary would show him – or better still, Casey. He'd need to work out how to shoot through the window: wasn't it one-way glass? Would it work? He needed to test it.

Okay. He'd be there at eight. Maybe there would even be some interesting changes to the type of people who frequent the precinct: maybe it was different early in the morning from the middle of the day. There was a thought. He should park himself near the doors and take shots at different times. Later in the evening might be really interesting. A link from the panhandlers to the police, perhaps. Hmmm. He scrawled that down on a post-it note, for later thought.

He was still considering all the technicalities about photographing through one-way glass, all the information he'd looked up on the web – strangely, the best information was from animal photographers, from hides – as he drifted into sleep, sprawled out in his plain, unpatterned covers. There wasn't much in his bedroom: only the basics: king size bed, closet, drawer unit with a mirror above it, a chair on which he tended to fling his clothes.

He didn't need more. All his effort and spending went on his cameras and lenses; the high-spec computer system he used; the top-class printer and inks. (It still didn't make a huge dent in the current royalties, no matter what Allan told him. Allan was a worrywart. A *well-paid* worrywart. Carval had a good financial adviser and despite Allan's fussing he did actually take advice. He had savings, and a retirement plan. He was never going to risk being broke.) His photography was everything to him. Sleep overtook him with ease, as he dreamed about his exhibitions.

***

Casey growled at the absence of warrants, even though they'd only requested them yesterday. On the other hand, Tyler had spent some happy time with Belvez's bank records yesterday, and she was looking forward to hearing about that. If there was something, that would be wonderful. If not, that started to clear him from the bad guys' list. She'd like the warrant for Merowin's bank records, and indeed Petersen's too. Despite the confusion of Mikes in Petersen's commentary, Casey was sure that Merowin was on the wrong side. She'd put it all together in her request, but if she got a picky judge, she might not have her warrant. Fingers firmly crossed, she tapped the wooden veneer on her desk.

Superstition didn't work. She'd only got some of her warrants. She scowled, tinged with ferocity at the thought of her next move.

"O'Leary," she called, as soon as she saw his mountainous form. "Intimidation time."

"Guess we're off to Brooklyn in the sunshine, then?"

"What sunshine?"

"The sunshine of catching a killer," Andy interjected on his way to his desk. "Seeing as Tyler and I don't get to go to Brooklyn, we aren't going to see any other sunshine all day."

"You get the fun of bank records," Casey noted. "Seeing as I got all those warrants. Not the landlord, yet." She scowled some more.

Andy bared his teeth nastily. "All of them? Whoop-de-do!"

"Merowin…" Casey enticed. "And if we can get him, maybe we can link it to Telagon, like you suggested? Follow the money, Andy. You're good with that."

Andy was pacified. Casey, on looking round to find O'Leary missing, was not.

"Where'd he go?"

"Dunno," Tyler answered. "Andy, we got all that footage round the Columbia labs and loading bays. You want square eyes or a money headache?"

"I've got a better idea. Let's give the techs square eyes cleaning up the footage so we only have to look at the important pieces. They can take out anything without people. Why waste our time?" They exchanged satisfied smiles.

Smiles faded rapidly when O'Leary reappeared, calling for Andy, and they got a good view of O'Leary's accompaniment.

***

Carval sprang out of bed when the alarm went off, full of thoughts and ideas and techniques he wanted to try. He packed a small camera bag with polarising filters and skirts to reduce reflections, but he was also interested to see whether he could achieve shots of interviews *with* reflections of the observers behind the glass. It might be astonishingly effective: Big Brother (who certainly would be big, if it was O'Leary, he thought with a grin) watching the suspect or witness.

He barely avoided cutting his throat when he shaved, such a hurry was he in; flung on the first t-shirt and pants he grabbed, a light sweater which fortunately toned, since he certainly wasn't paying attention to his choices; tugged on his usual leather jacket and was out the door, bouncing with eagerness and camera to hand, at a time of day which he might otherwise have scorned. He'd take shots at any hour, but he wasn't that fond of early mornings.

It was a very pleasant morning. The light was clear and fresh; there was a slight breeze. It was also rather before the eight a.m. at when he could present himself at the precinct. Carval stopped for coffee in the same small coffee bar to which he had followed Casey originally, and wasted some time in dealing with an Americano and a pastry, glancing at his watch every other second to see if it had moved on and fidgeting restlessly when the time unfairly refused to pass more quickly than its usual sixty seconds to each minute.

At eight precisely he pushed into the precinct and politely asked for O'Leary – definitely not Casey – at the desk.

"Carval," O'Leary's bass vibrato shivered his spine. The grin would have blinded the space station sensors.

"You said I could come."

"Sure. Wanna see our stylish pad?" he snickered.

Carval hesitated for a moment. "I do, but… I really wanna see how

163

Observation – was that what you call it? – works. If I'm going to be allowed to take shots through the glass, I want to see how to do it best. There are so many options. Reflections, lighting, all that."

O'Leary stared. "I think I'll get Andy. He's into all that stuff. Crazy for theatre, so he's likely best to help out." He blinked. "Hafta say, I thought you'd be all over Casey."

Carval flicked him a glance. "I need to take these shots," he said shortly. "Sure, I want to see all of you on home ground" – O'Leary's gaze speared him – "yeah, and Casey, too, but this is my work and I take it seriously."

"So I see," O'Leary said with respect. "So I surely see. C'mon, then. Let's go find Andy, and you'll get a quick look into the bullpen when we do."

Carval followed O'Leary upstairs and was inducted into a hive of apparent chaos. There was noise and buzz and movement, and without thought or memory of wanting to go to Observation he was already taking quick shots without remembering that he was supposed to ask permission of the subject cops first.

"Andy," O'Leary boomed. "Andy!"

The small Chinese-American arrived. "What d'you want, Bigfoot – oh. It's you." He grimaced. "I hope you've made your will."

"It's gonna be just fine," O'Leary rumbled.

His rumbling attracted the attention not just of the foursome but of several other cops as well, who clustered round to see what the new attraction was. Casey looked up, flicked a glance boredly across him, and bent to her work again.

"This is Carval," O'Leary announced happily, without benefit of first name. "He's takin' photos, iffen you want him to. You gotta tell him if you're okay with that. Iffen you ain't, it's no problem, he'll just leave you out. He's not gonna disturb us. Mebbe say if you're not cool with photos."

"Captain know about this?"

"Yep. Authorised it. Anyways, so's you c'n all get over the shock, Andy's gonna show him Observation. When he brings him back, if you're not cool, tell him."

"I'm cool."

"I like photos."

"I'm so good-lookin' I can't resist. I'll be a star."

And a whole lot of similar commentary. *Everyone* wanted to be a star. Casey continued to ignore the whole proceeding with magnificently chilly aplomb. It was so chilly she just *had* to be making an effort to be so.

"Great," Carval said. "I'll be sure and shoot you all, soon as I get back from Observation."

There was a tide of disgruntled mutterings as the chance of instant photography receded. "But I could take a few now, if you like?" Everyone was happy with that idea. "I get the best shots when you're all relaxed and normal. You'll all get to see them," he added. "So if you go back to normal, I'll start."

Amazingly, it worked, though that may have had something to do with O'Leary making shooing gestures at everyone and setting the example by going back to his desk. Carval wandered around for a minute or two, received a few stares, stared back, clowned a little, and then started to shoot when everyone was relaxed. After a few good shots, he wandered back to Andy.

"Can we go see Observation now?"

"Why're you so keen?"

"I need to know how the light works. How the reflections go. I need to see, and try things out. O'Leary said you'd be best because you like theatre, though I don't think I get that. What'd he mean?"

"I don't know. Maybe he thinks I'm good at spotting lighting effects. Come on, then."

Andy led Carval down a dingy corridor, not improved by harsh strip-lights, to a group of rooms. "Interrogation," he explained.

"Can I look in?"

"Sure. This one's empty."

This one was also the one that Carval remembered from his previous meeting with Casey. He didn't like it any better now. He exited.

"Cold," he said.

"We're not running a social centre," Andy said dryly, understanding instantly that Carval didn't mean the temperature. "Here's Observation."

"Would you – um – go sit in the room? So I can take a few shots and work out how this works?"

Andy shrugged. "Can't spare you more than five, ten minutes. We've got a homicide to hunt."

"I'll be quick."

Andy consulted his watch, very obviously. "You've got seven minutes." He whipped out and shortly reappeared in the interrogation room.

Carval spent six and a half minutes trying to work out how best to shoot through one-way glass, and decided that he needed another go later. He wasn't happy with any of it yet.

"How'd it go?"

"Ugh," he said gloomily. The team wasn't helpful.

"We're off to Brooklyn," Casey said unsympathetically, "so you're done with us for today." It sounded very like she'd meant *we are done with you for today*. Considering that she hadn't killed him for hugging her yesterday, that was a touch unkind.

"But we'll be back before lunchtime," O'Leary contradicted, mischief all over his face. "An' Tyler an' Andy'll be here." Casey stiffened, and then stalked back to her desk to collect her purse.

She maintained a flow of inconsequent conversation all the way to Brooklyn, which was not so much highly unusual as unique, covering the bullpen gossip, O'Leary's plans for the weekend (but not hers), the unfairness of them being on shift for any part of any weekend ever and whether it would be nice to go to MOMA. Casey, O'Leary knew, hated all forms of modern art and had been known to suggest that if Andy (naturally) liked it he needed his head examined. When she'd followed up with a comment that she would *open* his head for examination if he suggested she went, he'd desisted. O'Leary, therefore, was quite certain that she didn't want to talk about anything important, and specifically that she didn't want to talk about Carval. That was fine by him. As long as she wasn't doing anything dumb – such as killing any of them – and she was considering even a little light friendship, he was cool. Nudges, not picking them up and banging their lips together. He happily drove along and let her chatter, inserting occasional commentary where required.

They stepped out in Brooklyn into a light, persistent and annoying drizzle. O'Leary grumped as his buzz cut proved entirely insufficient to protect his head from the rain. Casey smirked.

"If you had hair, you wouldn't be complaining."

There was a grin. "Then you wouldn't get the beauty of my head," he drawled.

"You could wear flowers in it," she added mischievously. "That'd be cute."

"You never bring me flowers," he replied dolefully. "If you do, though, they gotta be pink. Suits me better than yellow or blue."

Casey snickered happily. "Let's go talk to Ahlbrechtssen again. I want to know about those cameras." She growled. "If we'd known last time, we'd be days further forward."

Mikael Ahlbrechtssen was not pleased to see them. "You again? What d'you want?"

"Same as last time. Ricky Belvez."

"I told you everything."

"Did you?" Casey enquired with a delicately nasty edge. "You didn't tell me you had hallway cameras."

"You never asked. I never thought about it."

Casey changed tack for a moment, to reduce her irritation. *They* should have noticed, and hadn't.

"What's Karlen Petersen to you?"

"Knew her back in the day in Minneapolis. Used to be, we were close. Didn't work out. Still, we're pals, sorta. She put Ricky on to me, but that was about it."

"She told you Belvez was looking for a rental."

"Yeah."

"But once he got in, she said you weren't so happy with his visitors."

"Wouldn't'a been. I don't allow extras, and Karlen told me that guy was there all the time."

"You check that out?"

"Naw. Belvez paid the rent on time and I had other things to do. She only said that a coupla weeks ago, maybe three. I'd'a got round to it, soon enough."

"She seeing someone here?" O'Leary asked.

"Dunno. Don't care." Two sets of cop eyebrows rose. "I got my own girlfriend. Lizbeth. She don't go wanting all sorts of expensive stuff I can't afford."

"That what Karlen did?"

"Sometimes. Liked the nice things."

Now there was an interesting side note for them to follow up. *If* Karlen was dating Merowin, she couldn't have been seeing much of the nice things in life on a post-doc's salary. *If* Merowin was on a post-doc salary. It was always possible he'd got a trust fund. Andy's work on his bank records would be interesting.

"I see. Okay. About these cameras." Casey took point again. O'Leary had stopped smiling, and when he didn't smile, he was a damn sight scarier than Tyler. Something about the buzz cut. O'Leary looked scary. She *was* scary, and Ahlbrechtssen was about to find that out.

"I want the camera footage, inside and out," she said bluntly.

"I want to see a warrant." He was instantly resistant. Casey's built-up irritation came to her aid.

"Sure you do. And I can get one no problem. But if I have to go away and get a warrant I'll make sure all your other tenants know that I'm looking at it. How's that going to go down? And if I find a single code violation I'll have the city down on you in a New York minute, *Mike.* So. Do you want to be the man who makes my life harder?"

Ahlbrechtssen cringed under the force of personality being projected, but didn't bend. "No," he emitted. "You ain't got the right an' my rentals deserve that you do it properly." He flinched at her stare, but still stood firm.

"Then I'll be back with a warrant as fast as I can get one. And when I look at the footage if there's anything else I'll deal with that too."

Casey stood up in a way that didn't so much imply as bellow her extreme annoyance. Ahlbrechtssen jerked to his feet and didn't quite run to his den as she left. O'Leary watched his scared scuttle with respect for Casey's laser-like intimidation.

They left, wrapped in Casey's considerable aura of complete dissatisfaction. "Why'd he have to know his rights," she bitched. "Now we need that and Terrison to run his tests. Why'd the judge not give me that one?"

"Yeah. Int'restin' about Karlen liking the high life."

"Wasn't it? I don't think Merowin gets paid that much, even if Telagon fund them with millions."

"Mebbe it's true love," O'Leary said with a sarcastic inflection that spoke volumes.

"Yeah, right. And maybe you're really a seven-stone weakling in a *lot* of make-up."

O'Leary's booming laughter filled the SUV. "Amazin' what they c'n do with plastic surgery these days." Casey snorted. "Or trick photos." The second snort was disgusted, but O'Leary didn't push his luck. "Let's get ourselves back an' see what Andy an' Tyler have managed."

***

As Casey left, Carval quietly entered into a discussion with Tyler, which resulted in the pair of them having a low-toned discussion with two other detectives, who had, up till that moment, appeared a tiny bit bored with their case files. Tyler sat back down at his desk just in time for Casey not to spot his discussions as she turned round and collected O'Leary.

Carval, having persuaded Tyler to find him two bored detectives who'd like to be in a photographic exhibition, had wandered off with them to pursue the technical difficulties of shooting from Observation. It took him a while to work it out to his satisfaction, but the two cops didn't seem to mind.

"What've you got?" one of them asked, and they all three spent another few minutes in discussing the interesting effects. Cops, Carval found, could be as interested in a completely different subject as he might be. They sauntered back to the bullpen as the best of pals.

Carval's main point of interest, however, was missing. He looked around, noted that the team was to be found in earnest discussion in a room with a closed door, and decided on a different tack, a little annoyed with himself for missing Casey and O'Leary's return. He sat at Casey's desk, snitched a sheet of paper from a handy pad, and scrawled.

Thanks for the time today. Got what I needed. He thought for a second. He wanted to encourage her to come out with him, even for a coffee, but it wasn't going to happen in work time. Oh, the hell with it. *Call me*, he added, and wrote his number clearly. *I want to show you the photos.* It was a little too close to come up and see my etchings for his liking, but he couldn't think of anything better and he wanted to download these shots and start to play around. He also wanted to know what Allan had so far managed to find on Marcol. Maybe if there was some progress there he'd be able to work out what the problem really was. Besides which, if Casey was on home ground – his home ground – she might not be quite so uptight. All those tiny little visual clues… He dashed off a signature under the words and waved goodbye generically to the bullpen. Some of them even waved back.

CHAPTER 23

Casey noticed that Carval wasn't present, shrugged off her tiny feeling of disappointment, which was entirely ridiculous, and descended upon Andy and Tyler.

"The landlord said Karlen liked the good life. She can't afford that on her salary, I guess, so what's Merowin's like?"

"Merowin's?"

"What's he got to do with Karlen?"

"I think he's her boyfriend." Casey said impatiently.

"Next time, how about telling us?"

"I did."

"Nope."

"I did! Look, it's up there on the board."

They looked. It was. In tiny little letters in a tiny little space, written with a pen that was barely functional, in writing that was hardly legible.

"Telling us?" Tyler said ominously. "That's not telling us."

"You can read. You all scrawl on the board. Told."

"I think you were told too," O'Leary drawled happily. Casey developed a grin. "Even if you need those guys at the museum to translate." The grin disappeared. "What do they call it? Hire o' spliffs? I always thought that sounded like somethin' naughty."

"Hieroglyphs," Andy corrected, and groaned as he saw O'Leary's immense smirk.

"Gotcha."

Andy fell for O'Leary's dumbass act nearly every time. He muttered and groused.

"Anyway, he is. Probably. So I want to know how come he can afford to give her the good life on an academic salary. Have you got his bank records?"

"We do," Andy answered, and spread them out on the desk. Casey peered at them.

"There's nothing obvious here. Not a bad pay-check, though – more than I'd have thought. I didn't see anything on Karlen that looked expensive, though."

"She was in a lab. Nothin's gonna be expensive. All those chemicals might spoil it."

"Didn't we find a Facebook account? Let's have another look at that." Casey smothered a snigger. "Tyler, seeing as you're our man in fashion, you can find it." Tyler pinned her with a hard stare. "Okay, okay. You get the street camera footage, I'll do Facebook." The hard stare dissipated. "Actually, let's just take over that room there and work out where we've got to."

And for the rest of the next hour, they argued and tested out theories and divided up the work between them, and then repaired back to their desks, all annoyed by the landlord's reliance on the law. Three of them were astonished that he did so under the Casey glare.

Casey could see a stray sheet of paper on her otherwise pristine desk from the moment she exited the conference room. She was initially intrigued – who would have left her a note? The bullpen would just yell across when she got back, or wander over. Kent would simply emerge from his office, rather in the manner of the bogeyman from the closet.

She read it with utter astonishment, some horror, and under all of that a small layer of warmth, which she tried very hard to ignore, because it was rapidly dissolving the horror. But instead of crumpling the note up and throwing it in the trash, she folded it neatly and tucked it into her blazer pocket. She had no idea why. No idea that she was letting hit her mind, anyway.

She turned to chasing up the warrant for all of the landlord's camera footage, and every time the note – and in particular the phone number – tried to creep into her mind she punched it away. By the end of the afternoon she might as well have gone twelve rounds with Muhammad Ali, she'd thrown so many ineffective punches. She hadn't had her warrant back, either, which was really annoying.

In fact, a lot of things were annoying about the afternoon. Mike Merowin's financials weren't showing up anything untoward, which was very, very surprising, because Karlen Petersen's Facebook was very, very active and revealing. If Merowin was dating her, what on earth was funding it?

"Second ID?" she said aloud.

"Bit unlikely," Tyler said. "Come'n look at Belvez's records."

Now *that* was interesting.

"Belvez's got two different accounts. Different banks. Different parts of town. One's normal – it's Chase, next to Columbia. One isn't: it's Popular Commercial Bank way up at 181st Street."

She followed Tyler's finger. One account – at Columbia - had all the usual entries – salary, rent, bills, cash, some socialising (not much). The other had quite a different profile. Big deposits from an unknown payer, big cash withdrawals.

"Wow," she said.

"Yeah."

The other two arrived. "Waallll, that's weird," O'Leary rumbled, which seemed to sum things up quite nicely.

"That's not weird, it's dumb," Andy pointed out. Being their resident technogeek seemed to have given him quite a facility with falsity. "So far we got formulae that shouldn't be outside the lab in his home, we got those lens cases hidden in his home, we got confidential formulae on his computer – in his home – and now we got a second bank account *in his own name?* Doesn't all this seem totally dumb to you too?"

They all regarded each other. Put like that, it certainly did. "You think someone's setting him up?"

"I think it's something we should look at. It's so dumb and he should have more brain than that. Bank account in his own name?"

"Someone's overplayed their hand."

"Might go see if Belvez's photo matches."

"Does the address on the statements match anyone else's address?"

"Naw, it's Belvez's too. But it's an internet account. No postal statements."

"Okay, Tyler, you thought of it, you get to go see if they recognise Belvez." Casey furrowed her brow. "You know, I thought Merowin was the man most likely. But how would he be able to do all this?"

"Students are good at fake ID."

"Yeah, but for opening bank accounts? That takes a bit more than just bluffing your way past the bartender or bouncers."

"How'd you know that?" Andy asked mischievously.

Casey gave him a bland face. "Gossip," she said. "Okay, Tyler, when are you going to do that?"

"It's after five thirty on Friday. Not going to be open when I get there." He tapped a search out. "Opens again at nine tomorrow. I'll call them now."

"Okay. Terrison should come back to us tomorrow too. I want that warrant," she sulked.

"Friday, yeah?"

"That's not the point. Criminals don't take the weekend off, and we don't get to, so why can't I have my warrant?"

"Bank's no help till Monday," Tyler said, returning. Casey growled.

O'Leary patted her on the head. He was the only one who'd dare. "They'll come through. Stop frettin'. Disturbs my chi."

Andy spluttered. "Bigfoots have *chi?*"

"Sure we do. Truckloads of it. How'd you think I'm always so relaxed?"

Andy descended into unimpressed muttering. The rest of the team discussed the possibility that it was all a somewhat clumsy set up for a while longer, but nothing they currently had – including the nothing of the non-existent warrant – was helping. Eventually, they left. Since they were on shift again tomorrow – though next Saturday they'd be off – no-one was receptive to the idea of beer. O'Leary's immense form drooped, but they weren't sympathetic.

Casey simply wanted to go home and consider the note which, now that she had no case to distract her, was burning a hole in her pocket.

She managed to resist re-reading it until she'd fixed her dinner and added a consoling soda. If she hadn't still been stung by her father's latest episode, she might have had a glass of wine, or a beer. Then she read the note again. *Call me,* and a number.

He was pushing. Not a lot, but coupled with the hand-brushing, he was pushing. And the hug. She couldn't forget the hug. She *wished* she could forget the hug, because then she'd know it hadn't affected her in the slightest. Unfortunately, her body was seriously overriding her brain, and it was saying *yes, again.* She put the note in her gun safe, and resolutely ignored it, all evening. It didn't make her feel any better.

***

"Allan? Allan!" Jamie called as he bounded downstairs to the office, early on Saturday, bypassing the studio. The office was empty. "Allan!"

"Up here," echoed down. "Looking at your board."

Jamie bounded back up. "Great, isn't it?" he enthused.

"I guess," Allan said. "For this stage. You'll need to do a lot more to get it ready for showing."

Jamie glared at him. "At this stage, it's amazing. I've never been this ready this early."

"Don't get carried away. You've got a lot still to do."

"Don't rain on my parade. Anyway, I've got more. I came back to download them and arrange them."

"Good," Allan said in a very parentally annoying fashion.

"You're not my mom, Allan," Jamie growled. "Stop it." His good mood considerably dented, he plugged in the camera and started it downloading.

"Did you get anything on Marcol yet?"

Allan smiled in an infuriatingly *I-know-something-you-don't-know* fashion, which didn't help Jamie's mood one tiny little bit.

"Allan, stop screwing around. I'm not in the mood."

"Okay. You've lost your sense of humour this week."

Jamie scowled. Allan carefully didn't ask *is she still avoiding you?*, mainly because Jamie's object of desire clearly was. Poking a bad-tempered Jamie was probably not his best plan.

"I've got some stuff. Only the basics, so far."

Jamie's scowl cleared. "Let's hear it, then."

"Mark Jarryd Marcol. 32 years old, based in Queens. Detective, in Narcotics. Well thought of. His family's all cops, too. Good professional record. I've got a photo, downstairs. Graduated second in his class. Guess who was first?"

"Don't need to guess. It was Casey. Aka Detective K. Clement."

"Yeah."

"Nothing else?"

"Not yet. Do you want anything else? You're paying."

Jamie thought, slow menace sliding through his eyes and curling his mouth unpleasantly. "Not yet," he decided, in unwitting repetition. "No. Not yet. We're going to do something different." That same hunched aggression shifted his shoulders. "You're going to write him one of your nice letters. You know the kind. The ones which accuse him of breach of copyright, mention damages – and yes, I know there's no loss, but he won't – and oh-so-politely make it clear that he's six feet deep in the shit. Let's see what that brings." His lips turned up, but Allan couldn't have called it a smile. "I want him scared." A few more teeth appeared. "Really scared." He smiled very nastily.

Allan really didn't like that idea. Messing with cops would be a bad plan from the get-go. Jamie was on a mission, however, and the only way to stop that would be for it to come to an end.

"Can we talk about this exhibition instead, now that's settled?"

"Yeah. What've you got?"

Allan started on the major points of hall, quantity, timing, cost… and after no more than five minutes it was obvious that Jamie had zoned out. He was printing out shots, which was a good guide to where his attention was.

"So I'll tell them you'll do it for free, next week?"

"Yeah – No!" Jamie woke up, and smiled apologetically. "Okay, I wasn't listening."

"You never do."

"But you fix it so well. Work your magic. I'll even promise not to take shots of you for a month."

"No, you'll promise not to nag me about wanting shots of me for a month."

Jamie laughed, and held his hands up in a placatory gesture. "Okay."

Allan tip-tapped downstairs, leaving Jamie to select and arrange.

***

Later on Saturday evening, still in a bad mood, entirely because Casey hadn't been in contact and he was completely unwilling to give in to his nagging impulse and ring her anyway, Carval was deep in rearrangement and storyboarding when his cell phone rang. He didn't recognise the number, and who would be calling him at after seven anyway? Allan had gone home long ago, and Carval was currently single. O'Leary would text to tell him any plan, not call.

"Jamie Carval," he answered, with an irritated edge at being disturbed. There was silence from the other side of the call. "Who is it?"

"It's Casey. Sounds like it's a bad time. No problem."

"Stop! Don't hang up."

It was Casey. She called. She'd actually called. And she was about to run away.

"It's okay."

"No, don't go. I'll call you back if you hang up. Where are you?"

"Precinct." She didn't sound particularly happy with the day.

"You want to see the photos?"

"Yeah."

"Okay. Come by." He gave the address of the apartment. "Buzz the second floor. That's the studio."

And his living space was just upstairs, but he didn't mention that. He also removed the initial photo that had started all this off. He didn't want her to see that one. He didn't ask himself why.

It took longer than he expected for her to buzz: the precinct wasn't that far away. He'd begun to think that she'd bailed; taken fright and run away. He'd almost called her back, but then decided that she'd definitely spook at that. *Take it easy, Jamie. Take it slow.* And he definitely would not think *take her slow.*

He let her into the building, and waited till there was a rap on the studio door. She was dressed in her normal professional garb, no hope of a skirt, or a dress, or even something more casual than dress pants and a blazer – well, of course she hadn't changed, when would she have? She'd said she'd been in the precinct. Her expression was very different, however. On the job, she was fiercely focused. Now, she was uncertain, doubt swirling in her eyes and her posture giving the impression that she was poised to flee rather than enter. Framed in the doorway, she could go either way. He clamped down on a burning desire to start taking shots.

She swallowed, and stepped in.

"Hey." There was no trace of her uncertainty in her voice. "I came to see your photos." The tone said *snaps*. The face still said that she was unsure whether she should be here, why she had come at all.

Carval closed the door behind her. There was another flicker across her face, a tiny movement of her gaze, as if she'd stopped herself turning round before her body could move.

"They're there." He pointed. "Want a coffee?"

"No, thank you."

"How was the day?"

"Cross-checking, analysis."

That didn't sound fascinating.

Two firm steps later, she was in front of his board: terrifyingly intent and silent. He looked from his shot of her to her in the flesh. Her gaze took it all in, studying, assessing; her frame motionless. She hadn't taken off her blazer.

Carval moved to stand a little behind her, not quite touching her; but he knew she was aware of his proximity: that same thin line of colour tinting her cheekbone; an infinitesimal hitch in her breathing; a nervous swipe of tongue over dry lips which he could see from the slight angle of his height and placement. Looking down, the clip confining her hair had worked a little loose and was slipping at an angle, a tendril escaping, curling softly down on to the nape of her neck. The air was hot around them, but there was no touching. All she'd have to do to break the spell, disperse the heat, would be to step away.

She didn't step away.

She had to have known he was there: closer than good manners might dictate, close enough for his breathing to ruffle the tiny wisps of hair at her ears. But she hadn't moved away, hadn't broken the gathering tension between them, hadn't stopped him.

He wouldn't stop himself.

He ran the errant lock through strong, sure fingers, and then moved up to release the clip. Her hair fell loose, waving silkily over his hand, and the shock of touch raced up his arm. She turned round, and looked up, mouth opening on words that were never said as he leaned down and in to kiss her, that same hand closing around her skull to hold her for his delicate exploration, his other arm around her waist.

And suddenly it wasn't gentle or delicate any more at all. It was intent, possessive, passionate: she was tight-held and heat rose in his body as she was close-caught against hard weight. He pulled her up on to her toes; lifted her and then with her still there landed in his chair; brought her down into his lap and never left her mouth.

He wasn't sure he *could* leave her mouth: lush and hot, soft on his; almost shy. He wasn't feeling shy. Anything but shy – but he needed not to lose control; not to push too fast and spook her. But again, she fit so perfectly in his lap: just the right size to curl in and tuck against his shoulder, raise her face to his for his hard, devouring kisses. He fought his own want; fought only to hold her close but not confined; to ensure that he would be able to tell the instant she backed off.

And yet she was tucked against him, not backing off, kissing him back like she might just mean it. He lifted off for a second, only to move around her cheek: butterfly kisses to tease and wind her higher until he nibbled a little at her ear and she squeaked and wriggled – *oh God, do that again, Casey, wriggle again* – and tried to force him back to her mouth.

"You're ticklish," he murmured, pleased appreciation in his voice. "It's cute." She growled at him, but there was an undertone of arousal, so he guessed she wasn't really cross. In revenge, she nipped at him. "That's not nice."

"Don't tickle me, then."

He stroked a hand through her hair, round and down to curve around her arm and keep her settled against him. Her head slipped on to his shoulder. He leaned back fractionally, taking her with him, and carefully cosseted her, so that she wouldn't notice that she was still here; still his. He tipped her chin up, and kissed her again; slipped her blazer from her to reveal the steel-blue silky t-shirt: again, no necklace, no bracelet, tiny stud earrings, dark navy dress pants. Stroking the t-shirt was irresistible. Her hand cupped his face: the elegant fingers curved around his jaw. Her tongue flirted with his lips, darted within and teased him to follow it back to its home.

So far, so good: he was taking it slow and easy.

Right up until his fingers slid under the silky fabric of her t-shirt on to the silky skin of her back, and she gasped. Her eyes sprang wide, realisation of where she was and what she was doing and with whom spilled in. He stopped his movement, but didn't remove his hands.

He sensed the instant she gave in again, and took hard, quick advantage, moving over the curve of her throat and down, exploring the scooped neck of her t-shirt and, carefully, his hand began to roam. She sighed softly and ran hands into his hair: he explored a little further, still cautious, but less so; another contented noise, close to a purr; and he palmed those particularly enticing curves. She flexed, and pushed against his fingers.

"Like that?" he murmured darkly. "So hot." He kissed her searchingly.

She curled closer, and delicate fingertips, those long, elegant digits, explored his jaw, neck, shoulders, the opening of his button-down. It was unbelievably arousing, but he couldn't lose control; couldn't take her upstairs and tumble her into bed and keep her there all night until he'd unlocked all her secrets. He was not going to treat this like it was only a one-night stand. Too much rode on it, and his exhibition wasn't going to be damaged because he was behaving like an over-sexed teen. He tried not to listen to the little voice that said *and you want more of Casey too.*

He lifted off and petted, at least until he worked out that petting would lead straight back to stroking and palming and…*stop*. Casey, curled in his clasp like a contented cat, made an irritated little noise and then blinked at him.

"I should go," were the first words from her mouth.

"No." It was reflex. Certainly there was no thought involved.

"Uh?"

"Don't go. Have some dinner, or a drink" – huh? Her face hadn't changed, but there was tension in the air – "coffee, or something." He smiled happily as the tension slipped away. "Tell me stories about being a cop. Surely it must be funny sometimes."

"Dinner?"

"Yeah. Food. Well, takeout. I don't cook that much."

She stared at him, as if a dinner invitation wasn't anything she expected. She wasn't saying *no* though. Not yet.

"C'mon. I'm hungry." Not surprising: it's after eight. "I've got menus upstairs." Still staring, from shocked silence. "You do eat?"

"Yes," she snipped.

"Well, c'mon then. I don't bite. Unless you ask nicely," he added, and smirked evilly. It raised a scowl. Carval, already impatient, stood her up, stood up himself, looked down, couldn't resist, crushed her in and kissed her again, hard, pressing against her. She really was mostly legs, because she was just not that tall, but she was perfectly aligned in that position. So he held her there, because it felt so good. *She* felt so good. His hand slid down and cupped her ass. More delicious curves, followed by a delightful wiggle.

"Kiss me," he murmured. "Kiss me, Casey."

And she *did*. So he did: taking her luscious mouth and teasing until she made soft, sexy noises and curved against him, not much above his shoulder: unbelievably soft and yielding. She fit: she could have been made to fit his form, and she was *hot*. His kiss continued, probing, searching; demanding a positive answer to the single question *do you want me?*

Finally he lifted off, not letting go, clinging to his self-restraint with his fingernails; clinging to Casey with both broad hands, enclosing her. She was still curved in, lax in his grip, sleepy-eyed and oh-so-sexy. He couldn't resist, and didn't try: ducking his head to explore her mouth again, the curve of her neck, the lobe of her ear, a nerve beneath it where she wriggled again; right where he wanted her.

"Come and have dinner," he said, in default of *have dinner and then let's go to bed*. Her eyes filled with doubt, erasing the warmth that had been there.

"I should go."

"Don't. Have some dinner, then go." *No, don't go at all.* Saying that would not help. "C'mon. Not eating is bad for you."

She slowly raised both eyebrows, eyes cool and cynical now. It was rather spoilt by the fact that she was still tucked neatly into his arms. He didn't point that out. She might have pulled away.

"I think I'm old enough to decide what's good for me."

Carval bit his tongue on *I'm good for you. Let me show you just how good.* He wouldn't have a tongue shortly, if he had to keep biting it. But she still hadn't moved away. He didn't push. He wanted to. He wanted to kiss her again; take her upstairs; take her – and then shoot her, tousled and tumbled and gorgeous against the sheets and pillows: a blaze of lush femininity against the plain, masculine linen and wood of his bed: perfect contrast. He could see it full-formed in his mind's eye –

And he couldn't ever do it. It would be perfect, and it was never going to happen.

CHAPTER 24

Casey had nearly not called, then almost put the phone down when he'd answered: irritable and annoyed – but he'd been surprised, and then there'd been an odd note of almost-desperation that she should have come round. But she'd still almost chickened out. Because she had known – knew – perfectly well that this had had nothing whatsoever to do with looking at the photos, and everything to do with how it had felt when she'd tripped and he'd caught her. She'd delayed her arrival: knowing that it was a step into something she wasn't sure she wanted; somewhere she wasn't sure she was ready or able to go.

So she'd hesitated in the doorway – she never hesitated: always decisive, cool and calm and clear and sure – she'd hesitated, and then walked in, certainty and assertion in her step, in her voice; butterflies flocking in her stomach. She could feel him watching her as she surveyed his board: the shots astonishing even in the raw; terrifyingly exposing. But none solely exposing her: where she was the focus it was her back or profile; where her face was fully on show it was as part of the team. It was bad, but it wasn't quite unbearable.

Then, prowling, he was behind her: tall, broad, looming without quite being intimidating. The tension rose between them; she was completely aware of him, standing a fraction too close. All she needed to do was step away.

She didn't step away, knowing it was making a choice, knowing she should have moved away, pretending she didn't notice or care.

When he stroked through a loose curl, and then undid her clip to free the dark locks; she turned to him, unsure whether the words gathering in her throat were protest or invitation; but he didn't wait: hand sliding surely into her hair and then mouth meeting hers; his other arm latching around her and bringing her in against a broad, firm chest. Her own hands slipped around his neck, and she opened to the gently searching kiss.

It was electric. As soon as she let him in, it fired up: sparking through her skin and down her veins: he bent to her – so much bigger than she: surrounding her, enfolding – and pulled her upward and against him to press against muscle and strength, before he descended into a chair and perforce took her with him, still searching her mouth with firm lips and demanding tongue, until he lifted off and nibbled round her neck and ear and *oh* that tickled and she *hated* being tickled anywhere but it felt so *good*. She squirmed in his lap and tried to turn to make him kiss her properly.

The overgrown *rat* was laughing. Worse, now he knew she was ticklish and that was *not* what she wanted. And she was *not* cute. She ignored the little tendril of heat that curled in her chest at his sleepy, sensual tone, and nipped him chidingly, to no effect. Instead, he petted her, a smooth stroke over her hair and round her shoulder to cosset her closer and *oh,* he was large and warm and just what she liked and wanted, a little male assertiveness to kiss her again, stroke over her t-shirt – didn't she have a blazer on? – and she glided her own hand up and round his jaw, a little stubbled that late in the day though he'd been clean-shaven earlier; stretched a smidgeon to bring her mouth to his and tease him in return. It had been a while since she bothered with a boyfriend: too busy to find someone, when she hadn't time or inclination to make any effort, nor time or inclination to a one night stand.

It was all good. Nothing that she couldn't explain away, or stop. Nothing too much, or too hot... but she shouldn't... she should stop this...

And then his hand was on her skin, and *everything* exploded, shattering her restraint and sense.

His fingertips were searing little circles into her skin: flame flickering through her nerves and over her back, and *how* had this exploded so quickly into scorching heat and hardness at her hip and if she wanted more all she'd have to do was copy his motion...

The hell with caution. He felt so *good*.

She yanked his head to hers and ravaged his mouth, taking as if she had the right, conquering him by sheer surprise and for a moment she had complete control and used it to flick his button-down open halfway, slip her hands inside and on to the firm frame of his shoulders – *ohhhh* that had worked. Carval's big frame and hard muscle suddenly turned on her and she was trapped: caught and held and control had flipped to him but she didn't mind that, loved the switch to assertive male possessiveness that allowed her to let go and simply enjoy. A wide hand spanned her back, the other kept her placed for her mouth to be taken back, and she surrendered the lead without a qualm or regret. He touched more assertively, she curled against the touch and he palmed her, murmuring velvet vice into her ear, then taking her mouth with complete conviction: intimate stroking that left her lax and purring, exploring on her own account and beginning to dip into the vee of his shirt to investigate some interestingly firm muscles.

And then he stopped. This was not the idea at all. She growled. And then she realised where she was and what was happening and what she was doing.

"I should go," she stated. Oh. That was not a popular statement. She didn't think he'd even realised that he was trying to give her orders, and surely not that his arms tightened as if to prevent her. But – dinner? That was…weird. She'd been expecting – oh. *Oh.* Oh yes. She melted and flowed and he was just *perfectly* fitting as he kissed her some more, paused: she was luxuriating in his broad frame and he was just what she liked.

What harm would dinner do?

"Okay," she said. "Dinner." Even though she knew that dinner wasn't the only option on offer.

Carval steered her upstairs with a large, warm hand on her waist, into a sparsely decorated apartment: a few (excellent) photos on the walls; comfortable furniture, a partly opened door to a bedroom. She didn't think about that. *Live in the moment.* She needed some unthinking moments.

She turned into Carval, reached up, and pulled his mouth to hers. His response was instant and effective, one hand in her loose hair, one bringing her tightly against hard body and an unmistakable arousal. She moved against him, opened under his lips, widened her stance just a fraction and he rolled against her which produced an incredibly erotic answering roll of her hips. It was too much, too good, and she succumbed to sweet sensation and temptation.

He walked her backwards, no longer caring that this was moving too fast, lost in the lush depths of her mouth and the luscious curves of her body, the little sexy noises as she kissed him just as hard as he was kissing her; lost in the moment and sheer desire. Her elegant fingers slipped down, flicking open his button-down; his hand slipped under her t-shirt where it had been loosened from her pants, broad span encompassing her back, the clip of her bra, leaving that for now; gliding round over smooth skin to encroach on those arousing curves, to make her gasp and push into his hands. Her own hands slid down to his ass, and *oh* this was a woman who knew what she wanted. Him. And he certainly wanted her.

He pushed her back on to the bed, her shoes falling from her feet; and toed his own shoes off to loom above her; her dark curls messy on the pillow and just as he'd imagined as he lowered himself to her, an arm beneath her neck, the other free to roam; and roam it did, opening the narrow belt, the dress pants, no less arousing than her hands on him. Hot became frantic, desperate for skin-to-skin, clothes were tugged away and while her fingers circled and slid, his dipped and found slick wet heat and as much need and want as he had. He growled, deep in his chest, and she gave a tiny mewl that fired him up and then he rose and she guided him home and *fuck* she was amazing as he brought her over and came himself.

After, she made a soft purring noise and snuggled in; quite unlike her workaday behaviour. He'd never expect her to be snuggly, but he liked it. He wrapped her in comfortably, and quite satisfied, drifted into sleep.

In the middle of the night, he woke, chilled, and with a feeling of space where space ought not to be. He reached out, and found nothing; listened, and heard nothing; switched on the light, and saw nothing. She had gone.

The damn woman had *run away*. He punched the pillow, fulminating all the while. Fulmination was fuelled by considerable frustration. He'd really thought that he'd got somewhere.

He'd really wanted to get somewhere, and – amazingly – somewhere hadn't just been bed; but as soon as they'd finished, she'd *run away*. He'd thought it was men who were only supposed to want a quick fuck. Well, he wasn't playing that game. He sulked industriously. He'd *liked* how she felt. And tasted. And kissed, and how she'd made little sexy kittenish noises and wriggled and curved and then sank against him. He'd liked how she was just right: just tall enough to kiss, short enough to be delicate and snuggled in. She had fit just right with her head on his chest, his arm around her, their legs tangled.

But then she'd *run away*.

He went to have an unpleasantly cool shower which did nothing to relieve his frustration and still less to erase the memory of a happy, sexy, responsive and above all *hot* Casey in his grasp. In fact, it didn't help in the slightest. Nor, when he woke again in the morning and attained the precinct, meaning to find explanations, did discovering that the team was off shift on Sunday.

Eventually, still seriously annoyed, he parked himself a little way from the precinct doors, far enough not to be noticed or noticeable, and took shots of all the forms of human life which entered. Supplicants and criminals; victims and perpetrators; cops and civilians; old and young. All human life passed through the portal. When he was done, he was somewhat happier. His work always soothed him.

And he wasn't giving up his exhibition just because she *ran away*.

***

Casey made it home in a highly suspect time largely induced by sheer panic, barely pausing at each stop light. She tore into a scaldingly hot shower, and tried desperately to put her wholesale stupidity behind her. All her intentions to stay away from complications, to keep a safe and sensible distance, not to open up any possibilities of having to reveal her life, had blown up the moment he'd made a move. Of course he had made a move. He'd been making moves from moment one. This move had simply been a lot less subtle and a lot more assertive, and she hadn't made the slightest objection.

The shower didn't help one little bit. Possibly a scalding shower hadn't been the best idea to cool her scalding shame. She huddled into a warm robe, and hoped that the ground would open up and swallow her before Monday. At least she was off shift tomorrow: she could go running – outside Manhattan. With her current luck, she'd run into Carval if she stayed in the city, which was the last thing she needed.

Her sleep was fractured and unrestful: the sheets were tangled in the morning from her tossing and turning. It wouldn't have been nearly as bad if her dreams hadn't been almost as hot as her shower. Eventually she took herself out to the Van Cortland Park, parked up, and ran for as long as she could stand, stretching out in the thin sunshine. It helped. A little. With every mile her car covered back into the city, however, she curled more tightly into herself: memory and shame pressing her inward. By the time she was home, all the good the run might have done her was gone, except for the calorie burn. It wouldn't make up for the planned ice-cream pity party, but she didn't care about that either.

Late on Sunday night, she fell into bed, not one whit consoled by running, ice-cream, hot shower or cool body lotion. At least tomorrow she'd have work. She could always lose herself in that. She firmly ignored any stupid little niggly voices telling her she had lost herself in Carval. That way lay disaster. The photographs he'd already taken were bad enough. He didn't even know her and he was exposing her inner life: it was like the old idiocy that a photograph stole a piece of your soul. She'd never believed in that nonsense, but seeing her – their – faces laid out on his board, she was beginning to wonder. She couldn't bear to let anyone more know about her history, know about her present. Her team knowing was quite enough.

By six a.m. on Monday, restless and sleepless, she was up and out. The precinct was empty, her coffee was strong, and burying herself in her work soothed her mixed emotions of appalled shame at how far she'd gone and an unpleasant feeling that she should be even more shamed by running away. She hunched into herself as she drank yet more espresso, and stayed head down until the rest of the team arrived. It was easy to hide in the plan for the day, and not one of the team asked her any difficult questions.

Tyler was disappearing in the direction of the bank as Casey's phone rang.

"Clement."

"Detective, it's John Terrison. Can you come and see me?"

"Sure. Why?"

"These gels aren't doing what I think they should."

"We'll be there shortly. Have you talked to anyone else about this?"

"No."

"Good. Don't."

"I'll be here. Bye."

"O'Leary, we're off to Columbia. Terrison's got a problem with those gels. He wants us down there."

Ten minutes later, they were at the university.

"Hey," Casey said. "What's up?"

"I can't replicate Merowin's results. I don't get it." He regarded Casey piteously.

"Okay," she soothed. O'Leary stood conveniently blocking the doorway. "Why don't you come for a little walk, and you can tell us about it in private." That meant: where Merowin – or anyone else – couldn't accidentally overhear. "We'll see you outside in a minute or two."

A few moments later Terrison joined them outside. "Where are we going?" he asked. "I can't be away from the lab for long. Mike wants to talk to me." Casey and O'Leary exchanged a very suspicious glance over his unwitting head. "He said he needs to discuss the Telagon funding. I can't put that off."

"We'll be quick, but we need to do this right. We'll bring you back, fast as we can."

They whisked up to the precinct and installed Terrison in a comfortable conference room, supplied him with their own coffee and got settled. O'Leary's phone tweeted as they brewed the coffee, but after a quick reply he put it away.

"So what's up?" Casey asked.

"I tried to make both syntheses," Terrison emitted unhappily, "and then tested them, but though I could replicate Ricky's results, I just can't make Mike's work at all. I don't know what's wrong. And there's no way Ricky's wasn't better than Mike's, when I synthesise them both. None of it makes any sense. Why would Ricky have *Mike's* papers, when Ricky's compound was so much better?"

It made an unfortunate amount of sense to the detectives: however, they weren't going to ruin Terrison's day.

"Thank you, Professor," Casey said. "O'Leary'll take you back down to Columbia, so you don't lose time."

"I really don't want to believe that Mike falsified his results," Terrison mourned. "It's just not how I thought of him."

"Mm," Casey hummed sympathetically. "Look, um, I don't want to spook you, but something's clearly going on around your lab. Try not to get left on your own, hmm, and don't discuss this with *anyone*."

Terrison stared at her, horrified. "Are you suggesting...?"

"I don't know anything, yet. I do know that you should be careful. It might be nothing. If it is, no harm done. If not..."

She let the implication hang in the air.

"Let us know when you're ready to go."

They gave Terrison a minute to collect himself. Outside the door, O'Leary looked grimly at Casey.

"Not lookin' too good for Merowin."

"No. If you're down at Columbia anyway, can you go talk to Karlen again?"

"Sure," O'Leary drawled. "She's got a bit of explainin' to do. Startin' with how she's fundin' her lifestyle. I can't afford smart restaurants an' cocktails ev'ry month, let alone ev'ry week."

"Precisely."

At that point, Terrison, white and depressed, emerged, and O'Leary gently swept him away.

Casey returned to the bullpen and bypassed her desk to hit the coffee machine. It was eleven, she'd already had five coffees, and not one of them had had the slightest impact on her dragging tiredness or her bitter disappointment at her own behaviour during the weekend.

"Nice machine," said an unwelcome voice.

"What are you doing here?"

"Getting a coffee."

"There's a bar down the street."

"I've been working with the one-way glass," Carval said bluntly. He did not say *and waiting for you to show up*.

"That's nice," she commented insincerely.

Carval lost his minimal patience. "What was up on Saturday?" he snapped. "You snuck out without a word."

"I wanted to go home."

Carval flicked a sharp glance at her, and changed his first, blistering response. "I wouldn't have stopped you," he said quietly. There was something in her voice…something under the hard shell. He thought she was about to answer, when Tyler strode in.

"Thought you were taking pictures in Interrogation?" he asked.

"I was. I wanted a drink."

Casey slid away, unnoticed.

"What's going on?" Tyler questioned, one half-tone short of accusation.

"Ask her. I don't know."

Tyler inspected him, and didn't trouble to conceal it. "No bruises. 'Kay. No issue."

"Uh?"

"You tried anything she didn't want, you'd have bruises. Or bullet wounds. You don't. No issue. Bigfoot'll want a word, later, though."

He left again. Carval took his coffee and went back to the known difficulties of shooting through one-way glass. It was less confusing than Casey and her team.

Tyler wandered back to his desk, thinking. He wouldn't tell Casey, but he'd heard Carval's first sentence, and Casey's reply. Looked like Casey'd found some distraction. Also looked like Carval was deeper in than she was. Hm. No reason to add words to that mix. He'd just watch. Casey was theirs, and they took care of their own. Carval could look after himself. They didn't know him. Yet.

Looked like they were going to, though.

CHAPTER 25

"Got it!" Casey emitted triumphantly. Finally, something had gone right today.

"What?"

"My warrant. Who wants to come with me to get the landlord's camera footage?"

"Me," said the still unwelcome voice behind her.

"Got the bank records," Tyler noted. "Gotta go through that with Andy." Andy was rather more surprised by that than Casey appreciated. O'Leary being Cupid was normal. Tyler getting in on the act was not. She growled.

"You've got to let me tag along," Carval pointed out. "Anyway, I've taken enough shots in here."

"Fine," she grated. "I'm going now."

She stalked out and down the stairs to her car, pursued by Carval's looming form and aura of befuddled annoyance. She just *knew* he was going to start a conversation about Saturday, and she really, really didn't want to have it.

By almost the whole of the way to Brooklyn, Carval hadn't said a word, though his camera had whirred and buzzed. Casey hadn't said anything either. The longer the silence endured, the more tense she became; and her fingers were tight on the steering wheel.

"Once you've got your footage, I'll buy you lunch."

"I can get my own lunch."

Carval huffed out an exasperated breath. "Fine. But we are sitting down and having lunch – and coffee, since that's actually what's in your veins instead of blood – and a break." *And a conversation*, he didn't say, very loudly indeed.

"I need to get back. Work."

"So do an hour of unpaid overtime. You do anyway, so it's not like you're going to miss out on your non-booked front row theatre seats. Anyway, you're supposed to get lunch."

"Solving this murder is far more important than having lunch." *And wasting time on you* hung in the air, unsaid but very audible.

She parked without a further word, until she'd exited the car and both of them were standing on the sidewalk.

"You'll have to wait here."

"Fine," Carval bit back.

Casey, in thunderous mood, stormed up the stairs to find Ahlbrechtssen in his office.

"Mr Ahlbrechtssen, I have the warrant," she stated, hammering down her anger at Carval to maintain her professional behaviour, and put it right under his nose. "Now, please give me the footage." Despite the addition of *please*, it was an order, not a request.

Ahlbrechtssen read through the warrant carefully, under Casey's harsh stare, and then handed her it back. "Fine. Give me ten minutes."

Ten minutes later, he appeared with three discs. "There you are. All the footage over that time."

"Thank you," Casey achieved, and left.

Carval, infuriatingly, was sitting on the hood of her car, humming to himself and gazing round. He seemed perfectly relaxed, right up until Casey unlocked the doors and he spotted her.

"Got them," she said briskly, and made to open the door.

"That didn't take long."

"No. Now I'm going back to review them."

Much to her surprise, Carval simply slid into the passenger seat. She'd expected another fight about lunch. Somewhat deflated, she started up and moved off without comment. Nothing was said, all the way back.

"Thanks for the ride," he said, as he got out, already checking his phone. His eyebrows lifted, and he tapped out a reply.

"No problem," Casey said, and, not just deflated but uncomfortably conscious that she should be trying to apologise for her behaviour, glanced uncomfortably at him. "Um… did you still want to get lunch?"

Carval almost dropped his phone. "You what now?" He recovered some game. "Thought you had work," he snipped.

"Fine. I do."

Casey turned on her heel and was four steps towards the precinct entrance before he caught her, a hand on her shoulder halting her charge.

"Yes, I want to get lunch. But only if you actually talk. You haven't said a word for the last hour and I'm not interested in Trappism."

His hand slid down from her shoulder to her wrist, and then slipped through her cold fingers. He looked down at her, but all he could see was the top of her head and an edge of ear.

"I need to drop the discs off."

"I'll wait."

He did: rather longer than he'd expected, and he was pretty much ready to walk away when she hurried out of the doors. From her expression, she hadn't expected him still to be there.

"O'Leary needed to bring me up to speed," she said. In no way was it an excuse, or apology. Simply this-is-how-it-was.

"Okay. Let's go up to Studebakers."

She shrugged. "Fine. As long as they're quick."

"What was up on Saturday?" Carval said, his limited patience at an end less than twenty yards from the precinct.

"I wanted to go home."

He hadn't got a response to that which wasn't *well I wanted you to stay.* Childish back-and-forth wasn't going to improve matters.

"Okay," he said instead, not particularly warmly.

"I should've left a note."

His jaw dropped. "Uh?"

But that was the extent of Casey's words. She'd retreated right back into her cool-cop shell, her walk clicking down hard on the sidewalk, a small but significant distance between them. Carval dropped back four strides, which Casey entirely failed to notice, pulled out his camera, and shot a few pictures; then caught up again just before they reached the café.

"Why didn't you leave a note?"

"I wanted to go home."

"That's getting old already. I get that. What was wrong anyway? It's not like there was anyone to interrupt."

"It...I never meant to."

"Didn't mean to leave or didn't mean to sleep with me?" Carval challenged, fed up and annoyed with her complete refusal to open up. "Because you were doing a pretty good job of pretending to enjoy it."

She spun round, eyes blazing, face white with fury. "I don't fake," she bit out. "Not like your photos."

"My photos are *not* faked," Carval bit straight back. "And if this is still about whoever stole my shot of you that's still not on *me.*" He drew an angry breath. "Anyway, it didn't matter. You think it was a mistake. Fine. It still doesn't get you out of me taking photos of the team. You can see them in the exhibition like everyone else. Or not. I don't care."

He marched off, leaving her by the café door, white and just as angry as he.

She slammed in, ordered, and stomped back to the precinct as furious as she had been at the café. Tyler looked up, clocked her mood, and made absolutely sure he didn't catch her coruscating gaze. Andy took the same route to continued existence. O'Leary, however, not only caught her eye but opened his mouth too.

"You gonna look at this footage, Casey?" he said, "'Cause I think you need to do somethin' that don't involve people. We solve murders, we don't commit them."

"Yes," she snapped, and retired to a room to watch the footage with the door firmly shut against the world.

"What happened there, then?" O'Leary asked generally.

"Sent her off to the landlord with Carval, she wasn't too happy first off, came back, spoke to you, went to get lunch." O'Leary waited. "Something happened between them over the weekend," Tyler added.

O'Leary's caterpillar-sized brows waggled curiously. "Did it now?" he drawled. "Do I need to have a chat?"

"No. No bruises." O'Leary translated Tyler's brevity perfectly accurately.

"Should I have a chat with her?"

"Wouldn't recommend it, 'less you're looking for ventilation holes through your head."

"Mm," O'Leary hummed, and returned to his work.

Half an hour later, Casey had not reappeared, and the metaphorical smoke and brimstone leaking from the room in which she was lurking had not notably diminished. O'Leary decided on a little big-brotherly interference.

"Casey?" he said, poking his massive head around the door. "What you got?"

"Nothing yet," she growled.

O'Leary inserted himself all the way in and closed the door behind him.

"Save it, O'Leary. I don't wanna hear it."

"Now, does that mean you know you've done somethin' dumb, or does it mean you ain't admittin' you've done somethin' dumb?"

"Not your affair," she said warningly. O'Leary, safely so sizeable that short of shooting with a semi-automatic Casey couldn't do anything that would damage him, ignored the warning.

"Sounds like it might've been yours," he noted with a very knowing grin. Casey blushed bright scarlet, and chased it with a searing glare.

"Still not your business."

"'Tis if you're mis'rable. I don't like it when my pals are mis'rable. Makes my desk soggy." He ambled over, and sat down. The chair creaked unhappily. "Now, whyn't you stop bein' mad an' tell him you're sorry?"

"I'm not."

"Mad or sorry?"

"Either. I'm fine."

"Bullshit." O'Leary rarely swore at her. "You ain't fine. You're as ready to blow as a live volcano an' you ain't doin' nothin' to calm down. Cap'n's goin' to notice pretty soon an' then you'll really be up the creek. First off, he's gonna notice that you ain't co-operatin' with the photographer. Since he's let him in, that's goin' to be the first black mark. An' then he'll notice that you ain't your normal sunny self, an' he'll start askin' questions, and takin' notice of thin's. An' if he does *that*, I won't bet a dime that he doesn't find out 'bout your pa, and I don't guess you want that happenin'. So kiss an' make up."

Casey turned her shoulder to O'Leary and stared at the camera footage. It ran for a few seconds. Suddenly she yelped. "Look at that!"

"Oh, boy. Oh, boy oh boy. Ain't that sweet?"

"Our friend Mike didn't tell us about that, did he?"

"Nope. An' Karlen di'n't tell me neither."

They stared jointly at the fuzzy footage. Fuzzy or not, that was quite definitely Mike Merowin and Karlen Petersen. Karlen was carrying a plastic bag, with something in it.

"I think we need to have another chat with Mike," Casey stated.

"Yeah. An' Karlen."

"And Terrison, because he said Mike wanted to talk to him about Telagon, and Telagon told me and Andy that Mike's syntheses were clearly better than Belvez's." She looked up. "Looking like money, isn't it? Telagon's money. Question is, were they in on it, turning a blind eye, or dupes?"

They watched the rest of the footage.

"You know, there's something else weird here."

"Mm?" O'Leary buzzed: the world's largest bumblebee.

"Karlen Petersen told us – and Ahlbrechtssen – that *that Troy dude was there all the time*. I don't see any *Troy dude* there all the time. I don't see any dude there *any* time."

"There're those exterminators."

"Yeah. Guess we'd better check that with the landlord, but I don't guess it's unusual."

"Sure is weird, Karlen sayin' there was this Troy dude when there wasn't."

"Maybe she was trying to get him thrown out?"

She surged out of the room and into the bullpen. "We got something," she announced. "Merowin was at Belvez's."

"When?"

"Three days after he got dead."

"That's interesting," Andy said, with sublime understatement.

"Isn't it? Time to have another little chat with Mike." She smiled edgily. "C'mon, O'Leary. Time for some terrorising."

"I love me a good bit of terrorisin'," he drawled. "Gimme a coupla minutes." He disappeared in the direction of the restrooms.

"What about us?"

"Can you get Merowin's home address? It might be a plan to go see if he's home. If he is, you get to do some terrorising too."

"Works for us," Tyler grinned.

***

Carval, having stomped off in a fine rage, mostly driven by hurt that he was being regarded as a *mistake*, found himself a bar in which to have lunch and chased it down with a couple of craft beers, none of which did much to soothe him.

Well, whatever *Casey* might think, he was damn well taking *his* photos and then putting them in *his* exhibition. And if she didn't like that, he didn't give a damn either. He chugged down his beer and tried very hard to forget the sensation of her in his arms, under his lips, under his body, and around him. He was not entirely successful. In fact, it was a complete failure. He left the bar in no better a mood than he had entered it.

As he marched down the street, his anger hardened into a settled intention that Casey would see that *she* was the one who'd made a mistake. He was going to keep hanging around to take his photos and be perfectly civil. Since she'd said she wasn't faking, she'd enjoyed it just as much as he had. So he was just going to play it cool, go anywhere he liked to take his shots, in the precinct or out of it, and she could just suck it up and choke on that stick up her excellent ass.

In pursuit of his goal, he called O'Leary to inform – not ask – him that he was going to come back to the precinct and take some more shots of the bullpen, and was left utterly infuriated that all he got was voicemail.

Carval was, in fact, suffering from the adult equivalent of a toddler tantrum, sparked by a nasty feeling of rejection and not a little hurt pride. He hadn't been knocked back for quite some time, and he didn't like it.

He was a hundred yards past the precinct doors and heading intemperately for home when his phone rang.

"Hey." The bass rumble shivering the circuits of his phone could only ever be O'Leary. "You wanna shoot in the precinct, or you wanna come chasing a suspect?"

"Who's chasing?"

"Me 'n' Casey."

"Precinct," Carval said, cutting off his nose to spite his face. Suspect chasing – or catching – would be an excellent series of shots, but, like a small child, he was sulking, and not inclined to make the first move.

"Aw, don't be like that. Just 'cause you two are fightin', don't mean I don't still like you."

"So tell your partner to play nice."

"I did."

"Say *what?*" Carval's feet stopped moving. "Can she hear you?" he blurted.

"Naw. I like me without extra holes." There was a pause. "So, you comin' or not?" Carval vacillated. "You got about one minute before I gotta go. Make your mind up."

"Where are you going?"

"Columbia."

"That professor? He didn't exactly look the type."

"Naw. One of the group."

"I'm in," Carval decided, completely reversing his position of three minutes ago. "I'm part way there already. See you at the entrance?"

"Sure," boomed Magog.

A fast yomp down the sidewalk later, Carval was leaning casually on the entrance pillars nicely in advance of the cops. Of course, he was still irritated with Casey. Well, he didn't have to talk to her. He could talk to the O'Leary mountain, and his camera could talk to Casey. It liked her. Right now, he didn't, particularly.

Casey's horrified expression when she spotted him indicated that O'Leary was still playing his own Machiavellian game. Simply to annoy, Carval very obviously took several shots of her changing expression – and O'Leary's smirk, above her head and behind her.

"What happened?" he asked O'Leary.

"Got the camera footage."

"I know that. I was there."

"Waalll, the guy who's top of our list just so happened to be at our victim's home."

Carval waited expectantly.

"Three days after he got dead."

"Are you coming, O'Leary? We got a killer to catch."

Casey paid exactly the same amount of attention to Carval as he had to her: none. O'Leary's smirk widened. She stalked off. Carval and O'Leary followed, catching her up in two strides, with O'Leary's bulk providing a dividing wall between them, or possibly a firebreak.

Unfortunately, proximity was not soothing Carval's temper, largely because the actual physical presence of Casey was simply reminding him of the actual physical presence of Casey-in-his-bed, which he wanted all over again.

"You can't come in," she said, on the steps of the hall.

"*You* can't stop me," Carval pointed out smugly. "This isn't the precinct and you don't have any authority to stop me." He only wished he'd realised that earlier, when he'd allowed her to prevent him following them.

O'Leary whistled. Casey ignored both men and marched through the halls towards Merowin's office. Carval, who regardless of his own high temper could still recognise a stunning sequence of shots when they appeared before him, raised his camera and started shooting continuously. He'd call it *on the hunt* – and hunt it was. The aura of focused ferocity was palpable; the sharp snap of authority echoed in every clack of heels on tiled floor. She was intensely intimidating – and it was, however little he liked it, intensely hot.

She flung open the door to a small office – and stopped dead.

"He's not here."

Carval captured the full astonishment and fury of the thwarting of her purpose, foursquare in his viewfinder: then the sag of surprised defeat.

"What?"

"Gone."

"Teaching?" O'Leary offered up.

"Maybe. Let's go find out, quickly."

She started down the hall, pursuing a new trail.

"Professor? Have you seen Mike Merowin?"

Terrison flicked a glance at his watch. "No, but he was in before me so maybe he went home early. He's not teaching today."

"Okay, thanks," Casey said, bitten off short, and turned on her heel before Terrison could ask any questions. She reached a quiet space outside and was already dialling before O'Leary or Carval could say a word.

"Tyler?"

"Yeah, gone. Can you get to his address?"

"Okay. Let me know. See you later."

She swiped off angrily. "What spooked him? There must have been something. I can't believe he's just taken an afternoon off."

"Coincidence usually ain't. Guess we'd better go back to the shop an' see what else we can do."

Casey made a noise of absolute disgust. Carval, slightly out of her sightline, kept taking shots. The sequence would be another excellent contrasting set of shots: the slump in her spine the opposite of her usual posture. As he shot, it dawned on him that she was far more disturbed by Merowin's absence than seemed reasonable, and certainly far more than O'Leary, who was mildly irritated but otherwise as generally equable as ever.

"I know what else we can do," she growled. "We can go to Telagon and shake the tree there. They knew more than they were saying."

"Better go back to the bullpen first," O'Leary coaxed. "Call them. Make like it's just an ordinary follow-up. Don't want to spook them too."

Casey consented to be persuaded – very reluctantly.

"An' I'll buy you coffee on the way. We'll go past that li'l shop you like." It sounded like a bribe to a tired child, and when Carval looked down at the shots he'd taken he could see why. Mixed in with her disappointment, he could see that her eyes were dark-circled and dull. He hadn't noticed, earlier. He didn't want to notice now: not inclined to sympathy when *she* had run out on *him*. Running out didn't seem to have done her any good, though. *She'd have slept better if she'd stayed*, he thought, and promptly squashed it.

She nodded at O'Leary. "Okay. Let's go."

In some mysterious fashion Carval found that he was on one side of Casey and O'Leary on the other. He was perfectly certain that O'Leary had arranged this, and didn't appreciate it. Not that Casey appeared to notice, or care.

Casey hadn't noticed, and if she had, she wouldn't currently have cared. All her attention and thought were directed to finding Mike Merowin, any way possible: so much so that O'Leary had to stop her as she passed her favourite coffee shop.

"What do you want?" he asked.

"You're paying?" she said, with very unflattering surprise. "Are you sick?"

"Naw. You need cheered up, an' I found a coupla quarters down the back of my couch. What d'you want?"

"Double espresso, please."

O'Leary flicked a glance at Carval. "Americano," he said. "But I'll buy my own."

"He'll never offer again," Casey pointed out. Carval ignored the interjection, and stared hard at O'Leary.

"Fine by me," the mountain rumbled. "I'll put it into my flower fund."

"Flowers?" Carval squeaked.

"Pete likes flowers. Puts colour into his grey suits."

"Grey suits?" he squeaked again.

"He's an accountant. Don't they wear grey suits?"

Carval snickered. O'Leary laughed. The men exchanged comfortably friendly looks as the barista concocted the coffees. Casey didn't notice. She was locked in her own head, running scenarios and what-ifs.

Just like she used to in the Academy, just like she did after her mother's death, just like…

Just like she always did when something hurt.

CHAPTER 26

"Mr Brewman? Detective Clement here."

"Yes?"

"I'd like to talk to you again. Just a few minor points to clear up."

There was a pause, and the hint of a gulp. "Yes, of course. Sure. When?"

"When are you free?" It was carefully calibrated to imply that it was not urgent, and that it was fine if it didn't happen right now. She was acting to the top of her bent. She *wanted* to get round there ten minutes ago and choke the answers out of Brewman.

"I'll need to check. I'll get back to you."

"Thank you."

She cut the call and swore viciously under her breath for a moment or two. Then she pulled herself back under her normal hard-shelled control and started assembling her thoughts, shutting out the world around her.

In the background O'Leary was quietly cutting Carval out of his photographic haze and steering him not-so-subtly to a conference room.

"Another intimidation party? I got that from Tyler already."

"Naw," O'Leary drawled. "Bit of advice."

"Not required."

Carval made to stand up. O'Leary put a massive paw on his shoulder and perforce he sat back down.

"I think it is," he said slowly. "'Cause my pal Casey's not right, an' while that ain't down to you, she ain't goin' to be any happier iffen she's on the outs with everyone."

"Why's that my problem? She doesn't want to make nice."

O'Leary looked pained. "Sure she does. She's just scared."

"Scared? Bullshit. She doesn't want to play, and that's fine with me."

"Scared," O'Leary said firmly. "Casey don't get into emotional stuff, an' she don't fall into bed with random guys either." Carval maintained an entirely blank face. "You don't blush like she do," he added mischievously. "Anyways, she don't do that. So, somethin's goin' on, an' she's spooked. So don't you spook too. She'll be back iffen you just wait. Watch the flowers grow, or somethin'." The sharp intelligence in O'Leary's eyes was directly contradictory to his down-home, dumb drawl. "Iffen she didn't wanna play with you, you'd know about it. An' so would we."

Carval shrugged. "You play Cupid if you want to. You're wrong, but that's not my problem either."

"'Kay. Wanna make it interesting? I'll bet ten that she's back in a week."

"Not taking it. Do you think I'm dumb? I won't bet on her behaviour."

The slow O'Leary smile appeared. "Naw. I don't think you're dumb. Havin' a bit of a sulk, mebbe. You go off an' have your sulk. Casey's havin' hers. Come back a bit later an' we'll all be pals again."

"I don't come when you call." He was not sulking. He was justifiably annoyed.

"Aww. An' here I thought we was pals."

"Can you *stop* behaving like you're as dumb as a rock? It's old already."

"It makes you listen. Anyway, *I* think we might all be found at the Abbey, later on. *I* think you might want to join us. If nothin' else, the beer's good and you can talk to the rest of us a bit."

Carval stared. Then he stood up, unhindered, and left behind the conference room, the precinct, and any idea that Casey's misfits team were in touch with sanity. They were *all* crazy.

O'Leary hummed happily to himself and reckoned that Carval'd be round for a drink this evening, by which time he'd have talked sense into Casey. He liked Carval, and he was rarely wrong in his judgements of people. He ambled back into the bullpen, shivering the walls as he went.

"You c'n come out now," he said cheerfully to Casey. "He's gone."

"I want to interview Brewman," Casey griped, ignoring O'Leary's statement. "But I can't afford to tip him off too. I've got to pretend it doesn't matter much."

"That's no fun."

"Where are Tyler and Andy? They should have found Merowin by now too."

At that point her phone rang. She snatched it up. "Clement."

"Detective Clement, Mr Brewman. I could see you tomorrow, at ten."

"Thank you. See you then." She glared impartially around. "One thing down. Where are the others?"

"Here," Andy groused. "That was a waste of everybody's time."

"Chi not working for you?"

"Shut up, Bigfoot."

"He wasn't there?"

"No," Tyler replied tersely.

There was a collective growl.

"Andy, we're going back to see Brewman tomorrow at ten. Telagon are in this up to their corporate necks and we're going to prove it. Let's get thinking."

The team gathered round the board and started to toss around ideas and trails to chase down. The board became coherent and logical, though there was still no proof as to who the murderer was. Merowin was very high up the list, but there were other options: Karlen, Brewman, and even the notorious random psycho killer.

"No random psychos," Casey said with a grin. "We leave them for Criminal Minds and other TV shows."

"Merowin," Tyler said.

"Hey, that's not fair. I didn't open the pool yet."

"Brewman," rumbled O'Leary.

"That wimp? He couldn't hit a barn door with a rock when he was ten."

"I'm betting on McDonald," Andy said, absolutely deadpan, and it took everyone a moment before they realised what he'd said and collectively sniggered.

"What about you?"

"I don't know," Casey said. "Merowin's a weasel, and I'm *sure* he's in on the fraud" –

"If there was a fraud" –

Casey made a face at Andy, "but he doesn't quite feel like a killer. I'm going for the unknown perp."

There were derisive noises all around her.

"If that's the best you c'n do, it's quitting time. C'mon. Beers."

Casey regarded him very suspiciously. "Why?"

"I'm thirsty, Tyler's even less talkative than usual, Andy's not goin' to the theatre, an' you've been in a sulk all day till now. So beers, to make us all feel better. C'mon."

O'Leary's breezy bossiness – and size – shortly had them all in the usual bar, with drinks. Somehow, Casey had been crammed into the corner, half-hidden in the gloom caused by O'Leary blocking the light. She was happy enough there, out of general view. It hadn't been a good couple of days, and if she were honest it was because she knew that she'd done something dumb and then compounded it with a fight; not that she would admit that to Big Brother Bigfoot O'Leary. Well, it was likely for the best. She'd got a murder to solve and her dad to look after. More complications were not required.

More complications had just walked in the door. Now what was she going to do? She couldn't escape – and she was dead sure that O'Leary had arranged it that way. She was going to kill him. She was fed up of his interference. She didn't need it.

And yet, watching Carval walking in, there was a little curl of happiness in her stomach that he was there. Which was ridiculous. O'Leary had *no right* to be correct. But she was happier. She even produced a smile as he looked around.

Maybe she could fix this.

Or maybe not, because that wasn't much of a smile he was giving back. Just a tight lipped half-effort that didn't exactly convey any enthusiasm. She drooped back into the corner, and hid her reaction behind the bottle of beer. He was only taking photos. That was it. Well, if that was what he wanted... She pulled herself back into herself and left only the work shell.

There was a general shuffling of chairs and placements which affected Casey not at all, and conversation turned to entertaining stories of dumb criminals and suspects. She let it all wash by, and participated in all the right places, and started dreaming about leaving just as soon as she possibly could. She began to plan a date with a very large carton of ice-cream.

Her phone rang.

"Clement," she said, over the noise of the boys and the bar.

"Detective, it's Sergeant Dawes." *Oh fuck no not already not again. It's too soon.*

She stood up and forced her way out of the corner and the group.

"Sergeant," she said as she moved. "I guess I need to come down?" Her voice didn't show a single hint of her feelings.

"'Fraid so, Detective." His pity bit.

"Okay. Forty minutes, I reckon. Sooner if I can."

She cut the call, realised she'd left her purse by her chair, and returned to collect it.

"I've got to go," she said, very neutrally. The three other cops flashed her a glance, and then exchanged a look with each other. "Pass my purse, please?"

"Okay," O'Leary rumbled. Carval's head came up.

"See you tomorrow," Andy added. "Tai-chi in the Park at six." She growled. Tyler managed a nod and waggle of fingers.

"Night," Carval emitted.

Casey disappeared, at speed.

The cops looked at each other again, and something passed between them that Carval entirely failed to understand.

"What's going on?" he asked.

"Nothing that affects you," Andy noted, in a very shut-it-down way. "Let's get another beer in and talk about culture."

"Let's not," Tyler said. "Beer, sure. Not culture."

Andy flipped him the bird. "You could do with some culture."

"Nah. You could do with some working out."

"I'll give you a workout," smirked O'Leary, "anytime you wanna hit the mats."

"Culture," wailed Andy. "Not workouts. You should all go see the new production of The Dolls House."

Tyler disagreed. Forcibly.

Carval had the very odd impression that the developing argument had been deliberately started to prevent him asking any more questions about Casey's departure, and when O'Leary provocatively weighed in with – of all the incongruities – a commentary on the social mores of Disney animations, he was sure of it. For now, he joined in, and ignored the heavy layer of subtext and not-discussing-it.

"I'm for home," Andy said, after a while.

"Guess I'd better go too," O'Leary said.

"Pete missing you?"

"Course he is," O'Leary grinned. "Can't really not miss me." There were various derisive noises. O'Leary unfolded himself to full height and stretched, which might well have been dangerous to street lights and geostationary satellites.

"I'll have another, if you want to," Tyler said to Carval. It didn't sound like a suggestion.

"Depends why you want to."

"Thought we could have a talk."

Carval's scepticism was patent.

"Not looking for a fight. Heard you earlier."

Carval said nothing.

"Unlike Bigfoot, I don't interfere. Up to you and Casey how you roll. But I think you're an okay guy, and Bigfoot likes you, which weighs on the right side, and you didn't ask why when we weren't saying." Tyler paused, clearly trying to make a decision. "She's dealing with some tough shit. Don't make it worse for her."

He relapsed into silence, which Carval didn't break, sipping his beer.

"She messed up."

"She can tell me that, then. Not you."

"Like you gave her the chance when you barely nodded this evening? She was smiling at you like she wanted to fix it."

Carval was brought up short.

"Wouldn't've noticed, except she did, and she shut down. Then she went off to deal with the shit. If you wanna fix it – and you don't have to – then you'd better work it out, 'cause she won't be trying now."

Tyler drained his beer. "Anyway. Enough of that. Up to you. Not my problem. How're you getting on with the one-way-glass?"

***

Casey deposited her father in his Brooklyn apartment, encouraged him to clean up, shower, drink a gallon of water, and went home to her solitary bed and her solitary life, utterly miserable. Her father hadn't been coherent enough to explain anything, and there would be no point in asking when she saw him on Sunday. She couldn't fix him, and she couldn't lose her life in trying.

Couldn't fix her dad, couldn't fix Carval, who'd clearly given up on her already. She got that. She would give up on her too. She wouldn't have wasted time on some guy who ran out on her without even a note, so why should she be stupidly hurt that he had quit the game? She'd brought it on herself. She'd just concentrate on the case. She could fix that. Starting with Telagon, tomorrow.

She spent the remainder of the evening with bubble-gum TV and as much ice-cream as she could eat. Neither helped. She hit the precinct as early as she could.

***

"Let's go, Andy," Casey instructed, Tuesday morning. "We don't want to be late, do we?"

"Nope."

"I want to scare them. I don't expect any answers, but I'm going to throw out some grenades and see what shakes loose."

Andy grinned. "Random frighteners? You? Ms Logical Detective?"

"Yep. I got the impression that they didn't think much of women. Let's make them think I'm a scatterbrain too."

Andy snickered evilly. "Just as well they've only met you once. That won't fly for long."

Not long later they'd pulled up at Telagon's offices and been ushered into another smart room. As before, Brewman was late.

He entered, followed by a big man, well dressed, but heavy set and somehow exuding underlying anger.

"Carl Sackson, Chief Research Officer."

That was surprising, and worrying. Maybe Brewman had seen through her act. Maybe they'd made a mistake. Why bring out the big guns for a casual clear-up chat?

"Thank you for seeing us again," Casey opened.

"Is this important, Detective?" Sackson asked aggressively.

"I wouldn't be here if it wasn't. Dr Ricardo Belvez was murdered, and I consider finding his killer important. Don't you?"

"Of course. But that has nothing to do with Telagon."

"You funded his research, and that of Dr Merowin."

"So what? We fund many research groups, so statistically – I assume you're familiar with basic statistics," Sackson bit with contempt, "sometimes there will be horrible accidents."

"Murder isn't normally an accident." She refused to be intimidated by Sackson's forward-leaning posture and aggression. "I don't want any other researcher to be hurt."

"Surely you're not suggesting we had anything to do with it?" Brewman asked mildly.

"Why would I do that?" She left that trailing, and started on a different track. "Just remind me, for reasons of confidentiality it's only you two who saw Merowin's results?"

"That's right."

"I see. There are some doubts around Belvez and Merowin. I thought you might have some insight."

"Doubts?" Sackson said sharply.

"Belvez had confidential information in his apartment. Highly irregular," Casey said, deliberately misleading. "Of course it's all secured now."

"That is our intellectual property," Brewman accused.

"Indeed it's not the property of the NYPD, which is why we are keeping it secure."

"What about Dr Merowin?" Brewman blurted. For an instant, Sackson looked furious.

"He and Belvez were good friends. We have to wonder whether he knows more than he's told us about Belvez." She left the implication hanging. Brewman, who was clearly the weaker link, took the bait.

"What do you mean?"

"Well, it seems that Merowin's results weren't quite as good as he thought."

Behind her, Andy's brown eyes were brightly intent on the two Telagon executives. Brewman had paled. Sackson's face was red with ire.

"What do you mean?"

"Seems he was overstating his compound's abilities, at the expense of Belvez's."

"Don't be ridiculous. Dr Merowin's results can't be challenged. We check everything. Unless you're implying we were involved? If that's the case, you'll be hearing from our lawyers by lunchtime, with a writ for professional misconduct. Our science is rock solid." So rock solid that Terrison destroyed the fakery in two days. Shouldn't they have been worried about *how* Casey knew Merowin was faking it?

From the tiny noise behind her, Andy was wondering why threatening them was their first thought, too. If they were innocent, surely they'd be panicking about the company and how Merowin could have fooled them?

"Why on earth would I think that?" she asked coolly. "You're a Dow-Jones stalwart. It's more than your company's worth to falsify results. The SEC would be all over you."

Both men stood down, which was interesting as well. So they were most worried about faking involving them? Casey scented support for her theory.

"We can't afford for any ridiculous rumours to get started," Sackson growled. "The media and the markets – they'd make a fuss about it and our share price would tank. Even if we weren't involved" – *if?* – "we'd be tainted. We can't afford that. No-one can afford that."

"If we sink, a lot of people suffer. Likely even you." Casey raised her eyebrows. "Your retirement plan is probably invested in us," Brewman added. "You could lose a lot of money." Now that had sounded almost as if they were suggesting she'd got a personal interest that they could exploit. Thankfully, she didn't.

"I see. Thank you for explaining."

"We'd be grateful if you would keep us out of this," Brewman noted, to another flash of fury across Sackson's face.

"If you're not involved, we won't be involving you." Casey paused. "But if Merowin contacts you, I want to know about it."

"Of course. Always happy to help the NYPD." Sackson's expression didn't indicate that he was happy at all.

"Has he been in touch in the last few days?"

"No."

Casey knew this was a lie, but she wasn't going after it now. Merowin's phone records included Telagon's number, several times in the last few days.

"Let us know if he does," she repeated. "Thank you for your time."

"I'm sure the NYPD will keep us informed, Detective."

Casey and Andy didn't say anything important until they were back in the car.

"Funny, I thought that last line sounded like a threat," Andy said. "Who do you think they know at 1PP?"

"Did you? I thought that suggesting our retirement plans were affected was leading up to something, too."

"Did we really learn anything?"

Casey smiled nastily. "Nothing definite, but that wasn't the idea. Sow a little dissension, throw a few curve balls, get them antsy."

"Sure managed that."

"I wonder why Sackson was in there?"

"There's a man who's used to getting his own way. He was pretty irritated. Brewman wasn't sticking to the script Sackson wanted."

"Mm. Didn't you think it was a bit odd how they reacted to Merowin faking? All about it wasn't possible and don't start rumours. Nothing about – you know – *oh shit what will this do to our results.*"

"Weird," Andy said with deep sarcasm. "Why, you might think they knew something they weren't telling us."

"You don't say," Casey drawled, with equal sarcasm.

Back in the bullpen, Casey and Andy relayed the morning's interview to Tyler and O'Leary, who received it with considerable interest. Scribbles were added to the board, thoughts were exchanged, and next steps discussed.

"We gotta find Merowin."

"Did he show up for work today?"

O'Leary squirmed, and then rapidly tapped at his phone. "No," he said a few minutes of conversation later, "but Terrison said that Karlen's in and that Merowin's done some work overnight."

"How'd we miss him?"

"Maybe he went to the movies."

"Yeah, to see The Great Escape," Casey said bitterly. "Tyler, O'Leary, you go get Karlen. Bring her in. We're going to scare her *shitless.*"

The men blinked.

"Showtime," Andy said, smiling nastily.

Tyler and O'Leary skedaddled. Casey wasn't in the mood for delays. More like in the mood for murder.

CHAPTER 27

"Where is he? Get hold of him and find out what the *fuck* is going on. They *dare* come interrogating us?"

"I'll call him."

"Wait – not yet. What does she know?"

"Nothing. She was all over the place. Didn't get it."

"You sure about that? Threatening us? That bitch, threatening *us*?"

"She didn't follow up anything. If she had a brain, she'd have picked up the points."

"I'm not so sure. She knows something. We can't afford that. Do you want to be indicted for fraud?"

"Never mind the fraud. What about…"

"What about it? We're not in the frame."

"But…"

"Keep your mouth shut. We've got our patsy. Why look further than the obvious?"

"But if she…. We could smear her. Say she slandered us. Leak and blame them? Or say she's – they've – been insider dealing on our confidential info, that they got on the investigation?"

"Won't work. Even my pal can't find anything on that lot. Believe me, I tried. And she didn't come alone. Two cops? Too much trouble."

"So what do we do?"

"They don't know anything about us, they're shooting in the dark. We've got to save ourselves here. Listen carefully. This is what we're going to do."

***

"Mike? Where are you? Are you okay?"

"Terence, I couldn't go home, the cops were there, and they were at the lab too. Terence, they're all over me. What am I going to do?"

"Don't worry, Mike. We'll fix it for you. We've got a solution. It's a bit out there, but if you can pull it off there's a big payoff in it. We'll be laughing and everything'll be fine. You just need to do this one thing.

"You sure?"

"Yep. Nothing to it. Bright guy like you, you'll be able to bamboozle her no problem. Listen up."

CHAPTER 28

Casey and Andy wrote up the next steps from the Telagon interview, and then Casey started to fidget and fret.

"You need to find your inner peace," Andy grinned. "Smooth out the bumps in your chi. Have you tried yoga?"

Casey rolled her eyes in a very put-upon fashion, at which point Tyler appeared.

"Petersen's in Interrogation, Casey. Took her prints already."

"Okay. Let's go do this. O'Leary, are you gonna watch or play?"

"Play. Tyler an' Andy can watch and learn."

They left to a chorus of imprecations.

Karlen Petersen was putting up a good show of indifference well mixed with an attitude of dumb insolence. It lasted for a whole three minutes, which was not coincidentally about how long it took Casey to work through the preliminaries and read Petersen her Miranda rights.

"Do you understand?"

"What?" Petersen had been shocked out her stained acrylic socks and sneakers. "I'm a suspect?"

"Yep," O'Leary said, with a show of teeth that wasn't a smile.

"Ms Petersen," Casey said, with intimidating formality, "you told me that Troy Bolton was always round at Dr Belvez's apartment. I've reviewed the camera footage, and there were no permanent visitors to the apartment. In fact, there were no visitors while he was living there."

Petersen stared bovinely at her, and said nothing. The intimidation level kicked up another notch.

"Why'd you lie about that?"

Still nothing.

"Okay, how do you explain these?" Casey pushed stills of Merowin and Petersen visiting the apartment across the table.

"Uh..."

Petersen looked about her frantically. O'Leary and Casey stayed entirely impassive. There was an ever-lengthening, ever more uncomfortable silence. Finally Casey broke it.

"If you won't answer that, then maybe you'll tell us what was in the Walgreens bag you were carrying?" Casey bared her teeth. It might, in some prehistoric monster, have been termed a smile. On Casey, it merely intimidated. Petersen was sweating copiously.

"Deodorant."

"Really?" Casey said sceptically, not concealing her utter disbelief in the slightest. "You left it there Friday 9th. He was murdered" – Petersen cringed at the blunt word – "Tuesday 6th. That was three days before you went. Dead guys don't need deodorant. Funny thing is, there wasn't any deodorant in his apartment."

She paused ominously. "Certainly not when CSU went through it."

"It was deodorant. I didn't know Ricky got dead till you told me."

Casey looked thoroughly sceptical. Petersen stayed obstinately dumb. Silence stretched out, which neither cop broke. Petersen stared at the door as if it would open and let her escape. It didn't. Another moment passed.

"You told me you knew Ahlbrechtssen" – Petersen looked bewildered at the sudden change of tack – "because you used to rent a room from him."

"Yeah, so? That's no crime."

Another pause, in which Petersen had plenty of time to sweat further.

"Why'd you tell him about the imaginary Troy Bolton? Were you trying to get him evicted? Why? Were you trying to frighten him off because he was better than your boyfriend?"

"No way that blow in was better than Mike," she cried, in the first sign of sincerity.

"No? All his results were better. His synthesis was better. Professor Terrison confirmed it."

"He was wrong. Mike was the top researcher. The results proved it. Mike's were better."

"Only when Mike was the one stating them. Soon as we got an independent eye to look, Belvez's were miles ahead. So what was your boyfriend doing?" Casey taunted. "I think he was faking, and Belvez caught him. You must have known, so you'll be going down with him."

Petersen gaped. "What?"

"Pretty much everything you told me first time was a lie," Casey said. "Hope you like company, because you'll have plenty of it in Bedford Hills. You'll be an accessory to murder, at a minimum."

"What? I wasn't. I'm not!"

"Belvez caught your boyfriend faking and now he's dead. You and Mike were in his apartment three days after and you took in something – and now I've got your prints we'll be checking for them on the canisters we found in there."

Casey smiled very nastily. "And since we can't find Mike, it looks like he's left you to take the rap. Not very loving, that. Looks like you were helping to make it look like Belvez was into industrial espionage, to cover up that you killed him."

She stood up. O'Leary followed.

"Nice meeting you," she said casually as they both moved to the door. "O'Leary, get them to take her into Booking, will you?"

"Sure."

Casey's hand hadn't even reached the door handle when Petersen caved. "It wasn't like that."

Casey turned slowly, exuding disbelief. "What was it like, then?" She didn't sit down, or move away from the door.

"Ricky had this compound, better than anything else around…"

***

Carval, completely ignoring anything Kent might have said about waiting to be asked, had texted O'Leary early that day to be allowed into the precinct. Tyler's words had pecked at him for most of the rest of the evening and the night, till he'd found sleep, and had then perched on the end of his bed to annoy him further in the morning. *She wanted to fix it. She won't be trying now.*

So there he was, casually greeted by Tyler since O'Leary was with Casey in Interrogation, and – as Tyler had put it – *it's show time. Wanna watch?* Of course he had. It had become a key part of his planned exhibition and it was the first chance he'd had to take real shots.

He couldn't stop shooting. The tension, even through the glass, was electric, and Casey was absolutely in command. The contrast between her palpable personality and the lumpen misery of the interviewee (no-one had told him who that was) was perfect: O'Leary's looming mass simply a backdrop: scenery to the clash in front of him. Casey was in her element, and that element was cold fire.

She kept interrogating, and he kept on shooting. He had to have these shots; he had to have *her*. She was his route to an outstanding exhibition: even better than his panhandlers, and he was *keeping* it.

And he was keeping her. If she wanted to make up, he'd take a step too. Something simple, easy, that didn't involve the blazing desire that had tumbled them into bed without as much as a date. Date. Hm. Dinner. Yes. Dinner. They hadn't had dinner.

Maybe that would be… neutral. Simple. Nothing too fancy: she'd not been impressed by his fame, so she was unlikely to want Nobu, or Jean-Georges, or Balthazar. Something she liked. When she was done he'd… see if she wanted a coffee. Neutral. Easy. Taking a step without taking a chance. He wasn't very keen on being shot down in flames in public.

Strategy set, he turned his full attention back to the small, cold, claustrophobic room where her victim was slowly being turned inside out.

***

Back in Interrogation, Casey was becoming happier and happier. Not that a single flicker showed upon her face. Oh no. That was stern and cold. Petersen, clearly terrified by the very real threat of prison, was spilling it. There was more spilling than at a toddler tea party.

"I just went with him. I didn't know he was leaving papers there, or his syntheses. He never told me anything. He loves me."

"Why was Merowin doing this?"

But that was where Petersen ran out of gas. She didn't know. No matter how much Casey and O'Leary tag teamed her, she didn't know. She went down to Holding, where her next stop was likely trying to make a deal with the DA. Good luck with that one. The DA was not a notably soft touch. More like concrete, really, and he was due for re-election shortly and wouldn't want to look soft on crime.

She strode back to the bullpen in full forward mode.

"We need to find Merowin," she rapped out.

"He's in the wind," Andy grimaced. "We've had uniforms at his apartment and at the department."

"Have you had anyone at the bank? What if he's trying to draw cash to disappear?"

Tyler was on the phone in an instant. Carval, quietly slipping in, started shooting again the instant he entered: seeing the team in action: one unit, one mind, one goal.

"Going up there," Tyler said. "Got a photo?"

Andy put one in his hand instantly. Tyler strode off at speed.

"Uh?" Carval queried.

"He's going to the bank, check if they've seen Merowin," O'Leary rumbled. "He doesn't need to tell us that. We know."

"What's Andy doing?" Andy's fingers were flying over his keyboard, faster than Carval had ever seen anyone type.

"He's gettin' street cam footage."

"Casey?"

"She's processin'."

That was an odd way of putting it. Carval had had the impression that Casey never stopped working.

"Processing?"

"Thinkin', if you like. Pullin' the threads together."

"Oh." Carval looked across to where Casey was staring at the board and her desk in equal shares. "D'you think she'd like some coffee?"

"If she don't, I'll call 9-1-1 for her." The Titan smiled. "Guess she would."

"You too?"

"Iffen you're offerin'."

Carval wandered off to the break room to concoct coffee: emerged with O'Leary's (having realised that he still had only two hands) and then returned with his own mug and Casey's double espresso.

"Coffee," he said, putting it down. She looked up, a brief flicker of surprise on her face, swiftly schooled away to cool civility.

"Thanks." She'd have provided as much emotion to a barista.

"Can't have you decaffeinated. The others tell me that's dangerous." He essayed a hopeful smile. "Who were you interrogating?"

"A suspect."

"Did she have a name?"

"Yes, but that's not your business. And" – she pierced him with a glare – "you *will* blur her face in any photos."

Carval was not happy about that. The whole *point* had been the contrasts, and without a face some of that was lost. While he digested that – and remembered, irritably, that he had agreed to it – Casey had returned to her board and papers.

"I did bring you a coffee," he tried.

"Yep, but that doesn't mean I can tell you who she is." Carval produced a tiny pout, and looked pleadingly at her. "Nope. Puppy eyes don't work on cops." He batted his eyelashes. "Nor that." But a smile was quirking at her lips. "Nor will more coffee." She drained her cup in one go.

"But you want more coffee."

Quirk turned to a genuine, if sardonic, smile. "Aren't photographers supposed to be observant? Of course."

Carval grinned at her. "Just checking. It might have been decaf."

Casey spluttered. "Decaf? What's the point of that?"

Carval snickered happily. "I don't get it either."

"You could get me another coffee, though," she smirked. "With caffeine."

He smirked back. "Would you even notice?"

"Yes."

She likely would, at that. He was almost tempted to try it, to see what would happen, but then considered that he liked his present, intact, unwounded and, critically, un-bullet holed life.

"Okay."

He dawdled off to construct another cup. When he returned, she was scowling at the board, though when she saw the cup she provided a genuine smile.

"What's wrong?"

"I want Merowin." Her fingers twisted. Without thinking, Carval snapped off a shot of them, curled and knotted around the coffee cup. "Stop that."

"It's just your hands and the cup."

"Stop it. Not now. It's distracting."

"Okay," he replied amiably. "If you'll do something for me?"

She looked instantly sceptical.

"It's easy. We didn't get dinner Saturday night. I owe you takeout. Come round when you're done and have takeout with me."

"What?"

Carval smiled very happily. "I can stay here and take more photos, and annoy you, or you can agree to come round for takeout later and I'll go away and not annoy you."

"Didn't we do this once already and all it got you was a chat with the team?"

"Worked for me, 'cause here I am. C'mon. I've got all the good menus. I'll even let you choose."

"Big of you," she said dryly. He grinned, suddenly boyish. Not that his build was *boyish*. A shiver ran down her nerves. His smile changed very slightly, to acquire a hint of male appreciation, but before her mind applied some common sense her body took control of her mouth and said, "Okay," without any permission from her brain at all.

"Great. See you later. Call."

And he was gone, before she'd really worked out what just happened, and then Tyler rang Andy from the bank and Merowin had drawn out $5,000 and she needed to be on top of her game.

"He did what?"

"Drew cash. Yesterday. He could be anywhere by now."

"Put out a BOLO. Andy, you got that footage?"

"Takes a few minutes. I'll have it in twenty."

"Okay. Where would he go? I'll check airports – five grand will buy a ticket to a lot of places."

"Doubt he'll go abroad," O'Leary rumbled. "If he was there last night – is anything missing?"

"Good thought. While we're waiting for footage, Andy, call Terrison and get Merowin's lab checked."

Andy jumped to.

"Anyways, if he was in his lab last night then he'd likely be gettin' a flight today, an' – oh. He could've got hundreds of flights by now."

"If I do airports, you look at the stations."

"Not till Andy's got me some footage. Too many stations, too many options. You do JFK. I'll start with Newark."

Tyler landed in the bullpen, not happy at all. "Missed him by hours," he bit angrily. "In there as soon's it opened, claimed the cash was for a car down payment, and it never raised a flag. Fuck."

"Yeah. But we know where he started, so as soon as Andy's magic tech gets us on his trail, we'll track him. You wanna take LaGuardia, while we're waiting?"

Tyler nodded. Very shortly, all three of them were on the phone to their respective airport security hubs. Shortly after that, all three of them were waiting for call-backs or e-mails. Andy was still waiting for his footage. Casey was tapping her fingers incessantly, and then went to make yet another coffee. Tyler paced. O'Leary shifted in his reinforced chair. Andy was perfectly calm, though his calmness exhibited an edge of being forced.

"Got it!" Andy exclaimed. "I've got the footage." They crowded around him as he started running through it. "Okay, there he is, coming out the bank." The grainy pictures kept moving on through. "Right there... *shit*." Profanity from Andy was unusual. "Into the subway. Bet he bought a ticket with cash."

"Hell. We're never going to be able to track him now."

The airports were no use either, no matter how hard they tried. The BOLO hadn't had any hits. Andy's station cam footage, when it finally turned up, was useless. All Merowin would have needed to do was put a hat on and they'd never have found him.

"Why are you all still here?" Kent asked icily. "Your shifts finished over an hour ago, and none of you have told me that there's a hot lead which requires overtime."

"Our suspect is in the wind," Casey said bitterly. "We're trying to get a hit."

"What have you tried?"

The team explained.

"Okay. You've covered all the bases. You're no good without some rest, so get out of here – I won't even bother telling you to keep an eye on your phones because short of taking them away I know you will – and come back fresh in the morning." He gestured at them. "And no sneaking in at midnight. Unless you've got a lead, of course."

He paused. Everyone inched to their desks to clear up. "Clement. A word in my office, please."

"Yes, sir."

She pulled on a brave face. That was not what she needed. She reviewed their case swiftly and hoped that Kent hadn't spotted some major error or missed opportunity.

"Clement."

"Sir?"

"Is that photographer bothering you?"

That – she did *not* see that one coming. "Sir?" she squeaked, flabbergasted.

"Is that photographer bothering you?" Kent repeated with a snap.

"No, sir."

"Good. Dismissed."

What was *that* all about?

***

Kent watched Clement depart and considered. If the photographer wasn't bothering her, then that was fine. If Clement wasn't upset by him, her team wouldn't be. They'd take their lead from her. Still, he seemed to have been around rather more than Kent had expected, which was not necessarily desirable. He pondered. The bullpen collectively didn't seem to mind him, and it wasn't like Kent himself had to be sociable or indeed photographed. And he did stay out the way. Messing with the one way glass, Kent had overheard. That was okay.

However, that didn't explain Clement's slightly strained air, which hadn't been improving with the photographer's presence. If she wasn't bothered by the photographer, it was something else. Kent remembered his investigations, and called up some information. There it was: two arrests of a David Clement in less than a month. Drunk. Incapably so. And there was Detective Clement down at the Eighth bailing him out. Hmm. She was coping. So far. He'd just let it be, for now. While maintaining a watchful eye, of course. He didn't want his stats dropping. Not at all.

***

By the time she'd cleared up her desk – not that Casey was deliberately being slow to see if a new lead arrived, no, of course not – and put her jacket on, the others had already gone. That was definitely deliberate. She didn't need to listen to their commentary – or indeed their lack of commentary, which frequently said a great deal more than actual speech. She certainly didn't need O'Leary's approving Cupid-playing, or Tyler's knowing half-smile. For once, she'd take Andy being cultural.

She pulled out her phone, tapped, stared at the number, paused. It was only dinner. Not even a cooked meal, but takeout. Nothing formal, no expectations. Really. She could leave right after dinner. Really she could. She was an adult woman and she shouldn't be behaving like a ditzy teen when it wasn't necessary.

She tapped the number.

"Is that takeout still on offer?"

215

CHAPTER 29

Half an hour after Casey's – well, not *un*expected, but still somewhat surprising – phone call, Carval's entry phone sounded and he buzzed her in.

"Come up to the studio," he directed. Half a minute later that door was briskly rapped and he opened to find a rather wind-blown Casey, her normally neatly clipped hair slightly ruffled and with little wisps curling round her ears and face. He was instantly reminded of her untidy curls across his pillow and his hands in her hair, and had to put said hands in his pockets to keep from simply hauling her in and kissing her.

That was *not* the plan. *Stick to the plan, Jamie. Stick to the plan.*

"C'mon up. All the menus are upstairs."

"Okay," she said. "What've you got?"

Oh, so much, Casey. How about I show you?

"Pretty much everything. I don't do much cooking."

"Lazy," she tsked, but there was a smile lurking at the corners of her lips and a sparkle in her eyes.

"Yep," he agreed comfortably. "I guess you cook a full home-made meal every night?"

She coloured up. "No time." Carval simply smiled knowingly, and tsked himself.

"Ow!" She'd punched his shoulder. "Don't do that. I bruise easily." Her eyebrows rose again. They generated a whole ocean of cynicism.

"Really?" The tone added another oceanful to join the first.

"Yes. Now come on, I'm hungry."

Mischief flashed through her face, lighting her eyes, but she didn't say anything, simply allowed herself to be tugged upstairs with considerable enthusiasm and towed into his living space.

By the time they were upstairs she had reverted to the same cool professionalism with which she'd entered, looking around with a focused, cop intensity. She hadn't exactly had a chance to pay attention last time, and now he was quietly watching how she did it. His fingers itched to have his camera to hand, but it was downstairs and anyway that would be well beyond the constricted boundaries of her tolerance. This was emphatically nothing to do with her work, and photographs were not her thing. *So don't ruin it, Jamie.*

He produced a pile of takeout menus. Casey supposed that might be better than her usual ready meals, though she'd have bet the microwave was faster than delivery. She looked around with rising interest: not having exactly had time or inclination to look at the apartment previously. It was fairly bare: only a few photos on the wall. She'd have expected half an exhibition hall, including quite a number of the glamour shots that had made his name originally. His reputation (and Google) would certainly have pointed her in that direction.

He hadn't much furniture, either. A large, comfortable couch, without scatter cushions or throws, toning with the neutral walls and the single rug on the floor; a small table in a corner, a larger one in front of the couch. There were no pieces of camera equipment up here, in contrast to the workroom downstairs, where almost every surface had been covered in lenses, prints, and other pieces of very expensive tech. It was oddly empty, and somewhat short of personality. She deduced that his living space really didn't matter to him. Comfort, but no soul. The half-glimpse of bedroom beyond the door, ajar, appeared much the same: she vaguely remembered it as stripped down and masculine.

"I don't need much in here," he said, behind her. She startled. He'd sneaked up without her noticing, which was truly unfair. "As long as I've got my cameras." She raised her brows at him.

"You don't like luxury?" she snipped.

"Sure, I like nice restaurants, and good wine – but that's nothing most adults don't like." He didn't mention good company. Company, which he knew would be exceptionally good, had arrived right here.

He distracted himself from Casey, currently prowling the room in a way which made him think of the restrained power of a sleek predator, by finding his extensive collection of takeout menus and checking that there was some beer in the fridge. There was even a bottle of white wine, though he wasn't sure how that had ended up there. Maybe better not to wonder. He probably didn't want to know the answer, and he was dead sure Casey wouldn't.

"Beer? Wine? Soda?"

She stopped, almost as far away as the room allowed, which prevented Carval definitively being able to say that she'd flinched.

"Beer," she replied: an odd defiance in her voice. "Where did you say those menus were?"

He collected two beers, popped the caps, and took them and the pile of menus back to Casey.

"Right here. What do you want for dinner?"

"Chinese," she said, and reached for the menus.

He spread them out on the coffee table and planted himself at one end of the couch. Much to his delight, Casey plopped down on the couch too: albeit a safe separation away. She started riffling through, found his favourite Chinese place, and started perusing the menu. That, too, was brisk. Casey, it seemed, didn't mess around being indecisive, which was good. Carval was not a patient man, generally, outside his photography (and frequently not even then, which was why he concentrated on people) and there was nothing he disliked more than constant changes of mind and *oh maybe I'd like this better* or *oh I'm not sure; does it come without calories?* or *you choose, I simply can't decide.*

"We could get a selection, and share," he said, a little provocatively, because normally he'd have been for a couple of dates with someone before trying that line.

Casey-the-cop simply blinked. Carval suddenly wondered if he'd read her mood correctly, or if there was something else going on. She was completely – well, blasé, about the blazing desire that had burned between them on the previous occasion, and might blaze again if she simply gave it a chance. It gradually dawned on him that mere physicality might have been what she'd expected, and the possibility that he'd want something else was what was giving her pause.

He was astounded by how much that bit. He wanted – okay, yes, he wanted to take her to bed again. A lot. But he wanted to know what she was like, too. He'd only just realised that he wanted that, as he'd realised that she might not be very keen on revealing herself.

"Share?" she eventually said. "Only if you don't steal all the lychees."

"Uh?"

"Andy always steals all my lychees."

"Not O'Leary?" Carval asked, astonished.

"Nope. He gets his own."

Carval was sure there was a story behind that, but Casey didn't seem inclined to elaborate.

"So what do you want?"

"Lychee chicken, and fried rice, please."

"Chopsticks or cutlery?"

She regarded him as if he was insane. "Chopsticks, of course."

Carval called in her order, added moo shu pork and more rice for himself, prawn spring rolls, and some chili salted ribs, and returned to the couch.

"I can't eat that much," she said peevishly.

"I can," he grinned. "I said I was hungry." His eyes darkened. "Very hungry." Casey blinked again, and made not one single solitary twitch of a move towards him.

"Here you are," Casey said when the door sounded and dinner arrived.

Carval stared at the bills in her outstretched hand. "What are you doing?"

"Paying my share," she said, as if he must be dumb.

"Uh?" he gaped blankly. His usual girlfriends – girlfriend? Casey wasn't exactly that – didn't bother offering, never mind regarding him with a gimlet glare that indicated that she expected her money to be accepted.

"I pay my share," she emitted impatiently, and shoved the bills into his astonished hand. His fingers closed around them automatically as she turned to the containers and investigated, locating her own in double quick time. "Chopsticks?"

"Here." He removed the chopsticks from the bag.

"Thanks." She was back on the couch before he'd blinked twice, delving for the lychees.

"Drink? Plate? Serviette?"

She looked up, captured lychee halfway to her mouth in experienced chopsticks, and lowered the fruit again. Suddenly, she blushed. "Sorry. Cops, you know? If we don't eat fast, we never get to finish. All of the above, please."

"Another beer? Soda? Water?"

"Soda, thanks."

She came back to take plate, soda can and serviette, still a little embarrassed. Carval smiled down at her.

"I never thought of that. I guess you're always in a hurry."

"Yeah. Especially if Andy's trying to steal my lychees," she grinned.

"I'm surprised he's still alive. Stealing your dinner seems like a short route to perdition." He smiled more widely. "I'm not that dumb. So why don't we sit down nicely and have our dinner. I promise not to steal any lychees." He waved his own chopsticks at her, and then brought himself and his stacked containers back to the couch, to find that he was indeed extremely hungry.

One hunger was rapidly replaced by another as Casey wielded her chopsticks with speedy aplomb and to considerable effect. *Erotic* effect. Casey sucking lychees into her lush lips would have aroused a corpse. By the time she'd eaten her dinner, Carval had nearly been driven crazy with the effort of not simply tumbling her on to her back and showing her for what her appetite should be used. He just about managed to clear the plates and takeout boxes away without exploding.

Then he noticed the bills lying crumpled where he'd put them down, distracted by the food.

"You don't need to pay for your dinner," he noted. "I asked you over."

"Yes, I should. My dinner, my share of the bill." That was uncompromising.

"But…"

"No."

She didn't know why she was making a fuss about this. It was only a few dollars, and Carval (per Google) had plenty of those. But she was. She didn't want to feel paid for. He'd already acquired a mutinous expression. This wasn't going to be like that. It wasn't a *date*. It was just… just… just not a date. Nothing important. Nothing *serious*. All of those would be a mistake.

He watched her carefully through those piercing blue eyes. She stared right back, not backing down. If she gave him a single inch, he'd take miles.

Suddenly the sulky, mutinous expression faded. "Have it your way," he conceded, and grinned, returning to the couch. "Stubborn cop." He sneaked up beside her. She quirked an eyebrow at him, but didn't protest.

"Yep." She smiled beautifully. "Wouldn't be much use if I was a pushover, would it?"

"Guess not. So if I can't give you dinner, what can I give you?" he flirted, a hand dancing over her shoulders and tracing a loose tendril of hair.

"Dessert?" she said hopefully, and smirked. He snickered.

"I might have some ice-cream."

He dug into the freezer. Right at the back, where he hadn't looked for months, was some chocolate ice-cream. He wasn't big on desserts, of the food variety. Usually his dessert had been of the female variety. He'd have *liked* tonight's dessert to be of the Casey variety.

"What've you got?"

He startled, flipped round, and quite without thinking ended up with her pinned against the counter with the chocolate ice-cream carton still in his hand. She stood very still: ice in her gaze and her hand – he gulped – on her holster. He stepped back, put the carton down.

"Sorry, you startled me."

She stood down; her eyes warming up again and her hands relaxing. "Okay. Just… doing that's not a good idea with a cop. We don't take well to being trapped unexpectedly."

Possibly that hadn't been the best thing to say.

"How do you feel about it if it's expected?" he purred.

"I might not put you on the floor."

"Might be fun, if you fell on top of me. I don't mind being on the bottom occasionally." She glared at him. He smirked. "What? I don't."

"Is that chocolate ice-cream or is it where you keep the next dose of bullshit?"

He faked a wince. "I'm hurt."

"Don't expect me to kiss it better."

He pouted hopefully. "No? But everyone knows kissing it better always works."

"When you're four. Not when you're an adult."

"I don't agree. I," he said annoyingly, "can prove it."

"That line is so lame you'll need to buy it a wheelchair. You're going to try and sucker me into saying *how*? Well, I know how. You were going to say *let's try it* and then claim it worked. Do you think I'm totally dumb?"

"No," he said, "that wasn't what I was going to do." It had been. Casey was annoyingly smart. She raised a very sardonic eyebrow at him. "But since you've suggested it" – her jaw dropped – "let's try it."

He took one step forward and slid his arms around her, leaned down and took her mouth. It was just as explosive as the last time. He'd intended to place a swift peck on her lips, draw back, and claim the win. Unfortunately, drawing back wasn't happening. *Unfortunately*? It didn't feel unfortunate to him. Not at all. In fact, it felt *fabulous*. He dived into her oh-so-receptive mouth and gloried in her instant response. Her curves fit his hands to perfection, and there was plenty of encouragement to experience said perfection.

She hadn't been going to do this. She had been going to have a civilised dinner and get back to a civilised interaction and then say goodnight in a civilised fashion. She hadn't been going to give in to the heat and desire and ridiculously flaring *need* for him. It was a mistake. It was too much, too close to serious.

And then she stopped thinking about serious or important or mistakes or anything at all but the feel of his mouth on hers and the heat between them and then the touch of skin on skin as his hand slipped under her t-shirt and on to her back, spanning almost from waist to neck.

She gasped when he picked her up, hoisting her so that she had to wrap legs around him or fall, and carried her through to the bedroom, still sparse and somehow male in the swift glance that was all she had time for before the only thing she could see was the ceiling: a room as bare and soulless as the main room. He laid her down, smiled wolfishly as he leaned over her, and fell to feast on her mouth.

She was as perfect as the first time: and this time he had time to look. A little curvy, as he'd liked last time, fit and toned; mostly legs; creamy, lush skin that he itched to shoot. Hot brown eyes, sparking with darker flecks, dilated pupils and a soft flush on her cheeks. He slipped off her t-shirt and whistled. That was *pretty*. Very pretty. And blowtorch hot.

"What're you waiting for," she murmured, and tugged him to her.

"Slow up," he chided. "We've got plenty of time. No need to rush." Something flickered through her gaze, and suddenly there was a tiny niggle of worry in his mind. But then she reached up, flexed against him, flicked his shirt off and his pants open, and everything was lost in scorching sensation and her: tight and hot and soaked beneath him and around him, taking everything and giving yet more back, over and again.

He snuggled her in, again, wrapped around her, cuddling her close. She sighed, and curled into the embrace; soft and lax and quiet. He petted gently, without intent; affection without demand – but letting her know that he wasn't sleeping; that she couldn't sneak away without a word. If she wanted to leave – when she wanted to leave – she'd need to say so. Till then, he was very happy to keep a soft, pettable Casey right there in his bed. She made a contented small noise.

Casey didn't want to move. She was happily tucked in, next to a large, warm form who'd provided some very spectacular sex. He was just the sort of big, broad man that made her feel protected and cosseted, which wasn't exactly how she normally met her day and her job. It was a very pleasant contrast. It did, of course, help that both times he'd been very – er – generous in bed. *So* nice to be with someone who took as much care of her as of himself. Okay, so she'd certainly taken care of him too, but still, a good start.

What? Start? *Start?* Oh, no no no. This was not a start to anything. This was… this was…

This was the second time and it was pretty clear that unless she actively discouraged Carval it wouldn't be the last, because it – he – felt really, really good and – *oh, for Chrissake, Casey, at least tell yourself the truth* – she wanted it. Him.

She just didn't want any complications, or talking about it, or anything that wasn't some nice, simple, fun. She wiggled slightly, and found that one particular kind of simple fun was very definitely on offer. She turned over, never leaving the haven of his arms, and draped herself on to his chest, one leg sliding over his. There was an interestingly predatory, pleased, growling noise. She put her head on his shoulder and relaxed. He fit her very nicely: just the right height to be a very acceptable pillow. He played with her hair, twisting the unruly curls through his fingers.

She slipped a hand up over his jaw. "Five o'clock shadow," she murmured, as it bristled against her palm.

"Mm," he hummed.

Her hand moved round, tracing his neck, under his nape, into the short, soft hair at the back of his head, and then pushed to bring his mouth to her waiting lips. Pleasingly, he kissed her gently, teasing, so she teased back, and slid the other hand down over firm muscle and the length of his torso. Mmmm. Nice. Just as nice as last time, though she hadn't taken the time to explore – it had been fast, hard and explosive, and then she'd – ugh – run for the hills as fast as she could. Not to be repeated. She really hadn't liked herself very much, after.

In return his hand stroked down to her rear, and then delicately explored her hip, her thigh – and nowhere *useful*. She wriggled to entice him closer, and then undertook some delicate exploring of her own, long fingers reaching downward, between their bodies, finding velvet skin over hardness and then playing: tantalising on her own account.

"Is that a hint?" he murmured darkly into her ear. "Happy to take it," and his hand slipped between her legs into slick heat. He played a little, flirted with entry and retreats, slid up a short distance and sent sensations shivering through her nerves. She mewed. He was so *good*, so soon. She rolled, and took him with her, so she was smiling up at him. He took that hint, too, and pushed home, perfectly fitting, perfectly sized. She arched up towards him, taking him deeper, and he groaned low down in his chest and took her mouth with sure possessiveness and total confidence, and then he moved and she did and his fingers found her and he swallowed down her noises with his and then she shattered.

That time, he pulled her over his chest and cuddled her under his chin, emitting pleased male rumbles without any real words at all. Casey was quite happy with that. Talking wasn't her thing.

She was beautifully, perfectly, peacefully snuggled in, when her thrice-damned phone rang.

CHAPTER 30

"What the *hell?*" she squawked. "Who's that?"

She scrambled out the bed, still completely naked, and dashed for her purse and the phone.

"Clement," she rapped.

Carval, still trying to catch up with the unwelcome turn of events, followed her. All he could hear was her end of the discussion.

"We've been looking for you."

"*Where* are you?"

"Proof? Proof that it was – *who*? Really?"

"Okay. Yes. If you tell me *everything* then I can protect you. Don't move from where you are, and don't contact anyone. I'll be there as fast as I can. I'll ring when I get there and you can get me in."

She swiped off.

"I've got to go. That was Merowin. He's holed up in the lab and wants to show me *proof* it wasn't him. It was all Brewman."

"Isn't that a bit convenient?"

"Sure it is. But I don't have a choice. I've got to go get him and take him in." She cast him a rather sidelong glance. "Don't suppose you wanna ride along?"

"Me?"

"Can't get O'Leary here in time. Merowin's right on the edge, the way he sounded, and if I wait for O'Leary to get here from right down the other end of Manhattan – he's in Alphabet City – then Merowin'll likely think better of it and then he's in the wind again. Andy and Tyler don't live in Manhattan and I can't wait for them either. So it's you or go solo. Which is it?"

While talking, she'd found all her clothes, been to the bathroom and unembarrassedly cleaned up, and started to dress.

"Okay. Can I bring a camera?"

"Sure. This is cop business. But you'll need to blur anything and you can't be there when I'm talking to him." She pulled her pants on. "C'mon, *move.*"

Bossy, in-charge Casey was surprisingly hot. However, she was on a mission and he already knew there was no room for distraction when the cops were on a hot trail. He hurried into his own clothes, and even though he dressed in a record-breaking time she was tapping her toes impatiently by the time he was at the door: her fingers fidgeting as he stopped by the studio for his camera.

"Why not use the lights or sirens?"

"I don't want to spook anyone, and if" – her tone spoke volumes of disbelief and scepticism – "Brewman really was the murderer" –

"You don't believe that."

"No – but if he is, I don't want to tip him off that the cops are coming. It doesn't usually go well, after that."

"Okay."

Carval sat silent for the rest of the short ride. They pulled up round the back of Columbia, in a darker side street that effectively disguised them as just another car. Casey tugged her jacket round her in order to hide her gun and shield.

"Right. You can't come in, and for God's sake don't freak out and dial my phone. That's the last thing we need. If this *is* a setup, I can take Merowin with one hand behind my back."

"What if there's two of them?"

Casey stopped. Being partnered with O'Leary tended to mean that anything short of the Giants' offensive line was not a problem. O'Leary was not here, and Carval was neither O'Leary nor Tyler. Nor, of course, was he a cop.

"Okay. If I haven't come out with Merowin inside thirty minutes you come in. Sneak. Can you sneak?"

"Sure I can sneak," Carval said, offended. "Some of my best shots have come from sneaking."

"Okay," she said again. "Out here, you can take any photos you like."

"But I can't take any in Merowin's lab."

"Right. At least, not unless you let me vet them after."

"Okay," Carval said without thinking, and then snapped his mouth shut. Let her *vet* them? What was he on? Fortunately, he didn't say that.

They skulked through the grounds of the Columbia campus, not talking, not making noises. Carval took a few non-flash shots, more in hope than expectation. That late at night – it was past ten, close to eleven – it was dark despite the streetlights, cold: the sky overcast and sullen with the sodium gloom below. The paths were shadowy.

"Belvez could have been hit with a rock from here," Casey murmured thoughtfully. "I didn't notice, before."

"Are you sure this isn't a set-up?"

"I'm pretty sure it is, but I can't ignore it."

Conversation lapsed again, after that flattening comment. When they reached the door, she pulled out her phone, and then stopped.

"We need some way of jamming the door open," she said. "Otherwise you won't be able to get in, and if he sees you he'll spook."

Carval looked entirely blank. Jamming open doors wasn't his thing. He preferred to be on the inside of them in the first place.

"Have you got a diary, or a notebook, or something in your pockets that I could use?"

"How's that going to work? He'll notice it. Can't you slide a rock into place?"

"I guess," Casey said doubtfully. It seemed very chancy.

"Why do you need to, anyway?"

"Uh? So that I know you can get in if it all goes wrong."

"I'm *backup*?"

"Do you see anyone else round here to be back up? Yes, you're back up. And before you get any ideas, you get my back up. Regularly."

"Aw, that's so sweet. You wouldn't be mean to me if you didn't like me."

"Shut up. Go find a stone or something."

"I've got a better idea."

"Yes?" she drawled, sceptically.

"Well, my trained observer's eye shows me a door wedge. Right there."

He pointed. There was indeed a door wedge.

"Okay. I'll kick it into place. Let's put it somewhere I can convincingly stumble over it and then tap it into the right position while he's fussing about me falling."

"Sneaky," Carval said admiringly.

"Brains are better than brawn."

"What's O'Leary?"

"A lot smarter than he pretends."

"I think I got that," Carval said very dryly.

Casey didn't dignify that with an answer, but carefully positioned the wooden door wedge so that she could stumble over it. Then she called Merowin, assuming a brisk, encouraging, slightly credulous tone: a cop looking for an easy solve.

A couple of minutes later the door opened and Merowin appeared. He didn't look around, and so there was no chance of him spotting Carval, a few feet away and buried in the shadows. Casey faked a stumble, caught herself on the door frame, and Merowin was sufficiently distracted by that and her annoyed squawk to miss her foot sliding the wedge into the way.

Carval thought for a moment, long enough to hear the fading of their steps, and then slipped inside and closed the door. Casey hadn't considered that the door not closing might trigger an alarm, but he, a veteran photographer of a thousand homeless hostels, had. He congratulated himself, and then concealed himself within a corner of the corridor, checked his watch, and waited.

And waited.

And waited.

Casey did not reappear.

The shriek of pain sent him off running, frantically searching through half-remembered routes.

***

Casey followed Merowin through the gloomy corridors. Clearly the evening shift – night shift, now – did not need much light. The shadows gathered in corners. She cursed softly as she realised that her faked fall had actually caused her to twist her ankle slightly, and it hurt. Not that it would stop her taking Merowin out, but she wasn't fond of being under par at any stage, and she was still ninety-five percent sure that this was a set up. She just didn't know how.

"I gotta show you the evidence," Merowin gabbled. He was sweating, and obviously had been for some time. She tried to shift further away, but the corridor was rather too narrow. "I can prove that I've been set up. I was played."

"Played?"

"It wasn't murder. I never killed anyone."

"Why'd you go off the grid?"

There was a sharp intake of breath. "I... we.... I needed the money. So I" – he gulped – "um... improved my results, and they knew but they were happy 'cause we all did well out of it." He swallowed again. "But then John brought Ricky on board. Stupid New Mexico hick, always watching what I was doing and wondering how I got better results than him." Another convulsive swallow. "If he'd just left well enough alone and not run my synthesis then we'd all have been just fine."

Ah. So Belvez *did* get suspicious, and did his own investigation – and had naively asked Merowin about it.

"We could have shared the cash. If he hadn't gone poking his nose in where he wasn't wanted it would all have been fine."

"So he told you he couldn't duplicate your results?"

"Yeah." Merowin sounded more sulky than anything else. "I was just as good as him. He just got the break and I didn't. I could have done it too."

But you didn't, Casey thought. *You were jealous.* She hummed

227

sympathetically, and was grateful that he couldn't see her expression in the dim corridor.

"So I told Brewman and he said not to worry and then the next thing I knew you were telling us Ricky was dead."

"Mm?"

"And then I got scared 'cause it was obvious you thought I had something to do with it but I didn't, and I can prove it."

"But you and Karlen took those lens cases to Ricky's apartment."

"Yes, but that's what I'm trying to tell you. Brewman *told* me to. He was going to pin it all on Ricky and then it would all be fine."

Are you actually on this planet? You'll be under SEC investigation for fraud in half an instant.

"I've got the e-mails."

Okay, now he'd gone past the point of believability. *Nobody* kept that sort of e-mail. Nobody *sent* that sort of e-mail. Brewman hadn't struck Casey as dumb. Arrogant and weak, but not dumb.

"You've got to believe me. I didn't kill Ricky."

That had almost sounded like truth. Almost.

"So what was going on?"

Merowin hesitated. "I don't know what happened to Ricky but someone made it look like it was here in the lab."

How did he know that? They hadn't told anyone how Ricky had actually died. Casey began to feel really nervous.

"We're just about to my lab. You'll see. I can prove it wasn't me."

Casey suddenly had a very bad feeling. Something was wrong. She wasn't sure what, but something was off. Her cop senses were twitching. She surreptitiously reached for her phone, and tried to swipe it on as they reached Merowin's small domain.

"What are you doing?" Merowin asked, nervously. "Why're you touching your phone? Leave it off. You promised you'd protect me. Who are you calling?" He reached for her phone, and she tried to duck out of his range. She did, but he was between her and the exit, and the only way out was further in. She moved in to take him down, but someone struck from the door behind her, rabbit-punching her hard so that she was off balance and falling: the twisted ankle gave under her and she landed hard on hands and knees. After that, it was a flurry of blows as she desperately shrieked in the vain hope that Carval would hear: hands and arms around her head to protect it; her knees curling up, but it still left her opened to fists and feet.

The last thing she felt was the boot to her stomach that left her gasping. She didn't feel the blow that knocked her out.

"No time to dispose of her. We've got to get out of here."

"But – she knows."

"She doesn't know. She didn't see me. You didn't admit anything except the fake results. We'll get you out of here. Don't worry. You'll be safe. You'll never have to worry again. *Don't* kick her head again. Kill her and they'll never stop looking. We've done enough."

Even so, a few more kicks to the body went in. Two men hurried out, leaving Casey crumpled unconscious on the corridor floor.

***

Carval heard fast, heavy footsteps and ducked behind a door into a small office. With abrupt, terror induced inspiration, he whipped out his camera, still with the flash disabled, and held it high, hoping that he'd capture enough to allow some chance of identification. He hid himself, and kept snapping, praying that they wouldn't spot the pale patch of his hand or the door being ajar. He barely breathed as they went by: Merowin, and a thickset bruiser of a man whom he didn't recognise. As soon as they were safely past, he dashed down from where they came, terrified by the silence they'd left behind.

He skidded to a halt just in time to avoid falling over the still form. She was breathing. For an instant, that was all he knew. She was breathing.

And then his mind started to function and he dialled 9-1-1 and then, the ambulance summoned, O'Leary's number.

"Carval? Why're you callin' this time of night?"

"Casey," he forced out. "They beat her up and I called the ambulance but" –

"Where are you?" O'Leary rapped sharply, all hayseed gone.

"Havemeyer Hall. Inside."

"Okay. Stay there till the bus comes. If it gets there before I do, call me and tell me which hospital."

"I might have got photos of them."

"Say what? Photos?"

"I don't know. I tried."

"Anything's better than nothing. Stay put. Be there soon's I can." There was a microsecond pause. "You did good. And you called the bus first, so you're in credit."

The call was cut.

He took shots of Casey, not sure whether they'd be evidence or exhibition – he couldn't not: the prone form ghastly in its limp unconsciousness, the marks on her clothes: mud, from boots or shoes, and he was furious and terrified at once, gazing at his camera blankly, and then sliding down the wall to sit on the floor and try to dissipate the adrenaline and the shaking of his hands.

He was scared to do anything that might move Casey, so he compromised with fingers lightly touching hers and absolutely nothing more, during the endless minutes till the ambulance staff called his phone and he could go and let them in, rather than listening for every shallow breath as her eyes didn't open and her limp form didn't move.

He wasn't actually sure that it was an improvement, as the medics brought a stretcher, immobilised Casey's neck, and asked him a lot of questions which he couldn't answer. It took him another moment to realise that they were suspicious of *him*.

"Why would I hang around waiting for you if *I* did this," he growled furiously. "Do I look that dumb?"

The medics simply raised eyebrows and carried on, while managing to give Carval the clear impression that he was still the primary suspect. In all the fuss and bustle, Casey didn't move or give any indication of consciousness.

The medics took her out, very cautiously, and started loading her into the ambulance. Just as they were shutting the rear doors, O'Leary strode up, covering at least two yards per step. Carval had never seen anyone short of an Olympic athlete covering so much ground so fast. It was like watching a fast-forwarded angry Ent.

"Carval," he boomed. "Where is she?"

"In the ambulance," he emitted, beginning to fall apart once O'Leary had arrived here. "They…. I don't know, these guys think I beat her up but I think she's really badly hurt."

"Nah. She's too mean. Only the good die young."

Carval snickered, very shakily. O'Leary approached the medics, and flashed his badge. "This guy's one of us," he said, which was a considerable stretch in Carval's view but gave him a very warm feeling. "What's the damage?"

"We don't know. We'll take her in and check her out."

"Where? We'll follow you in."

"Presbyterian-Columbia. You can walk. She needs the bus."

O'Leary spun on his elephantine heel and started. Carval scrambled to catch up.

"Now," O'Leary said, "while we're walkin', whyn't you just tell me the story. Startin' with why Casey's here an' you're with her. Last time I looked, you weren't a cop."

Carval gave O'Leary a rather extensively edited version of the evening, leaving out a substantial proportion of the detail. From O'Leary's sceptical regard, he'd managed to fill in all the missing details with remarkable accuracy, but fortunately refrained from commenting.

"Okay. An' here we are."

It wasn't entirely clear whether O'Leary meant there at Presbyterian or there in the actual situation.

"I've got photos," Carval reminded him, in an effort to be useful.

"Yeah. We've lost them anyway, for now. Let's see how our girl's doin', and then we'll take a look. We'll give the other two a call."

"I couldn't leave her," Carval said defensively.

"Never said you should. Anyways, what could you've done? You ain't a cop, an' you couldn't arrest 'em. You called the bus an' you called me. Don't need to do more'n that to be in credit." O'Leary peered around inside the ER waiting room. "Where've they put her?" Since no-one answered, he wandered up to the nearest nurse and made enquiries.

"They'll tell us," he rumbled. "We just gotta wait. Let's get a look at these photos."

Carval pulled up the pictures. By his standards, they were appalling. Not centred, chopped off heads, several were blurred: he'd have been ashamed that he took them – except that O'Leary was muttering to himself in terms that, translated, seemed to imply that he could make an identification from them, if they patched them together.

He was still muttering to himself until he saw the shots of Casey unconscious, when his growl cleared a two yard space around them.

He paused, and produced an evidence bag. "You better gimme your camera, for now."

"We can clean them up at my studio," Carval offered. "Probably quicker than whatever you would do."

"We c'n mebbe do that, but first off, we gotta get your memory card copied by one of our guys. Chain of evidence, you know? We don't want anyone sayin' we faked it in your studio."

"That why you just took the camera?"

"Yup."

"But after that we can go and clean it up at mine?"

"Might just take you up on that. Where is it? I c'n tell Tyler an' Andy to meet us there." He smiled, a quick flash of mammoth teeth. "Hope you don't need any more sleep this evenin'. You ain't gonna be doin' too much more of it." He grinned evilly, and let that say everything he didn't voice. Carval declined to rise to the bait.

It took another several minutes before a harassed nurse, five-foot-nothing tall and seven-foot-eight in bossiness and personality, arrived in front of them.

"Contact for Katrina Clement?"

"Guess so."

"She's okay. Lots of bruising. We're keeping her in tonight, in case of damage to her kidneys or spleen. Someone kicked hell out of her. Nothing broken, maybe cracked ribs. Can't do anything about that. Just give them time." The nurse sped off to the next emergency.

"How are you the contact?" Carval asked. He didn't remember Casey saying anything other than that her mom had passed. Surely she had a father?

"Circumstances," said O'Leary, forbiddingly. Carval took the hint. "I'm gonna call the others and they can meet us at yours. What's the address?"

Carval provided it, O'Leary made two terse calls to Tyler and Andy, added a further one to CSU for them to try to recover any samples from Casey's hands, nails and clothes, and shortly they were on the way again, starting at the Thirty-Sixth's bullpen. A lanky tech copied the camera, with all due attention to evidence requirements, and then Carval trailed after O'Leary to his SUV.

"Casey's car is parked on the side street," he told O'Leary.

"We'll get it tomorrow. One of us c'n bring it home for her."

CHAPTER 31

"That was easy enough. Don't know why you were spooked. Dumb bitch cop thought she was so smart and didn't even bring anyone as back up. She never saw me. Deserved the beating."

"Yeah..." It sounded doubtful.

"She'll never be able to prove a thing. You gave her enough to pin it on Brewman, and there's no-one to say otherwise. He was getting greedy, and now he's finished. Even if they can't prove murder they'll get him for fraud."

The men took a few more steps, out on to Broadway, across it, into the side streets.

"Where are we going?"

"Getting you out of here away from the street cameras. You don't want to be arrested, do you? That was the whole point."

"But – look, I drew out cash. I can catch a cab, buy a ticket and be gone."

"Sure you can. You've done your bit. Everything's going to be okay. The cops don't know anything they didn't already suspect, and they can't pin anything on either of us."

"Where'll I go?"

"You've got enough money to go anywhere. Tour Europe, or Asia. Get out of the country for a few months, and it'll all be forgotten as soon as Brewman's indicted."

He stared around. "You sure?"

"Yeah. Take a train and go down to DC, get a flight from there."

The other man slowed up a little, falling behind, then catching up again.

"Okay. Out of New York. Yeah. I can do that."

"Nothing to worry about. Everything's going to be just fine."

"Why are we here?" he asked, staring at the dark movement of the

Hudson. "I can't get a cab to Penn Station from here. What's going on?"
    "Trust me. You don't need to worry about anything any more."
    "But…"
"I'm going to solve all your problems."

CHAPTER 32

"Int'restin' place you got here."

"Workroom.   My studio.   There's an office downstairs and I live upstairs."

O'Leary shuffled around, trying not to knock into anything delicate, such as desks, cabinets or walls, and stared at the huge board on the wall with the shots arranged on it.

"You really caught us," he said. "Didn't expect that. Sure, they said you were good an' all, but this – scary accurate." He stared some more. The entry system sounded, and Carval let Andy up. He stared at the board, too. Lastly, Tyler arrived. He flicked a glance across the board and then turned to Carval.

"Where's the central one?"

Carval blinked. "Uh?"

"No focal point. You need a focal point. It's not here. Where is it?"

"How... uh.... How did you *know*?"

"Always had a focus. Gotta have a central point to centre your eye."

O'Leary and Andy regarded Tyler rather oddly.

"Yeah, I've got one. Trade you. *Were* you a sniper?"

"You were there for Casey, you deserve an answer. Yeah."

No further questions were invited or asked.

"You can show us it later," Tyler said, in a tone that implied that Carval *would* show them it, whether he liked it or not.

"Let's get on with these photos," Andy said, grim menace in his tone and eyes back to a thousand years old.

They crowded around as Carval efficiently downloaded the card and brought up the photos on one of his larger screens, sorting as he went. Shortly, the shots were grouped, those that were truly useless discarded, those of unconscious Casey tucked away before Tyler and O'Leary started to break things, and the four men considered the remnants.

"That looks a lot like Carl Sackson," Andy said, almost immediately.

"Huh?"

"Sackson. Big bruiser, chief research officer at Telagon."

"How can you tell it's him from that?"

"Talent," he said, with a rather bitter edge which Carval didn't get. "I recognise the type. He was an arrogant bully when Casey and I went over, with added misogyny and probably racism."

"Easy," Tyler said soothingly, which also didn't compute with Carval.

"C'n we clean it up a bit?"

"I can try."

Carval started to work. The three cops looming over his shoulder didn't help. "Go get coffee or something," he said irritably. "I can't do this with you there watching every move. There's a machine in the corner."

O'Leary padded over, and poked hopefully at some buttons. Shortly, Andy joined him. Tyler, however, pulled up a chair and stayed put.

"I don't need an audience."

"I don't drink coffee."

"Keep quiet, then." Carval, still disturbed by the evening and desperate to know how Casey was, was not inclined to manners. Tyler leaned back, and said nothing. Carval returned to his work, trying to bring the fuzzed shots into better focus and to improve the contrast to try and clarify the faces. He couldn't yet do much about the shots which only had parts of the attackers.

When he had a set of cleaner shots, he started to look at the part-photos, as if it were a jigsaw puzzle, and began to patch them together. In all the time he'd taken, Tyler hadn't said a word, but when it came to matching bits of face, he started to point.

"Goes there," he said laconically.

"This one next to it," Carval followed.

"That one there."

"Plus this."

Over in the corner with the coffee machine, Andy and O'Leary watched in confusion and some awe.

"Guess the sniper and the shooter got somethin' in common."

"Visual types," Andy said, and shrugged. "Though I thought he was your new best pal."

"He's a good guy," O'Leary said comfortably. "Don't lose his head in a crisis. Anyways" – he smirked evilly – "he's Casey's new best pal."

Andy smirked back at him. "Just don't try your Cupid role on me, or I'll take you to a year's worth of high-end culture."

"You can't take me anywhere, little man."

"Bigfoot."

The amicable squabble continued, though Tyler and Carval were oblivious. Finally Carval leaned back and stretched widely. Tyler stood and stretched equally widely.

"We got it. It's as good as it's going to get."

Little and large were straight over to inspect the results.

"Definitely Sackson," Andy stated flatly.

"He's not going to have a shiny happy day tomorrow," O'Leary added. Menace pervaded his huge frame. "Thinks he's such a big man. An' Merowin. What a dick."

"Won't think he's a big man when he meets Bigfoot." Tyler bared his teeth in a non-grin, matched by the other cops, and then turned. "You okay, Carval?"

"Yeah," he dragged, unconvincingly. "It's been an interesting day."

"Like the Chinese curse," Andy said.

"Yeah."

"You don't look okay. Get some sleep. No-one's going to be allowed to see Casey till tomorrow, an' she won't thank you for tryin'." O'Leary smiled reminiscently. "I tried, one time. She wasn't happy."

"As I remember, she called you an over-protective idiot – with a few extra adjectives that weren't fit to print – and threatened to call security to throw you out, till you pointed out you could pick them all up in one paw and throw *them* out."

"Yeah, but she didn't stop yellin' at me till I left. She don't like bein' fussed over. Took the chocolates fast enough, though," he added mournfully, "an' didn't share."

"Casey never shares her chocolate. You know that. You've known her longest."

"Wasn't fair," O'Leary pouted.

"What are you going to do?" Carval asked.

"Go an' hole up in the precinct, catch some sleep in the break room" –

"He's got a mat there. He doesn't fit on the couch."

"– and get started first thing. This Sackson guy isn't going to know what hit him."

"Now, Bigfoot. No hitting. You know you're not allowed to hit people."

O'Leary appeared deeply disappointed by this, then grinned stupidly. "He ain't gonna like bein' arrested by some dumb, oversized cop, is he?"

"You're going to use that one *again*? Doesn't it ever get old?"

"Nope. Works every time," he replied, smiling seraphically. "They never expect I got a brain."

"Time we went," Andy pointed out. "Good work, Carval."

"Yeah," O'Leary agreed. Tyler merely nodded once.

"Can I come along for the arrest?"

They looked at each other.

"Seems a shame not to let him when he got the evidence," Andy lilted.

O'Leary and Tyler nodded.

"Done," the mountain pronounced. "I'll call you. Iffen you go to the hospital" – he smirked evilly – "don't switch your phone off. Or get distracted."

Carval let them all out and hoped he wasn't blushing. From their amused collective demeanour, he had been. As they clattered down the stairs, he locked up behind them and went to wash before bedtime.

An hour later, he was no closer to sleep than he had been when the cops left, and with every dark moment in which his eyes didn't close his photographer's imagination showed him pixel-perfect pictures of Casey bleeding out, of her face beaten and broken, of her body ruined and crumpled and smashed by a thug in three-thousand dollar suits, who thought money – and his avaricious love thereof – could buy him freedom.

Oh, shit!

"O'Leary!"

"You're supposed to be sleepin'."

"No, but that was Merowin with the other guy. And they went out together after…"

"An'?"

"If Sackson's in on this, and if he thinks no-one knows he was there, then how long d'you think Merowin's gonna last?"

"Waallll," O'Leary drawled, "seein' as we're cops, and nat'rally cynical sorts, we already thought of that one. We're trying to find them. Andy's all over the cameras, an' we got canvassers out."

"Oh." Carval deflated.

"Good thought, though. 'Nother tick on the good side. Now, get some sleep, or I won't tell you where Casey is."

Carval growled, not markedly improved by a yawn. "'Night."

"Night. Come by tomorrow. After you've seen Casey."

The call was cut. Carval, suddenly utterly exhausted, slipped under his plain bedcovers and crashed into sleep, in which, quite astoundingly, he dreamed not at all.

When he woke the next morning, almost as early as he'd wanted, he hardly paused to grab his camera before he was out, scrawling a hurried note to Allan on the way, who wouldn't appreciate it but was used to his fits and starts. Not twenty minutes later, he was entering Presbyterian-Columbia, with a box of chocolates of expensive brand and tasteful wrapping.

The reception desk staff begrudgingly admitted to a Detective Clement being there, but only after Carval had been forced to dial O'Leary so that he could give permission. Patient confidentiality was a *bitch*, he decided.

When he entered her room, her eyes were shut. The contrast of her dark hair against pallid skin and white hospital linens was too much for him, and he took two or three well-constructed shots before the inappropriateness of his conduct even had a chance to dawn. He didn't delete them, though.

Closer to the bed, he could see the violent bruising on her arm, some – less, not that that was a consolation – on her face. Lightly, he ran a fingertip over her cheek, avoiding the splotched lividity, then traced down to her arm and ended up with his fingers twined in hers, sitting down beside her and stroking his thumb repetitively over the back of her hand.

After far too long, her lashes fluttered, then opened. Her brown eyes were unfocused and hazy, briefly, then clear.

"What happened?" she asked, in a pained half-whisper, as if it hurt to speak, and then, "You?"

"Me," Carval said, a little surprised at her surprise, and more than a little hurt – at least, till her fingers tightened on his. "O'Leary and the others are a bit busy finding them."

"How? Never saw them," she slurred.

"I took photos."

"Photos?" Life, albeit fuzzy, slammed into her voice. "How'd you get photos?"

"Hid," he muttered uncomfortably. "No flash. They didn't see me, and I just kept shooting and hoping it would work."

"Chain of evidence?"

"O'Leary did all that."

"Good. You did good."

Her eyes drifted shut again, but her fingers were still twined into his. A few moments later, a brisk nurse arrived. Carval took the line of least resistance and cleared out until the nurse was done, much happier.

It didn't occur to him at any stage that he'd never have sat quietly for that long – it felt that long, but truthfully it was likely only half an hour or so – with any of his previous girlfriends; certainly not while they were asleep or otherwise unresponsive.

When he went back in, Casey had spotted the chocolates, and, from the way she was wriggling uncomfortably, had been trying to sit up without causing herself serious pain. She looked very like a sulky five-year old who couldn't get at a treat which was out of reach. It was cute – it would have been cute, without the livid bruising.

"Something you want?" he asked cheerfully, with a slightly lecherous grin.

"You brought chocolate." Casey was stating the obvious, there. And she'd completely ignored the grin while focusing completely on the chocolates.

"Yep. It was that or grapes, and chocolate is almost never wrong."

"Chocolate is a fundamental human right," she stated flatly. She sounded clearer.

"Are they going to let you out?"

"Hope so. They don't think there's any real damage."

That wasn't damage? She looked like an accident in a paint factory, and that was just the bits he could see.

"I wasn't shot. Nothing's broken. No real damage," she said briskly, recovering Casey-ness with every moment that passed.

"But you're hurt."

"Temporary. I'll be fine by the weekend."

Carval, not a fan of pain, winced.

"I'll be a lot finer as soon as we take these guys down. Who was it?"

"Merowin" –

"I *knew* that much" –

"And Sackson?"

"Sackson? The research chief? Not Brewman?"

"Brewman wasn't there."

"Hm," Casey hummed thoughtfully. "Who did the beating?" She was entirely dispassionate about it: as if it hadn't been her at all.

"I don't know. They were escaping when I took the photos."

Casey thought. Carval did something profoundly useful and opened the box of chocolates, then looked at Casey, still lying flat. Her pained wriggling had not achieved any form of verticality.

"Shall I prop you up?" he asked.

"Yes. Thanks."

Very cautiously, he found her waist, swathed in a too-large hospital gown. She winced. He tried a little higher up, which was no better, and then her hips, which seemed far too intimate for a semi-public setting, but had fewer winces. He hoisted rapidly, stuffed two pillows in behind her, and withdrew his hands.

"That's better," she said more happily, and examined the chocolate selection carefully. "Want one?" There was a distinct implication that one was all that he would be allowed.

"Please."

Casey chose, and chewed cheerfully. "So," she pondered aloud, when the chocolate had been swallowed, "Sackson must have put the first hit in, and then it was all over. I couldn't do anything once he kicked me in the gut."

"But" –

"It's not like the movies. If you get kicked that hard, you don't turn round and suddenly you're able to beat hell out them."

"Oh."

240

"Try as O'Leary might, we're not superheroes. He ought to be The Thing from the Fantastic Four," she added dryly. "I offered to do his make-up, but he wouldn't let me." She made a disappointed moue. "Totally unfair." To salve the wound, she munched another chocolate.

"Anyway, I got photos of them. Then I called 9-1-1 and O'Leary."

"'Kay. Sackson's prints'll be in Merowin's lab, then. Or there'll be something. A hair, anything. O'Leary better have sent CSU in, stat." Her eyes lit up. "Do you know where my phone is?"

"No."

"Oh. Well, can I borrow yours then? You've got O'Leary's number."

Carval unlocked it and handed it over with some resignation. Clearly Casey, rather than being a pathetically pained patient, intended to run her investigation and her team from her hospital bed. This seemed a little...um...*dedicated*. In his own defence, he snitched another chocolate, and avoided Casey's swipe at his thieving fingers.

"Mine!" she squawked, and then, "O'Leary, it's me."

"You're supposed to be recoverin'," the big man rumbled. "Whatcha doin' callin' me up?"

"I want to know what's going on," she fired back. "C'mon. What've we got?"

"Your boy took good enough shots that we could ID them. Tracked 'em on street cams, as far's we could, lost 'em at Riverside and 108th. Uniforms are out there."

"Sackson's going to dispose of Merowin first chance he gets. Why didn't you go after them last night?"

"Didn't have an ID till Carval an' Tyler patched the faces together. Took a while." Casey made an angry-turkeycock noise. "None of that, Casey. Was as fast as it could be done. Faster than the techs would've been." She subsided. "Anyways, couldn't go anywhere till I'd cleared up the little misunderstanding with the medics."

"Uh?"

"They thought your boy had somethin' to do with the beatin' you took. Needed to sort them first. Didn't want him suspected."

"Dumbasses," Casey bit. "Like he'd've hung around for it if he had."

"Yeah, well. Anyways," O'Leary said again, "uniforms are out, CSU have swept Merowin's office an' are off doin' their magic tricks, we got photo ID, all we need is Merowin an' Sackson."

"You'll only find Sackson. Merowin's dead and in the Hudson by now."

"Most like."

"We need to pull in Brewman, too. Conspiracy – to defraud, if not to murder. Even if we can't pin anything on him, the SEC will."

"On that too. Don't you trust me or somethin'? I got it all under total control." There was a rude noise in the background. Casey attributed it to

Andy.

"It's my case," she said somewhat sulkily.

"It's your recovery. Kent'll have your head if you come in when you should be in the hospital."

"Bully," Casey grumbled. "I wanna take these bastards *down*."

"Hurry up an' get fixed, then. If you c'n walk okay, you c'n come with me."

"If I can lift my gun, *you* can come with *me*. You can carry me."

O'Leary's deep bass belly laugh rang out of the phone. "Sure I can. It'll be like a sci-fi movie where they ride on an exoskeleton."

"Oops, got to go. Doctor just walked in. See you."

"Bye."

Casey handed the phone back, and regarded the doctor hopefully.

"I'll discharge you," she said. "No exertion, no heavy lifting, and let your boyfriend do everything for you."

Casey was speechless. Carval, fortunately, didn't emit any of his thoughts, most of which were *Yes!*

Papers were signed, clothes – very grubby – produced, and Casey regarded her smashed phone with despair as Carval steered her out.

"I hope they can recover it," she said unhappily. "I don't like being in the bullpen without a phone."

"What?"

"I'm going to the bullpen."

"You can barely walk."

"Don't have to walk. The boys'll get my coffees, and I can sit at my desk." Her face was set mutinously. "This is *my* case and *I'm* taking them down."

"But the doctor" –

"The hell with the doctor. I'm going to the precinct. You coming with me or not?"

I think I'd better, Carval thought. *Catch you when you fall over.* He swiped up the remainder of the chocolates, on the grounds that she would surely be cross if they went missing.

Carval sated his deep desire to sweep Casey up and kidnap her, to prevent her acting on her insane view that she should go to work, by hailing a cab and inserting her into it, during which process she only winced every half second and squeaked painfully a mere dozen times. This was clearly unworthy of comment, and so Carval didn't comment. He was rather looking forward to the commentary of the rest of the team, which he expected would be pointed, if not extensive.

He wasn't wrong.

"What the *hell*, Casey?" was the opening salvo, from the ever-articulate Andy.

"My case."

"Your dumb ass," Tyler growled. "You should be home resting."

"Don't you trust us?" O'Leary tried plaintively. "We got this."

"Have you got Sackson yet?"

"Waallll" –

"No. So no, you haven't got this, so I'm on it too."

"Everything's being done," Andy pointed out. "There's nothing for you to do, except sit and glower and make the bullpen look like a modern art installation."

Casey growled and did indeed glower.

"See?"

"You're spoilin' our rep." She raised a quizzical eyebrow. "Ev'ryone knows we're the good-lookin' team. An' here you are all shades of yellow an' purple."

"Those colours don't suit you, and they don't go either," Andy jibed gently. "You gotta get a better colour consultant. And a personal shopper, because those clothes look like they belong in the nearest Dumpster."

Casey growled some more, but a grin was twitching at her mouth.

"Need some arnica," was Tyler's only contribution.

"That come in blue?" O'Leary asked. "Might improve the yellow."

Casey snickered, and stopped with an abrupt, pained gasp. The three cops shifted into a defensive, protective group around her.

"Don't let Kent hear that," Andy said. "You'll be in deep shit."

"Sit down all nice-like an' mebbe he won't notice too much."

Tyler grunted, disbelievingly.

"If he doesn't look at her face," Andy pointed out.

Casey lowered herself very cautiously into her chair and sighed.

"Tell me what we've got," she ordered, and they began.

CHAPTER 33

Two hours later, Captain Kent had not been seen, much to the team's relief. Unfortunately, Sackson and/or Merowin had not been seen either. Brewman had been located, picked up, and left to cool his heels in Holding for the moment. Andy and Tyler volunteered to get lunch for everyone, including Carval, who had stuck around, taking occasional shots of the bullpen and anything else that caught his eye, but always circling back to Casey: making her coffee, getting her water, and – just once – helping her to stand up. She had declined his assistance in going to the restroom, and had shuffled off without comment or too many pained noises.

It hadn't been for want of pain. She *hurt*. It wasn't the first time she'd been hurt, of course, but it was the first time she'd really been beaten up – the advantage of being paired with O'Leary, who could take out grizzlies with a single punch, and who merely needed to unfold to his full height and width for problems magically to disappear and aggressive types to discover inner and outer peace and harmony.

She leaned heavily on the restroom sinks after she was comfortable again (she'd waited as long as she could) and bleakly surveyed the damage. The last time she'd had that shade of acid-mustard yellow on her face she'd been five and at a face painting stall. The purple – well, maybe when she was first trying out make-up. It hadn't suited her skin tone then either.

She tentatively pulled up her t-shirt, gasped, and tucked it straight back down. Ugh. That was vile. She wouldn't be running for a while, or practising yoga, or indeed taking any form of exercise, which thought reminded her of the exceedingly pleasant exercise early the night before. Much better. That was a nice thought. At least it would have been, if there were any chance of repeating it in the next few weeks.

What? Again? *More?* Was that really a good plan, Casey?

Yes, it damn well was. She had no fun in her life. She had nowhere to go that didn't make demands. And Carval didn't make demands, except that they had considerable fun. So as long as it didn't get *complicated*, that was just fine. Better than friends-with-benefits, but nothing that might be a serious emotional commitment, on either side. Yep. That sounded just perfect.

She shuffled out of the restroom, firmly controlling her desire to wince and wishing, for the first time ever, that she kept a full make-up kit in her desk.

She wished it even harder ten seconds later.

"Clement!"

Aw, *shit!*

"My office. Now."

Captain Kent had arrived at the most inconvenient time possible, and worse, had actually paid some attention. Why couldn't he go straight to his office rather than interfering with Casey and her case? They were doing just fine.

She creaked up, exceedingly slowly – fortunately Carval didn't hoist her out of her chair again, but regardless of that Kent was watching her with unpleasantly beady eyes – and shuffled yet more, towards the Captain's domain. Or possibly towards the place of execution.

"Explain," Kent said coldly. He regarded her for an instant. "Sit down, then explain."

She did, with some relief. The next few minutes would not have been improved by having to ask to sit, or worse, falling down.

"The main suspect in the murder of Belvez, Merowin, called me last night saying that he had proof that the perpetrator was someone else. I met him, with back up in place but out of sight, and a second man, who we have identified as Carl Sackson, beat me up."

"I see."

"We're doing everything possible to find Sackson and Merowin. Brewman has already been picked up. It appears that the three of them conspired to falsify results to inflate Telagon's share price so they all made money. When Belvez found out the results had been faked, one of them killed him. I thought it was Merowin at first, but actually now I think it's likely Sackson."

"I see," Kent said again. "As it happens, Clement, I am entirely uninterested in the irrelevant details of how you are closing this case. I have no doubt that you and your team will do so in their normal efficient fashion."

Casey winced.

"I am, however, exceedingly interested in the exceedingly *relevant* details of your injuries, whether you have attended an ER, and the advice that they might have given you about, say, resting" – Kent's tone took on a bitingly sarcastic inflection – "not undertaking anything strenuous, or indeed requesting medical leave."

"I did go to the ER."

"I require a rather more complete answer than that, Detective. Alternatively, I can request the records from the healthcare plan, and if I find you to have been less than forthcoming there will be consequences."

Casey winced again. Consequences, in that tone, would *start* with flaying, and then continue with evisceration and salting.

"They checked me over, kept me in overnight in case there was damage to my spleen or kidneys, found nothing broken and no serious damage, and released me this morning. I'm not to exert myself or do any heavy lifting."

"And which part of *not exerting yourself* do you consider that attending work falls under?" Kent asked, very nastily.

Casey opened and shut her mouth a few times, without finding an answer which would satisfy Kent or indeed basic sanity.

"While you're considering that point, I also notice that that photographer is fussing around rather more than expected. Is there anything you would like to tell me?"

"No, sir." At least that was easy. "He keeps out of the way of the job and doesn't talk much."

Kent raised his eyebrows and regarded her piercingly. It had no effect. She hadn't told a single lie.

"You will stay in the bullpen. You will not go to arrest these lowlifes. You may interrogate them, when they arrive here. You will do so with Detective O'Leary, who *might* be able to insert some sense into you. And you will leave promptly at shift end, regardless of any arrests."

"But sir, if I'm interrogating…" Casey trailed off under Kent's icy glare.

"You may finish. That single interrogation of that single suspect. There will be no further interrogations. Other members of your team are equally competent and can take over. You *will* go home, voluntarily. Or I will bench you."

"Yes, sir." There wasn't really anything else to say.

"Dismissed."

Casey heaved herself up under Kent's acid gaze and shuffled out.

Behind her, Kent shook his head ruefully. Sending her home now, which had certainly been his first thought, wouldn't have helped. She'd just have been on the phone every five minutes, which was not conducive to efficiency or clear up stats. Still, she'd be out of here on the dot of shift end or he would know the reason why.

Casey trudged back to her desk in less than happy mood. She'd wanted to see that pair arrested. It would have been better than morphine for her pain. Humph. At least Kent hadn't asked about her back-up. That would have been very undesirable.

"Still alive?" O'Leary chortled. "Thought he'd send you home."

"She'd call," Tyler pointed out dispassionately. "Get in the way." Casey emitted a strangled noise of fury.

"We got Sackson," Andy cheered.

"We got him?"

"Turned up at Telagon. Alone. Uniforms are escorting him in."

"Awwwww," whimpered O'Leary. "I wanted to bring him in. 'S not fair." Everyone ignored the ten-ton-toddler act.

"He went to work? He's crazy."

"No, he didn't know we had photos of him. As far as he knows, Casey's in hospital or on sick leave – which is where you should be, Casey" – she stuck her tongue out at Andy, childishly – "and she never got a glimpse of him, only Merowin."

"According to the uniforms there was a lot of *do you know who I am I'll have all your badges for this* going on."

"Did they find Merowin?" Casey asked.

"No."

"Anyone looked in the river yet?"

"No. Let's deal with this guy first."

"Okay. O'Leary, you and me are up."

"How d'you wanna do it? Iffen he sees you creakin' in like a dead tree he'll know he got you."

"Yeah. We're going to use it. *Someone* beat me up. Someone with Merowin. After Merowin admitted fraud and that he and Brewman were part of it. Whoever beat me up will be going down for that, as well as fraud." She paused, and despite her facial bruising managed an extremely nasty smile. "But we're going to make him wait. He thinks he's such a big man. He's so important. By the time we remember about him he'll be really mad. And then I'll take the lead and be really mean to him. He won't like that, either. Not a man who's used to women in charge, Sackson."

"Do I get to be all pally?" O'Leary asked hopefully.

"Not this time. You get to look mean. Big and mean. Bigger than him."

"I get to be bad cop?" O'Leary appeared utterly delighted. "You never let me be bad cop."

"You get to be bad cop. I get to be worse cop."

They smiled at each other, perfectly satisfied. Carval, lurking in the corner out of the way, snapped the identically vicious smiles.

"Shall we go practice on Brewman? I need to warm up to bein' bad cop."

"We could do that. Not forgetting to let Sackson know that he's waiting because we're dealing with his junior. Tyler, Andy, you wanna do that?"

The twin nasty smiles became even nastier. Carval took another few shots.

"Let's go," Casey said very happily. "Tyler, Andy, can you get Brewman into Interrogation, and read him his rights – let's hope he doesn't ask for a lawyer – and then Sackson straight there after he's been booked? Not forgetting taking his prints, and a mugshot. It'd be a shame to deny him the full experience, don't you think?" Her face fell into cold, hard lines. "After all, he didn't deny me the full beating up experience."

The instant drop in the team's temperature was palpable even to Carval, who therefore didn't make the mistakes of speaking, getting into their way or even their sightlines, or helping Casey out of her chair.

Nor did anyone else help Casey out of her chair, though the exchanges of rolled eyes and twitching of three sets of fingers inclined Carval to think that all of them wanted to help. He remembered O'Leary's words about hospital visiting, and decided that they'd all been trained – or more likely threatened – out of it. Still, it was hard to watch. Somewhere in Carval's subconscious was a hardwired desire to protect women – er, no, not women in general, this woman in particular – which was emphatically not required right now. He didn't understand it. He was a modern man, and women didn't need to be protected. This woman especially didn't need to be protected: she was as tough as they come.

Oh. Yes, she was as tough as they come – but then she'd been soft and snuggly and pettable and she'd *wanted* to be cuddled and cosseted and petted. Off duty. Which was still not the same as protected. That was nearly a massive mistake: he could totally see the outline of that discussion and it involved pain. His.

Right now, however, Casey had locked down cold, and she looked like she was shrouded in the wrath of God. This couldn't be omitted: he had to capture it. He began shooting: Casey's glacier demeanour; O'Leary's massive, looming, ominous scale. They were terrifying. Even Tyler, who was not exactly cuddly, looked as friendly as Big Bird beside them.

"Showtime," Casey said, as Andy gave her the thumbs up. Carval, Andy and Tyler whisked themselves to Observation. Casey shuffled out of the bullpen, O'Leary thudding menacingly behind her.

From the one-way window, Carval could see Brewman, sweating, white and nervous: jumping when the door opened. There was no lawyer. Casey strode in – and he guessed that would cost her three super-strength Advil, but it worked. Brewman took one look at her, a further desperate glance at O'Leary's impassive, monolithical bulk, and crumpled into his chair.

"Terence Brewman," Casey bit contemptuously. "Fraudster, thief, and murderer. I get you first, and then we'll let the SEC take what's left. Not that you'll need any cash or assets in Rikers, and since you'll never get out, you won't need any afterwards either."

"What? I never murdered anyone."

Casey looked coldly sceptical.

"Ricardo Belvez is dead. You, Michael Merowin, and Carl Sackson were involved in a major fraud which he discovered. And Merowin has told me that you were part of the conspiracy that left Dr Belvez dead. Conspiracy to murder is the same as if you killed the man yourself."

Brewman stared at her, mouth unattractively agape. Damp patches spread beneath his arms into his expensive cotton shirt.

"Rikers is waiting for you," O'Leary said, no hint of his hayseed drawl. He sounded menacing. "You're pretty enough for them. Nice uptown accent. They'll like you." He bared his teeth. It wasn't a smile.

"There's no death penalty in New York," Casey picked up the rhythm. "You'll have plenty of time to contemplate your mistakes."

"I didn't! I didn't kill anyone!"

"They all say that," O'Leary growled, deep in his barrel chest. "Don't they?"

"Sure they do," Casey replied acidly. "And they all end up doing life without parole just the same."

"I *didn't*," Brewman half shrieked. "Carl said don't be a problem. We were just going to scare you off."

"Do I look scared off?" Casey enquired frigidly. "And you've just admitted assaulting a police detective."

Brewman paled even further. He was already panicked and they'd barely begun.

"That'll look good in court," O'Leary remarked casually.

"I wasn't there. I never did it."

"Someone did." That hung heavy in the still, cold air: as frozen as Casey's bruised face. "And all of it is documented."

"What? How? I wasn't *there*."

"But you knew about it. You just said so."

"But I wasn't there!"

"That's not relevant. You knew it was going to happen and you didn't stop it. You knew about the fraud and you didn't stop that. So why don't you just admit that you knew about Belvez's murder and you didn't stop that either, and then we've got our trifecta and we can all go home." She paused. "Except you, of course. You can go to Rikers." She everted her lips, which was also not a smile. "You can share a cell with your pal Sackson.

"Might even add Merowin, if we can find him," O'Leary added. "Unless you want to tell us where he is?" Menace pervaded the small room, thick and suffocating. Brewman took quick, shallow, desperate breaths.

"I don't *know*. He went with Carl last night and I didn't see either of them after Carl left and I *wasn't there*. It wasn't me. I didn't do anything."

The rhythm of the interrogation was hitting Brewman like a series of

Muhammad Ali jabs: relentless, metronomic. He already looked punch-drunk: unable to appreciate that he'd already admitted his guilt and that Casey and O'Leary were now drilling into Sackson and Merowin.

"Whose idea was faking the results?"

"When did you know Belvez was joining?"

"What did Merowin think of Belvez?"

"Did you try to bring Belvez in on your scam?"

Tick-tock, tick-tock, as regular as a pendulum.

"Who killed Belvez?"

"Was it you?"

"Was it Merowin?"

"Was it Sackson?"

"Mike called us," Brewman whimpered pathetically. "He said Belvez knew he was faking. He'd hit him. But he wasn't dead. He *wasn't* dead. Mike said he was still alive."

"Who went to see?"

"Carl. Carl could always calm Mike down. Mike got hysterical."

"So Carl went to see Mike the night Belvez died?"

"Yes, yes he did. I wasn't there. Carl went but I didn't and I wasn't there."

He was frantic: pleading and pathetic and petrified. The cops were impassive. The pleas fell on cold, deaf ears.

"I think we're done for the moment."

It didn't sound like they were giving Brewman a break.

"You're going back to Holding. We'll be talking to you again." Casey paused a beat. "After we've talked to Sackson." Another pause. "Thanks to you, we've got a lot to talk to him about."

Brewman's colour drained entirely. Casey stalked out, O'Leary massive behind her.

As soon as she was through the door, she stumbled: O'Leary caught her with one huge paw and concealed her pained steps from the interrogation rooms. They arrived in Observation, and Casey leaned on the wall, face tight, wincing.

"Hurts?" O'Leary rumbled.

"Yeah," she breathed out: breathed in again, slowly; out and in. "But we're going to get these bastards."

"As long as you don't faint," Andy sniped.

"That's not me, it's you," Casey flipped back: but she was still leaning heavily on the wall, and O'Leary was bare inches away from her.

"Advil," Tyler said, and magically produced a pack from his pocket. "Take them."

"They make my head fuzzy," Casey complained.

"Take them."

"One."

"Okay," Tyler said. It sounded to Carval as if it was a game they played. Casey swallowed it dry, and made another face. The men were unobtrusively around her. Carval didn't think they meant to be protective, but the team bond was very obvious. He felt almost shut out. None of them noticed.

"Sackson next," Casey said coldly. "After he's had some time to chill."

"Don't think he's going to be cool when you've kept him waiting an hour."

"Shame he's not as important as he thinks he is," Andy snipped. "He's not going to like it when you tell him that, is he?"

"Shouldn't think so." All four smiled their very nasty, identical smiles. It was as good as Carval saying, "Say cheese," which he had never in his entire photographic career let pass his lips. He didn't pass up the opportunity, though. Oh no. Ten fast shots later, he was sure he'd got another piece of the hunt: the pack, ready to go in for the kill. Teeth bared, as it were, ready to rip out the jugular.

"He sure didn't like it when we said you were busy with Brewman. He needs to calm down, do some meditation. He didn't have very harmonious chi."

Muffled sniggers emanated from everyone.

"I got harmonious chi," O'Leary resonated happily. "Ev'ry time I lock one of 'em up I get more harmonious." More sniggers echoed in the cramped space.

"Let's improve the harmony of Bigfoot's chi by tipping off the SEC," Casey suggested, and everyone agreed with that too. Andy wandered off to achieve that, and shortly wandered back again with another new outfit from the team's dressing-up box of nasty smiles.

Carval noticed that the few moments taken to discuss the luckless Sackson and call the SEC had provided just enough time for the Advil to start to kick in. Casey was already less white and the tight lines around her mouth had relaxed, which was reassuring, and also lessened his intense desire to hug her. Hugging her was not likely to be well received, right now: they were at work and in front of her team. Maybe later. He stayed quiet and out of the way.

After a few minutes more, in which Casey downed a strong coffee, then creaked out and creaked back again, they observed Sackson through the one-way mirror as he fidgeted, paced, and glanced at his watch. His temper didn't appear to be calming.

"Another minute?" Casey wondered.

"It'll take you that long to stagger there, seein' as you c'n barely walk."

"I guess. Okay, O'Leary, show time again. Feeling like a big bad cop?"

"Can't be a little one," he pointed out with a grin. "Let's go play,

Casey."

Their progress towards Interrogation was halted by a uniformed officer.

"Detective Clement?" he said, trying hard not to stare at her multi-coloured bruising. "We got a Dr Michael Merowin" –

"Great. Put him in a cell for now."

"Uh, he's dead."

"Dead?"

"Shot. First up, looked like suicide, but ME McDonald's on the scene."

"Okay," Casey said slowly, neurons firing frantically. "Andy, Tyler, on me. We need to rethink this."

She staggered back to her chair. The team gathered around her desk, perching on corners, except O'Leary, who collected his chair to prevent everyone having to yell the long way up to his ears.

"If this is a suicide I'll quit chocolate for a month," she said, to exaggerated gasps. "It's got to be faked."

"Yeah."

"So. Tyler, you go peer over McDonald's shoulder. Tell him we think it was Sackson. Andy, you make sure Sackson's booking-in details get to CSU and McDonald so they can try matching them up a bit faster than usual."

"Sure thing."

Tyler simply nodded.

"O'Leary, think we've got enough for a warrant on Sackson?"

"Most likely. Let's add it all up, an' see what his bill looks like."

Carval regarded the sudden anthill of activity, and rapidly assessed his own interests.

"Tyler, can I come with you?" he asked.

"Okay," he said, laconically.

"You're not shooting more in Interrogation?"

"You're not going back to interrogate Sackson now."

All four cops stared at him as if he'd grown another head.

"Huh?"

"If you're doing all this on Merowin, you're going to put Sackson back in Holding till you get some of these results back and then you're going to hit him with them when he lies."

Their stares turned faintly impressed. "Yep. We sure are."

"Seems like you've learned a bit, photographer." O'Leary was approving. "You 'n' Tyler run along now." He made to pat them on the head, which they rapidly dodged.

Andy was already on the move. Casey and O'Leary instructed a pair of very burly uniforms to put Sackson back in a cell and then rapidly started to construct a warrant. Carval followed Tyler.

CHAPTER 34

A couple of hours later, Tyler and Carval returned, Carval looking exceedingly satisfied and Tyler with an undoubtedly McDonald-induced expression of irritation. Tyler's irritation didn't improve when he was met with a barrage of shark-like smiles.

"We got our warrant. Uniforms are executing it now."

"Just waiting for CSU to give me preliminary results."

"How was McDonald?"

"Usual."

"Did he say anything useful?"

"Barely." They groaned. "But…"

"But what?"

"Yes. But what, Detective Tyler?" Kent had padded up to the team. "I have a very high-powered attorney demanding that I release Carl Sackson. Tell me we have some evidence to hold him."

"We do," Casey said, a bright smile illuminating her bruises. "We know that Sackson was the man who helped beat me up."

"How?"

"Photos," she said with vicious delight.

"*Photos?*" Kent repeated – and then stopped cold with a very unpleasant expression of realisation dawning. Uh-oh. "We will be discussing exactly how those *photos* were obtained later." He turned to Tyler. "But what, Detective?"

"ME McDonald confirmed it wasn't suicide, sir."

"We have street camera footage of Merowin and Sackson leaving the lab together, too," Casey added. "Circumstantial, but he was the last person to be seen with Merowin."

"Time of death estimated at about midnight to two a.m., sir," Tyler noted.

"Last camera footage was just after midnight," O'Leary's bass joined in. "So it's right in the window."

"I see," Kent said thoughtfully.

"And we got a warrant for Sackson's apartment, Merowin's apartment, and Merowin's room at the lab," Casey put in. "So the judge thought that we had enough, sir."

Kent acquired a rare hint of approval. "I see," he said again. "I can certainly refuse release on all of those grounds. However, don't delay your interrogation much longer. And be aware that this attorney will be present."

"Yes, sir," came in chorus.

Kent turned away.

"Captain Kent?"

"You? What is it?"

"Er," Carval said, for the first time in years a little intimidated, "er, could I take photos of you?"

That was in the way of asking for forgiveness, not permission, since he already had done, without actually requesting consent.

Kent's face coloured. "Photos?" he repeated. It was his word of the day, at that point. He regarded Carval with a laser-like glare. The detectives made themselves very unobtrusive, and O'Leary, who couldn't be unobtrusive, did his best impression of a motionless mountain.

"Yes. You in charge of your detectives, keeping a watchful eye."

Kent harrumphed. "I shall think about it." He stalked off, stiff-backed. Carval let sleeping Captains lie. Kent was scary, up close, but…. He took a surreptitious look at the shots. Yep, those worked. He felt a sudden desire to go back to his studio and print them: rearrange his board and shots – and then he remembered that there would be the key interrogation to watch, and the momentary urge died unmourned.

"Are we ready?" O'Leary asked, tolling the bass knell of doom without any of his usual humour or lazy, yokel drawl.

"Oh, yes," Casey bit. "Let's *do* this."

The team rose as one, and moved at Casey's limping pace towards Interrogation. Carval's observant eye noted that she was moving no more easily than earlier, and was less than happy that he could do nothing about it.

Three of them parked themselves in Observation. Two moved on to the door of an Interrogation room.

Casey entered first, and noted a flash of hidden, vicious satisfaction on Sackson's face as he saw the livid bruising. The attorney was merely shocked. When O'Leary thumped in behind her, stone faced, both of them quailed. Sackson's mouth opened, but then closed again. It was pretty clear that Sackson didn't like meeting someone bigger than he was. Bullies rarely did.

"Carl Sackson?" Casey began, and read him his Miranda rights, perfectly and precisely enunciated. "Do you understand?"

"Yes," he snapped, and jammed his lips together. The attorney looked satisfied.

"You are a suspect in the murders of Ricardo Belvez and Michael Merowin, and in the assault of Detective Katrina Clement," O'Leary thundered. "Have you anything to say?"

"No."

"My client is unjustly accused," the sharp-faced attorney pinched out, each word carrying the full value of its extortionate charge out rate. "You have no evidence."

"Oh?" Casey took up the rhythm.

"My client is a senior executive of a major corporation. It's quite ridiculous that he can be accused of this nonsense."

"Has he told you about his fraud yet?" Casey enquired. "Hope your retirement plans aren't invested in Telagon."

"What has that to do with anything? You're accusing him of murder."

"And assault on a police detective," O'Leary reminded them.

"Your client," Casey stated, focusing only on the attorney, "is about to be the subject of an SEC investigation into falsifying the results of the latest Telagon research in order to manipulate the market and for his own personal gain. His colleague is already in a cell. We interviewed him earlier. He admitted it."

"Hope someone else is paying your bill," O'Leary jibed. "Mr" – that carried sheer contempt – "Sackson here won't have a cent when the SEC finish." The attorney went a little pale. "We already informed them." He went white.

"Fraud?" he said weakly.

"Yes," Casey confirmed. "Michael Merowin was part of a conspiracy to fake critical results, thereby inflating Telagon's profits and misleading the markets, reporting only to Mr Brewman – who is already in custody – and Mr Sackson. Ricardo Belvez discovered the problem. He's dead. Merowin is dead. And I was lured to Merowin's office late last night to listen to his confession – so he said – and someone jumped me, with Merowin's assistance. I guess I'm lucky I'm not dead, too."

"You dumb cops couldn't read research with a grade school primer. The results weren't falsified. They were straight as a die. This is a tissue of lies and unfounded assertions. By the time we're finished here your careers'll be in the dirt."

Casey and O'Leary looked at each other, turned back to Sackson and smiled like matched knives. "I didn't say *we* proved the research was fake. As you correctly point out, we are not opto-electronics experts. Professor

John Terrison, at Columbia, who is both Merowin and Belvez's boss and is in charge of that group, tried to replicate both their results, supervised by CSU. He couldn't replicate Merowin's. He's prepared to testify. Are you going to call him dumb?"

Sackson's face was suffused with fury. "Terrison? That stick-in-the-mud fossil? He won't testify. We fund them $20 million a year. He knows what's good" – rather too late, the attorney elbowed him.

"So you're saying you're going to threaten Terrison not to testify in a murder trial? I don't think that's going to go down well in evidence."

"You have no evidence."

"This is an interrogation in which we have read you your rights. Everything is recorded. You've just admitted that you'll try to tamper with witnesses. That's a felony."

The attorney went whiter. "I would like some time to confer with my client," he said.

"Sure," O'Leary's bass growl answered. "We can wait. Just like Rikers is waiting for him."

Casey very obviously winced and creaked as she stood up, leaning hard on her chair. O'Leary put a massive hand under her arm to assist her, and she leaned almost her whole weight on him. It made no apparent difference to O'Leary, who appeared to half-carry her out of Interrogation.

"You can put me down now, Bigfoot," Casey complained as soon as the door to Observation had shut behind her.

"Aw, c'mon. I didn't get to the gym this mornin', seein' as I was investigatin' this dirtbag. You'll do, 'stead of weights." Casey growled. "Now, you're a good bit lighter than my usual, but…"

"Shut up, O'Leary." She grinned nastily at Tyler and Andy. "Did he buy it?"

"Sure did. He was watching you all the way out the door. Really liked it every time you wobbled."

"That was a *performance*?" Carval gasped.

"Of course it was," Casey scoffed at him. "You think I'd let a thug like that see he'd hurt me if I didn't want him to?"

"Oh," Carval said flatly. She'd totally fooled him.

"She was *so* leanin' on me," O'Leary whispered. "Don't tell her I told you. That wasn't all an act. She's hurtin' pretty bad."

"Oh," he said again. Casey glared suspiciously at them.

"Just don't let on. We'll fix it all later." O'Leary dropped an umbrella-sized eyelid in a wink of unparalleled salaciousness. "Or you will."

Carval preserved an entirely bland face, which O'Leary greeted with an expression of total scepticism.

In Interrogation, Sackson and his attorney were having something that appeared to be an exceedingly animated discussion. Sackson's infuriated face was crimson and contorted, and he was pounding on the table. The attorney was trying to calm him, with no success at all.

Finally the attorney threw his hands up in a very *do-what-the-hell-you-want-then* gesture, and flumped backwards in his chair. Another moment passed, and then the attorney, at an aggressive gesture from Sackson, opened the door and said something to the uniform outside.

"They've finished," the uniform said. "You're clear to start again." She grinned. "Can I watch?" she asked hopefully.

"Sure," Casey said. "Enjoy." She limped out, followed by the protective mountain of O'Leary.

"Who's this?" the uniform asked Andy.

"Photographer. Haven't you seen him buzzing around the bullpen?"

"No." She turned to the one-way glass.

"Watch?" Carval asked.

"Watch the floor show. Casey interrogating is, um, entertaining."

"If you like horror shows," Tyler noted cynically.

"Blood on the floor is the least of it," Andy smirked. "She's really gentle with those who deserve it, but somehow no-one who's a suspect ever deserves it."

"Gentle?"

"Okay, she went *aww* at a cute kitten once. That counts, in our world."

Tyler snickered. Carval's attention snapped back to the interrogation room as he saw the door start to open. Casey had exaggerated her discomfort again, and this time Carval noted the flash of cruel pleasure in Sackson's face.

Inside, Casey sank into her chair.

"All you've got is circumstantial," Sackson said. "I haven't done anything wrong so you can't pin anything on me."

Casey and O'Leary raised eyebrows. "You think?"

"Sure I do," he said with overweening confidence. "The SEC won't find anything on me either, because I didn't do anything."

"Really? Brewman's testimony said you knew about all of it. He said you went out with Merowin last evening – same evening someone beat me up and Merowin got dead."

"If Merowin was faking and Brewman was in on it of course they'd try to drag me in. If Merowin's dead he did it himself. Shame at his behaviour."

"Mm," Casey said thoughtfully. "That's your story, is it?"

"It's no story, it's the truth." Sackson regarded her with a smugly satisfied smile. The attorney, clearly more sensitive to atmosphere, still looked worried. "So since you got no evidence, let me go. If you apologise for being such a dumb woman, maybe I won't sue."

"Why do you think I don't have evidence?" Casey enquired coldly.

"If you had evidence you'd have produced it. You're bluffing and you can't even do that right."

O'Leary bared his teeth in a ferocious smile.

"I have photographs of you in Havemeyer Hall with Merowin last night," Casey said with satisfaction. "I had enough evidence to get a warrant for your apartment, Merowin's lab and Merowin's apartment, which is being executed as we speak. I've got footage of the hall cameras outside Belvez's apartment, and I think I'm going to be able to match you, Brewman and Merowin – or any two from three – to the pest control operatives two days after Belvez got dead." She stared coldly at Sackson. "Amazing what facial recognition technology can do. Not that you'd expect *dumb women* to know that, would you?"

"You're lying. There's no photos. No-one was there."

"How do you know?" Casey enquired.

"I wasn't there so I couldn't have been photographed."

The attorney looked happier. Sackson looked as if that was a clincher.

"So how do you explain these?"

Casey slid copies of Carval's patched together photos across the table. There was a terrible silence.

"And this. This is street camera footage – note the time and date stamps – of you leaving Columbia with Merowin, and walking along with him to Riverside Drive." She let that fall heavily between them. O'Leary, massive and menacing, stayed silent. "Your prints and DNA are already with CSU and the ME's office, so as soon as we find a single trace of you on Merowin you're dead meat."

Sackson's face shaded purple.

"So now that you've tried telling us nothing but lies, how about trying the truth? Let's summarise. You've beaten me up, you've conspired to defraud, you've conspired in Belvez's murder and you murdered Merowin. Quite a record for a desk driver." She looked at him with bored contempt. "Such a big man. Beating up women and stealing money, and then blaming it all on someone else. You don't even have the courage to own your own acts. Pathetic" –

"You stupid, stuck up bitch!" Sackson yelled, stung to furious admission. "You fucking deserved it. I wish I'd killed you like that pathetic dickless idiot Merowin. If he'd just kept his head we'd never have been found out. I should have gassed him like the other one."

The attorney put his head in his hands.

"Carl Sackson, you are under arrest for the murder of Michael Merowin, the murder of Ricardo Belvez, conspiracy to defraud, and assaulting a police officer in the execution of her duty."

O'Leary stood up to his immense full height, ungently spun Sackson and cuffed him, then walked him out to Booking. The attorney scuttled out.

Casey stayed seated. Now it was over, all the adrenaline had drained and all her bruises were forcibly reminding her of their painful presence.

Footsteps became audible, and shortly Tyler and Andy appeared at the door, followed by the inevitable figure of Carval. A moment later the O'Leary continental drift joined them.

"Got him," Tyler said approvingly.

"Another uniform terrorised," Andy noted, not quite as approvingly.

"Naw. She wanted to be like you."

"Don't think she'd want the bruises," Casey dragged out. "Got another Advil, Tyler?"

Tyler handed the pack over without comment, though his expression spoke volumes. Andy slipped out and slipped back again on silent, delicate feet, bearing a plastic cup of water. Casey downed two tablets and the water, made a face, and stayed sitting down. Nobody said anything, so it was a mystery why everyone could hear the words *Go home, Casey* as clear as day. Carval became aware of a weight of expectation upon him, emanating from the massed ranks of the men in the team.

"Let's get the loose ends tied up," Casey said into the silence.

The three cops looked around. *You, no you, no him, no you, not me, no way* passed through the air as they glanced at each other. Eventually O'Leary shrugged, in a *she-can't-shoot-me-I-guess* fashion which was not entirely convincing.

"We'll tie up the loose ends. You're goin' home, like you were meant to. Iffen you go now, an' let Carval here make sure you make it out the door without fallin' over, we won't eat your chocolates."

Casey squawked. "You touch *my* chocolate and I'll" –

"I c'n get there before you c'n stand up, way you look. You couldn't beat a dead snail in a race, right now. Go home, have a hot bath or somethin', find some Icy Hot."

"C'mon," Tyler added. "Home. We'll check."

"Not just yet, Clement," arrived a chilly voice from the door. "I want to understand how there were photos of the perpetrator. I wasn't aware that your regulation equipment" – Kent's gaze seared around the four cowering cops – "included sophisticated cameras?" He paused. "I might, of course, be wrong."

He wasn't wrong, and everyone knew it.

"I was there too," Carval admitted, choosing his words carefully to imply but never state that there was other back up. "I hid. When I heard something I took shots."

Kent's face betrayed an interesting war between considerable approval and considerable outrage.

"Carval and me patched them together after the techs got a copy – chain of evidence," Tyler said. Without telling a single lie, it vaguely implied that

Tyler had been there too. "O'Leary was about till the bus took Casey away."

Kent emitted a truly disgusted *pah* noise. He was sure he was being misled, but there was nothing he could put a finger on, and anyway his band of misfits had scored the big scalp *and* found something that would put the SEC a little in his debt.

"Okay," he said. "Well done, all." He spotted Carval, who was semi-hiding in the shadow of O'Leary. "You can take shots. Just don't tell me when you're doing it."

"Thank you."

"Clement, you get out and go home now. Take two days' leave. Come back when you don't look like a circus clown. It's bad for our reputation."

"Yes, sir," she agreed.

Kent's beady eye watched her as she heaved herself to her feet, slowly, and aimed for her desk. "The rest of you, tidy up the paperwork – I won't be authorising overtime, so if you're not finished by shift end – which is in less than half an hour – finish it first thing tomorrow."

"Yessir," they chorused, and fled.

Casey sat desultorily packing her purse and clearing her desk, accompanied by short, shallow breaths. Suddenly, she looked small and fragile: with the focused ferocity switched off, the commanding presence that made her seem so much larger than she really was had dropped away. She wasn't tall: she merely seemed so.

"I could use a beer," she said generically to the team.

"Guess it's better than Advil," Andy agreed. "Do we have to carry you, though? I'm not buying beer if I have to carry you. You buy it." She growled at him.

"Yeah. Even Bigfoot can't carry you that far. If you start now, you'll get there first."

O'Leary's ice-shelf smile appeared. "You go get the beers in. By the time you've gotten them, we'll be almost there." The smile became a broad grin. "Snail."

"Bigfoot." But she rose to a hunched position, pulled on her coat without any unnecessary movement, and picked up her small purse.

"Carry your chocolates?" Carval teased: the only way he could stop himself from picking her up and cosseting her. She flicked him a tired look. "What? You've got enough to manage carrying yourself. You don't think I'm going to carry you, do you? I'm not your weightlifting pet Bigfoot."

"I wouldn't let him carry me either," she snipped. "I can walk just fine."

"Sure you can. I'm going to enter you in the annual Giant Snail race, too." He smirked evilly. "I'm betting on the snails."

The three male cops regarded Carval meaningfully. He grinned back at them all over Casey's oblivious head. "See you there," he said. "Okay, let's get a cab." She seemed to be about to object. "Stop being difficult. If I don't make sure you get there in one piece your team will make sure I die painfully and then they'll hide the body."

"If you babysit me *I'll* make sure you die painfully and hide the body."

"Oh," murmured Carval in a very different tone, "I don't want to *babysit* you." Casey blushed crimson, which clashed horribly with the bruising. He whistled down a convenient cab, ushered her in, and followed.

CHAPTER 35

Five minutes later, in which Carval had not-so-gradually taken full advantage of Casey's inability to wreak revenge on him and had assumed a protectively cosseting posture including an exceedingly gentle arm curled around her shoulders, they pulled up at the Abbey pub. Carval paid the driver without so much as a questioning look at Casey, who didn't appear to notice his action, exited the cab, opened the door for her and then, on listening to the hurting pattern of her breathing as she moved, took the line of least annoyance and carefully assisted her to get out.

It took her a minute to straighten up, and even then she was leaning on Carval, at least until she realised she was, at which point she also realised that he had an arm around her. That was not particularly popular.

"I can walk," she noted irritably.

"Sure. And I can cuddle you."

"That doesn't follow."

"Why does it need to? Anyway, you didn't complain in the taxi so stop complaining now."

"I don't need to be babied."

"I don't want to baby you. I don't like babies. Or women who behave like babies. Or men who do, for that matter."

"Good. I don't do babyish."

"You do amaze me," Carval drawled sarcastically. "How could I have missed your complete lack of need for any care?"

Casey produced a small smirk. "Too busy looking through your lens."

"Nah. Must have been because you're little." He looked down at her dark hair. "Or maybe it's the curly hair. It's cute."

Casey emitted a spine-chilling growl and glare, by which Carval was entirely *not* frightened.

"That's cute too. I mean, it would be scary if I didn't know that you can barely stand up, but since I do, I'm not scared at all." To prove it, he tightened his arm around her just enough to notice, without hurting her bruises or pressing on cracked ribs. "And if you weren't bruised to bits, I'd prove how cute you are." He leered happily. She glared. "C'mon. Let's get you inside before someone thinks it was me who hit you."

"You couldn't lay a finger on me."

"Wouldn't. Not couldn't. Though I couldn't either because either you'd have shot me or the gang would have. I'll happily spar with you if you promise not to hurt me," he added, "but not now. Let's get you some beer, instead."

She raised a tired half-smile. "Or coffee. I can't do without good coffee."

"I noticed." He grinned. "I'm surprised your bruises aren't brown and black. You must have coffee in your veins."

"Might hurt less if I did," she muttered, which Carval was certain he wasn't supposed to hear. They perambulated awkwardly into the Abbey pub and found a comfortable corner where Casey could collapse into a soft couch.

"Beer or coffee?"

She considered. "Beer."

"Advil aren't an admission of weakness, you know. And they don't cost more than diamonds, so you don't have to ration them."

"Can't take any more for another hour."

Which was not entirely an answer, Carval noted. Rather than get himself into trouble by commenting, he acquired beers, sat down next to Casey and calmly wrapped his free arm around her shoulders again. Surprisingly, she executed a tiny, getting-comfortable wriggle, and didn't object. Even more surprisingly, she didn't wince. Much.

"You need a hot water bottle."

"Don't have one. I'm fine."

Carval gave a disbelieving huff. "Yeah, because being beaten black and blue with cracked ribs is fine. Still, if you don't have a hot water bottle you'll just have to stick with me."

"Huh?"

"I'm hot." She made a scoffing noise. "So you should stay curled up to me," he said provocatively.

"Yeah, right. I had a teddy bear. When I was five." She shifted slightly away from him. "Anyway. I'm going to drink my beer and go home."

Before Carval could open his mouth and stick both size elevens inside, the others clattered in, demanding beer and chips and complaining that Casey was spoiling their collective good looks and perfect skin.

"We can't have you ruining our rep. No-one'll talk to us."

"No-one talks to us anyway," Casey pointed out sardonically.

"No-one likes us, we don't care," Andy singsonged.

"Nah," Tyler put in. "Jealous."

"Can't match our solve rate. Can't match our good looks. Can't match up, that's all there is to it."

"And we won the bullpen quiz, too," Andy grinned.

"That was the real clincher."

"Quiz?"

"Pub quiz," O'Leary grinned. "We won."

"They were *toast*," Andy added.

"Not that we're competitive or anythin'. No sirree."

Sure you're not, Carval thought. *Just like tigers aren't jungle-dwelling.*

"Anyway. Here's to success and another two lowlifes into Rikers."

O'Leary was the first to lift his bottle. "Yep." Andy and Tyler clinked their bottles with O'Leary and Casey. Everybody smiled at each other, and Carval was included in the general happiness. He shifted back, pulled out his camera, and took a few unposed shots of the team.

"Still takin' shots?" O'Leary queried. "Thought you'd be done with us."

Carval frankly stared. "Done? No way. I've only just gotten started."

"*What?*" arrived in surround sound from four totally shocked cops. "You're *not* done?"

Carval tried a pathetic look and, "Don't you love me?" and received only four matching disgusted glares.

"How are you not done?"

"Anyone would think you didn't like me hanging around," he grumped. The glares became steely. "Okay. To have a proper exhibition I need thousands of shots covering a lot more than a short period. My panhandlers took me six months of shooting. You're..." he picked his words "...bigger. More complex. More *interesting*. There's just so much more. I can't do it with what I've already got. I need the rest."

They gaped at him. "More?" O'Leary said faintly, and faked collapse. "Guys, we gotta talk about this."

"Damn straight," Tyler added, with a hard stare at Carval.

"I'm pretty keen on culture," Andy said, to derisive noises. "If he keeps shooting, I get to be it not just see it. Of course, I'm better looking than the rest of you."

"Better-lookin' than colour-card Casey there, sure. Better-lookin' than me, ain't no way. Look at my lovely big muscles." O'Leary flexed. Tyler groaned.

"Bigfoots" –

"Bigfeet" –

"Bigfoots aren't good looking. They're a ten foot vertical sheepskin. Cuddly. Not handsome." O'Leary made a face at Andy.

Casey sipped her beer and watched the fun. The boys were amusing themselves with Carval, and she wasn't inclined to intervene. She didn't like the idea of more photos at all.

"You wanna keep hanging around?"

"I can't get shots if I don't. But... next time, can I get shots at the crime scene? You wouldn't let me near it this time."

Three faces consulted each other. "We gotta think about it," O'Leary rumbled. "This ain't the time." Carval's face fell. "But I'm leanin' to yes." He grinned.

"You're just messing with me," Carval noted coolly. "Just wait. Next time one of you slips on a banana skin, I'll be right there shooting it."

Everyone snickered. Casey decided that the boys were all friends, and further decided that her beer being finished, now was a good time to get a cab the short distance home. She wasn't in any state to walk, and, decision made, she was the good kind of tired.

"I'm out," she announced. "Going home, cuddling up to my Icy Hot. See you all tomorrow."

"Saturday," Tyler said laconically. "Except we're off Saturday and Sunday, so Monday."

"No bullpen for you, Casey. Kent told you two days off, then back on the roster. That's Monday."

Casey pouted.

"None of that, now. Take the time. Sleep. Go see a movie."

"I'll give you some good movies," Andy smirked.

"That arthouse shit?" Tyler got in first.

"No, thank you." She heaved herself up. "I'll stick to Dwayne Johnson." Andy choked. Casey smirked. "See you all."

Carval looked indecisively at her retreating, hunched back. He shifted to follow her – and was prevented by O'Leary's massive meaty paw on one shoulder and Tyler's hard grip on the other.

"Nuh-uh. You're stayin' here."

"Uh?"

"We want to talk to you."

"Oh, for Chrissake. I thought we were done with the intimidation go-around."

"Focal point," Tyler said briefly.

"We're all goin' back to yours to have a look at this focal point."

"You said you'd show us it."

"So time to pony up."

"Drink up, guys. Time to go."

Carval shrugged. "Why couldn't you just say that?"

"More fun to mess with you."

"An' Casey needed to be gone."

Carval looked around all three of them. "Uh?" he said articulately.

"She don't like photos. No point upsetting her."

Tyler nodded, firmly. "We like you. We're cool if you hang around a bit longer."

"But if Casey takes against you 'cause of the photographs, she won't be."

"You're still It," Tyler said.

"Tagged."

"An' if Casey finds out, prob'ly bagged."

"Thanks," Carval replied sardonically. "Good to know about my imminent demise" –

"Hey, that's cop talk" –

"Shhh" –

"I can make sure they get all the good bits in my obituary." Everyone laughed. "C'mon then. Let's go. We can walk down to mine. It's about twenty minutes."

Twenty minutes later, not without considerable grumblings from three slightly breathless men and smug smirks from one Bigfoot, they arrived at Carval's building.

"Jamie?"

"Hey, Allan."

Allan appeared from the office, and regarded the motley crew with none-too-well concealed horror. "Jamie?" he said feebly.

"These" –

"Are the cops you're shooting."

"Hey, I'm famous," O'Leary drawled. "He recognised me."

"There's only one six-ten Bigfoot in the NYPD. It's not difficult."

Allan's gaze disapproved. "Jamie, what's going on?"

"They've come to see the board."

Allan threw his hands up. "How're you ever going to get paying visitors if you invite everyone to see it before it's done? I swear, if you were directing Ibsen you'd let half Manhattan watch rehearsals. Why do I bother?"

"Ibsen?" said Andy, spotting a potential friend. "Do you like culture?"

"Do you?" asked Allan, in his prissiest tone.

"Yes. Season ticket for La Mama."

"Really? I've got one too."

They regarded each other with respect, tinged with liking. Allan magnificently ignored Carval and gestured Andy into his own domain.

Carval sneaked quietly past Allan, trailing O'Leary, who couldn't sneak, and Tyler, who was quietly unobtrusive. Behind him, he could hear the opening of a discussion on a production of The Dolls House.

"Coffee?" said O'Leary hopefully.

"You know where the machine is," Carval flicked back.

"Focal point."

"'Kay." He pulled out the central shot. "Close your eyes," he added childishly. Amazingly, they did, albeit with a cynical expression. He pinned it in its place. "You can look."

"Shit." Tyler stared.

"Waaaalllllll now."

"Wow," Andy said, getting the full effect as he walked in.

"Hell of a focal point."

"Casey is not gonna like that."

"Too damn right she won't."

"Hell no."

Carval regarded them all coldly. "Too damn bad," he said bluntly. "This is the centrepiece of the whole show and like it or not it's staying the centrepiece."

There was a deathly silence. The three cops simply kept staring at the picture of Casey, head perfectly centred, framed by the grimy walls and service doors of the alley, the drying puddles on the sidewalk; contrasted with the sharp blue sky above, their faces a fraction unfocused, leaving hers pinpoint clear among them. Her expression was fierce, intent; focused on the crime scene just out of shot.

Finally they exchanged looks, and silent communications. O'Leary nodded once, sharply, as if agreement had been reached with never a word being said.

"Okay," he said. "We ain't gonna interfere. This is between you 'n' Casey, an' *we* think you're an' okay guy to have around. We won't tattle." The others nodded in turn. "You c'n come to scenes. One of us'll call you." He smiled mischievously, the world's largest imp. "Mebbe Casey'll call. If not, we will." The grin wrapped round his face. "Now, you got some beer here? I need a drink after seein' Tyler's face that size. It's scary."

Quietly, he left a business card of Casey's on Carval's desk. Carval raised an eyebrow, and didn't comment, though the card wasn't necessary. He'd already stored Casey's number: the first time she'd called him. The others didn't notice, still staring at the board.

"Sure," Carval said, took the centrepiece down again, and led them upstairs, where the evening descended into shop talk, sports talk, and plenty of beer and pizza.

***

Casey woke very late on Thursday, and rapidly discovered that she was very, very sore. A hot shower loosened her up just enough to get her to the kitchen and coffee, after which she spent the day surrounded by the aroma of Icy Hot and barely moved from her couch until she had another scaldingly hot shower and went to bed to sleep, unusually, like a log.

She woke late again, but less sore, and looking in the mirror after she'd showered, the bruising was less appallingly livid, beginning to fade. Not fast enough, though. She was going to have to explain it to her father when she saw him on Sunday, which was unappealing. She parked that thought, and found another one which she liked better. This thought said that she could go and get her car. She had some coffee, toasted a frozen bagel, dressed casually in jeans and a soft t-shirt, and cautiously slipped on her jacket to leave.

A slow amble later, she'd retrieved her cruiser. That was one positive, she supposed, as she found that the seatbelt hit every bruise from shoulder to hip, every time she hit one of Manhattan's copious quantity of potholes. She returned to her apartment in need of Advil, another coating of Icy Hot, and, to soothe her soreness, copious quantities of hot coffee and cold ice cream. She was flopped on her couch with a good book, wishing rather pathetically that someone (she carefully tried not to think who) was there to cosset her for a while, when her phone chirped.

"Hello?" she said cautiously, not recognising the number.

"Are you feeling any better?"

"Uh…yes?" she replied, frantically trying to place the familiar voice – "*Carval?* How did you get my number?"

"From when you called," he answered.

"Oh. Why're you calling?"

"I wanted a colour contrast card for green and purple."

Casey snickered. "Not here. I only do yellow and purple today."

"Oh. Can I come see you anyway?"

Casey considered, and couldn't find a reason to say no. "Okay." She gave her address.

"There shortly."

The call was cut. Casey curled up on her couch and waited, intrigued. Very shortly there was a buzz on her entry phone, and then a rap on her apartment door. She shuffled over to open it.

"Hey," she said.

"Hi." He inspected her. "You look a lot better. Has it stopped hurting?"

"Mostly."

Carval took a couple of steps inside, which were conveniently also towards Casey, cast a quick glance around, approved of the comfortable atmosphere and cosy décor, and ignored it all in favour of gathering her gently into him and massaging soothingly over her back. She made a funny little noise: not quite a purr, not quite a groan, and didn't stop him. Her head leaned on his shoulder, and she eased against him. He nuzzled into her hair, and added a soft kiss.

After a while, Carval unobtrusively moved them towards the couch, and ended up exactly as he'd wanted: Casey curled against him in the crook of his arm. He continued his petting. Kissing her would have been a much better pastime, but he wasn't an oaf and she was in no state to play.

"Better?" he asked.

"Yeah. Nice." She wriggled her shoulders. "Much better."

"Nice to know I can do something you like."

"Mm."

"Mm? That it?"

"You have some good points. You called the bus and O'Leary. *And* you brought me chocolate. You're in credit."

"Er... good?" Carval collected up his courage. He'd had a purpose in coming round, but soothing Casey had come first. "Casey, um..."

"Yeah?"

"You know I said I need more shots, well, are you happy about that?" he blurted out on one nervy breath. He wanted her to be at least okay with it. He had to keep shooting the team, and he wasn't going to give up that gig, but it was going to be easier and better if she was okay with it.

A void opened into which his words disappeared, and Casey hunched away from him.

"You said I was in credit," he tried, pathetically.

"I don't like photographs," she said bleakly. More silence followed. "But you'll take them anyway. I can see it. You can't stop photographing any more than I could stop trying to solve a murder." She stopped.

"Yes." He wouldn't lie to her. He never lied about his photography, and anyway, somewhere down in his back-brain a still small voice was telling him that lying would put this on entirely the wrong footing. He'd never cared enough to lie, before, and now, terrifyingly, he cared too much to lie. This had to start off *right*. "I can't *not* shoot you. All of you, not just you: the whole team, but they all spin around you."

She hunched further into herself. "So I'm going to be front and centre?"

"Yes." No point shading the truth.

"I see."

The cosy apartment was suddenly bleak and chilly.

"Why *me*?" she spat out. "Why not anyone else?"

Anyone else, Carval thought, *would have been delighted to be the focus of my show.* Saying that would not help.

"I don't know why you. The shots just *work*, okay? There's no reason why sometimes it all comes together." He reached for her, tipping her face up and meeting her dark, chill eyes. "Maybe it would have been better if it hadn't been you, but it is. I can't – I *won't* – change that."

"Even though the last time you did that it was used against me?" It was a challenge.

"Yes. I'm not being blamed for something I didn't do. This is my life, same as murder is yours."

Something in her expression shifted. "Artistic integrity," she murmured. "Who knew?" She straightened up. "I won't stop you," she said definitively, which was a concession Carval was certainly not expecting. "But I'm not going to change anything about how I work."

"I don't want you to. I don't do fake. I want real."

Yes. He wanted real. Shots, and, it dawned on him, a real woman. Oh. Oh, no. No no no. This was not the plan. No no no. He couldn't be falling for her this hard, this soon. This was plain dumb.

"Okay. I won't stop you," she said again.

"Okay." He took her hand and shook firmly. "Deal."

She looked a little confused, but shook back, equally firmly. "Deal," she agreed.

"And to seal the deal..." He turned towards her, leaned down, and planted a brief kiss on her lips. "There. You can't back out now."

"I don't welch on a commitment," she said crossly.

"Nice to know," Carval noted, and took a chance. "Come out to dinner with me." She gaped. "C'mon. I'm good company."

"And *so* modest."

He grinned. "You don't like fake any more than I do. So c'mon. Let's go to dinner and actually talk. I wanna know why you like being a cop."

"You're not going to stop fussing till I agree, are you?" she said with resignation.

"I don't fuss. That's what Allan is for."

"Allan?"

"My agent. He fusses."

"Mm. Wonder why?"

"How unkind. Still, I won't stop till you agree. So agree now, and I'll stop asking."

"Or I could shoot you," she snarked. "Then you'll stop asking."

"That wouldn't be any fun. You'd have to come visit me in hospital – though at least that way I might get to eat the chocolates – and we couldn't do anything nice at all." Buoyed on the snark, Carval took another chance, leaned down and kissed her again, drawing her in. "We couldn't do this." Another kiss, and another, and Casey softened into his arm and consented to some very mutual petting and kissing. Once more, she was cuddlesome and snuggly.

"So come for dinner," he said to the warm bundle of Casey in his lap, where she had migrated over the course of the last few minutes.

"Like this?" she asked disbelievingly, pointing at her face.

"Oh. Maybe not." He drooped a little around her, somehow managing to swaddle her in more closely. "When you're healed up. I don't want to be arrested."

"You'd get some interesting experiences, for sure."

"I prefer different kinds of experience," he oozed, and demonstrated.

Some time later, he reluctantly pulled himself away.

"So you'll call me?" he asked hopefully, as he left. "Here's my number." He handed over a card. "In case you've lost it."

She smiled, inscrutably. "We'll see."

Saturday and Sunday passed without a word. Monday rolled around, and rolled away again. Carval seriously considered calling O'Leary, and then decided that he wasn't a puppy to chase after the gang. Tuesday slithered into view, by which time his mood was so foul that even Allan wouldn't come near him and his shots had an edge of cruelty that he'd normally have eschewed.

On Wednesday, his phone rang, and he picked it up without looking, hurt and angry.

"I've got a case," Casey's voice arrived in his ear. "Kent finally let me have a new one." All his ire drained. She paused. "Wanna tag along?"

"On my way."

The End.

ABOUT THE AUTHOR

SR Garrae lives in London with her family.

Manufactured by Amazon.ca
Bolton, ON

22732061R00162